Louise Kean was born ▓▓▓▓▓▓▓▓▓▓▓▓▓▓▓▓▓▓▓▓ A graduate of the University of East Anglia, she worked as a marketing manager at an international film company in London for five years. Her first novel, *Toasting Eros*, was published in 2002 to great acclaim.

By the same author

Toasting Eros

LOUISE KEAN

Boyfriend in a Dress

HarperCollins*Publishers*

HarperCollins*Publishers*
77–85 Fulham Palace Road,
Hammersmith, London W6 8JB

www.**fire**and**water**.com

A Paperback Original 2003
1 3 5 7 9 8 6 4 2

A catalogue record for this book
is available from the British Library

ISBN 0 00 711464 8

Typeset in Sabon by Palimpsest Book Production Limited,
Polmont, Stirlingshire

Printed and bound in Great Britain by
Clays Ltd, St Ives plc

Acknowledgements

Thanks to Jen for being wise and wonderful, and to Max for being fabulous. Also to Sara, Kelly, Fiona, Jane Harris, Martin Palmer, Nick Sayers and all at HarperCollins. And of course a continued big thank you to my agent Ali, Carole, and everybody at Curtis Brown.

To Ken, Alice and Karen, for caring, wisdom, and fun, in that order – am I anything yet? To Nix, for always reminding me what I am at the end of a phone line, Jules, Nat, Nim, Claire, Marc (for adding value), to JP for making me think, to Jamie for inspiration (which surprised me more than anyone), and to Watson, for his penis – now you see, how does that look?

And as always my love and thanks to my family: Amy, an adult now and taking it seriously, to Laura and Jase, for their constant support, and to Mum & Dad, for always being where I need them to be.

For Mum & Dad

Contents

I used to be Snow White . . . then I drifted

MAE WEST

It takes two to speak the truth – one to speak, and another to hear

HENRY DAVID THOREAU

The First Time I Ran Away

'I'm sorry, what?'

'We should just know zat ze ghost is zere, we shouldn't be able to see it! 'Ave it taken out of ze script. Get somebody else to do it. Sack 'im first.'

You can barely even make out the Spanish accent now, although when my boss first came to this country two years ago, when he first took the job as the head of television development, it was actually impossible to understand three out of four words he said. He told me six months ago, through a toothy Spanish smile, that he swore a lot in those early days, at all of the producers and scriptwriters he worked with, and got away with it. I know that is a lie. He thinks it ingratiates himself with me, with 'the team'. We know that he would eat his own hands if it pleased the producers. José isn't fooling anybody any more. It only takes a couple of months for the political animal to show its face.

'José, I can't just sack him, I need a reason.' I don't know how many times I have had this conversation with him. He still cannot grasp the fact that somebody has to do something wrong before you give them their marching orders.

'Look at 'iz 'air! It is all wrong. 'E 'as to go!' José thumps the boardroom table violently.

'You want me to sack him because of his hair? I don't think hairstyles are specified in the contract, José – besides, what's wrong with his hair?'

'Oh, everything. It is so . . . so British. 'E 'as no flair.' He sighs wearily. I too am British, I will never understand. José has slicked back black hair. That apparently is the hair to have.

'José, why don't we just ask him to rewrite, if you don't like it, but in all honesty, I have to say I don't know how we are going to make the sequel to *Evil Ghost* without an actual ghost.'

'Yes, but zis is for TV, it is very different, Nicola.'

'I know, we've got a tenth of the budget.'

'I cannot work like zis,' José says, as he holds his head in his hands.

'Look, why don't I just tell him to make the ghost a bit more . . . subtle.'

'Yes, maybe zat will work.' José comes alive again.

'Tell 'im it should be more like . . . more like a big gap.'

'Just a big gap,' I repeat, although I know I am pushing my luck, but it's just such a stupid thing to say. We are not a TV company who lets our audience 'sense' anything any more. If you can't see it, in all its graphically-enhanced, action-packed splendour, it ain't us. Subtlety went out with the sequel. And promotional tie-ins. Both of which we are very good at, I might add.

'Zat's what I said.' The toothy grin is warping into gritted teeth.

'You don't think we might need to be a bit more blatant than that? You don't think we could show something a bit scarier than . . . a big space? You don't think it will just look like we had no budget and ran out of money before we could do the effects?'

'No, it will intrigue zem.'

'You think it will intrigue young males, fifteen to twenty-five, our primary audience?'

'Zee audience are more sophisticated zan you give zem credit for, Nicola.'

'Fine.' The only thing he can't do in a perfect English accent now is any word beginning with 'th' or 'h'. It kills him, I know. But I give up. I will be told to change it eventually, or be ultimately blamed myself for the idea of leaving a big 'space' in our TV movie, if it ever actually makes it onto TV, probably cable at this rate. Play the game, I remind myself, as I click my pen, and write in large letters on my notepad – LEAVE A BIG SPACE. I massage the side of my head slightly, and try not to project 'attitude'. José stares at me pointedly, daring me to tell him what an idiot he is, but I don't bite.

'Maybe a big space is going too far,' José says, and I realize he is coming to his senses.

''Ow about a cloud of white fog instead. Try zat.' He smiles at me. I smile back. It's obviously happy hour at the idiot farm.

'A cloud of white fog?' I ask, trying not to sound numb.

'Yes, like a mist.' He makes a circular motion in front of him with his hands, and then nods at me to somehow 'write that down'.

'You want me to tell him to write a mist in. What kind of mist?'

'A ghostly mist.' Jesus wept!

'Look, it's called *Evil Ghost 2: The Return*. We need a ghost in it. Come on, he's doing a good job. If the script is lacking, maybe we need another character or something. Maybe there's something wrong with the second act . . . .'

'Yes! We need . . . we need . . . something sinister – who are sinister? Work with me, Nix, work with me . . . the old, the old are sinister, if zey 'ave lost zer teeth . . . An old lady

3

mist! It should be an old lady ghostly mist,' he shouts, his personal Eureka. We have been doing this for over an hour.

'An old lady?' There are no old ladies in our script.

'Yes, shoot it tomorrow, get me a visual, I know it will work. You can use Ángela! It will be cheap.'

'José, we can't use Angela.' Angela is his PA.

'Why not?' He looks at me, confused.

'Because she's thirty-nine. She might be offended.'

'Thirty-nine? She looks older zan zat.' He looks down solemnly; I have burst his bubble. José only employs young women, and by young, I mean under twenty-five. Luckily, Angela and I were here before him, and he hasn't sacked us yet. I'm twenty-eight, but that is middle-aged in José's book.

'So?' He looks at me expectantly, waiting for a solution. By my side, Phil, my assistant, has a blank look on his face that lets me know he has been asleep with his eyes open for the last half an hour.

'Okay, I'll drop in an old lady, a proper old lady – she'll be like, eighty, José.' He practically retches at the thought.

'I'll have it worked up by the designers, so we can see how it looks.' I surrender, trying to draw the meeting to an end.

'No, organize a shoot. I won't attend.' There's a surprise.

'You want me to organize a shoot – for an old woman in mist?'

'Zat's what I said.' I'm going to get told off after this meeting. I'm being 'negative'.

'But it'll cost twenty times as much as just working it up on the Mac.'

'Yes, but it 'as to be realistic.' He gives me a patronizing smile.

I sigh, as José sucks on a biscuit with a smile.

'Set it up for tomorrow. I'm in Spain on Friday,' José says through a mouth full of Digestive.

'Tomorrow? But it's five-thirty now!'

'Nicola, 'ow 'ard can it be? It's just mist, and an old woman.' He smiles at Phil, and raises his eyes to heaven at me. Phil doesn't respond.

'We'll have to get a smoke machine.' I nudge Phil, whose pen darts towards his pad, and just draws a line.

José thumps the table with his hand, and looks straight at me.

'No, for fuck's sake – it 'as to be realistic for fuck's sake!'

'But we're in the middle of a heatwave; where am I supposed to find mist by tomorrow?' I ask coldly, trying not to lose my temper.

For emphasis, I wipe the beads of sweat off the back of my neck, and blow a hair off my cheek that has stuck.

'I'm sure you'll find a way.' José regains his composure and smiles at me again, through gritted teeth. He hasn't broken a sweat for the last two weeks, in the middle of this freakishly hot May. The man is ice. You could pour vodka down his ear and watch it come straight out of the other end, with your mouth open beneath what I am sure is a below-average length penis, while everybody cheers and claps. I am left with a horrible mental image. If it wasn't eighty-five degrees outside, I'd shudder.

'Are we done zen?' José asks cheerily, and pushes back his chair.

'I suppose. So for now, the scriptwriter can stay?' I say, as confirmation.

'Yes, but tell 'im to cut 'iz 'air.' José pulls a face, and saunters out without a care in the world.

I nudge Phil again – his pen darts towards his pad and underlines the line he made earlier.

'Phil,' I say, losing my temper.

'Wha?' he says, as his eyes desperately try to focus.

'I'm going for a cigarette. Go downstairs and conference in Naomi and Jules.'

'Your mates?' he asks, confused, even though he has done it a thousand times before.

'Yes, you have their numbers. I'll be back in five minutes.'

'Get me a Twix,' I hear him shout after me as I head for the lifts.

I sigh and hit the button for 'ground', and try desperately to ignore the mirrors on all sides of me in the lift, reflecting my shiny face back at me. It is too hot for May. I love it and hate it. If it holds until the weekend, I'll love it. If it breaks on Friday, it'll just be a pain in the arse. There is nothing worse than working in the summer. Actually, there are a lot of things which are much worse – torture with acid and sandpaper isn't great, I've heard – but this is . . . frustrating.

I lean against the side of our building, with the sun pouring onto my eyelids, and inhale.

I was fourteen, dressed in my school uniform, and hiding behind a petrol pump. My exasperated parents drove up and down the road in front of me. I could see the car crawling back past the church, past the petrol station opposite. I didn't want to go to my first confirmation meeting. My friends were all at the cinema, but I was ducking behind the four star. After too many arguments to go into, I had succumbed to being driven to St Jude's, our church, because my parents didn't trust me to get there on my own. I waved at them as they pulled away in our old Orange Datsun that my mum swore had 'character', and walked up the few steps to the door, but didn't ring the bell, waiting for the car to recede into the distance so I could make a run for it. But the door suddenly flew open, and Sister Margarita sprung out of nowhere, grinning like the village idiot: she'd been at the holy wine . . . again.

'Jesus Christ!' was my unfortunate cry of shock.

'Nicola Ellis!' she managed to slur back in mock outrage –

she'd heard worse, hell, she'd said worse herself, but she was obliged to at least seem offended.

'Sorry, Sister,' I mumbled and made a break for it. I dashed off down the steps, and stood, half excited, looking both ways deciding which new path to follow. Which is when I noticed the mobile baked bean tin handbrake turn at the end of the road, and suddenly my mum and dad were on my tail like the Dukes of Hazzard hit Kent. I managed to make it to the petrol station before they drove past – my dad may have been angry, he may even have done an illegal turn, but he wasn't going to do more than thirty in a built-up area. So I ducked and dived as they went along and their sixth parental sense stopped them driving off in the other direction. They were going to track me down. It was a matter of principle, and it would make my nanny happy.

As they cruised past the church again, looking like a pair of terribly respectable kerb crawlers, I found my feet and dashed off in the other direction. The Datsun caught me as I sprinted towards the park, and I heard my mother's voice say wearily from behind a wound down window,

'Nicola, get in the car, please.'

There was no point fighting it. For me the compulsion to run has always been there, but when I am caught, as I am always caught, a tidal wave of guilt at doing what *I* want to do manifests itself in a desperate need to make amends. My dad walked me up the steps and rang the doorbell to the nuns' house, as I hung my head in shame.

'Don't run off again – it's getting dark, it's not safe,' was all he said. And I obeyed. Sister Margarita swung open the door again, still smiling like she had a Wagon Wheel stuck in her mouth. At the sight of me she managed to say,

'Blasphemer!' covering my father in a shower of holy saliva.

'Sorry, Sister,' I said again, as my dad eyed her nervously, and wiped himself off. Her cheeks were purple and riddled with veins, and her nose was bright red, her wimple lopsided, with an ear popping out of one side.

'I'll pick you up in an hour and a half. Be here,' my dad said, and kissed me goodbye. I waved to my mum, who waved back, smiling that it would be okay. So I end up doing the thing I'm running from anyway, just with the added bonus of feeling like a bad person for daring not to please somebody else. I was the only latecomer, but I was already feeling guilty, so I was instantly top of the class.

I go back upstairs, and throw the Twix at Phil on my way past his desk, and he catches it with cricket hands and cries 'Howzat!'

Phil follows me into my office mumbling 'not out!' as I slump at my desk.

'We should throw more things in the office, it brightens my day,' he says, and lingers near the door.

'Are they on?' I ask, ignoring him, looking at flashing buttons on my phone.

'Yep, they're holding. Is Naomi the fit one?' he asks seriously.

'They're both fit, they're my friends,' I reply, wearily.

'Yes, but not girl "they are both lovely and funny" fit, bloke fit?'

'I wouldn't know,' I say, and hit the red button and mouth 'shut the door,' at Phil, who slumps out of the room. He really would prefer just to sit and listen to my conversation for twenty minutes.

When nothing happens – I can't work this damn phone, it's like something out of *Star Trek* – I press the button again, and instantly hear the girls talking at the other end.

'Oi, I'm here,' I say, and press some buttons on my keyboard, checking new emails for anything important.

'"Oi"? How rude is that? She keeps us waiting, and then says "Oi"!' Naomi is indignant.

'Sorry, hello, I apologize for my lateness, I was in some stupid bloody meeting for hours, at the end of which we established we are going to put an old lady in fog to scare people.'

'Like *Last Of the Summer Wine*?' Nim asks.

'Yes, just like that. Are we still on for tonight?'

'I am, but I'm going to be late. I have to meet the Countess of Wessex.' Jules is a fundraiser, she keeps meeting royalty; we don't ask why.

'What time are you going to be finished?' Nim asks.

'About seven.'

'Cool, that's good for me,' I say, turning my attention to the photos on my desk that have been sent through by our agency of young wannabes to play our leading man. They are all useless. I wanted gritty and urban, I've got sons of Lionel Blair.

'Shit, I'm finished at six, what am I supposed to do for an hour?' Nim works in the City, meaning she works normal hours, unlike myself and Jules, who chose 'interesting' careers, instead of being well paid and working sociable hours. Nim has both, and even though she has to put up with banking arseholes all day, she has pots of cash, and wants to go out every night. I have to talk to her about that. I don't want her to end up like Charlie.

'Shop, write personal emails, go to the gym, whatever,' Jules is saying at the other end of the phone.

'I should go to the gym.'

'Well, there you go, do that,' I say, as an email entitled 'Play this now!' flashes up from Phil. I open it, distracted, and try and smack a monkey with a hand as fast as I can by pulling back my mouse and then whizzing it across my desk.

9

'So seven? Dinner or drinks?' I say, as I swing my mouse into my in-tray, sending papers flying everywhere, and swing it back.

'Shit, hold on.' I find and press hold, and shout out for Phil, who opens the door seconds later,

'Phil, what's your fastest smack?'

'Four hundred and thirty-six miles an hour,' he replies, and wanders over to stand behind my PC.

'Bloody hell,' I say and pull my mouse back, determined to beat his score. I whack the mouse and a tune plays and the computer declares I have smacked the monkey at five hundred and two miles per hour.

'Shit,' Phil says, and grabs my mouse from me, and has a go himself, as I press hold again.

'Sorry, did we decide?' I ask.

'Yep, drinks and dinner, Café Bohème,' Jules says.

'Cool, I'll see you later.'

'Can I bring some guys from my office?' Nim asks.

'Who?' Jules asks suspiciously, knowing full well that she doesn't want to run into at least two of them.

'Neither of them,' Nim pre-empts her.

'They're nice,' as some sort of explanation.

'And they work at your office?' I ask, incredulous. I know some of the guys who work with Nim; they know Charlie.

'Yes, some of them are nice.'

'None that I've met,' I say.

'They've just started.'

'Oh, okay, cool.'

'See you later then, I've got to go,' I say, as I see Phil smack the monkey at six hundred miles an hour.

'Cool, byeeeee,' we all squeal off the phone, trying to go higher than each other.

'Give me that.' I grab the mouse off Phil, who is looking smug. I smack it a couple more times, but can't beat his score.

He strolls around to the front of my desk, wipes the sweat off his forehead, and throws himself into a chair.

'Are you going out with them tonight?' he asks, the picture of innocence.

'Yep.'

'What time?'

'Seven.' I start going over the photos again, trying to see past the crowned teeth and sunbed tans.

'Can I come for a couple? I'm meeting the boys at eight.'

'Yep,' I say, and then, 'these are shit.' I throw the photos across my desk, lean back in my chair, and sigh. 'What time is it?'

Phil checks his watch.

'Ten to six.'

'Have you got any more games?' I ask wearily.

'Of course, but aren't we supposed to set up that shoot or something?'

'Shit, SHIT, yes! Well done! Call Tony, get him on the case. I'll make some calls.'

I grab my numbers.

'What exactly am I supposed to ask him?' Phil hasn't moved from the chair.

I look at him and feel bad at the prospect of making him work hard for the next hour. 'Don't worry, I'll call him.' I plug the number into my phone, as Phil closes his eyes in front of me, deciding it's time for a well-earned nap.

'Out,' I shout at him and point at the door.

'Alright, darlin'.' I hear Tony's Scouse greeting on the hands free and pick up the receiver. 'I was just about to leave – whattdaya need?'

'Tone, I need a massive favour, hon. A shoot tomorrow. I need mist. For *Evil Ghost 2*.'

'Not a problem, you tell me how much.'

'And an old lady.'

11

'Eh?'

'I need an old woman, but I'd rather not pay for her, I haven't got the cash. Is there anybody that you know – how old is your mother?'

'Not old enough, I'm from Liverpool, remember.'

'Of course, she's probably younger than me.'

'Pack it in.'

'Okay, but you have to find me some old dear, preferably one without her own teeth, who'll work for a hundred quid tops tomorrow morning.'

'Not a problem, darlin'.'

'You are a star.'

I go over the details with Tony for the next twenty minutes, try my best to discuss last night's Liverpool game with him without sounding bored, make some more calls, and then head for the toilets to sort my make-up out. I catch Phil chatting to the boys at the end of the corridor, playing imaginary cricket shots and laughing. I don't bother telling him to do what he should be doing: actual work. I'm done for the day.

At seven Phil and I wander up the road into Soho, dodging tourists and drinkers, completely oblivious to the pace at which everything moves around us, or the gulps of steaming pollution-filled air we are inhaling. It is still hot, but becoming bearable. The restaurant is cool inside, and Nim is already at the bar. I kiss her hello, and Phil looks like he wants to do the same, but she turns back to the barman.

'What are you having?' she asks over her shoulder, while gesturing with a twenty-pound note at the young French guy behind the bar with a mole on his cheek that looks like eyeliner. These are vain days. Everybody's caking it on, and moisturizing themselves into a slippery mess that enables us to slide past each other down the street. I can't remember the last time I saw a real spot on anybody I actually know. Strangers have them, but they don't count. Hell, even Phil hides his blemishes now. I had to buy him blackhead strips from the chemist because he was too embarrassed to buy them himself. It used to be condoms. The world is spinning differently these days.

'Dry Martini,' I say.

'Phil?' she asks, as he shifts uncomfortably, about to reach for his wallet.

'Oh, I'll have a pint of Stella, thanks.'

'Did you go to the gym?' I ask, over her shoulder at the bar.

'No, played some monkey-slapping game and then came over here.'

We sip our drinks, and I catch Phil staring as Nim takes her jacket off.

'I don't know how you work in a suit in this weather,' I say as a distraction.

'It's not so bad, the blokes aren't even allowed to take off their ties,' she says, and sips her gin and tonic.

Phil is chatting to the guys from Nim's office about last night's Liverpool game. I could join in, but I've done my football talk already today. The boys wear make-up and the girls know the offside rule. Mostly due to the fact that the footballers seem to have got better looking, and the boys need to look like them to get a girlfriend. The icecaps are melting – the sea is the only thing today that is growing less shallow.

'How's work?' Nim asks.

'Shit – you?'

'Boring,' she says, and we move onto more interesting topics.

'How's Charlie?' she asks eventually.

I turn my nose up, but say 'fine.' We move on again to more interesting topics.

Jules turns up late, and we are seated at our table.

Two hours later, we are lashed on some new cocktail one of the guys from Nim's work has introduced us to. But it's the tequila that really pushes us all over the edge – the implication that we got drunk by mistake on some new and peculiar concoction is a lie. We wanted to get drunk, so we drank tequila. There are no real mistakes any more, not where losing yourself is concerned. In every other facet of your life maybe, but the pursuit of oblivion is a knowledgeable one. Nobody is snorting that coke for you. Phil has completely forgotten about his mates, and is falling asleep at one end of the table, while Nim shrugs his head off her shoulder. The whole place is giggling in the end of the day heat, and I start to think about going home. We kiss our goodbyes outside, making the responsible decision not to go dancing on a school night, and Nim's mates help me put Phil in a cab back to his grandfather's house in some leafy south-west London road where car insurance is still affordable. I walk to the tube with one of them, Craig, who is a few years younger than I am.

'So, Naomi tells me your boyfriend works around the corner from us.'

'Yep, at Frank and Sturney, he's been there for a few years, started there straight out of university – like you,' I say, and hope to hell that this sweet, funny, young guy doesn't turn out the same way.

'Are you enjoying the job?' I ask, at the same time as he decides to ask for my number.

We stop outside the tube and look at each other uncomfortably.

'I don't think so,' I say, and he looks down at his smart City shoes, embarrassed.

I lean forward and catch him with a kiss, and he is surprisingly quick to react and kiss me back. As we stand on the street, kissing, I feel his tongue and his breath, and let it drag me back five years, out of London, into the country, onto a campus, surrounded by friends. It is a young kiss, not cynical, not dirty, but the kind of kiss you got at the end of

14

the night back in the days of lectures, of drinking all day on a Wednesday, and taking your washing home to your mum.

'That's just because of the sun,' I say, as I pull back and smile, remembering I have grown up since then. He smiles back.

'Are you sure?' he says, all of a sudden the confident young City thing, stepping into a new world of arrogance fuelled by an ever-growing bank account. He will turn out like Charlie, they can't help themselves – it's a breeding ground, almost a social experiment.

'Yep, I've got . . . Charlie.' The words 'relationship' and 'boyfriend' stick in my throat and refuse to come out. Neither my head nor my heart will let them.

I sit on the tube home, drunk, and try not to get upset. I only ever let myself get really upset when I'm drunk. My head flops from side to side, and the heads of all the other drunk people around me, opposite me, do the same. The middle-aged couple who came up to town to see a show squirm in their seats in the corner, and pray they won't get leaned on, making mental notes not to come again until at least Christmas. It's our city now, us drunk young things on the tube late at night, it stopped being their's years ago, when people started to ignore the beggars instead of acknowledging them with a turned-up nose or an incensed disgusted remark. Nobody says anything any more. They are as much a part of life as Switch and internet shopping.

I phone Nim as I get off the train, staggering in the dark towards my flat.

'Why are you crying?' she asks straight away.

'I'm just being stupid,' I say as I wipe the tears away from my face, and try to stop them reappearing immediately in the corners of my eyes.

'It must be something,' she says, and I can't help myself saying something stupid.

'I'm alone, aren't I!'

I hear Nim laugh slightly.

'How melodramatic, Miss Ellis. Besides, you have Charlie.'

'I don't "have" Charlie at all. We just keep going, like the Queen Mum. But even she died in the end.'

'Well, then do something,' she says.

'I will, thanks, hon, I'll speak to you at the weekend.'

I fall through my front door, and into bed.

I should do something.

Amen to That

When I was sixteen a kiss was a wonderful thing. The mere idea of pressing my open lips to some boy's mouth lit a fuse of excitement within me that sizzled its way through my bloodstream, and I could only imagine the joyride that would follow when I realized what to do with my hands. A kiss was a great step forward into the world of people who drove cars and owned their own houses and had babies. I was still learning, still believed I could somehow 'do it wrong'. A kiss was enough for me then. It was the world.

At twenty-eight, a kiss just never seems to be enough. Today it's all about sex. I have sex because I can, I am allowed, I have that house, I drive a car. I know that nice girls only kiss on the first date, but the whole notion of being a 'nice girl' is relegated to my teens, when it passed out of my consciousness, and I realized I was perfectly within my rights to go further than that without stigma, because stigma was just sexism, and I am a liberated woman. That's my excuse at least.

Sex can be many things, and about many things. It can be animal, fatal, it is political, natural, it is a weapon, it is illegal in some countries, it is about control: there is even some particularly vicious propaganda out there that says it is

17

something to do with love. It is easy to become obsessed with it, and its emotional effects, and the physical realities it can leave behind. I live in a world obsessed with something it still finds it hard to talk about. Religion stamps its ugly muddied footprints all over the sex act for so many of us, and it is this notion that true love waits that muddles my subconscious time and time again. The very fact that I should postpone some random physical act for three weeks because then I will know that it is 'right' makes a rebel of me. Do anything too soon and you are cheating yourself, you have low self esteem, you are desperate, you are, in a word, a 'slag'. I don't want those rules to apply to me, but still I feel them hanging over my head like the 'snood' my grandmother knitted me when I was fourteen.

I've realized recently, as you've probably already guessed, that a good Catholic schooling has affected me more than I previously thought. I never labelled my hang-ups before, but now I do and I name them 'convent school'. Guilt is like a sperm stain on a suede skirt – it shouldn't be there, you want to get rid of it, but even dry cleaning won't get it out – basically, if you want to keep wearing the skirt, you're stuck with it. You can try to ignore it, but accept that it is always going to be there, making everything not quite perfect.

I feel guilty about everything – about the big things and the small things, the things I haven't done, the things I should have done. Rationally, I know I should really focus on the actions of my hooded teenage tormentors rather than their words.

The nuns mostly seemed angry, and I seriously believe it was due to their 'lifestyle choice'. Their major release of emotion, as far as I could see, was belting out a good hymn. Now I can only manage to hit a high 'C' with a little help from the man of my choice, and yet they manage it most days in church, but I honestly doubt we're feeling quite as good when it happens.

18

Although it's very possible that there are 'nun exercises' that compensate for their chastity and produce the same 'reaction' – you can probably even buy the video in Woolworth's – it's why they are always so keen to sing everything an octave too high. Bless 'em for trying, I suppose. You've got to get your kicks somewhere, and one bonus is that they don't get itching diseases their way, or mild concussion from an unforgiving headboard.

But their frustration, or restraint, or choice, or whatever it is, has had a knock-on effect. They managed to get to me at a particularly vulnerable stage in my mental and emotional development, and even though I personally have chosen to pursue a life where sex is allowed, I still feel guilty about doing it the first time, the next time, too many times with too many people, not loving the one I'm with. I can't help feeling that if only somebody had p-p-picked up these penguins once or twice, I'd have a much healthier sexual mindset now.

And even though I can admit that, with regard to this particular incident, the incident in question, the sex itself isn't the only thing I have to feel guilty about, and that there are feelings and emotional repercussions that weigh just as heavily on my mind, it is still a big part of my guilt. No need to hide the truth from everybody, including my mother, but most importantly, Charlie. I could have been so much happier. But I can't change it now. This is me.

You wouldn't know to look at me that I am so terribly mixed-up – my hair is long, my eyes are brown. I burn first, then tan. I stand five feet seven in bare feet. I look perfectly normal, perfectly average. I don't know my vital statistics. This is the measure of me, I suppose.

I like ordinary things: red wine, whisky goes down smoothly, Martinis the most. Lychee Martinis are my favourite – swollen with vodka like a juicy alcohol eyeball.

I like to go dancing, any kind. I have a few drinks and do

stupid things. Once at a summer barbecue in the garden of one of my friend's houses, as we all fought the chill and the need to go inside at nine p.m., I tried to do a front roll over a piece of plastic cord that had been hung between a tree branch and some guttering as a makeshift washing line. We had been drinking since three. It was positioned over paving stones nearly two metres off the ground. I got halfway over and the cord snapped. I fell face down onto the paving, and chipped my front tooth. I still have a lump on the back of my head from that one, which I should probably get checked out. The tooth got fixed the next day obviously; you can see that.

I wake up early the next day, another wild warm day when you feel like big things are supposed to happen. The sky is bright blue, even at eight in the morning, dusted with fairy-tale clouds, and the air already smells of cut grass – the community servicers have been out early – and I fight the urge to have ice cream for breakfast.

I wake up on my own. I spend the first twenty minutes breathing in the heat and the sun and the silence. The phone doesn't ring, I am left alone, the way it should be on a day like this. Everybody is praying for something to happen to their lives, to whisk them away on the sunshine express to a much better time.

Instead of ice cream, I light a cigarette, and hang over my balcony which overlooks the communal gardens that nobody uses, in case they have to sit twenty feet from somebody they don't know. A breeze creeps up, and everything sways, including me. A spider stuck in the middle of its cobweb rocks to and fro, and seems to enjoy it, and the hairs on my arms search up for the sun. I feel it, where I always feel it, in the small of my back, and the heat closes my eyes, and I dream, standing. I breathe warm air, think I hear music somewhere, not here. It is a small bliss. It is a beautiful day. I know

20

something should happen today. It makes me feel giddy. I should do something. This thought snaps me back to reality, and the moment is gone.

'I don't want to go to fucking work,' I complain to myself, in a staccato voice, accentuating every word, as if somebody, God, maybe, might hear me and say 'that's ok, you don't have to – take your passport and run away!' It doesn't happen, nobody says anything to me, and I sigh, facing the inevitable, and move back into my flat to get dressed.

The doorbell buzzes while I am pulling on yesterday's jeans, having the age-old footwear debate in my head as I look at my strappy sandals sitting prettily next to my starting-to-reek trainers: longer legs, or still being able to walk by lunchtime?

'Package for you,' my intercom says.

'I'm coming down.'

I button up my shirt as I run down the stairs. The delivery boy is waiting by the door – a kid really, maybe five years younger than me, but a world away. He looks like he has fun in the evenings. He likes his job in that it gives him no hassle, but it is the evenings that are his. A young black guy, good-looking and charming. He smiles, I smile back.

'Do you need me to sign for it?'

'Nah, it's fine.'

He walks off as I shut the door, saunters back to his van. He looks like he gets a lot of sex. He looks like he has them queuing up. You can tell he is good in bed, in a young excitable way.

I thought my parcel would be from the book club, but it's not. It's the organic meat my father keeps ordering for me and having sent directly to my house. He is worried about contaminants, about what they put into beef these days. If I refuse to become a vegan, like my dad, he is going to keep ordering me 'clean cow' as Charlie calls it, which just makes me want to chuck it straight in the bin. Somewhere deep inside of me I know I don't want to eat meat any more. If Charlie calls our bacon sandwich 'pig' I retch. I can't eat the animal, and hear or say the animal's name at the same time. Unfortunately I just really like the taste. It's yet another issue I'm avoiding, I know, but today isn't a day for confrontations, especially with myself. I just put the meat in the fridge, in the knowledge that it will probably have gone bad, organic or not, by the time I get around to cooking for myself in my own flat. Cooking for one demands minimal effort, and therefore the use of either the toaster or the microwave, and I don't think I can put steak in either of them. Of course I don't know for sure.

My neighbours are out now, going to work, going to the shops. I say good morning to a couple of them, the older ones. I smile at the young guy who has moved into the flat on the first floor. He is tall and broad and looks like he does a lot of sport. He is wearing a suit, which puts me off slightly, and swings a gym bag by his side. He will work out today, at the gym at work, with the other City boys, but in his own little world, picturing his muscles expanding with every bench press. I can picture his lungs, clean and clear, the little hairs swaying, not tarred and blackened like the anti-smoking programmes show me mine will be by now. He'll sweat a lot, maybe get a little red in the face, exactly the look he'd have after sex; not that I know.

Walking is only ever a pleasure for me on a day like today, with the sun out and sensible trainers on my feet. Today is a day to smile. The man on the fruit and veg stall by the station makes a remark about melons, which I choose to ignore, my bubble will not be burst this early at least, if at all on a day like today. If I could just wander around all day, in my comfortable footwear, getting a tan, smiling to myself

22

and not having to talk to anybody I know, it would be heaven. But I have to go to work. And even if I manage to make it through the political minefield that has become making TV programmes for a living, it won't last. Tonight I am going over to Charlie's, and I will cook for us both, and sit out on his much bigger balcony – with a glass of wine afterwards. It's amazing how easy it is to ignore a problem. You just don't say it, and it doesn't matter. I've done it for years.

I was going to do something. I decided, somewhere in my sleep, to talk to Charlie about us, but on waking, today doesn't seem to be the right day. I just want to enjoy it. I want the entire day to go without a hitch, without a raised voice or argument. Maybe I'll leave it and talk to him next week. I've been seeing Charlie for nearly six years. I met him in America, but we are both British. It's not working out. It's more than a bad patch . . .

I work in Covent Garden – it's a lovely place to be based, apart from all the fucking tourists. I know that might seem a bit strong, but I am smacked by an oversized rucksack at least three times a day, just walking from the tube to work, and back again.

By the time Tony arrives to drive us to the shoot in a studio in Islington, José has still not turned up at work. He'll think I was running late and went straight to the shoot, which pisses me off, so I send him a quick innocuous e-mail, asking him when the video for *Evil Ghost,* the original film, is due for release, so that we can tie up our TV sales. We haven't even made the film yet. This is the way that it works. By the time we get around to actually making this damn sequel we are going to have about six weeks to finish the thing. We have been teaser trailering for months on the front of all our other videos. And the thing isn't even made. The marketing comes first, then we film. I don't know my job title exactly. There are only thirty of us in total. We do a lot of everything, masters of all trades.

I am left to direct the shooting of the foggy woman myself. She is very sweet, actually – Tony hung up the phone after he spoke to me last night, and caught the first bus he saw. He spoke to three OAPs before he found us this one. She is grateful for the money – she lives on her pension, and after Tony proved he was legitimate, and I don't ask him how he did this, but it had something to do with carrying shopping and playing gin rummy at her 'Home', she agreed to come along. She asks if she can sit behind the fog machine, because her legs aren't as strong as they used to be, and I almost feel bad saying no, she has to stand. An old woman sitting in a cloud of smoke just doesn't scream 'horror' to me.

To be honest, there are only so many ways you can shoot it. But the day itself will still cost about five grand. Tony and I spend most of the time sitting outside on the steps of the studio, smoking cigarettes and eating the muffins that were supplied by some eager beaver production assistant keen to impress the television lady. It embarrasses me slightly – I am not quite so impressed with myself. Not fresh muffin impressed. My phone rings, and I check the number before answering – it's Phil.

'Yep?'

'Nicola, it's me,' he says.

'I know, what's wrong?'

'There's a problem with the teaser trailer.' He sounds panicked. It's rare to hear him this worried, which panics me.

'Oh what now?' I ask, and close my eyes, ready to concentrate on today's catastrophe.

'Somebody has called it porn.'

'What?'

'It's been put on the front end of the new *Bristo the*

24

Badger videos, and some mum has written in and called it porn.'

'It's what?' I say again; I don't know why, I heard him the first time.

'Somebody's put it on the new *Bristo the Badger* video and José's going mad. He says it's your fault. And then he asked if you had got me to send him an email from your computer this morning. I said no.' Phil goes quiet at the other end of the phone.

Evil Ghost: The Return is going to be the equivalent of an eighteen certificate for television – it will be strictly post-watershed. Needless to say, the trailer that I cut was very much an eighteen certificate. Some young model, who I now have to write into the film, practically naked but for a wet bra, but it's fine because we would have had one in there somewhere. I spliced in shots from the first film, the one with a decent budget and a film release, the one we didn't get to make. This is what I do; you've got to hook your audience. And we stick it all over our adult comedy videos, our soft porn videos. It raises awareness, so when we finally come to sell the thing, we can say we already have a market. But my audience is not three- to five-year-old kids, or their mums, who stick their pride and joy in front of our bestselling kids' video franchise, *Bristo the Badger*, for an hour's peace in the mornings. As usual it has nothing to do with me. Some bright spark in the mastering department, some doped up operations type, has got confused. It's a publicity nightmare. Not that anybody is going to care so much about that. What José is obviously doing his nut about right now is the fact that it's going to cost us tens of thousands of pounds to recall all the tapes, and replace the trailer with something a little more three-to-five-year-old friendly. Saying that, I doubt it's the kids themselves that have complained. More likely some young mum with a rich husband, who gets to sit about all day thinking about playing tennis, has happened to catch a glimpse of our original *Evil Ghost*, after hearing her offspring having a good old giggle at the naked lady on the television. Again, this is not my fault. Why doesn't she just take her kid to the park, instead of sticking it in front of a box all morning? I have a feeling they won't let me send a letter back saying that. And even though José knows it has nothing to do with me, you can bet he is damn well telling anybody who will listen back at the office that it is, because I am the person who doesn't happen to be there. I am the one out, on his orders, photographing an old bird in smog.

'Phil, I'm coming back. Don't worry about it, it's nothing to do with us.'

'One last thing.'

'What?' Surely nothing else can be wrong.

'Charlie called.' I catch the tone of his voice, but ignore it. I am more surprised than anything. Charlie doesn't call my work any more.

'Really? Charlie? What did he want?'

'I don't know, but he sounded weird. I answered the phone, and he asked me if I was you. Obviously I said no, and he hung up.'

'That's not weird, Phil, that's just him,' I say. Obviously he doesn't even recognize my voice any more.

'Yeah, but he sounded really strange, like he was upset or something.'

'It's probably just the coke,' I say, and hang up. I don't even know if he still does it. I know he was doing a lot, a couple of months ago. I've stopped asking now.

I go over to Charlie's apartment early, just to get away from José, who is making vaguely disguised accusations in my direction about 'Badgergate', as it has already become known by the time I get back to the office. Charlie lives in East London. We live on opposite sides of town – Charlie in his urban wasteland outer and minimalism inner on one side, and me amongst the trees and families and pubs with gardens, on the other.

If I lived with him, I'd have to see him shagging other women, and that might force me to confront things. I wouldn't be able to ignore an orgasm in our bed.

I wonder at what point love became so trivial. I wonder when I began to deride my heart, instead of feeding it, when I decided it didn't matter and wrote it off. I wonder when the loneliness and despair became almost laughable. I wonder when we learnt to dismiss the pathetic who went back again and again to have their hearts trampled on. I wonder when they became 'pathetic'.

When romance does break through all the walls these days, it leaves me in tears. If people sing in tune, or run the marathon, or exemplify any kind of harmony or commitment it leaves me crying, in private of course. Because these are the things my life lacks, and I cry that I wasn't more careful to hold onto them.

I wonder why starvation, or racism, are so much more weighty issues, so much less pathetic than the emotional heartburn caused by the one you love trampling all over your feelings, and your heart. Why is this not deemed just as bad as an earthquake? Sure it affects just you, and not ten thousand people, but you can bet your life there is more than one person in the world at any given moment feeling like their world has ended, because they have been unbearably hurt by the one they love. There must be at least ten thousand at any one time. An earthquake for every day of the year. We are told to spend our whole lives looking for real love, and then if we find it and lose it again, we are supposed to underplay it, pull ourselves together, and get on with life.

When did love become a joke?

When did I?

Psycho

I was at university in America for a year, the autumn of 1995 to the summer of 1996, and so was Charlie, but we were from different universities back home in Britain. I had to walk through the quad to get to most of my lectures – a huge rectangle of grass and crossing paths, of students with backpacks, and haggy-sac games, flicking tiny bean bags off their feet and ankles and heads and shoulders, and smelling of illegal substances and youth. Massive trees spotlighting the season, framing buildings that seemed older than everything else in town. The library was at one end and the theatre at the other, where I had seen a particularly gratuitous performance of *Hair*, students making a big deal of being naked, to prove that being naked wasn't a big deal. On either side were the humanities buildings – the science buildings were off to one side, supposedly in case of explosions, but mostly because science students don't mesh well with other students, and there would be too much bullying between lectures.

The day Charlie and I met had been eventful. It was November, and freezing outside. The weather in Urbana-Champaign was a curious set of extremes; ninety percent humidity in the summer – asthmatics didn't make it through July – and minus forty in the winter, when the wind chill could freeze up the water in your eyes given two minutes. And either side, in spring and fall, were the tornadoes – green silent skies before a killer wind whipped through town. I strongly believe in the effect of the weather. It makes you do things you normally wouldn't, it's the backdrop to all our greatest dramas. More than anything it affects the moods. Bad things shouldn't happen on sunny days, it's confusing.

It was an exchange year, with an American student who got to be conscientious in England while I pissed it up in Illinois for three terms. The only downside was that I had to stay in university accommodation, which meant sharing a room with a complete stranger.

And my roommate was trained to kill. This was the thought most prevalent in my mind early on the day I met Charlie. Her face, contorting with rage, her mouth screaming random obscenities, and she was trained to kill: not just chickens after two days of starvation in some mosquito swarm of a jungle, but real people, actual humans, in battle. She had spent two years in the American Army Reserves, and they let her have a knife, and probably a gun, which she had no doubt stolen and kept. She was trained to kill, and in the process of throwing my stuff around the room, beating my bed with her pillow, twisting and snarling at me, and screaming abuse. This was not the first time, but certainly I had never actually feared for my life before. Trained in the art of slitting a man's throat in the dead of night, and she was very much pissed off with me. I knew for a fact that she was seeing a counsellor. My roommate, Joleen, mentally, medically unstable, able to slit my throat, and barely two feet away from me. The last time she was mad, which wasn't even this mad, I had been nearer to the door. But on this particular day, I was practically pinned against my debunked bunk bed, while she held the sides of her head, palms wide, pressing her temples, as if the pain wouldn't stop, as if the voices wouldn't stop. Did she hear voices? I'm not sure, but I would never bet against it. J. Edgar Hoover? Probably. He was a psychopath in women's clothing as well. Like attracts like they say.

Joleen turned to face me, and started screaming. I was petrified.

'You fucking bitch, you are like a dog on the street, I have less respect for you than a fucking dog on the street, you fucking piece of shit, you fucking bitch.'

She was pretty much repeating this over and over. I don't know what the voices in her head were telling her, but they were anti-me, that much I deduced.

'Joleen, simmer down and at least tell me what I have done!'

I tried desperately to keep the situation reasonably calm – no rising to the bait and feeding her fury. I felt it was important not to make direct eye contact with a psychotic, so I looked at her forehead with one eye, while sizing up the door with the other.

'You can't use my fridge, it's my fucking fridge, don't put your stuff in there, you bitch!' she screamed back, her face turning a yellowy red, the colour of serious illness.

'Oh, right.'

At least now I knew why she was angry. She hadn't said anything before. And it was only some beers to drink while I got ready that night, and an eye mask.

'Don't you think you're blowing this all out of proportion, Joleen? It's a couple of beers, for a couple of hours. Let's talk about what this is really about. It's Dale, right?'

The last time Joleen had actually tried to do me harm was because of Dale. Dale was her friend, her only friend. She loved him, I knew that much. You could tell from every sideways glance, every admiring beam in his direction, every distracted glazed daydream of what they could be together. But he did not love her. He used her. He used her car, used her soap powder, used her phone. He had a room in our dorm, not two hundred feet away, yet he was never there. He wore Bryan Ferry suits. He quiffed his hair, but rarely washed it. He was a five feet six, nine-stone weasel of a man. He wore second-hand winkle-pickers, which were so badly scuffed at the front it looked like he kicked dustbins for a living. He chain-smoked Marlboro Reds, and he wrote poetry on a bashed-up old typewriter with keys missing. None of his poems contained the letter J, he said, through choice. He was a womanizer, of sorts. He preyed on the insecure; he lured the weak ones with romantic ramblings, and implied sensitivity, and had sex with them when nobody else would. Or else he lucked out and got a cheerleader who was looking for something 'deeper' and 'darker' and ultimately dirtier. And if Dale looked one thing, it was dirty.

Dale had five women on the go at any one time. They left messages for him on Joleen's answerphone. The messages weren't just 'meet me at six o'clock in the coffee house'. They were nearly always sexual, mostly bordering on the perverse. 'I want to lick you from the tips of your toes to the tip of your . . .' or 'I want you to dip your fingers in honey and push them up my . . .' The challenge was always stopping the message before anything truly disgusting was disclosed. I could make it from one side of the room to the other in a quarter of a second. He enjoyed both sides of the coin – getting them to say things to a machine they would never say to somebody's face, and having Joleen listen to them after a hard day of lectures and taking the bus because Dale had her car. Sometimes he even had the luck to see her face drop, and witness first hand any dismal light in her fade.

But Joleen loved him anyway. She saw how he treated these women, saw them fall in love with him as he kissed parts of their body that had never been kissed, whispered things to them that they longed to be true, and then he turned on them. One day he was their hero, the next their only hope, as he told them nobody else would want them, told them how fucked-up they were, how neurotic, how stupid, how insecure, how pathetic, how boring, how unintelligent, how unworthy. Joleen thought he did this for sport, for some Machiavellian fun: in the mixed-up world that was her mind, Dale was some twentieth-century Marquis de Sade, playing games with whores and handmaidens who somehow deserved it.

Joleen looked at me in sheer horror at the audacity of my even saying his name in her presence. Seconds lapsed but time stood still, and then she hit me with the full verbal force of her startling originality: 'You fucking bitch.'

She glared at me, and I half-expected to see venom fly from the sides of her mouth. This was all a real shame, as despite the hate campaign waged against me since day three, I didn't dislike her . . . that much. I felt sorry for her, I wished she'd go out more, I wished she'd see Dale for what he was, but I didn't hate her. How can you hate somebody that fucked up? Everything she did to me, every perverse stab in my direction, was fuelled by jealousy, and jealousy is a terrible affliction. It hurts its victim most, and I was getting the easy bit compared to what must have been going on in her head. The room was quiet, but the silence itself seemed loud. The threat of impending noise seemed to hang everywhere, in the air around the two desks, our beds, our book-filled shelves, the wardrobes on either side of the door, my shoes kicked off under my bed, the papers on my desk, the photos of her naked scrambling up a tree (I know!) on her desk, everywhere.

The phone began to ring, and we both jumped a little. She was nearest, with her back to it. I didn't move to answer it. Joleen stared at me, daring me to grab for it, so in one swift

33

movement she could get me in a head lock and flash her blade in front of my dying eyes while blood oozed from the slit in my throat; she'd claim it was self-defence because I 'lunged' towards her. I decided not to move, and let the answerphone get it. It was, after all, exactly this kind of situation that answerphones were created for. The phone kept ringing. We both waited for the sixth ring and the click. We stared at each other and mentally counted, although I swear I saw her fingers folding in one by one, and her lips moving. At last, the answerphone kicked in. A male voice, young but gruff. It was Big John from the dorm upstairs.

'Dale, if you leave one more death threat on my answerphone, I swear to God I will kick your ass. Get a fucking life!'

Joleen and I both turned and stared at the answerphone incredulously for a moment, before she turned back to face me, but a little less angry, a little more concerned. She was worried for Dale and rightly so. I don't know what the sick little shit had been up to but, by the sounds of it, it was no good. And more frightening still, for Joleen and Dale at least, Big John's nickname was not ironic.

'Don't do it again,' Joleen hissed at me, turned and grabbed her keys. I flinched and covered my face – oh the vanity! – but I don't think she even noticed. She snatched her coat and goose-stepped out the door.

Joleen believed that deep down Dale loved her too. She would come up behind him and hug him, the only real outlet of affection I ever saw her indulge in, at which point he would push her away with absolute disgust. It takes real love to keep coming back for more of that kind of treatment. She saw a twisted black prince – I saw a pretender, intent on making everybody feel as bad as he did about his failed notions of poetic greatness, about rejection from a father who wanted a son with a crew cut and a football in his hand.

34

And despite his sexual indifference towards her, Dale had long since convinced Joleen that she needed him like oxygen. Every time it started to dawn on her that he was a destructive force in her life, and in fact scaring away any new friends she seemed on the verge of making, he sensed it, and offered her some weak branch of hope that he might actually feel something for her too. She was hooked again. The previous year he had changed his surname from Woodfood to Curse for the devilish connotations. I don't need to say 'wanker', but I will.

I shared my room with Joleen, not through choice, but through a complete lack thereof. I had requested a smoking room, and I had got hers. This was America, after all; they weren't all lighting up down the corridor. We were a grim novelty at the end of the hall, hippies or beatniks or freaks or arseholes, depending on who you asked. Smoking was our badge, and we wore it like a cloud of smoke around our heads at all times. Nobody had a single room; they were like gold-dust. I was obliged to stay in halls of residence and I had nowhere else to go. It was a battle of wills, mostly. I didn't realize she was a fruitcake on day one. Maybe day three, when all my pictures got mysteriously smashed during dinner. It was about the same time that Dale started to make advances towards me. He was in our room twenty hours a day and I literally had to ask him to step outside while I changed my clothes, which he found amusing more than inconvenient. I broached it with Joleen.

'Dale's here a lot, isn't he?'

'Yes.'

'What's his roommate like? Don't they get on?'

'He's a moron.'

'Who, Dale or his roommate?' I laughed, but Joleen didn't get the joke.

'His roommate of course.'

'So do you think he might mind not coming round if neither of us is here – I don't know, it just makes me feel uncomfortable if you're not here and I come back, and he's already hanging out here.'

Joleen stopped sorting her socks, and was completely still. I seriously thought she had slipped into a coma. Or was suffering some minor epileptic fit at least.

'Joleen?' I edged forward.

'He's got nowhere else to go.'

'What about his room? He could hang out there, I mean, until you got back at least.'

The conversation was starting to make me fell uncomfortable. Joleen was not being as receptive to my feelings as I anticipated.

'Joleen?' I asked again, as she fell silent.

'Dale stays.'

'Oh come on, don't you think you're being just a little unreasonable?'

'Fuck off.'

'Sorry?'

I heard her the first time. I shouldn't have asked her to repeat it.

She leapt up from her bed, dumped the basket of freshly washed clothes on the floor, screamed 'Fuck off' at me again, and left the room. I was a little shocked if I'm honest.

I stayed, because it was my room too. In this land of democracy, I wasn't about to surrender my rights. But mostly, and despite my political high-mindedness, I stayed to prove I could. I should have asked for a transfer in week one, but some weird sense of determination and fairness kicked in, and I decided that I would not be driven out by a fruit loop and her twisted sidekick – Batmad and Dobin.

*   *   *

Whether Dale was actually attracted to me was up for debate, but he feigned it regularly and I admired his persistence at least. I could see it was about Joleen and not me, but this was unfortunately only clear to the sane. He just delighted in pushing her to the edge, and she hated me for it. As is often the case, instead of naming her enemy 'man' she named it 'woman'. On the third day of my stay at the University of Illinois, about an hour before dinner, as the sun sank like an American football behind our halls, Dale sat in a chair in the corner of our ten-foot by fifteen-foot room, and Joleen sprawled across her bottom bunk. They were both seemingly transfixed by a re-run of *The X-Files* on TV, as I attempted to put the cover on my duvet. Is something really out there? They were hoping it was their mother race. But I noticed Dale staring at me, giving me sideways, strange, twisted smiles, and pointing his winkle-pickers in my direction. I pretended not to notice. But Joleen noticed. Eventually, as Mulder and Scully took a break for the adverts, he piped up,

'Nicola, can I do that for you?' Dale gave me a nonchalant sneer accompanied by a nasty twinkle in his eye that he labelled 'mischievous'.

'No, I'm fine thanks,' I replied, attempting to deflect his attention back to the TV, and simultaneously ignore the scowl that was threatening to make Joleen the ugliest woman I had ever seen, as opposed to just one of the top ten. She was scrawny, and ratty-looking, with dyed black hair and brown roots, curling and kinking in the strangest, driest places, and with a front tooth significantly more brown than the rest. She was pale in that unwashed way: she looked like she needed to be taken outside and hosed down with disinfectant.

'Nicola, I'd really like to do that for you though.' Dale continued to leer and Joleen's face morphed into rage.

'Why, Dale?' I asked, feigning innocence.

'So that I can say I've at least done *something* in your bed.'

'Funny guy.'

I looked away and carried on struggling with my duvet, Dale turned back to the TV with a grin, and Joleen broke a cigarette in half. After another ten minutes had lapsed, and I had finally dealt with my bedding, I jumped down and admired my handiwork. I was wearing battered old Levis that I had triumphantly paid thirty dollars for and an old T-shirt that said 'Cuba' across my chest – I was dressing the part of an American student. I turned to pick up the discarded packaging and Dale muttered, just loudly enough for us all to hear,

'Hmmm, Cuba, I'd like to go *there*.'

I ignored it, but Joleen couldn't manage the same restraint, and kicked over her Coke can with a scream. The room went silent, and then we all carried on as normal. I headed for dinner in the canteen pretty much straight away, and it was only when I returned to our room that I found my pictures, previously hanging innocently on the wall, smashed on the floor with glass everywhere. Joleen and Dale were top and toeing on the bottom bunk, seemingly asleep. There had been no effort made to clear up – my mum and dad, my sisters, my friends, all covered in shards of glass on the floor.

It got steadily worse from then on. I tried to talk to Joleen about the fact that his advances towards me, which went so far as trying to lick my shoulder after I'd had a shower, were not genuine affection, but a twisted theatre on her behalf. But again she would hear none of it.

And her fury only grew.

The room itself was the usual testament to the authorities who believed that if they treated us like kids we'd act like them and not have sex. We had bunk beds.

The beds were 'debunked' upon my request – they were too high to jump down from, particularly if, like me, you have weak netball ankles caused by a thousand sprains from the ages of eight to eighteen. Besides, I just don't think bunk beds are dignified at twenty-one, especially if you have an overnight guest. The likelihood of serious injury during any kind of sexual experimentation is increased at least tenfold. Joleen grudgingly agreed. My bed was still higher than hers, as it was the top bunk, the one with the longer legs, the one that would have suspended me six feet in the air given the chance. Now I could jump easily down to the floor by putting my foot on the wood of the end of her bed. This was the piece of wood where the metal rod would slot in a hole in the centre to connect the two beds when they were in their naturally 'bunked' state. This was the hole I stepped on nearly every day with bare feet as I climbed out of bed. This was the hole that Joleen chose to put an upright compass in, without my knowledge, which I missed by a fraction, and at the very last minute, one day while she was at lectures. I don't need to say the word 'freak', but I will.

I tried to talk to Dale about it as well. One afternoon, early in my stay, I arrived back at the room to find Dale lying seemingly asleep on Joleen's bed. I tip-toed across the room, annoyed at myself for not confronting the situation, for being quiet on his behalf, and in truth I just couldn't be arsed to wake him. But he wasn't asleep.

'Hmmm, you're back, I knew I could smell you.'

'Dale, it's not Joleen, it's me,' I laughed, pretending he'd made a mistake.

I saw his lids open slightly.

'Joleen doesn't smell like vanilla and baby moisturizer.' He was speaking so quietly that the air in the room was suddenly saturated with an intimacy I didn't like.

'Oh right. Sorry.' I was becoming increasingly cross with myself for not telling him to stop, but I didn't want an argument.

Dale's half-open eyes closed again, and I kicked off my boots. I decided to go straight back out, to my friend Jake's room, and reached under my bed for my slippers.

'I can't think of anything more wonderful right now than if you just curled up here with me, pressed yourself into my chest.'

He was testing my limits. I took a deliberate step towards the door, to put a decent amount of distance between us, and turned to fiddle with something on my desk.

'Look, Dale, I don't really appreciate you saying stuff like that.' It sounded half-hearted, but I still barely knew him, and you don't shout at people you barely know. I was interrupted.

'I bet your neck tastes like ice cream.'

'Dale, enough!' I turned to face him, but he kept his eyes closed. 'I'm serious, stop it! You're being a prick. I don't want to have to get you banned from the hall, but I will.'

'I've stopped. I'm just trying to get some sleep.' And somehow he made me feel like the fool.

'Oh whatever.' I dumped the contents of my bag onto the bed to find my keys and cigarettes. The room was quiet now.

He mumbled and I ignored it. But then I heard it again, a little louder, and I distinctly heard the word 'nipple'.

'Jesus, when do you stop?'

'Can I help it if I talk in my sleep?' His eyes were still closed, but there was a smile creeping across his face.

'Who says they talk in their sleep, in their sleep?'

'Touché.' He smiled. And I erupted.

'I will never be interested in you, you tiny little man! You're making me feel uncomfortable in my own room, and that's not fair! Why are you being such an arsehole?' I stared at him until he was eventually forced to open one eye.

'Because, Nicola, Nix,' he propped himself up on one

elbow, and spat my name out like a joke, 'other men just don't understand you like I do.' He stared at me intently. It occurred to me for the first time that he might seriously want to add me to the menagerie of feather-brains that fell for his routine.

'You don't even know me, for God's sake. You don't know anything about me. I'm not bloody interested. Get it through your head.'

'Nobody gets your sense of humour, how much passion you have.'

'How would you know?' His flattery meant nothing given that he couldn't possibly know after such a short amount of time and no decent conversation how funny and passionate I considered myself to be.

'I don't think you understand how beautiful you are, Nicola.'

He stared at me, and I finally lost it.

'Don't try your twisted shit on me, Dale, I'm secure enough, thanks. I don't need your nasty little routine, I'm not Joleen!'

Something in his face hardened as I said the words. I wasn't scared, but nervous maybe.

When he spoke, it was quietly, but with a controlled anger:

'Other men might think your ass is too big, but I can see its merits.'

'Oh, touched a nerve have I, Dale? Well, merits or not, if I see you looking at my arse again, I will report you to the Resident Tutor and have you banned from the hall. And I'll get Jake to kick your skinny arse, an arse that, by the way, I see no merit in whatsoever.'

I stormed out of the room, shaking, and slammed the door behind me. I went straight to Jake's room, and forced him to stop snogging his new girlfriend and listen to what a dick Dale was. He offered to do the arse kicking straight away, mostly to impress his new girlfriend, but I decided not to take him up on it just yet.

But Dale didn't stop, and Jake never got round to kicking his arse. If he was in the room when I got there, I would sigh and swear under my breath, and he would just sneer, turn back to his battered old typewriter, and start typing furiously. Sometimes he cried out, as if in pain, and then scrambled for a piece of paper to note down some thought or other. Sometimes it was just a word on a page that I'd find lying around the floor, discarded. 'Brambles' was one, 'Pigmy' another. I accidentally found and looked at (purely by mistake) some of his poetry, while he and Joleen were, for once, both elsewhere. I accidentally found it in his plastic bag that he carried with him, which I happened upon, purely by coincidence, at the back of Joleen's wardrobe where he always stashed it.

In Autumn,
We dance around the leaves,
Until she comes.

Not exactly Wordsworth. And given how long he had been working on it, not exactly a masterpiece. I asked him after some petty jibe in my direction if his poetry ever rhymed, and how could it be poetry if it *didn't* rhyme? He looked at me like I was the fool. I asked if he ever wrote any limericks, at which point he pretended not to hear.

Despite her almost fatal self-esteem issues, maybe because of them, Joleen didn't seem to realize that in the twisted world that was her and Dale, she had the power. He relied on her completely. If he left, she'd be sad for a couple of weeks, maybe even months. Maybe she'd muster a half-arsed attempt at suicide, but only then with pills, and eventually she'd be fine. But Dale would be the one out on a ledge, with nothing to cling to, nobody to validate him, nobody to assure him that he was the thing that he wanted so badly to be – a poetic, sexually liberated soul: a 'character'. If Joleen left and he didn't have her adoring looks and unfaltering declarations of his massive talent supporting his ego, reality would slap him so hard in the face he'd be bruised for life. And he'd look in the mirror and see what the rest of the world saw – a guy who was a disappointment to his father, a guy who had never fitted in, who had been bullied at school. In short, a guy who felt unloved. Dale was so desperate to prove how he could never have been that thing that his father wanted, that he persisted in acting out a fantasy that didn't even make him happy. He had enough intelligence to know he'd been hurt, yet he had spent the last ten years hurting other people because of it. Joleen would eventually be fine. Dale, on the other hand, would fall apart at the seams of his replica Bryan Ferry suits.

Look back and back and you can always see where the hurt comes from. For some it's more recent than others, just over the horizon, barely out of sight, but you can always trace anybody's pain back to the actions of another. Somebody hurt you once. Somebody always does. Whether you choose to hurt other people because of it is a whole different story. Is it a choice, or can't we help ourselves? Answers on a postcard. But I have Dale to thank for something at least. He was my first living, breathing example of a man who hurts a woman, not because he particularly wants to, but merely because he can.

I took a shower in the communal bathroom after Joleen had gone. I got back to my room and Dale, who hadn't been there when I left, had since arrived. He was staring off into space, looking out the window of our little room, through the mosquito mesh, at the trees and the dorm rooms opposite, with his winkle-pickers squarely on Joleen's desk. He was wearing a shiny green suit with an ironed-on dirty glaze that I just knew somebody had died in. Even from the doorway, I could see the flecks of last week's gel in his hair and on his shoulders. Nick Cave and the Bad Seeds played from Joleen's battered old tape machine: a small courtesy, at least, was that Dale never disturbed my newly acquired American CD player. I don't think he owned any CDs anyway – Dale made it a point to fight technology like a matador fights a bull: all suited and booted, but looking small and stupid in the process. Every time I suggested he get a laptop, instead of banging away on his archaic typewriter and disturbing us all, he informed me that a laptop could 'have no character', and thus whatever he wrote would 'have no soul'. I said I doubted anybody would notice, given that as far as I could see he had no character and no soul, and they would just attribute it to that. He had laughed in a way that implied I loved him really. I really didn't.

I coughed and broke his daydream – probably of being well adjusted – and he acknowledged me with a glance over his shoulder.

'Oh, you're back, are you?' he said, with a trace of irritation – he wasn't nearly as nice to me if Joleen wasn't in the room.

'Yep, and I've just had a shower, so can you leave, please, while I get ready?'

'Going anywhere nice? Another frat party, is it? You're such a joiner,' he said, without a hint of interest. I had only been to two fraternity parties in the four months since I had arrived – pathetic affairs full of seventeen-year-old girls not used to drinking, and a house full of frat boys all lashed on keg beer, and a makeshift jacuzzi out front for concealed groping. The University of Illinois, my home for that year, had the largest Greek system in the States, meaning it had the most fraternities and sororities. It's a quaint little system, whereby you get to buy your friends for four years because you're too damn scared to make them on your own, but it's all dressed up as tradition and fun. It's a system that reeks of the 'American Dream', rotting. One girl in my dorm, a gorgeous looking, athletic, popular, intelligent freshman named Joanna discussed the ins and outs of trying to get into one of the sororities, over bagels one day in the canteen. Joanna had a shortlist of three. The one she most wanted to get into, Pi Kappa whatever, was her favourite, the top of her list, but she was a little nervous. She didn't think she would get in, the reason being she was Jewish, and Pi Krappy whatever didn't usually take Jewish girls. I practically threw my lunch up all over her. She was desperate to get into some mock Tudor shit-hole of a house with a bunch of tight arsed wasps who wouldn't like her anyway because she was Jewish. I told her you would never get it in Britain. We make our own friends when we get to college I explained, trying hard not to sound like her rabbi. We go down to the pub and have a legal drink at a sensible age, and make friends that way, half cut. We don't discuss how much our parents earn. What about the class system in England she had said? I told her I had a lecture to go to, and she was too bright a girl to be doing something so stupid as join a sorority.

I wasn't going to a fraternity party, therefore, that evening, but to the pub, Henry's, where all the 'foreigners' went – Aussies, Brits, Kiwis, Paddies – for the birthday of one of the guys from university back home. You see I hadn't braved this new world on my own – there were at least fifteen students from my university with me, and that's not even counting all those from the other British universities. What with not actually having to pass any courses, it was more like a multi-cultural holiday camp with racial tension and inadequate air conditioning, than work. It was Jon's birthday, and we all congregated in the pub, which we did most nights anyway. It wasn't like all the other bars – the 'sports bars' – with their neon lights and blonde-haired waitresses, and TV screens and dozens of pool tables. It was dirtier, dingier – all the bar staff looked slightly tortured and, if not unattractive, they all had tattoos at least. The tables were made of old battered wood and engraved with fifty years' worth of drunken etchings by students missing lectures. It reminded us of home. On these occasions, we would drink until the birthday boy or girl threw up. This was generally about ten p.m., as they had invariably been in the pub all day. I don't know why I told Dale this, but I did.

'No actually, Dale, I am not going to a fraternity party, I'm just not in that date-rape mood tonight. And besides, I'm always scared I'll spot you hiding in the bushes, weeping in loneliness and wanking over bikini-clad freshers – and that's just the boys.'

Dale swore at me under his breath.

'I am actually going to the pub.' I continued to stand and stare expectantly at him, waiting for him to leave, nodding towards the door, holding up my towel, wet hair dripping all over the floor, as I needed him to go before I could put the towel covering my body on my head.

'I don't see why I have to leave. I won't look; I'm working.' Dale stared down at the letters on his typewriter, supposedly in concentration.

'Oh Dale, just get out, will you – I shouldn't have to walk on eggshells to get a little fucking privacy in my *own* room. Joleen's not even here,' and with that, Joleen walked in and practically had a seizure at the sight of me in my towel, standing in front of Dale, begging him for something, even if the something was his speedy exit.

She turned on me straight away. 'What the fuck are you

doing – can't you put some fucking clothes on?' She spat the words at me, which she pretty much did whenever she talked anyway.

Joleen's sudden appearance in the room meant Dale's attitude towards me changed completely.

'Nicola, can't I stay for a little while? I yearn to kiss your milky white shoulders.' He looked at me, looked at Joleen, and then back at me again, a smile playing on his lips.

'They are not milky white. Get out.'

And for once, Joleen agreed with me.

'Yeah, Dale, leave while she gets dressed for God's sake, she's just a prick tease.'

Dale grabbed his Marlboros from the desk and pushed past me, his proximity immediately making me want to get straight back in the shower.

'Thank you, Jesus, at last!' I muttered as he left.

'What was that? What did you say?' He spun around and, for a moment, he was a froth of anger and spite, but almost instantly he recovered himself, and forced a smile. 'Oh Nicola, remember, you'll never meet an American who loves you like I do. They don't get how ironic you are – they're all assholes. They think you're just some uptight Brit who wouldn't know her ass from her elbow in bed, but I know you'd go like a greyhound.'

And with that, Dale stalked off down the hall to sit in his room for the rest of the evening, watching sci-fi shit on TV.

My Penis Is . . .

I pushed my way into the pub, past the moronic doorman who maintained every time I went in there and showed him my ID, that I had 'forged it wrong', and got my dates mixed up. There was no fourteenth month he said, every time. And every time I calmly explained to him that I was British, and we write our days and months the other way round, the right way round. The aisles were narrow, and crowded, and it took me ten minutes to get to the big seats at the back where my friends were sitting. Jon had been there most of the day, and was looking a little worse for wear. In American terms, anybody who goes to the pub at lunchtime is a drunk, pure and simple, even if you only drink lemonade all day. Jon was at the finding it hard to speak and control his limbs stage. The boys were all playing 'My Penis Is', their favourite game. I pushed in beside Jake, grabbed a glass and filled it from the pitcher in the middle of the table. 'My Penis Is' was a game that Martin had brought with him from home. They sat around, started with the letter A, and then described their penis, but they had to 'drink as they think'. So Martin would start and say 'My penis is aromatic,' at which point the boys would cheer, and it would be someone else's turn.

'My penis is astronomical' the next guy would say, and the cheering would start again, and so on. They obviously hadn't been playing for long, because they were only on the letter B. Jon had just said 'My penis is bacon' and the game had stopped for twenty minutes while the boys cried with laughter. I didn't get it, but then I hadn't been in the pub since midday. Sitting opposite Jon was a guy I hadn't seen before.

He was obviously tall, but sitting down, so I couldn't tell quite how tall. He had the body of a footballer who drank too much – slim, with vague muscle definition that he was already losing with every sip of beer he took. The top three buttons of his shirt were undone and I could see a mildly hairy chest poking out from beneath the denim. His hair was spiked at the front, and he had obviously been nurturing his sideburns for a good year. What I noticed most was his laugh. It was loud. And the smile that preceded the laugh almost made me dizzy. It was a huge, face-altering smile. It was a smile that could capsize small boats. He was obviously good-looking, but, more than that, he seemed over the moon with the world, with himself. When he laughed, as the boys all laughed at how funny all their 'peni' – plural of penis? – were turning out to be, it was the closest I had come to a religious experience since school.

When he stood up and got his wallet out to get another four pitchers of beer, he did something peculiar – he jogged to the bar. And all the people seemed to let him through. It was a casual jog, not hurrying to get beer, or to go for a 'slash' as the boys endearingly put it. He just jogged because his body seemed to want to, it seemed the most natural thing to do. I had to fight the blush from taking over my cheeks as I watched him. I asked Jake who he was.

'Oh, haven't you met Charlie?'

I knew I would have remembered.

I watched him as he made his way back from the bar,

somehow balancing four pitchers of beer, spilling a little on people's shoes, but faced with that smile nobody seemed to care. It was a Tom Cruise, fifty million dollar, all-encompassing, I own the world and the world loves me smile. Of course, none of this was going to mean a thing if he was stupid. I couldn't do stupid; it was just too depressing. It was going to hinge on his answer to 'My Penis Is' .

The boys decided you couldn't top 'bacon' and moved onto the letter C. Charlie was drinking a lot of his pint, trying to think of what his penis 'was'.

'Come on, Charlie, ss'get ss move on!' Jon shouted a little too enthusiastically.

Charlie was still drinking, his eyes widening as he thought, spluttering out beer as he laughed at the others all staring at him and laughing, banging their palms on the table to hurry him up. He slammed his pint down suddenly,

'My penis is cathartic!' he yelled, and all the boys went a little quiet. A couple of them tittered embarrassed, and Jon went, 'Eh? It's what?'

'You know, cathartic, like relaxing, you know,' Charlie justified.

'Nah, mate, haven't got a s'clue what you're talking about,' Jon said.

'I know what he means, they can be . . . cathartic . . .' I said, without thinking, forgetting my 'play it cool' rules straight away.

But the boys all cheered, and I drank some beer, caught Charlie's eye, and he winked at me, and mouthed 'thanks'. I honestly, literally, nearly fell off my chair. If there hadn't been a big wooden armrest between me and the floor, I would have been face down in the grime and beer and cigarette butts. Which would have been a good look.

'Nah, mate, I don't think we should let him have it – he's

got to think of s'another one.' Jon was lashed, but it was his birthday, his game, his rules.

'Alright, alright, Jon, mate, it is your birthday.' Charlie took a sip of his beer, put it squarely back on the table, and announced, 'My penis is crooked.'

The boys cheered and raised their glasses, and I raised my eyebrows at Charlie, who raised his glass at me. I downed my beer, looked away at the rest of the bar, and felt my neck. I looked back at Charlie, who was watching me, as intended. I wondered how desperate I had become, whether it had been so long that anybody was looking good, and whether I was actually dreaming this perfectly ordinary guy into the man I wanted to meet. I put my beer down, and resolved not to drink too much, to ensure I was seeing straight. The game continued, but my concentration was shot to hell.

Later on in the evening, when Jon had passed out, and was proudly propped up at a table in the corner, his glasses falling off one side of his face, I was chatting to Jake about who had missed the most lectures that week. We were almost proud; no we actually were proud. I just don't know what we managed to do with our time – we had ten hours a week, maximum, yet I couldn't make it to half of them. Unfortunately we weren't actually required to pass the exams at the end of it, just attend the lectures. But the lectures were all so crowded, nobody knew if you were there or not, and if we didn't have to pass the exam at the end of it, our reasoning was simple: we didn't need to go, so we weren't going to go.

I kept one eye on Charlie as he wandered back from the bar again, a couple of drinks in hand, smiling at everybody around him, including a couple of cheerleader types who stared at him as he walked past. Jake noticed my eye wandering, and before I could protest, was calling him over. Charlie put the drinks down on the table, grabbed his beer, and squeezed in next to me.

'I preferred cathartic to crooked, so much less graphic.' I gave him a grimace.

'But no less accurate. We haven't been introduced – I'm Charlie,' and he held out his hand. I offered him my hand back, and we shook on it.

'Are you here for the year?'

This was the most important question – if he was only here for one term, as were some of the other Brits abroad that we had met, I felt my world would crumble. It was already Halloween. He would have to go home soon

'Yeah, you?' he smiled, and I resolved to look down at the table instead of directly at him, at least until I could relax.

'Yep, but I'm looking forward to going home for Christmas. Just not finding the accent appealing. I need to talk to some English men.'

'What am I, Scotch mist?' he asked.

'No, but yours is crooked, remember?' I practically coughed my answer out. He was having a bizarre effect on me. I just didn't get like this around men; I was always the one in control. Jake was looking at me out of the corner of his eye, with horror, as if I had morphed into a pigtailed, giggling schoolgirl freak in the space of an evening. I tried to fight it as best I could.

'It isn't crooked at all actually, it's straight as a pool cue – that was just a game.'

'Oh right, well you would say that, who wants to be crooked?' I managed.

'Are you going to make me prove it?' he asked, trying to catch my eye as I looked sternly at a knot in the wood of our table. I coughed slightly.

'Maybe later,' I mustered, and looked up, and into, those eyes. Which is when I saw that they were different colours – one dark brown, the colour of old wood, almost dull, one bright blue, the colour of Greek pottery, a bright summery glistening blue, seeming to reflect sunlight that wasn't even there.

'Your eyes are different colours,' I said, without thinking. I'm sure he hadn't realized, and was grateful to me for pointing it out.

'Yeah, I know,' he replied and looked away. And suddenly I knew I had blown it. It's not as if it was a disability, but it was very possible that he was sensitive about it, or defensive, and I had just thrown it out there. I may as well have called him 'freak.'

Except it wasn't freaky; it wasn't unattractive at all. Even the smallest defects aren't tolerated these days. The beauty is in the details, the flaws, the imperfections that make us different, somebody once said, but it isn't true any more. If you have a problem, in this plastic-coated world, just fix it. Have your teeth straightened, your nose fixed, your ears pinned. The surface should be pretty, almost bland, even if underneath there is a mess of scars and emotional tears. If you had told me previously that I would find somebody with different-coloured eyes attractive, I would have been surprised. But with Charlie, it just seemed right. It stopped his face from being completely perfect, but made it so at the same time. I had to correct my outburst, I had to rectify my massive faux pas.

My cheeks suddenly burned with the blood rushing to my face, and I bit my lip and tried to maintain eye contact without getting embarrassed.

'I'm sorry – I didn't mean to be rude. It's just, well, you don't see many like it!'

I was making it worse, he sounded like the bearded lady at the circus, or the smallest man on earth.

'It's fine, your eyes are brown, one of mine is blue, one's brown. It's nothing.' He shrugged, but with a serious look on his face. He looked away, and I looked at the table, at the graffiti that had been etched in with penknives over the years, and swore in my head. Charlie adjusted himself in his seat, and I prepared myself for him to get up and leave. He stood up, and stretched his legs. I turned to talk to Jake, to mask my crushing disappointment, and suddenly heard Charlie's voice in my ear. I moved slightly, to face him, as he leaned in and whispered,

'So, what halls are you in?'

'I'm over in Toulouse. You?'

'Just opposite – Parker Hall.'

'I'm surprised I haven't noticed you before . . . and not because of the eyes or anything.' Jesus! What was wrong with me? I sounded like a Nazi!

But Charlie ignored it and carried on talking.

'Shall I walk you home?' He cut straight to the chase.

'Okay, I think there'll be a few of us though, Jake is in Parker as well.'

'I meant now.' Charlie stared me straight in the eye.

'Sure, why not, I've had enough.' I mustered all my confidence, flushed slightly, grabbed my coat and, with my head down, squeezed myself out of the bar, with Charlie breathing down my neck the whole way.

It was cold as we walked towards the quad, which was the quickest way to get home. We chatted, nowhere near touching each other, and at points he even jogged backwards, trying to expel some of the energy that obviously whizzed around his body at all times. We joked, and made a vague date to see a film together that we both claimed to want to see, but no date was fixed as we passed the library. The cold had really started to set in, and I felt my nose turning red. In the dark I couldn't make out his smile as readily, but I could hear his laugh, which sounded smaller out here, underneath the huge Illinois sky.

'I'm surprised I haven't met you before,' I said, to fill a

55

sudden silence as we started to walk past the law buildings, towards the flower conservatory.

'I've only met Jon a couple of times,' Charlie said.

'Oh, I thought you knew all those guys really well.'

'No, I only met some of them for the first time tonight.' He didn't smile at this, but slapped himself to keep warm. I prayed inside I wasn't boring him, that he hadn't expected me to be a much funnier, livelier person than I was.

'Who have you been hanging out with then?' I asked, for something to say, boring even myself.

'Oh, some fraternity boys – my roommate is in Pi Kappa Chi, so I kind of got in with them.'

'Right, great – been to many parties?' I sounded far more impressed than I had discussing them with Dale. In truth, I was massively disappointed – he wasn't part of our gang, not really, our Brits-abroad gang, us against the world, failing to bond quite properly with our hosts.

'A few, they're all kind of the same. They aren't great actually. They all act like they're your best mate, straight away, just because you can play basketball or whatever.'

'Maybe they just liked you.' I don't know why I was making excuses for the frat boys, something to say again, I suppose, and I couldn't imagine anybody not loving him. I was actually sticking up for myself, in a twisted way.

'Maybe,' and he smiled again.

'Just loveable, I guess,' he said quickly, and then looked down, embarrassed at himself, at something he seemed to know about himself, that didn't sit well with him. And instantly I knew that Charlie wasn't quite as confident as I had first thought – but the world loved him anyway, and chose to overlook all the flaws he felt in himself, for the good stuff they could see. For the world, that smile was everything. For Charlie, that wasn't quite right.

'Well, it takes a while to get to know people, I suppose,'

was all I could say. I felt desperate to let him know that I understood, and not to reveal that I too had instantly fallen victim to his smile as well. I didn't want him to think of me as shallow as the rest of the world. I wanted him to know that I could go deeper, and that we wouldn't be shallow together. Somehow, in my silent desperation, he understood.

'Hold on,' he said suddenly, and grabbed my arm.

'What?' I asked, surprised.

'Look up,' he said, and I had a sinking feeling that he was going to make me gaze at the stars. For somebody fighting for his own depths, it was a mistake.

'What am I looking at?' I asked, suddenly tired, and aware that maybe this wasn't going to work out.

'Whatever you want,' he shouted, from a little way away, and I turned to see him dash behind a tree.

'I had to take a . . . piss,' he said weakly, walking back moments later. 'I didn't want you to see.'

I started to laugh with relief, and chanced my arm.

'Thank God, I thought you were going to start talking about the stars!'

'Hell no!' Charlie laughed too, and then caught me off guard with a kiss. Before I knew it, his tongue was in my mouth, and his arms were around me, and we were kissing each other softly, and fiercely, and he was kissing me exactly the way I wanted to kiss him, and for the first time that evening I regained some control. I realized that something in me had hooked him, the way I had been taken by his smile. I just wasn't sure exactly what.

We didn't make it to either of our rooms. We ended up somewhere behind the cactus conservatory, about two hundred feet from our halls. It was a quick, passionate, gorgeous start. Not seedy, despite the building we were leaning on. We went back to his, and stayed there for most of that first term.

*   *   *

But innocence fades, and sexy starts to a relationship are long forgotten six years later. We wouldn't have sex against that laboratory now – I'd be worried about my heels getting stuck in the grass and mud on suede, and Charlie would have trouble after that much drink. Things aren't as hard as they used to be.

Stripped Bare

January is always a depressing month, I never manage to save money over Christmas for the sales, which is the only thing that January has going for it. I blow it all on champagne parties through Advent, and a hugely extravagant New Year trip, so I can get back to work on the second day of a fresh year and tell everybody that I was somewhere other than London for 31st of December. 00.01 on New Year's Day isn't even an anti-climax, as most people will say, it's just a fucking relief. As soon as Big Ben has chimed, you feel a nation of people relax – they have their story, their setting for those fateful twelve gongs, and now they can go to bed, or carry on getting drunk. But whatever they do, they don't have to worry about how much fun they are having for one particular minute for another year. It's a night when you actually question yourself, your friends, your relationships, your ability to enjoy yourself. Staying in just doesn't cut it, no matter how 'chilled' it supposedly is, it will always sound pathetic until New Year's Eve itself is banned. You can opt out of Christmas Day without seeming pathetic – on religious grounds, on practical grounds, it can almost seem cool not to sit around and eat poultry and pull crackers with your parents.

But New Year is just about 'having fun'. There is no credible reason to opt out. Unless you simply don't have any friends, or don't know how to enjoy yourself, which makes you feel like a failure. There are parties all over the world that night, and you aren't at any of them.

So last January, five months ago now, my friends and I did what we always do and put at least three nights in the diary that wouldn't break the bank, but would enable us to look forward to the following weekend.

Which is how we ended up in Shivers, a lap-dancing club on the Edgware Road at one o'clock in the morning, whooping at the women on the stage, and trying to persuade Jake to have a lap-dance. He was having none of it. The room itself was strange – stages like catwalks with, sticking up from them, poles which looked kind of smudged and grubby and greasy in the pinkish neon lights that shone from above. Around the stages were tables and chairs, not exactly tatty, but not stylish either. The bar was very pink, very neon, with a vase at one end holding what looked like plastic lilies. It wasn't seedy, it just looked cheap. But we were drunk, so what the hell did we care – I hadn't expected it to be something out of *Elle Deco*. All that glass, however, looking slightly grubby, slightly smeared, reflected the core business of the place back at me a little too much. It was essentially a sex club, but I didn't want to have it spelt out for me. I wanted to convince myself that it was really very innocent, and fun, and frivolous, and that no bodily juices were actually involved. Initially, we didn't think the doormen were going to let us in, until Nim convinced them that we were all bisexual, apart from Jake, who was a red-blooded male, and that we would all be chucking around a lot of money. If it hadn't been January, a quiet month for lap-dancing clubs apparently, I don't think they would have let us in. They could tell we were just there to giggle, and would be spending hardly any cash, but they needed anything we were prepared to give.

Jake was the most uncomfortable from the start. He couldn't look at any of the women parading around in their underwear, or sliding down poles, while we were there. Somehow our presence made him feel sleazy, we knew that, and he couldn't leer at women with his female friends around. But we adjourned to the bar, and just whistled from a distance, paying for extortionately priced drinks on our credit cards. We were playing some stupid game that Jules had got from a guy she'd been seeing – you have to name somebody you would have sex with, and then the next person has to name somebody they would have sex with, but their first name has to begin with the first letter of the surname of the person you have said you will have sex with. I started with 'Jeremy Paxman' – I would – and Jules, who always panics, because you have to drink as you think, said,

'Pope John Paul.'

'You disgust me,' Nim said, weeping with laughter and wiping the tears from her eyes, while I tried to stop my drink coming out of my nose.

'Is it me? Is it "P"?' Amy, my big sister, asked – she had loosened up since earlier, relaxed with my friends and not hers.

'Yep – let's try and stay away from leaders of world religions from now on though,' Nim said, and Jules apologized again.

'Paul Newman,' Amy said after a gulp of drink. She was clever, and married, and measured. She was what I hoped I would be in a couple of years' time, but I knew I never actually would. She didn't take shit from people, but she was lovely as well. I took shit from some people and not others, but lost my temper a lot more often. It's like she left all the bad genes in my mum's womb for me to suck

61

up when it was my turn two years later to burst out into the world.

Nim started to drink and think, but was still laughing about the Pope exclamation, and sputtered out her drink as she said,

'Nigel Lawson.' We laughed again, and then fell into a quick silence, as the mental image refused to dislodge itself from all of our brains. We all seemed to neck our drinks quickly, at the same time.

I turned to the bar to order more drinks from a topless smiling woman, who stopped smiling when she saw us in our work clothes. Instantly I felt bad, like I was ridiculing her place of work, her work itself. I knew she thought we were smug and patronizing, and I avoided her stern eye as I handed over another forty quid for five drinks. Jake came back from the toilet, looking concerned.

He whispered something in Amy's ear, and I saw her jaw lock slightly, in anger, and she nodded. I turned to pick up the drinks and pass them around, and caught Jake mouthing something to Jules, but they both stopped guiltily when they saw me looking.

'Hey, I'm tired, shall we go?' Jules said suddenly, smiling at me, and picking up her bag.

'I've just got another round of drinks in!' I said, feeling confused.

'I don't think I can drink any more,' Jake said quickly, grabbing his coat.

'Well, you could have told me that before I paid out forty quid,' I snapped, starting to lose my temper, as an uneasy feeling crept up my back and tension spread across my shoulders, stiffening my neck.

'What?' I said to them all, suddenly feeling sober.

Nim looked from me to them, confused, and Jake and Jules gave each other 'meaningful' looks. It was Amy who spoke.

'Jake thinks he saw Charlie over there, with some guys.' She pointed in the direction of a large group of noisy men on the other side of the room, barely visible through the smoke and the neon.

I heard my jaw click, as I reached to massage the tension in my neck, and looked down at the floor, not wanting to meet any of their gazes. I wasn't surprised, just mortified. I knew damn well that nothing was past Charlie now, but I had never shared it with my friends. I didn't want them feeling sorry for me. I didn't feel sorry for me, why should they? But I wanted to see for myself, some morbid curiosity wanted to at least see his face, see who he was with. He had told me he was seeing his brother tonight, and I wanted to see if it was true. Earlier in the day, when he had told me that, I wondered why he had felt the need to pass the information on – I had started to lose track of Charlie's movements, and didn't care to be told. I had heard whispers from various people, that they didn't think he was 'happy', asking me if we were, as a couple, 'ok?' Asking indirect questions to which they didn't want an answer, fulfilling an obligation to somehow alert me to what was going on, without having to get actually involved in what was at the end of the day a 'domestic' issue, somebody else's relationship. Amy looked shocked. I felt slapped in the face – I don't care how ironic it was that we were in this sleazy hole, which now looked rotten to the core, old and haggard and flabby and bruised. He shouldn't be here, in front of my friends, making me look like an idiot.

Nim, Jules and Jake had picked up their coats and bags, as well as mine, and were trying to usher me to the door. Amy was staring at me, trying to work out what she could reasonably say about my boyfriend, who she at first really quite liked, but had recently come to almost despise. I could tell from her eyes that she was framing sentences in her head that wouldn't upset me, but which would get her point across as well – I could also tell it wasn't easy.

'Hold on a minute,' I said, and marched towards where Charlie was supposed to be, hearing Jules whispering to the others behind me, 'he really has changed, hasn't he. Poor Nix.' I shuddered at the pity of it all.

As I got closer to the group of guys, I could hear a laugh coming from within their circle. His laugh had always been too loud. I was five feet away when I saw one of the guys he worked with clock me coming towards them, and shove the guy sitting in front of him, obscured by one of the others. I could see notes flying towards a girl on the stage, who was kneeling close to the guys, massaging her plastic tits, and licking her lips, and pulling at her G-string as if she might take it off. She looked . . . hairless. Suddenly, an arm sprang into view, waving a fifty pound note at the stripper, and then the crowd seemed to clear, and I could see the note was attached to a hand, to a suited arm, to a man with spiky hair and sideburns, with the top button of his shirt undone, and his tie, knotted around his head like an idiot. The man was leering at the kneeling woman, and it was a smile I didn't recognize – it was seedy and sordid and desperate and arrogant and awful. It was still Charlie, though.

All the other boys were staring at me now, not the stripper, and one of them was nudging Charlie hard on the arm, but his attention couldn't be dragged from the bare breasts in front of him, pushed together to receive his fifty pound note. I stood and watched his mates desperately try and get his attention, with my hands on my hips, just waiting. Finally one of them said 'Charlie' loudly, and he turned quickly.

'I'm fucking busy, what?' and then he looked past his comrade, and saw me, his girlfriend, standing a few feet away.

I didn't say anything, I just looked at him, his hand still outstretched, holding the note. The stripper moved away quickly to another group of guys, glancing back over her shoulder at me once, in sympathy. Charlie seemed to click into life suddenly, and stood up, stuffing the note into his pocket, pulling his tie off his head, and throwing it on the chair behind him. He looked at me, ran his hand through his hair, ashamed, but not guilty. I looked back at him, and almost cried. His hair was blonder now than it had ever been. His suit was bespoke. He looked ten years older than he ever had before. I could see sweaty patches on his shirt, where the cotton stuck to his body.

'Alright?' I said. The rest of the boys looked terribly uncomfortable. I heard one of them whisper to another 'it's his old lady,' but I ignored it. I saw him flinch slightly as he heard it.

'I was out with the girls, I don't know how we ended up here. But I'm going now.' I carried on looking at him, and he stared back, and then looked down, hands on hips, with nothing to say. I turned to go, and then spun around quickly. 'Is your brother with you?'

'No.' Charlie shook his head slowly as he answered.

'Okay, I'll see you later.' I turned and walked away, and didn't look around until I was outside. They were all waiting for me at the top of the stairs, looking concerned.

'It's fine, he's just out with some clients.' I laughed and looked away, and we started to walk down the road towards a cab. Amy tried to hold my hand, but I shook it off.

I didn't see Charlie for a week after that, and I began to wonder if we had somehow called it quits, without even speaking about it. But then he phoned, the following week, to check that I was still coming with him to his boss's birthday party and, for whatever reason, I said I was. We didn't mention it again. We both just knew.

Some people get married, have kids, are divorced in six years. Charlie and I have been through a lot, although appearing to have been through nothing at all. Our start was promising and, God knows, we've stuck it out. It seemed more sensible to stay together than be apart. We have both hung in there. But we've driven each other quietly mad, despite never admitting it. It never seemed that important at the time.

My Green-Eyed Monster

Vittorio De Sica was an Italian film director who said 'moral indignation is in most cases two percent moral, forty-eight percent indignation, and fifty percent envy.' I want to have Charlie's laidback attitude to fucking about, fucking around, acting like an overgrown boy. I envy his ability not to care more than anything. I just can't help myself caring, in some small part, about everything. I like to call it passion, a passion that seeps through me and won't be silenced on so many topics.

Phil has it too, the ability not to care about the little things, to take life easily, and let the troubles fall away from him as he strolls through his years. I pretend that I am shocked, but in truth I am only angry that I can't do the same. Phil's easiness doesn't seem quite so mindless, or destructive, mostly because I am not having a relationship with him, and his actions can't hurt me. Charlie's still do.

But sexual envy is, of course, not the only kind. We envy other people's lives, mostly the lives with more money in them, that seem less like hard work. The general populace spends most of its time envying one small band of break-out characters, who are managing to escape the humdrum existence of the rest of us with our money worries and failed relationships. We envy them, and criticize them, and throw abuse in their general direction, and are repelled at their sexual shenanigans, while secretly, and not so secretly, we all want what they've got. We all seem to want to be famous. Is it just the money that we want, or the ability to make ourselves look prettier with the cosmetic surgery that they can afford? Being famous seems to me to be a lot of hard work, so it isn't their schedule that we want – how many of us have to work a twenty-hour day on a regular basis? Our moral outrage when another one of them is arrested for mucking about with fully-grown adults at midnight on Hampstead Heath when there are honestly no kids about is in most parts envy, and that's what we have to understand. These most beautiful powerful creatures that move about in a world we glimpse but can never touch have a different set of rules to us, rules that apply once you have got past the celebrity gates, and not been blackballed for wanting it too much, or being undeserving. They don't have to worry about what their boss will think, or their friends. They don't have to worry about the norms of our society, they are not applicable to them. They move in a world of the most beautiful, desirable creatures on earth, all of whom offer themselves up for the taking. And they dip their fingers in whichever pies suit for the day. A man here, a woman there, they are not the ugly Joes we pass on the street, they look like angels. Given a world where nothing is frowned upon, where you are powerful enough to move from person to person without fear or shame or recrimination, where your sexuality, in private at least, is not an issue, wouldn't you do the same? If you truly had the ability to sleep with all of these angels, would you turn them down based on the fact that you couldn't have kids together, or some ancient book says you can't? I don't think so.

Of course as we envy their lives, and their cash and their

cars, we never stop to think that they envy us. They envy us our freedom to move from our front door to our car door without having a camera stuck in our face, but in some way their huge amounts of cash are supposed to compensate for this. They lusted for fame and therefore they deserve to have the flashlight of our envy in their faces every minute of their waking lives. I'm not sure, when you actually think long and hard about it, what is more valuable – the cars, or the privacy. I'd like a Ferrari and a holiday home on the Med, but I don't want my sexual moves to be plastered all over the papers for my mother to read. We can only stop our insane jealousy dressed up as outrage when we decide that we are happy with what we are, that we are where we want to be, and doing all the things we want to do. But who is? Just those famous elusive souls. And maybe they aren't so happy after all, because whenever they slip up, everybody gets to hear about it.

Dressed to Kill

The sun burns down on me as I walk along Charlie's road, swinging my bag full of vegetables and Martini. Maybe, if the sun goes down, I will talk to him about it. It's time to end it.

I turn the key in the door, holding my purse in my mouth, and juggling bags. I shove the door with my shoulder, and kick it closed behind me. But I am stopped in my tracks by the sight in front of me. I drop everything, and the Martini bottle clinks on the floorboards, mercifully not breaking, when I see Charlie sitting on the sofa, staring off into space. As the light from the window catches his face, I can see tear stains on his cheeks, damp red eyes, glazed. I see his hands and feet, twitching slightly, and hear the almost imperceptible noise of teeth chattering, as Charlie shakes, slightly, without control. My mind does immediate grotesque calculations. It can only be drugs. The only time I have ever seen Charlie in this state was after a really bad pill a couple of years ago in Brighton. He had moaned and shook and plummeted from deliriousness to despair in seconds and back again. I don't remember him crying though, even then. He doesn't acknowledge my entrance, or the bags crashing to the floor.

He doesn't even realize I am here. A splinter of me entertains an impulse, for whatever reason, to grab the Martini and run back out of the room as quickly as I entered it. But my feet are stuck to the spot. It is one of those few occasions when fatigue instantly takes you, and your body is already aware that the emotional effort needed for the next half an hour at least is going to leave you spent.

The good me, the moral me, rushes to the surface before the real me grabs the chance to leg it, and I whisper, 'Charlie, what have you taken?' This room does not need noise – it might crack something vital and the whole building will collapse. I don't want to disturb anything that isn't already quite clearly disturbed.

I see a flicker in Charlie's eyes, fear, I think, behind the tears. I don't know what to think, or do. I feel suddenly helpless, faced with a stranger in a bad way, equipped only with my alcoholic beverage of choice to handle the situation. But it would be rude of me to swig straight from the bottle lying on the floor, and I certainly don't think I should offer anything to Charlie. I have never seen him actually afraid, but there is no doubt that he is scared. I am too. I can't move towards him, I have no idea how he will react. My veins feel taut, about to snap.

'Charlie, is it coke? A trip? How much have you done? Should I call a doctor?' I say, still whispering.

'Charlie? Charlie!' I raise my voice slightly. 'Charlie, can you hear me?'

I take a step towards him, and then stop in my tracks as I see his lips moving, mouthing words neither of us can hear.

'What?' I ask quietly.

'It's not . . . drugs . . . but . . . I can't . . . move.'

The tears are flowing now, down his face, and his eyes shift to focus on me, imploring me through the blue and the brown, to do something, to grab him, or hit him, or something. But this is an alien situation for me, I don't know whether to grab his tongue, or guide his limbs, or bandage splints to the sides of his legs. Or should I just keep him completely stationary? Maybe his neck is broken – you aren't supposed to move the injured, I remember that from some ancient first aid lesson years ago. I should cover him with a blanket, and call an ambulance. First I need to be sure what he has taken, otherwise I am effectively shopping him to the police.

'Charlie, can you move your toes, can you move at all? Your hands are shaking, I mean, they're moving. Did you fall? Have you banged your head, or your back, or . .'

'No.'

Twisting his head down, moving for the first time, he looks at his hands, brings them up to his head, and rests his face in them. He can move – he is not paralysed. I don't need to call an ambulance or make the splints. I hear him start to sob. Blond strands of hair, mixed with a white powder, hang stiff with sweat round his eyes. I am still standing ten feet away, staring at him, blankly. He is crying slowly, gently. This boy who became a man with me, who does nothing softly these days – not lovemaking, not talking, not breathing – is crying, gently. My impulse is to hold him, but I don't know how any more – we haven't held each other for a long time, like we cared. I take a tentative step forwards, and when he doesn't react with some kind of animal instinct karate lunge, I step over the bags and move swiftly to the couch, sitting awkwardly on the end. I reach out for one of his hands and he takes it, and for a while we sit quite still. I get a little bored as I realize there is probably nothing wrong with Charlie that is not self- or stupidity-induced, and I feel my lack of patience rise up my throat. I stare out of the window for something to do, as he cries onto my now soggy hand. It is still so hot outside, as the sun makes its way down but seems desperate

73

not to leave. I look directly at it until it hurts my eyes, and I have to close them.

My mind wanders and I picture myself saying what I was going to say to Charlie tonight as he clutches my hand tightly, and I look back at him. He says something, but I can't hear.

'What?' This time I say it with a little less patience. He has ruined my day with his silliness. He's got pissed at work or something similarly stupid and is now feeling sorry for himself, and I don't get to say what all of a sudden seems the most important thing in the world to say. After weeks, months of delaying it, I feel I am ready, mostly because there is no possible way I can do it. It's some false bravado on my part.

'Something's happened,' he says gravely. I can see that. I just don't want to know what it is yet I suppose, what folly has brought this little pantomime on.

'It's fine. We'll talk about it later.' I hear myself, speaking in clichés, but this whole situation dictates them. I don't know how to react to this other than through somebody else's words. If they were good enough for somebody else, before me, in a difficult place, and a strange time, they are fine for now. I have nothing to say to him now.

Here's what I was going to say.

'Charlie, I think it's time we stopped seeing each other. I think it's time we stopped mucking about. Neither of us is getting any younger, and you don't like me any more, and you've changed from the person I liked. It's not enough. We have nothing in common other than America, history, sex. I don't think we should be together any more.'

That is what I had planned to say, later that night if the sun had gone down and left a chill, and I had mustered up the courage, and not been bothered about ruining my sunny day. I had worked it all out in my head. For something that was supposed to mean so little, I had been surprisingly nervous. I had rehearsed it enough to have it almost word-perfect. I'd pictured the various outcomes as well. The first was Charlie completely nonchalant, shrugging his shoulders and brightly asking for one last shag, for the road. The second was Charlie mildly unsettled that I am ending it before him, and getting a bit arsey, telling me he was going to do the same thing but he was too bored to care, which is a possibility, and one that I have convinced myself I could live with. The final version was a devastated Charlie, telling me he has loved me all along, and he doesn't know what has gone wrong, clutching onto me and begging to give it another try. I don't know why I even entertain this one, but entertain it I do. Quite a few times actually. I'm not sure if it makes me happy or sad. Whether I want it to happen to give some meaning to the whole mess of the last year, or to prove that I have always meant something to him after all. I could console myself with the fact that I am uncontrollably loveable, and even he who seems now to care so little, and who has slept with half of London in the last six months, can't bear to be without me. This last version is more a cushion than the truth.

And you may ask why now and not six months ago when he started being unfaithful on a regular basis? Or even before that, last year, the year before, as we drifted apart and failed to talk about things any more, why not then? What has triggered me to break the routine? And why has Charlie picked today to fall apart? Had he sensed it somehow, and is just putting on this bizarre act to throw me off course, to get me to feel sorry for him and drop my guard so he can spring up, save face, and finish it quick before I can get the words out first. I change my mind – we will talk now. I'll make sure for certain he's not falling into a coma or something equally as awful, and then I'll do it.

I lean forward and whisper in his ear,

'What have you done? What's wrong with you? You look . . . weird.' I search for a better word.

'You seem ill, Charlie – I've never seen you like this.'

There is no response, he just carries on staring at the floor, almost vacantly, like a victim of something he can't put into words. He is almost absent, from the room, from himself, the only sign that he is alive now are the tears trickling slowly down the sides of his nose, mingling eventually with the blood sliding from the cut at the side of his eye and meeting in a small puddle, via his sideburn, on my hand. The eye itself, his blue eye, blackens by the second, growing more purple, more bruised, more swollen.

I try to whisper again, but my voice becomes a little more strained, a little more frustrated with every word.

'Charlie, please, tell me what's wrong. Have you been in a fight? Has something happened at work? Have you lost a deal? Just tell me if you're sick or not!' I raise my voice.

And still no response, nothing. I feel my temper rising, and I make little effort to control it.

'Charlie, the least you can tell me, the very least, is why the hell you are wearing my dress!'

What Charlie Has to Say for Himself

Charlie just sits there, staring at the floor, clutching onto my hand, lean football muscles that regained some of their polish when he started going to his work gym a couple of years ago, now bursting out of a terrible, cheap blue Lycra dress that I bought last summer when I had split my top in a cab on the way to a barbecue. It is an awful dress that didn't suit me at the time and that I threw off as soon as I got back to Charlie's that night and have never worn since. Today, stretched over his chest, his thighs, it is apparent he is wearing nothing underneath. The hem skims his hips, but his flaccid third eye is poking out from underneath, resting on the sofa cushion like some whole other person in the room. It's a distraction, even though I have obviously seen it countless times before. I have held it in my hands, and my mouth, it has been inside me a thousand times, but it doesn't look right. It looks like a mistake, something I shouldn't be seeing. Something about it makes me want to recoil. So does Charlie himself. He is certainly not his recent self; a ridiculous, shagging, supremely good-looking drinking monster, aloof, out with the boys, revelling in the shallow, a million miles away from what he used to be, when I fell in love with him. When he fought that side of his character, when he was unhappy with the world for loving him just because he looked good, and had a great smile. Charlie is living, breathing proof that people change, or give up fighting at least.

'Jesus, Charlie, if you won't tell me, what am I supposed to think? How can I help you?'

We are still holding hands and he starts to cry again, as I gaze out at the city, and the evening heat, and the smog mixing with the last rays of the day, landscaping East London. Charlie squeezes my hand tighter, and carries on resting his wet face against it. I make a decision. It's just a hunch, but I don't think now is the time to break up with him.

After about half an hour, I realize I have been watching the world get dark out of the window, and that Charlie has stopped crying. Uncomfortably, I feel my hand in his, and we both sense the tension simultaneously. Suddenly my hand is stiff and unyielding. We never hold hands any more. We have dinner sometimes, I cook, we read the papers, we pretend we don't know what is going on in the other's head. But still he holds onto me. The blood has dried on his face, and he reaches up and scrapes it away. He catches my eye, and I smile at him nervously. I'm not sure what to do, but he speaks for us both. I don't turn the lamp on; I just listen.

'I want to tell you, I need to tell you, what happened.'

'Fine, Charlie, tell me. I'm listening.'

'You don't understand, it's important that you be the person to hear this – I need to know you understand, and that you can forgive me. More than anyone.' He has gone from silence to a strange eloquence in one easy step. I am a little anxious, but he can't be telling me anything I don't already know. Unless he is gay – I have never entertained that. I shock myself with the thought, purely because this is Charlie, and he has always been so . . . straight. He doesn't have the personality to be gay. Maybe he is just a transvestite. I think I would find it weird, hard to understand, but not unacceptable in the slightest. Whatever floats your boat these days.

'Charlie, tell me, it can't be that bad.'

'You don't understand, it is big!' He widens his eyes, as if whatever he is going to tell me is going to blow me away.

'Charlie, for God's sake – just tell me! I just want to know now!'

'Ok, last night . . . I slept with someone else last night.'

Is that it? That barely even raises my interest – I could have told him that the odds are on it these days. He must be getting his sex from somewhere, his sex drive is ridiculous, and he sure as hell hasn't had any from me recently.

'And?' I ask him, raising an eyebrow, and shaking off his hand. I don't particularly want to hear the gory details, no matter how unsurprising I find it.

'And I was out in town with the boys, at a bar. We'd been drinking all day, and I saw this girl, she was blonde.' I hear my jaw click. He has mentioned the 'B' word. He looks at me, uncertain as to whether to carry on, but I don't think a freight train could actually stop him now. He wants to confess.

'I fed her some drinks. She came back here. She left about three a.m. I didn't want her to stay.'

He looks me straight in the eye.

'I never want them to stay.' If I look even remotely shocked it is only because it's the first time he himself has told me. I've heard it from everybody but Charlie.

'She left and I went out on to the balcony, with a beer. It's been so hot, I couldn't go to bed, I couldn't sleep. The sheets needed changing, so I put them in the machine and came out for a beer. It was still so light out. You know how light it can be, with all the street-lamps, and it was like the sun was already up. It was so hot.' He looks giddy, and closes his eyes, picturing it in his head. This is turning into some kind of love

79

story – the sun was beating down, I've found somebody else – just get on with it! I cross my arms subconsciously.

'I leaned on the balcony for a while and just watched her go.' He pauses. I clear my throat to interrupt, tell him not to bother going on, I know where this is heading – he has found somebody else, somebody permanent, but he talks quickly, to stop me butting in.

'And I saw her walking down the road. She was swinging her arse, still drunk, strutting, looking like a tart in her bikini top.' A look of disgust sweeps his face, and I am a little taken aback. Maybe this isn't going where I thought.

'And I thought at the time that women shouldn't walk around on their own like that at night. If she'd have asked me, I would have called her a cab,' he says, like an apology, 'but she looked confident.' Charlie takes a deep breath.

'I saw the guy, a normal guy, a guy from the City, a guy like me. I saw him grab her from behind, spin her around, and hit her, throw her against the wall.'

My mouth hangs open and I say 'shit' involuntarily. His words are like exclamation marks, hanging in the air. He is trying, and managing, to impress on me how serious this is. This poor girl has been attacked, and Charlie feels responsible. So this is why he is so all over the place. I blink deliberately to take it in – the world is not safe any more. But as I take it in, Charlie starts talking again.

'I saw the rage in his face, as he dragged her into the alley. I saw him hit her, and her eye kind of exploded, and went blue. I didn't know what to do. She fell back against the wall. He wasn't holding her, he just hit her. But I didn't know what he would do if I didn't stop him.' Charlie's pupils dilate as he speaks, and so do mine. This is all getting a bit gruesome. Alarm bells are ringing everywhere.

'I put my beer down, grabbed my keys. They were in my jacket pocket. I didn't need the jacket because it was still so

80

hot outside.' Charlie's words quicken, as he talks at the pace of the events he is telling. I don't want to interrupt now. Has he stopped an attack? Has he become somebody's hero?

'I went out and pressed for the lift, and the lifts are good here, you know that, and it came right away.' His hands gesture, as if he is telling an audience of one hundred, and not just me.

'It was so quiet going down in the lift, apart from that music – music to watch girls go by. It's been the same music for weeks. I liked it at first but now it's just starting to annoy me. And all I could think of were those lyrics, I couldn't get them out of my head, and the girl in the street.' He pauses suddenly. I gesture with my eyes for him to carry on, and he whispers, through fresh tears,

'I don't even know her name.' How has he managed to make me feel sorry for him suddenly, as he tells me about last night's antics with another woman? But I do feel sorry for him, somehow. He looks heartbroken.

'I could see her lying in the alley. There was blood running from her nose, but her clothes weren't ripped. She was unconscious. I was in front of her, and I tried to wake her up, but she wouldn't wake up. The guy was gone. She wasn't dead, because I checked her pulse. She was breathing, she just wasn't awake.

'I had lost my mobile again, left it in a cab going to Lloyds, and then to Deutsche Bank, I had so many meetings that day. We had got the Lloyds deal. Four million. That's why we'd been out. I walked to the payphone, I had never seen it before, but there's a payphone right by the newsagent's.' He points out of the window to prove his point.

'And I called the police and said that I needed an ambulance.'

'Good for you, Charlie – good for you.' I smile at him, and feel a lump in my throat – I am strangely proud. He stopped

81

something awful happening. He ignores me, he is in full flow, he doesn't want my praise yet.

'But I didn't think it would do any good to wait with her, I couldn't make a statement, because what if you found out, and then I'd have to admit that I'd slept with her, and then if they had done tests, well, you know.' Charlie is pleading with me to understand this bit, the bit that signifies she meant nothing to him. I find it hard to swallow, maybe because of the lump in my throat.

'I came back up here and watched them arrive, a couple of minutes later. They found her, but then the ambulance blocked my view and I couldn't see anything after that, so I went to bed.' His last words are like a full stop to everything. He went to bed? I swallow hard, and the lump in my throat disappears. He went to bed! Charlie isn't looking at me, and luckily, because he would see the look of disbelief on my face – how can he go from a hero to an insensitive arsehole in the space of ten words?

He obviously doesn't think anything of this, as he carries on, but I feel my back stiffen and my chest tighten at everything he is going to say to me now.

'But this morning I felt strange, I felt bad. I felt like it was my fault somehow. I felt nauseous.' Well, that's something at least. He realizes it was wrong to just bugger off to bed.

'I got on the tube, but it was so hot. I don't know why I got the tube; I should have got a cab. There was this old woman, like an old-fashioned secretary, standing next to me and her perfume was so strong it turned my stomach even more.' He wrinkles his nose. 'I only had to stay on for a few stops, but by the time I got off, I felt so hot and sticky, and sweaty and sick, and my head was itching.'

Charlie is talking with his whole body now, animatedly,

reliving it all. He is quietly buzzing, and the room, in darkness, doesn't seem dark at all.

'I ran to the toilets in the mainline station, but the door wouldn't open. I could feel the sickness rising up my throat, and I tried to hold it down, while I barged the door. But I felt so weak and hot. I got it open on the fourth go, but then this terrible smell came out.' Charlie puts his hand over his mouth and I think he is going to be sick when he gags. I pull away slightly, and move my feet out of firing distance.

But from behind his hand, he continues. 'I had never smelt anything like it, and there was this guy, just slumped into the dirty sink. He was stiff as a board. His face was blue, and his fingers were all twisted at weird angles.'

'Jesus,' I say again, completely involuntarily.

Charlie hangs his head in shame. 'I threw up all over him.'

The thought of it makes him retch again.

'Somebody shouted out, and then people started coming, the station attendants, all holding their noses, their eyes watering from the smell of my sick and his death. I had to get away, and I pushed past the guard and up the escalators, and outside.'

We both catch our breath – Charlie has certainly had a terrible day. I rub the back of my neck, and try and unknot the tension that has built in the last twenty minutes listening to Charlie's story.

'What happened then?' I ask, hungry for more dreadful gossip.

'I thought I felt better – I got to work and had some water, but then some guy, Piers, from the backroom, just some fucking research guy, he made a crack about me having thrown up on my suit. I had been sick on the bottom of my Armani trousers. Sick all over them. They told me to cool off, after I hit him, so I came home.'

83

'You hit somebody at work?' I ask, incredulous. Charlie would never normally do anything to jeopardize his work – he lives for his work.

'Yeah, I did – I'm not proud of it! Anyway, I tried to change but I couldn't find anything. Everything needed washing.' Charlie turns and looks at the kitchen behind him, and then looks back at me, gesturing behind him. 'I started washing all my clothes.'

He sounds like a child who has been caught doing something they shouldn't, getting his nice, expensive, dry-clean only work suits all wet. I look towards the kitchen and sure enough the floor is covered with water, and all of Charlie's suits are spread, sopping wet, across the floor.

'This dress was the only thing I could find, that didn't need cleaning. You must have left it here one night. I don't know, it was here, so I put it on.'

'Charlie, stop!' I put a hand up. 'Charlie, this is all absolutely awful, don't get me wrong – but the dress? That bit I don't get – why put on a dress?' I search his face for an answer, but he looks at me with impatience.

'I just told you – everything else needed washing!' He looks at me like I'm the idiot. I am starting to worry. He thinks there is logic there.

'Anyway, I ran out of soap powder so I went downstairs to the newsagent's, and the guy told me to get out, that he didn't want to serve me! I told him he had served me hundreds of times before, but he pushed me out onto the street, and that's when I fell and banged my eye on the kerb.' He points to the dried-up slit above his eye. 'I had the washing powder, though, I just hadn't paid for it. So I brought it back up. And then, I don't know, I sat here for a while . . . and then you came in.'

I look down and for the first time register that Charlie has a packet of soap powder by his side. It has half spilled out onto the carpet.

I make my deduction quickly – he has completely lost it. This whole strange sequence of events has made him snap, and he has turned into a dress-wearing, hygiene freak, class 'A' nutter. Is this what happens when people go mad? I always thought it would be a steady process and you would notice them changing over a period of months, making occasional bird noises, or claiming to be Mother Teresa, or you'd catch them eating compost. But Charlie appears to have leap-frogged the progressive type of madness, and just gone straight for the looney tunes version of boys in ill-fitting dresses talking gibberish. Nobody would blame me for dumping a mad man, surely? Or would they think me cold? I do a quick mental tot up in my head and draw the conclusion that I would need to look supportive for about three weeks, and then I could claim strain and give him the heave-ho, as long as he is safely ensconced in a home, with some crayons, where he can't get to me in one last rational act of anger and passion. It's amazing how quickly you plan the next month of your life, four seconds to be precise. But then I've always been an A grade student; it might take somebody else a little longer. I have forgotten Charlie is still in the room, as I make my getaway plans, but he speaks and I jump slightly in surprise.

'I need to get away for a few days, Nicola. I think I'm cracking up.'

It's the understatement of the year – 'I think I'm cracking up' from the guy in the hot blue Lycra and no pants, with tear stains down his cheeks from half an hour's bawling.

'Charlie, will you be alright, just going off by yourself? Go and stay with your brother or something instead.' I am relieved to hear him say he wants to get away, and he isn't expecting me to stick around. It would be hypocritical of us both. Maybe he's not so mad after all, and has just had a bad couple of days. Don't get me wrong, I am horrified by his experience, but I can't pretend I wasn't about to end this twisted relationship, and I can't pretend our problems have just disappeared. I want him to get out of London, clear his head of the trauma of the last few days, and then come back, either still completely mad, although this is obviously not my wish, or more realistically, insensitive and tactless as ever. I dread breaking up with people, even though I haven't had to do it for years, I can still remember how horrible it is. I hate the weeks leading up to it, when you can feel it coming, when you haven't admitted it to yourself yet, but you know what you are going to do. The sentences are already forming in your mind, you just aren't quite ready to say them out loud yet. And then gradually, you find yourself rehearsing it in your head at night, like some school production of Shakespeare, stumbling over your lines. By the time it comes to actually doing it, you are a professional. Then he pleads with you, with his eyes, and his words. He reaches out and grabs your hand, just a little too roughly, and tries to stop his voice from breaking, and grabs at the tears at the sides of his eyes.

Except that's not how it turns out at all. You fluff up your lines, your own voice breaks with emotion, he just sits, no dramatic response, understanding that it's been on the cards for a while. And he is reasonable. It's not romantic, it's pathetic and he is stronger than you. You know you have done the right thing, and that you weren't compatible and you hadn't been happy. But even so you have just, and of your own volition, completely ostracized one of your best friends, the person you have spent most of your time with for the last six months or whatever.

I have always felt better being dumped. You have no choice in that matter. At least you can get on with it, spurred on by rage or pride or secret relief that he has done it now and not waited a couple of weeks, by which time you would have been forced to do it yourself.

'Charlie, where are you going to go?'

He looks at me desperately, and grabs my hand again, too quickly for me to pull it away. His voice rises. The madness is back again, I just know it, he's about to say something stupid:

'I need you to come with me. Nicola, come with me, you have to. I'm losing it. I can't ask anybody else. Nix, please – I don't know what's happening to me.'

I hadn't expected this. It's not the best time for us to take a weekend break. Maybe I should tell him . . . confess all.

'Nicola, if the last six years mean anything to you at all, please come with me.'

I can't go with him, I just can't. I can't tell him I don't want to see him any more, but I can't swing the other way. He has pushed it too far for this – he has spent the last year showing no thought for my feelings, and yet now he expects me to pick up the pieces during some early midlife crisis. This isn't fair. He can't expect me to do this – he can't be this selfish.

'The thing is, Charlie, and kind of on that subject . . . maybe it would be better if you stay with your parents? Or with your brother, or down in Devon at the cottage? Don't you think that would be better? Come on, Charlie, be honest, I don't know how we'd cope for a weekend together. I think that maybe I'm not the best person for you to be with, while you sort your head out.'

He wrings my hands with his, and his eyes plead with me. 'Nicola, please. I promise I won't touch you. We'll go just as friends. You were going to finish with me, I know that.' Again, I am shocked. I didn't realize he knew. His sudden insanity is lending him a clarity that is quite off-putting, especially considering that, before today, it has been known to take him three weeks to notice I've had my hair coloured. Now, now he manages to guess what I am about to say before I say it! He's got some kind of Uri Geller thing going on. I contemplate getting a spoon, to test it out properly, but then realize I don't really want to be handing him metal implements, no matter how blunt.

'It's fine,' he says, as he registers my surprise as guilty shock. 'And I promise, after this, you never have to see me again. But please, Nix, do this for me. Help me out. I know I've been a cheating arsehole shit, thoughtless and insensitive, but please. Just help me. I can't stop crying . . . I feel like my head's going to cave in.' On cue, he starts sobbing again. I don't know what the hell to do.

'Charlie, I really don't think it's a good idea, plus, you know, *Evil Ghost 2* is playing up, José is going to have my arse if it goes over budget, and. . .' Charlie grabs the sides of my face and pulls me close to him, forcing me to look into his eyes. There's a deep fear in there, and he genuinely believes he is losing it. I feel my body, previously stiff with tension, soften slightly at those eyes . There is something familiar in them that I haven't seen for an age, or maybe I just feel needed.

'Charlie, how about this,' I whisper, 'we'll go away. We'll go down to Devon, stay in your parents' cottage, and just sort you out. Because I know you are scared now, but I really, honestly, truly believe that all you need is some sleep, and some clean air, and some perspective, and you will be fine. But then, hon, then we don't have to have the conversation we were going to have. Then we don't see each other as much. Do you understand what I am saying?'

'Thank you, thank you so much,' Charlie whispers back, and doesn't seem to have heard anything other than my agreeing to look after him for the next couple of days.

'But Charlie . . .' I have to get this clear now, if I am going to do it.

'Charlie, when we are done – Charlie, look at me.' I hold his chin and pull his head up, so he is looking at me with his teary eyes.

'When Devon is done and we come back, and you are your old self again,' I force a smile, 'then we're done, ok?' I nod my head at him, as if to encourage agreement. 'Then we go our separate ways, ok? You'll feel better, I promise. And we should go just as friends, just like you said. Separate rooms, separate beds, we'll just chill out, and get you better.' A wave of relief sweeps over me – I don't have to have the conversation after all. This conversation that I have been putting off for nearly a year doesn't need to happen now. Thank God!

Charlie drops his head into my lap and says, all of a sudden, 'Of course, thank you. Now can I go in this? I feel comfortable in this.' He gestures down at the dress. It was obviously my turn for a moment of madness. What have I let myself in for?

'No, Charlie, I think you should get changed.'

'But,' he points like a child towards the kitchen, then says pathetically, on the brink of tears again, 'I have nothing to wear! Do you have anything I can borrow? What about that sundress I bought you last year?'

The wave subsides. Shit.

I'm With Stupid

I pay the cabbie, tell him to keep the twenty, and try to direct Charlie into Paddington without too much fuss. He keeps trying to take off the Burberry mac I have made him wear, pulling at it like Houdini in chains. Underneath, he is still in the blue Lycra number. We have been unable to find anything else that wasn't soaking wet or covered in dried-on soap suds. His hair has flopped, all the blond spikes now stuck to his forehead, and his sideburns are still covered in soap powder. Even his out of work clothes, his FCUK jeans, his trendy clothes that so few men can pull off, were soaking wet on the kitchen floor. The eggshell blue lambswool Nicole Farhi jumper my parents bought him last Christmas lay crushed and shrunken and ruined forever in a pile on the tiles. I am incredibly self-conscious about his almost nakedness, and the fact that he has refused to put any underpants on before leaving the flat. He is intermittently laughing and sobbing, and it was all I could do to make the taxi driver take us in the first place. I had hailed a few cabs which had slowed down and pulled over and then accelerated quickly as soon as they caught sight of Charlie giggling like a schoolgirl and waving his arms around like a mad scientist. I resolutely shouted out after each one of them, 'I've taken your plate numbers! I'm reporting you!' but they were long gone, and I don't blame them. I wouldn't have picked us up. A big blond guy with blood on his face and a blue dress popping out from under his flasher's mac, and a stressed-looking girl carrying all the bags and chain-smoking. We're hardly Posh and Becks.

Charlie is wrestling with the belt I have triple-knotted around his waist, like a child. I want to pop into WH Smith's and get some magazines for the journey, but I think it may be a mistake to leave him on his own.

A woman brushes past us with a German Shepherd, and I consider offering her fifty quid for the lead, before realizing that, conceivably, I have nothing on Charlie to attach it to that he isn't likely to strip off, or try and get at with his teeth. He is swinging between sane and absolutely crazy. At least if he was acting consistently mad, I could eliminate the element of surprise. I think he might just be doing it for attention.

I push him into Smith's and tell him to keep quiet. I have no idea if he is going to cry or scream like a girl at any moment. In the cab, he kept putting his head on my shoulder, and trying to nuzzle under my arm and fall asleep. I slapped him on the face every time his breathing started getting deeper. I wasn't going to let him fall asleep while I had to live through this nightmare. This is going to be a long few days.

I phoned Charlie's brother, Peter, from the flat to check that the cottage was free. The family has a beautiful pile of slate and wooden beams down on the South Coast, in Salcombe. I have only been there once before, for the wedding of one of Charlie's cousins, and we stayed with Charlie's parents and Peter and his wife, and their two sons, who are Charlie's godsons. Even then, Charlie's mother had been suspicious of our relationship, treating me with mild disdain, like some kind of impersonation of a girlfriend. I'm sure she noticed that we didn't hold hands any more, never touched each other unless it was completely necessary, never exchanged distracted kisses in the kitchen, or sat with legs entwined on the sofa. Mentally she was putting two and two together: either Charlie was gay, and I was his ruse, or the relationship was dead, and I was refusing to walk. From the way she acted towards me, and the death glares I was getting, I'm not sure which one she would have preferred. In both, I was at fault, and I had either made him gay, or I wouldn't leave him alone, while Charlie was merely incorrigible, no matter what the outcome. It was apparent we had lost whatever we had. We sat as far away from each other as possible, only having perfunctory conversations if pressed.

Iris, Charlie's mother, had quizzed me that afternoon.

'So how long has it been now, Nicola?' she asked me in the kitchen as I made myself a sandwich and she made herself a peppermint tea.

'A while.' I didn't actually want to say the number of years out loud; I knew where she was going.

'Yes, a *long* while. Peter and his wife were married and expecting after three years, you know.' Iris picked up a cloth.

'I don't think we're the marrying kind.' I took a big bite of my sandwich in defiance of the dinner that would be ready in an hour and that Iris had spent all afternoon cooking.

'No, maybe *you're* not.' She emphasized the word 'you're' just to let me know that Charlie was the marrying kind, and I was the fly in the ointment, not her precious son.

'I think Charlie's calling me,' I said as a means of escape.

'I don't think so, dear. Charlie brought some of his friends up for the weekend last month. Lovely bunch of boys, do you know them?'

'I've met them, yes.'

'What were their names, Nicola, I forget?'

93

'Harry, Deacon, do you mean that lot?'

'Yes, that's it.' Iris gave me a quizzical look, surprised that I was passing her impromptu test.

'And his office in the City?'

'Frank and Sturney,' I offered, to save her from the indignity of actually having to ask its name.

'Ye-ss. That's right. Charlie tells me it's very impressive.'

'I suppose,' I shrugged. 'If you like that kind of thing.'

Iris wiped a surface, and spoke without looking up. 'You don't like that kind of thing? I'd think most girls would be pleased to have a boyfriend who's so successful.'

'It's fine, whatever. I'm going outside.'

I sensed Iris stop wiping as I walked out.

Of course I could answer all her questions, but with a little sadness. I felt like I was deceiving her in a way. A mother only wants her kids to be happy, and she could see we weren't. I was profoundly aware that if my mother had asked the same questions of Charlie, he wouldn't have been able to answer any of them. But it was nice to see him with the kids who brought out the most natural and least pretentious side of him – a side I hadn't seen for a long time.

I walked outside to watch the cricket game the boys were playing on the lawn: Charlie bowling, Peter and the kids fielding, Charlie's dad Tom wielding his cricket bat like a professional.

And as I watched, Charlie seemed to romp instead of run. Tom hit an easy catch to one of the boys and Charlie screamed, ''Owzat!', threw his head back and started laughing.

'Good bowling,' I shouted, surprising myself, and Charlie held up a hand to me in acknowledgement.

He looked so happy, so relaxed, the smile didn't seem so dirty or deceitful any more.

As I watched Charlie pick up one of his nephews and spin

94

him around, I felt an urge to be the one being swung around by him. I believe I could have forgiven him everything if he had. If he could just persuade me that there was still some depth there, that he wasn't the sum of his hair and his smile, his bank account, and his suit.

Iris stuck her head out of the window and called out that dinner was nearly ready, and smashed my daydream. Peter and the boys ran past me, and Tom winked and touched my arm as he went in. I smiled over at Charlie, who retrieved the bat and ball, and he jogged over, grinning, pleased with his performance. I folded my arms and looked at my feet as he got closer, and he slowed to a walk, until I sensed him only a few paces away. I looked up and into his eyes and felt a rush of courage. But Iris's head darted back out of the window.

'Charlie, I need you for drinks,' she shouted, and I turned sharply to face her.

'For Christ's sake, can't she open a bottle of wine herself?' I muttered, and turned back to Charlie, but he was already walking past me into the house.

'She can do it!' I practically pleaded with him, and he spun around.

'Don't start on my mother now as well,' Charlie sighed, as if that last sentence had tired him out, and went inside.

Iris had given me a pitying look through the window, which my pride had dismissed as her having a headache, and I had put all thoughts of a real relationship to the back of my mind for the rest of the evening.

Later, when the kids were tucked up safely and everybody had a glass of wine, we played Trivial Pursuit, and I won. Iris said, 'Isn't Nicola clever! You've done well, Charlie, to get somebody pretty and clever to put up with you for *all this time*,' in a strange voice, obviously to make a point, or try and catch us out and get us to admit something we otherwise wouldn't. It had embarrassed the hell out of me, but Charlie had shrugged it off, although he gave me a funny look like he barely knew me, as if I was the one responsible, the one who had changed. That night I went to bed before Charlie, pleading fatigue and found myself daydreaming again that he might make his excuses and come to bed and hold me. Maybe he would just chat to me for a while. But he stayed in front of the TV, not crawling into bed until two. He didn't even touch me. Some masochistic urge made me turn and stroke his arm to let him know I was awake, but he had merely said, 'I don't think we should have sex with my parents in the next room,' snuggled into his side of the duvet, and was snoring within seconds. He managed somehow to turn it around, make me feel that I was the one who only wanted to be there for the sex. Or maybe that was my conscience knocking. I never voiced my daydreams. We never gave an inch to each other on the control stakes; it was political, it was a tiny war. The whole relationship was an exercise in who could look like they cared the least. I wasn't as brave as I am now. I hadn't got used to his disinterest.

The next day at the wedding, I had started to come to my senses. I caught him chatting up one of the after-dinner guests later in the evening. Some little redhead, probably no more than eighteen – he was actually showing her his credit cards. I told myself it was the wine that had made me tearful, but I wandered around in the grounds for a while to get it out of my system. Peter found me sitting outside the barn, a little red-eyed, and topped up my champagne with his.

'He's a different person out here, isn't he? Until he gets drunk, of course. I'd almost forgotten how much of an arse he's become,' I said. I don't know why I chose to spill my beans to Peter, who would obviously defend him, but surprisingly, he agreed.

'I know,' he said. 'I've been out with him a couple of times in town, with his work posse, and they can be a bunch of arseholes.' We had both laughed uneasily and nodded our heads.

'I don't know why you put up with it, Nicola, you have to cope with him in his natural habitat, day in, day out, and he's different now . . .' He trailed off and I thought I caught a trace of sadness in his eyes, too. I could see he felt sorry for me.

'Oh, don't feel sorry for me,' I mustered. 'I'm just the same at home. We've both changed, Pete; London does things to people, it brings out the arsehole in them. Believe me, I can be just as bad. I barely even see him, I shop far too much for a woman in an adult relationship. We've both grown up, I suppose – grown up and grown apart.' I tried to laugh it off; I didn't actually believe what I was saying. But he shoved me along slightly and sat down next to me. We both stared out at the fields for a while; it was one of those nights when it's so much nicer to be in love. I should have been sitting there with Charlie.

'Look, honestly, don't feel bad for me, I really am fine. This is just wedding rubbish.' I pointed at my puffy red eyes. 'Most of the time I'm happier than he is. I think I'm just realizing that I've stuck around a bit too long.' I got a strange lump in my throat at that point, and had to gulp it down. 'We won't work out, you know.' I shrugged and looked down at my half empty glass, then took a massive swig and finished it off.

'Well,' I said, brushing off my trousers, and standing up, 'I'm going to get another drink.'

'You know,' Peter had looked at me over his shoulder, 'he's not ready to settle down yet, but one day he will be. I know what you two have got going, and maybe it *is* time for you to move on for a while.'

I half-smiled at him, raising my eyes to heaven. 'Just maybe?' Another lump in my throat.

'But I think he'll come back to you, Nicola, one day. He

used to be close to people, and he will be again, and I think then he'll be a person you could . . . love again!' Peter laughed at the embarrassment of saying it out loud. 'He's going to drop back down to earth at some point, with a bang. He can't be everybody's golden boy forever.'

'I wouldn't count on it! But thanks, Pete. Do you want another drink?'

'No, sweetheart, I'm fine. I need some more air.'

With that, he had staggered off down the lawn to the field below, clutching his champagne flute, singing some old tune. I had watched him go as I leaned on the barn door, thinking about what he had said. It was so obvious to anybody with eyes that one of us should leave soon.

Moments later, Charlie staggered towards me from behind the door, bashing into me, sending me tripping forwards. He had obviously caught the end of my conversation with Peter.

'Not making a pass at my brother are you?' Charlie shot his accusation right at me.

'Oh fuck off, Charlie. I could never get a man that nice.'

Charlie's half closed, drunken eyes tried to focus in my general direction.

'You're right, you don't have the conversation any more,' and it was like a punch in the stomach when he said it.

I walked back into the reception, gulping down the lump in my throat, hearing the commotion of him falling face first into the flower border behind me. He was an arse, who looked like a person I used to love.

The memories slap me in the face as I leave Smith's and force Charlie out in front of me. He has gone strangely quiet, but I'm not complaining.

By the time we board the train, Charlie hasn't said anything for half an hour. The train is almost empty, at eleven on a Thursday night, and I find the smoking carriage practically deserted with only two people sitting at the other end. Charlie slumps into his seat, staring down at the Formica table in front of him. I position myself opposite him, and offer him a cigarette, sticking the pack under his eyes, but he just shakes his head. I inhale before we have even left the platform.

We're All Going On a . . .

I wake up with my head against the train window, my mouth pressed awkwardly on one side; half of my face clings to the glass, while the other hangs out into the carriage for everybody to see. I focus on the outside, and try and look past the darkness and see the houses and trees and parks and offices and lives that are slipping past me by the second, never to be seen again. My eyes slide with the occasional lights that appear and disappear just as quickly. I close my eyes again.

I can feel my contact lenses stuck to my eyeballs, only slightly uncomfortable now: they'll be ok if I just keep my eyes shut. I want to go back to sleep and pretend I'm somewhere else. I don't want to open my eyes and admit I am in the middle of the smoking carriage, on the middle of a train, in the middle of the West Country, in the middle of the night, in the middle of Charlie's breakdown, in the middle of a situation I am not equipped to deal with, mentally or physically. In the middle of Charlie's nightmare. I want to drift back into sleep with the gentle rocking of the 120mph train, and be back in my old school hall, in uniform, except it's the McDonald's uniform now, during assembly, but with all my new friends, not my school friends, bar one for no reason whatsoever, and

101

then be ushered to the front of the hall and climb up the ladder and fly the trapeze to be caught by the priest who gave me my first holy communion, and then land and run over the bridge and go to the dentist's and begin kissing the dentist who becomes the sexy internet guy I met at a work party not so long ago, and who I didn't end up going home with, didn't even kiss goodnight, because I had to leave to go to another work thing, pissed in a cab on dry Martinis and bottles of beer, and the whole time wishing I'd stayed at the last work thing, because that guy was really sexy, and has occupied my thoughts a little since, although he wasn't really into me, but he could have been convinced, he just wasn't playing along, but I could have coerced him with a little more time and a fresh coat of lipstick, although I was talking shit by that time, randomly thinking up questions in my head while he answered the last one I'd posed, so he probably thought I was an idiot, but I should have stayed because, judging by our current action in the dentist's chair, he is a bloody good kisser and he is convincing me it is real, that I am feeling the feelings, kissing him when I am not. And now I realize I have slipped into that dream, and out of it again, and I'm back, looking into the darkness, with dry eyes, dry lenses, a dry mouth. And an idiot for company.

I am covered by something, a makeshift duvet, and I focus on the flimsy brown arms of the mac I had made Charlie wear before we left my flat which is now making a half-hearted attempt to cover my shoulders and torso, and which Charlie has obviously placed over me. With a resolve I know will be tested to the limit in the next few minutes, no doubt the next few days, I look up and over at Charlie. He is looking out of the window, still in the dress, shivering slightly, with his hands flat on the Formica train table in front of him. He looks calm, less wild than before. His eyes look big and tired, reflected in the train window, and I stare at his reflection. He seems to be studying himself, intently, and using the fleeting countryside as some weird transvestite backdrop , framing his Lycra, his sad eyes, his flattened hair. He can't see past himself right now.

I sit up sleepily and as Charlie realizes I am awake, his reflection gives me a sad smile.

'Charlie, take back your coat, you're freezing.' My mouth is so dry I can barely get the words out, they scratch at my throat as they form, and come out sounding strange and lazy. 'Look at you, you're shivering, have the coat.'

I unwrap the arms and belt from my limbs and hold it above the table so as not to dip it in the coffee or makeshift plastic coffee-cup-lid-ashtrays, and Charlie accepts it with another smile.

'You looked cold, and I thought one of us might as well be comfortable,' he says. 'You were asleep at least. Do you feel ok?' Charlie speaks to me quietly, and I notice that the lights have somehow dipped in our carriage, and yet he seems to be radiating with heat. His face is bright red, and he's sweating.

'Oh I'm fine, but, Charlie, are you hot or cold? You look really warm,' and I reach across to touch his forehead, like a child, or my little sister Charlotte when she's been drinking and I'm scared she'll fall into some kind of liver-collapsed coma. I'm behaving like his mother, and he doesn't flinch, but offers his head to be felt, glad for the comfort, and the care.

'I am a little hot . . . and a little cold as well,' he says with a confused laugh, while trying to put on the coat and pull it away from his burning skin at the same time. My palm is damp with the sweat of Charlie's head and I wipe it sleepily on my jeans. I breathe in deeply before speaking again, preparing myself for the madness to begin once more, (and also to at least try and project an air of knowing what I am going to say next). But I am winging it, and we both know it. I am doing my damnedest to be the one in control here, the one I always am with everyone but Charlie.

I am the strong one. I am the one doing a near-perfect impression of Atlas, the independent, the impassable, the uncrushable. Charlie is the only one I've stopped bothering with, the one I haven't tried to save for a while, leaving him to his own devices; he doesn't need me to do it any more.

'How are *you* feeling?' I ask, not wanting the answer at all.

'I'm alright,' he says, but quietly, not confidently, and we both know it's not true. His voice breaks slightly as he says it, the way it always does with me when I am feeling bad, mixed-up, confused, wanting to cry, just waiting for somebody to trigger it off by asking me how I am, and then repaying their feigned sincerity with a bucketful of tears.

'Okay, well, that's obviously not the whole truth,' I say, 'but are you semi-okay? Are you okay enough to go back to London okay? Or . . .' I don't want to sound like I am desperate to get off this train, and get back to town, and my flat and a big bed, and lie star-shaped as a single in a double, and sleep. But of course I am desperate for all of those things. I'm trying to convince him this train ride was all it would take to make him feel better, and a couple of hours of scenic Intercity action would make him calm down, and long for his job, and his lads, and the drink, and the drugs, and his London.

'I'm . . . not great.' Charlie's voice breaks again as he says it, and I sit watching his eyes welling up, seeing them go red, wanting to hold his hand and make them stop, but feeling a thousand miles away from him. I don't know what is going on inside his head, and I don't know if I'm going to find out. Charlie is speeding further away from me, and I feel like I have been left behind in London.

The interlinking carriage door opens behind us automatically with a vacuumed swish, and a youngish student stumbles up the aisle in battered denim, an army shirt, and a year-old haircut. He spots Charlie in his dress and smirks. We both turn our heads towards him and catch the smile he seems unable to hide. But I don't say anything; I don't have the energy or the words to defend us right now. And Charlie just looks down, embarrassed. Charlie who, these days at least, doesn't need an invitation to start a fight. When I first met him, he was the last person to throw a punch, always breaking up fights with a smile, blocking attackers, calming things down. People listened to him, they still do. He's just saying different things now. And his fists are a lot more ready to do the talking for him. Not with me, he's never raised a fist to me.

'Charlie, don't get me wrong, I think we should stay in Devon, just for a couple of days, and just sleep, you know? I don't want to go back to London yet.' I backtrack quickly.

'Just get some rest, get some perspective, and I promise you'll feel a thousand times better. And you know I could do with the sleep as well. *Evil Ghost* has been keeping me awake at night! We might even get some sun. Besides, it's Friday tomorrow.' I check my watch. 'Well, it's Friday today. I'll just take a day off and then it's the weekend and we can come back up on Sunday, how does that sound?'

'That sounds good, if that's okay with you,' he says.

'Of course. Jesus, it's only a couple of days; let's get you okay, but for God's sake, remind me to phone work tomorrow morning.' I can't believe the words are coming out of my mouth, even as I say them. I can't believe I am agreeing to three days of this, but I do know that I want him, even now, to see me in a good light. I want to reflect well in his confused eyes, want to believe I am a good person. I don't know who I'm trying to convince. I do want to get him better, get him through this baby breakdown. He thinks he's having a breakdown, but it's not real. He'd be frothing or rocking, not showing himself off in a jaunty thigh-exposing number.

But I don't want to come away from this with any guilt. Any more guilt.

It will be fine. I'm sure it will be fine. Or maybe it won't.

Mind My Decanter!

In a cab on the way to the cottage in the middle of the night, we bump along roads that have seen better days – probably World War One – and bounce up and down in the back while the cabbie chats to me and ignores Charlie, who is still conspicuously silent. The cabbie is somebody's grandfather, with shirt sleeves rolled up in the twenty degree heat of the night, and a handkerchief to wipe his forehead. A faint odour of sweat and the country and old car hang in the air, and scramble up my nose. I put the back of my hand up against my nostrils to stop it. Gerry and the Pacemakers are playing quietly on the radio and I start to feel depressed, sticky and, ultimately, fucked off. I pay the taxi driver – Charlie doesn't appear to have a penny on him. It costs me two pounds thirty – we're not in London any more, Toto. The cottage is one of about ten dotted along a stretch of grass that separates them from the beach, surrounded by trees, and flowers, just over-grown enough to look romantic, not quite out of hand. Paint flakes off in places, and inside none of the sofas match.

I scramble around behind a row of potted geraniums to find the spare key, while Charlie sits on my overnight bag, squashing everything in it.

'Careful, Charlie, my decanter is in there,' I joke, but he doesn't even look up. I sigh and picture his parents' drinks cabinet on the other side of the door.

After a *Krypton Factor* struggle with the key, I eventually get us in. I remember that I've always wanted to know how to pick a lock, a minor nod to a wilder side of life that I'll never know.

I dump the bags, and make straight for the kitchen. I don't even bother to rinse out a glass that has been sitting in the cupboard untouched for four months. I find the ice trays, mercifully full to the brim, and dump two in my glass and one in my hand, which I run up and down my neck, around my hairline, as I unscrew the whisky bottle with one hand. Resisting the urge just to neck it from the bottle, I pour myself a large double, and finish it off in two gulps. I breathe out heavily, pour myself another large double, and slump onto the sofa, kicking my shoes off. Sweat trickles down the back of my neck, and another line escapes down my breastbone. My legs feel damp in my jeans. I will literally be peeling my clothes off tonight. Somewhere in the back of the cottage, I can hear Charlie retching, but the compulsion to go and help loses out to my compulsion to not move and not smell vomit.

'Charlie, hon, are you okay?' I shout out as a compromise. 'Do you need me to do anything?'

A muffled reply comes back.

'What?' I ask, but still don't move.

'I'm okay.' His mouth sounds full of something, and I hear him throw up again. I grimace and take another sip of my drink. I try to turn the TV on with the remote, but the batteries must have gone, so I leave it off. My head lolls back against the cushion, and my eyes close, my head swaying slightly with the effects of the whisky.

'Shout if you need anything,' I call out to Charlie, and continue to doze and sip my drink.

I wake up about half an hour later with a wet sensation on my thighs, the effects of falling asleep with a half-full glass in my hand. Charlie is sitting opposite me on his dad's big armchair, with a beach towel wrapped around his waist.

'Shit,' I say and pull at my wet jeans, but then give up. 'Nice towel; did you throw up on my dress?'

Charlie doesn't answer, just looks intently at me.

'What are you looking at?' I ask him.

'You drink too much', he says sadly.

'Well, it's been a long day.' I sigh, playing with my empty glass, pushing my hair off my damp forehead.

'You should cut down, it's not good for you, physically and emotionally,' Charlie says in a monotone.

'Charlie, you drink more than I do.'

'Not any more,' he says, and gets up. 'I'm going to bed.'

I haven't thought about the sleeping situation since we've arrived, but now it occurs to me. 'Charlie, where are you sleeping?' My awkwardness projects across the room to him. I don't think we should be in the same bed, and I want to make sure all his declarations of innocence before we left have held fast. I don't want this to turn into some bizarre pity- and angst-ridden dirty weekend, one for the road and all that. Besides which, he might be sick again . . .

'I'll sleep in my parents' bed, and you can take our . . . my room.'

'Okay, thanks. Are you going to be ok, I mean, tonight?'

'I'll be fine,' he says, sadly again. He turns and heads towards the room.

'Charlie?' I shout out, as he reaches the bedroom door.

'Yes?' he says, expectantly, and turns to face me. I pause.

'Do you need a bucket?'

'I've got one.' His shoulders drop and with his head down, he goes in and shuts the door behind him.

I hear him shuffling around his parents' room for a moment or two, and then the light goes out.

My eyes close, my head nods, and I just don't seem able to move. My legs feel like whisky-soaked, denim-clad tree trunks, and even moving my fingers requires too much concentration and effort. My head nods back again.

You do what you do, right? No rules, no judgements, just fun. But thinking about it now, I acknowledge my life hasn't been like that for a while. I thought I was still carefree, living it up, but I haven't been recently, not since I started work, not since university. Not since America. I thought I was putting up with Charlie because we were still twenty-one at heart. That was the last time I can truly remember the honest pursuit of a good time. I had hardly any money, a stranger in a bloody strange land, but God, I had fun. We wanted the same things. Now we think about what time we have to get up, our mortgages, the fact we are being shafted by a boss who is taking all the credit for work that's ours. We just think too much.

I remember one night back in the States, a couple of months before I left. Joleen had gone home because her dog had died. Dale and I were sitting in the room watching a film, *The Jerk*, on TV. He was ok now, if Joleen wasn't there, almost courteous. I think maybe he felt exposed, or lonely, in her absence. I was tired from playing tennis all afternoon, and Charlie was coming over with a takeaway. I assumed Dale would leave when he arrived, so I wasn't too bothered by him being there. I had a bit of a tidy up on my side of the room during the ad breaks and Dale, without my asking, emptied the bin, the ever-overflowing ashtray, and made Joleen's bed that was a pile of sheets and green scratchy blankets. I said thanks, he said no problem. We sat down on opposite sides of the room to carry on watching the film. We laughed in the same places, and relaxed.

'I wish I was British,' he said, out of the blue, while more adverts played.

'Sorry, Dale?' I wasn't sure I'd heard him right. He didn't answer.

He was two different people by then. The sleazy innuendoes and come ons stopped as soon as Joleen left. When she returned, he would start back up again, but almost as if it were obligatory, and even with an apologetic look to me if she turned her back.

It was March by then, and the weather was getting only slightly better. Charlie had gone home for two weeks for his brother's wedding, and I had missed him quite stupidly, especially as we had agreed that we were just having fun really, no major ties, no unnecessary commitment. We had both cottoned on, however, during the time we spent apart, that we liked each other more than we had admitted.

Whenever Charlie came over, Dale would make his apologies and leave. It wasn't rude, it was almost chivalrous, acknowledging that we wanted to be alone. Joleen would generally follow him, for a couple of hours at least. Dale and I had come to some kind of undeclared understanding. I think Dale actually liked me, had some small amount of respect for my consistent rebuffs of his advances.

One afternoon, as I pulled my hair back into a ponytail for a game of tennis with Jake in the new spring sunshine, I noticed Dale's eyes rise from a battered second-hand copy of *A Hero of Our Time*, and caught his smile as I applied lipgloss.

'You're about to play tennis,' he said as I stared back at him in the mirror.

'Hey, perceptive boy!'

He let his book rest on his chest, taking care not to crumple

111

his piano key tie, adjusted his feet on Joleen's desk, and lit a Marlboro.

'Why in God's name do you need lipstick for sports?'

'It's lipgloss, Dale – you have so much to learn about women.'

'Oh is that right?'

'Hell yes!'

Joleen coughed loudly and scowled from the corner of her bed, and Dale raised his eyes in exasperation.

But that was his sport.

'Nicola, tell me again, why we can't be together?'

I bent down to do up my trainers.

'Because, Dale, as I have explained already, I'm in love with Joleen. I've been trying to mount her for weeks, but she's got wicked sleep reflexes!'

'Damn those sleep reflexes!' Dale laughed out loud.

'Tell me about it.' I grabbed my tennis racquet.

'Just fuck off,' Joleen spat from the corner.

'My pleasure.' I smiled at Dale as I left, and he winked back.

It was almost a challenge, coming up with new putdowns for his requests. It kept me on my toes, like waiting for a fast serve. I also noticed that Dale was never anything but polite to Charlie. He shook his hand whenever he came into the room, made up some excuse and left, with Joleen hurtling behind him.

That night, when Charlie arrived, Dale had just opened a beer, and the film was two-thirds of the way through.

But as I kissed Charlie hello, still weakened at the sight of him, and he settled down next to me on the bed, putting the cartons of Chinese on the newspaper I had put down over my sheets, Dale stood up.

'Well, I've got to see a woman about some sex,' he said.

'Dale,' I said, 'you haven't eaten, have you? Do you want

112

some Chinese – Charlie has, as per usual,' I poked him in the stomach, 'bought far too much.'

Dale looked a little taken aback.

'No, no, I never eat that stuff – too little grease for me. Far too healthy.' He seemed almost shy.

'Honestly, mate, at least finish your beer – you don't have to leave just because I'm here.' Charlie smiled, and I think it won Dale over. Everybody wanted to be Charlie's friend, and he knew it, with a sadness that he only told me about. I was the first person he said, who hadn't just taken him at face value, who had listened when he explained how hard it was to have people forgive anything you did because they just liked you too much. Charlie added. 'Besides which, how interesting is female conversation, really?' and squeezed my hand in apology. He was making Dale feel important, better.

'He is right, Dale, I do bore him. Stay and finish your drink at least. Have a slice of prawn toast.'

Dale looked a little awkward, but then he smiled at us both, and without a word, nodded his head and sat back down, put his feet up on the table, and continued watching the film.

As the credits finally rolled, I said to Charlie, 'Dale wishes he was British, you know. Can you believe that, the American poet wishing he was part of the mother race?!'

I smiled at Dale to let him know I wasn't being nasty.

'I can understand it, mate,' Charlie said. 'You don't even play cricket over here, do you? Best reason for being British there is!'

'My God, you're deep,' I said, and wiped sweet and sour sauce off his cheek.

Charlie gave me a sudden hurtful look, and I smiled quickly back, squeezed his hand, a little scared. Just as quickly he regained his composure.

'Damn right I'm deep!' and opened his mouth and showed me half-eaten beef in black bean sauce and egg fried rice.

113

'Charming!' I said, and looked straight at him. He smiled. I was forgiven.

Dale laughed. 'You guys just seem to have the good stuff. You have the history, the culture. We have turkey in November and American Football!' Dale sighed, pretending to be depressed.

'You've got a bigger nuclear arsenal, mate.' Charlie talked with his mouth full of Chinese.

'I know, I know,' Dale smiled, 'and aren't you scared! The British, you have an arrogance, a confidence to you. You honestly believe you are better than the rest of the world. It's not right, of course, but it makes you comfortable in your own skin. You skip around the world with your stiff upper lips, and you just seem . . . like you can handle it, you can handle the world. We just shout at the world like idiots, feeling inferior, no matter how great we are supposed to be.' Dale trailed off, his last words almost whispered, and he seemed to remember himself suddenly, and leapt up from his chair, startling Charlie, who dropped his fork. I stared at him in confusion. I wanted him to stay. I wanted him to tell us what was wrong. He stared back at me for a moment, and his eyes seemed so massively hurt, it made me want to cry. It felt like he only needed one right word from me, but I didn't have a clue what the word was.

'Fuck me, I'm stuffed!' Charlie announced, rubbing his stomach, stretching out his legs. 'Give me ten minutes, my love, and we'll burn it off!'

He tried to tickle me, but I pushed him off, and muttered 'For fuck's sake' under my breath. I was annoyed with him, my fear of upsetting him gone. Dale was trying to tell us something, and Charlie's claimed depths weren't showing their face now. Dale saw how effortless Charlie's life was, and it was alien to him, the little guy in the suits who tried too hard at everything.

114

I looked back at Dale who was standing with his head down, smiling at the floor.

'Dale, you don't have to go yet, if you don't want to,' I said.

He looked up at me, still smiling.

'I have women to bed and small children to upset,' he replied.

'Okay, I'll see you tomorrow, have a good night,' I said.

'Yeah, see ya, mate,' Charlie said, and jumped down off the bed to shake off the crumbs.

'See ya,' and Dale span out of the room.

I sat and stared at the door for a minute, until Charlie noticed, and stopped dusting himself down.

'What?' he asked, and reached for my hand.

I looked at him, and couldn't be angry – he would never understand.

'I feel sorry for him,' I said.

'I thought you hated him.'

'I know.'

Bowls!

I dream I am running away from something, although I can't remember what. I wake, with a start when I fall off a kerb on Charing Cross Road. It startles me so much I am wide awake. For a moment, as is always the case in an unfamiliar bedroom, I have no idea where I am, and I stare at the wardrobe and the curtains in scared surprise. A moment of terror, and then a moment of recollection, followed by relief. Same old, same old. I roll over, hook the duvet under my leg, and close my eyes. It is already too hot to be in bed, and the sun creeps in from beneath the curtains, lighting up all my stuff dumped under the window in the corner. I can hear a faint ringing somewhere, and realize it's my mobile phone, deep within my bag. I belt out of bed, naked, and trip over the rug, landing clumsily in a pile of breasts and limbs. I scramble towards my bag, turn it upside down, empty the contents onto the floor and grab for my phone. It could be important, it could be somebody desperately needing me back in London straight away: our old lady in the mists could be suing for sexual harassment because Tony has told her in his native Scouse that she's done a 'boss job', something that has caught me out in the past. It could be an emergency – I want to go home! I don't want to be here, I've only just woken up and I'm already shattered at the thought of going and seeing if Charlie is up and about, depressed, or worse, doing wild crazy man things.

I flip the phone open, and the screen says 'anonymous'.

'Hello,' I say, out of breath, with half a ring to go before I lose the call to the answerphone.

'Hello,' a man's voice, old, West Country.

'Who is this?' I ask – the amount of wrong numbers I get on my mobile is ridiculous.

'Yes, hello, this is Salcombe Bowls club. Can I speak to Nicola Ellis, please?'

'Speaking.' I'm a little confused. I check the clock – it's late, I've slept until ten forty-five and I haven't phoned work yet.

'We have a bit of a situation down here, and this is the number the young man gave me. Charles Lloyd said I could contact you.'

My heart is sinking already. I close my eyes to prepare, and hold my head in one hand. 'Yes, where is he – is something wrong?' It's going to be a long day.

'Well, he's here. He's out on the green.'

'Right, sorry, who am I speaking to?'

'My name's William.'

'Okay, William, what has he done?' William sounds like a nice man. God only knows what Charlie has done to him.

'Well, he's a . . . buoyant young man, and he's not in any trouble, I just thought I should give someone a call, and he asked me to call you.'

'Right, William, what has he done?'

'Well, he's out on the green, you see.'

'On the bowls green?' I ask, although I don't know what other green he'd be talking about.

'Yes, out on the green, and he's having a lovely time, but he's refusing to put his trousers back on, and he's actually

118

trying to get some of our members to take theirs off, and, you see, I wouldn't mind, but we have strict dress codes on the green. He should really be in white, but he's only in his undershorts, and they are black.'

'He's taken his clothes off?' I don't know why I am repeating this, rubbing my forehead to make this information go in, as I sit stark naked on the floor.

'Yes, most of them, yes. To begin with, he just insisted on keeping score and shouting out encouragement – we had a couple of complaints from the usual old sticks, but everybody else found it quite amusing and we don't get many youngsters down here, so in truth, my love, it was actually quite refreshing. But then, you see, he started taking his clothes off every time somebody knocked out, and now he's down to his undershorts, as I say, and he's started singing songs.' Poor William sounds quite apologetic, and I feel the anger rising up inside me. How dare Charlie go and ruin these people's day with his stupidity and shock value tactics! Poor William has been nominated to phone me and is embarrassed as hell by all of this. I am going to kill Charlie. I am going to break both his thumbs.

'William, I'll come and get him. Whereabouts are you based?'

'On the Salcombe road, just before the beach huts.'

'Is that just up the road from the Seaview cottages?' I ask, fingers crossed.

'Yes, that's right. Just before you turn to go down to the coast road.'

'Great, William, I'll be there in ten minutes. Can you tell him I'm coming for him, and, William, can you tell him I'm angry.'

'Oh well, I'll tell him you're on your way at least. Thanks. Bye.'

I'm fuming. What the hell is wrong with him? For Christ's

sake, you don't strip off in front of old people – William probably fought in the war! It's all very well going off the rails a bit, but you have to maintain some sense of personal responsibility, and you can't just go around showing no respect for senior citizens in the twilight of their lives. He's gone too far. I'm going to kick his arse.

I jog down the road in my hanging around the house tracksuit bottoms which I had the sense to stuff in my bag as we hurriedly packed in London, and a vest top I normally wear in bed. I'm wearing my flip-flops with flowers on the front which keep threatening to trip me up. Hair scraped back, sunglasses on, jaw set, in need of a shower, key and mobile in one hand, purse in the other, in case the bowlers need some kind of cash incentive to keep the peace. They may be old, but the old can be cunning. As a rule, I don't trust them. They are far too knowing for my liking.

I see the bowling club set back from the road, and trying to keep calm, I slow down to a swift walk, and try to work out what I am going to say. He may have completely lost it, in which case I'll just call an ambulance and keep well back. But if not, if there is even the possibility that his sanity has not completely left him, if he is not dribbling and slapping himself, I am going to rip his throat out. They'll think I'm his girlfriend – officially, I suppose I still am – and they'll feel sorry for me. The thing I hate most in the world is pity. I can't stand it, and Charlie has put me in this position. I don't understand what's wrong with him.

I can hear him singing as I open the door to the clubhouse. It's coming from the back. It's dark as I walk in and, as my eyes adjust to the light, I head towards the patio doors, where a lot of old people appear to have congregated, like an OAP Persil advert, all dressed in white, pleated skirts, little hats, tank tops over short-sleeved shirts. It amazes me how much old people can wear in the heat and not sweat – if I wear closed-in shoes and it's more than seventy degrees, I'm mopping my forehead.

The whole herd turns and stares at me as I walk through them and outside, ignoring their mutterings and remarks. They may not have been bothered before, but they are outraged now. I take a deep breath and stride towards Charlie, who is singing 'Feelings' in the middle of the lawn, holding a bowl in each hand and gesturing to the sky with every word. A couple of old men are about twenty paces away from him, talking quietly together. I can see the skin on his shoulders turning red in the sun, and the glow from behind him makes him look almost angelic . . . almost. Angels generally don't wear black jockey shorts, not in the pictures I've seen at least. I wonder when exactly Charlie went from the epitome of cool to an idiot.

'I'm looking for William, he called me,' I say.

'Yes, that's me.' A well-presented old man in glasses and a starched shirt turns towards me. The creases in the front of his trousers seem even whiter than the rest of him.

'I'm sorry about this. If I take him away, will you guys forget this ever happened.' I am practically begging them.

'Well, yes, I suppose,' he says, looking uncomfortably at Charlie, wondering how the hell I'm going to get the singing crazy man off his lawn.

'Thanks, William, I owe you a drink,' I say, and walk towards Charlie. He is singing skywards but out of the corner of his eye he sees me approaching. The singing quietens a little, then stops, his arms out at his sides like a bowling green crucifixion. He looks at me uncertainly, nervously. He knows he's been bad. He looks like a man, with the face of a guilty child. I feel something in me weaken as I storm towards him. He looks really scared. I get to within two feet, and stop and stare at him.

'Hi,' he says quietly.

'What the bloody hell are you doing?' I ask through gritted teeth.

'I was just, I just felt like ... I just needed to ...' He trails off.

'Are you angry with me?' he asks, and I feel like his mother.

'No, Charlie, I'm not angry. Exasperated maybe. I don't understand what you're doing. I don't know what to say to you, I don't feel like I know you, I don't know what's got into you. Are you, do you feel like you're cracking up?' I ask him quietly, my teeth and jaw loosening, the anger fading.

'I just wanted to feel like a cloud,' he says quietly, head down.

'You wanted to feed cows?' I ask, incredulous.

'I wanted to feel like a cloud, I wanted to float away, I wanted to be clean,' he says, not raising his head, not looking at me.

'Let's go back to the cottage.' I bend down to make eye contact, as he's still staring at the grass.

'We'll have a shower, have some lunch, and have a talk. How does that sound?'

'Fine,' he says, without looking at me.

'Okay, let's go. I'll get your shirt, you get your shorts.'

'Okay,' he says, and walks over to where he flung his shorts at the side of the green. I walk over and pick up his shirt, and hand it to him. They are both still damp – we had stuffed them in a bag last night, the unshrinkable cotton clothes that had survived Charlie's impromptu laundry-fest. He starts to walk off.

'No, Charlie, put them on first.'

'Oh, okay.' And he climbs into his clothes.

We walk back past William, and Charlie hangs his head.

'Thanks, William,' I say.

'My pleasure, bye, Charlie,' William offers, but Charlie just walks towards the clubhouse, head down, ashamed now.

The old people mutter as we push our way through them to the door at the front. I hear their little jibes, and choose to ignore them, until I hear a particularly blue rinse say, 'She could have brushed her hair.'

'Alright love, at least I've got my own teeth!' I snap back.

We leave to the sound of geriatric tutting.

Food for Thought

I make Charlie promise he will not leave the cottage, and he agrees sheepishly, as I deliver him to the front door and head off in the direction of the village shop. It's always been the same down here – loaves of bread, but no croissants, chunks of Edam, but no Mozzarella; you check the sell-by date on everything. I manage to cobble together a breakfast slash lunch fit for a loon and his ex-girlfriend – somehow they manage to have a single melon for sale, and two tubs of strawberries that haven't gone mouldy yet, but my requests for bagels are met with incredulous stares.

I think maybe, with regard to breakfast, lunch, dinner, and 'supper', for God's sake, we've got out of hand in London; we expect every meal to be a feast. We don't just sit down and eat cheese on toast any more. It has to be sundried tomato bread, and three cheeses at least one of which has to have a name whose pronunciation is up for debate, pepper, ground, not just dusted on (God forbid!), and a tub of olives and Feta chunks in olive oil to accompany. And generally we have champagne with it, or mineral water – sparkling, of course. Why can't we just have Cheddar? What's wrong with sliced white bread? The world's gone mad. I live in constant fear of one of my friends spontaneously crashing at my house one night, and waking up in the morning only to be met with a stale loaf and some two-week-old Anchor butter. For shame!

Charlie has managed to have a shower by the time I get back, and is in his jeans. He dances around behind me in the kitchen as I unpack our food.

I spin round to put water in the fridge, and Charlie jumps back.

'Charlie, are you ok? You seem a little edgy.'

'No, I'm fine, I mean, I feel alright.' He gives me a weak smile and rather than get into it, I carry on unpacking our breakfast.

'Can I help?' Charlie darts forward, and picks up a knife and a melon simultaneously.

'Jesus!' I jump back, and Charlie looks confused.

'What's wrong? I can cut a melon, I'm not an idiot.'

'I'm not sure, Charlie . . . do you think you'll be okay . . . with a sharp object?'

'I'll be fine.'

'Fair enough. Look, I'm going to have a quick shower. You cut the melon, but Charlie, if the knife scares you at any point, just put it down and walk away.'

I leave the kitchen, but glance back to see Charlie gingerly cutting the melon at arm's length.

I'm not even going to think about it.

I grab a towel out of his parents' airing cupboard. They have at least ten matching towels in different sizes and textures – soft, super soft, want to make love to it soft, want to give birth to it, it smells so good. They are all neatly folded in the airing cupboard, which smells of roses and babies' heads, not damp or mould. And they come to this house for one month a year. My towels in my flat back in London, in which I live twelve months of the year, are generally damp, on my radiator which isn't radiating, and in three different colours, none of them big enough to cover my front and back. The middle-aged can organize their time so much better than the rest of us – it's either years of practice, or boredom. It's either part of their strictly adhered to daily routine, or the only thing they have to do.

Blasting away the sweat with a slightly cold shower, I just begin to relax when the door opens, and I hear Charlie come in.

'Charlie, what the hell are you doing? Did you cut yourself doing the melon?' I poke my head out of the shower curtain. I don't want him to see me naked. I can't remember the last time he soberly saw me with no clothes on. We hide away from each other these days, unless we are too drunk to care, and having sex. I haven't had sober sex with Charlie in over six months. I haven't had sex with him at all for two months.

He puts the toilet seat down and slumps down on it.

'I just felt like talking,' he says, leaning forward, elbows on his knees, head in his hands.

'Yes, okay, but Charlie, is now really the time?' I ask, holding the shower curtain around my neck.

'I don't know, I just keep losing myself, like back there at the bowling green. What was I thinking?' Charlie runs his hands through his hair. He looks despondent.

'I know, and I do want to talk, but can I get dressed first?'

'Sure, I'll get the stuff ready,' and he mopes out, leaving the door open.

I dash out and close the door behind him, and kick the mat up against it to stop it opening from the outside.

But now my shower is quick; I can't enjoy the getting clean experience, because I am worried about what he is doing.

I pull my shorts on over still damp legs, and my wet body sticks to the material. It'll dry in the sun. I put my bikini top on, towel dry my hair, apply concealer, grab my sunglasses, and head outside. Charlie is lying down on the throw that usually covers the bottom of his parents' bed; the melon is cut into quarters – not slices. Not chunks, no design of any description. It looks great, it's the way melon should be eaten, with your hands, juice dripping all over your chin. I sit down on the blanket next to him, but he seems to be dozing. He looks great in just his jeans, with his sunglasses on. His face looks troubled, but the rest of him looks good. I still find him attractive, I still like the look of his body, but it's like the history we share now coats him with a 'do not touch' Vaseline. If he was anybody else, looking that good lying next to me in the sun, I would be distracted. If it were still the beginning. But it's not like that any more with us, because to kiss him isn't just to kiss his mouth, it's to kiss what we were in the beginning, what we became, and what we are now: it's to open up a body full of issues and accept them pouring into me. Sometimes there are just too many complications for the simple things to be possible, particularly a kiss. It's a tragedy.

But even without all the history and just dealing with the here and now, I don't like the person he is any more. This weekend with Charlie being so weak and so confused, it's confusing *me*. He isn't a different person at all, he's just having a minor breakdown, but in a few days we'll be back in London, and he'll be whoring about town again, not wanting to have a two-line conversation with me any more. It's easy to forget it lying in the sun in the middle of nowhere, with the faint sound of the sea ebbing and flowing as a soundtrack. I am still a romantic, God knows how, but Charlie isn't my knight in shining Armani, he is not hero material any more.

This weekend pretence and the confusion it's throwing my way makes me hate him slightly, and I 'accidentally' spill lemonade on his chest while I am pouring myself a glass, and he jumps up from his daydream. I almost feel bad for disturbing him, but why should he relax? Charlie isn't the only one with feelings all over the place. He sits up and crosses his legs like a kid in assembly. I offer him a glass and a piece of melon. He takes it and says thank you. We sit in silence for a while, and the heat makes even the slightest conversation seem exhausting. After half an hour, all our problems drift to the back of my mind, and I begin to think of sunscreen and wrinkles, and the normal things I think of in the sun. Generally, when I think of suntan lotion, I am abroad – being at home doesn't seem to warrant it – the sun is so rare in this country. I don't associate 'holidays' with England; the people are too familiar, the smell isn't right. Holidays always smell the same – suntan lotion and moisturizer and chlorine, slight damp and dry heat.

Holidays smell different in the evenings: desperation and sunburn, too much hairspray, and po-faced English girls storming down neon strips, glaring off sleaze filled assaults by the locals, and sternly pretending not to hear the equally sunburnt heckles of their male compatriots who have some-how got lucky, got beer, got sun, got cheap quick sex at four a.m. the night before with an underage girl who has crept out of the villa window while her sangria-filled parents slept off their holiday excesses.

These holidays are pink – be they Spain, any of the Greek Islands, the Canaries. The faces are pink, the Lycra is pink, the drinks are pink. It is not a girly pretty shade, it is not baby pink. It's the holiday bleached out version of hooker red.

And every conversation you have with a stranger is fuelled with having to say a major yes or no at some point, usually NO! to the opportunists, who can't take a hint. Every con-versation is one rather avoided, and brought to as hasty an end as politeness allows. No I don't want to talk to you, no I don't want you to rub cream in my back, no I don't want to see your menu, or your tan line, or come into your bar no

129

matter how many shots of cheap local shit you are offering. And no, of course I don't want to have sex with you – do I look that drunk? Are you mad? Is the sun in your eyes? Can you see me? Now remember what you look like – put two and two together and make fuck off. Of course you rarely say it that bluntly. I try to be polite. I say no thanks very much.

There was one holiday that was different. Spring Break of our American year. There were groups of people going everywhere – Florida Keys, Cancun, party resorts. But Charlie and I just wanted to be on our own and experience somewhere distinct together. We booked a cheap-looking hotel over the internet, and two flights to . . . San Francisco. It was a surprisingly small city, but fantastic, intimate. And we were the golden couple, getting on so well. Charlie laughed and made me feel loved and admired by this gorgeous man, and I listened to him as he flustered his way through thoughts he had never voiced before, trying to make sense of being a child and feeling loved, but alone. Of people never really wanting to listen to what he had to say, of not being needed, just being seen. It was something that had never occurred to me. I knew what it was like to get admiring glances, to feel eyes following me across a room, but I had never entertained that it was the sum of me, or that anybody would ever feel that it was the sum of me. I have always had something to say, and have always had people to listen. Charlie said he hadn't. It broke my heart. We don't generally feel sorry for the ones whose lives seem to be too smooth, too blessed, who genetically struck gold, who have an innate charm that wins the world over at a glance. Who would have thought they were desperate for something else, to feel weighty, and deep, and necessary, and valued as something more? Too many people love them, for any of it to count.

We went to Alcatraz, on our one stormy day, and we wandered around the tiny island with headphones on, listening to the misery of people's lives like gossip. We wandered around Fisherman's Wharf, and strolled with the tourists through Haight-Ashbury, wondering how different it had been when it was Love Street, and people believed in things. We didn't pretend to understand. We passed the greatest preponderance of same-sex couples wandering down the street holding hands that we had ever seen. It was a very personal city.

We took one very special day, and walked our way from Ghirardelli Square to the Golden Gate Bridge, and watched the sun go down over the Pacific. We skimmed stones and ate a picnic; Charlie dragged me up a hill I never thought I could climb. It was just the two of us, walking all day – a dog tried to hump Charlie's backpack while we took our shoes off and kicked through the sand of the beach. We found what looked like a Roman monument and stood in the shadows and the sun. We smoked and talked and held hands the whole way. It was young love indeed.

'Sorry?' I am roused from my dozing by Charlie mumbling.

'I wonder what happened to us?' he says, not looking at me, but taking his sunglasses off, shielding red eyes from the sun with his forearm.

I feel a lump in my throat. I am not good at 'emotional'. If things aren't going well, if it's personal. It always makes me want to cry. Especially if the person I am talking to may be about to pay me some misplaced compliment and tell me that they love me. I either feel awkward or suddenly tearful.

I shrug, with my head down, and make a face that I hope says I don't know, but covers up my quivering chin.

'We were great to begin with, in the States. We had a great laugh. And we were in love, weren't we?' Charlie knows we were. I nod my head.

'And I know when we left, well, it wasn't great for a while, but we stayed together, and we came through it, didn't we?

131

We were okay for a couple of years, we wanted to be together, so what has happened to us?' I am shocked that he has brought that up. We had agreed never to talk about it. We have hardly acknowledged it since it happened.

'Charlie, I think we just drifted apart. People do! You get jobs, you meet different people, you pay bills. It's not as much fun as it was.' It sounds lame.

'But, Nix, I thought we would last, I really did, if we could get past what happened.'

'Charlie, I really don't want to talk about that, ok?' I snap at him. 'Fine, so you are feeling shitty, and confused and depressed, but don't drag me down, this is your crisis not mine, I'm here to help.' I cross my arms, and then uncross them, fearing tan lines.

'Nix, you know it's part of the problem. You know it's part of the reason we've ended up hating each other,' Charlie says.

'I don't . . . hate you,' I say, upset, confused. All of a sudden this has become about me.

'I think maybe you do, a little bit. I hate you, a little bit. We've never talked about the abortion, just ignored it, and these things build up inside you.'

I get up, grabbing my cigarettes, and walk away. Angry, tears streaming down the side of my face, I storm into the house, and out the back door, into the garden behind the house. It's much more cultivated than the front, much neater, much more like an old person's garden, like the Blue Peter garden. It's not relaxing at all. You feel like all the ants are marching in line, along the rock borders.

I light a cigarette, and breathe it in heavily. I wasn't ready for that, Charlie has never brought it up, not since the day I asked him not to. I don't want to talk about it. It happened two months after we got back from America. I wasn't even going to tell him, but he guessed. You can't ignore morning

132

sickness. Charlie might think he is getting in touch with his emotions at last, and that's up to him, but my emotions are just fine, I don't need him lashing out at me too.

Then I hear Charlie walk up behind me. 'I'm sorry,' he says. 'I didn't mean to upset you. I've just been doing some thinking. I haven't thought about anything really, for ages, it's easier not to. I didn't mean to drag it all up again.'

I turn around and smile at him, wiping the tears off my face.

'It's fine, Charlie, it's just, you know I don't like to . . . I can't talk about things like that.'

Charlie just stares at me, and I can tell what he is thinking. He doesn't say he actually 'blames' me, but he thinks it's my fault. I don't think I'm here by accident. I think Charlie is after saving us both.

'Let's go swimming, shall we?' he asks suddenly, like it's the first idea he's ever had.

'Let's go down to the beach, it'll be great. Nix, do you fancy it?'

It's about three o'clock. It's a good time to go swimming. I see him trying to make it right. He is bursting with an old innocence, a need for fun. He isn't hungover, or silent.

'Sure. Let me grab some towels.'

He doesn't move out of the way as I walk past him back into the house, and the hairs on my arms bristle slightly as they brush past his skin.

We walk down the beach road, both of us with a towel in hand, a couple of feet apart, and we run down the grassy sand to the beach itself. There are a couple of people about, old folks in deckchairs about thirty feet up from us, and a couple of kids with buckets dancing around the edge of the water as it laps their little legs.

We both run in, and dive under the water, which is cold

133

and slaps us both simultaneously. We come up for air at the same time.

We make our way out further into the sea, to jump waves, that lap at us to begin with, but then start to carry us into the air with them. Charlie looks back over his shoulder and laughs at me as he gets pulled backwards by the water. I think of San Francisco, I think of the way we used to talk, I look at him laughing and I feel something stirring inside me. I forget where I am, until the wave snatches me and drags me under. My mouth is full of water, my head pushed back by the force of the wave, my legs drag along the bottom, cut and scratched by sand. I feel my limbs twist and unceremoniously I am dumped back on the beach by the sea, now bored with me. I cough and wipe my eyes, feeling sick and shocked by what has happened. Charlie is running towards me, frightened. He dives onto his knees by my side, and stops himself at the last second from hugging me. He jumps up quickly, and then falls onto his knees again, a little further away.

'What happened – I looked around and you were gone!'

'I didn't time my jump right,' I say, wanting to laugh now, with relief.

'Jeeesus,' Charlie whistles and looks out at the sea, then turns back to me. 'Are you okay?' He reaches out to touch my arm, but doesn't.

'I'm fine, Charlie. I just scared myself. That's enough swimming for me today.'

I clamber to my feet, relieved that at least my bikini didn't get dragged off. I feel sand in the fresh cuts on the back of my legs stinging already. Salt is getting into all my wounds.

Highlights

It was a month before we were due to leave the States, and I began to feel sad about leaving this town I had been complaining about for the past year. I realized I was in a strangely happy bubble, and when we left of course everything would change. Joleen had even become almost bearable, if I ignored the swearing tantrums, which were less frequent, partly because we had both grown tired of it, but mostly because the end was in sight. Charlie and I were getting along fantastically. We had already agreed that we were going to keep on seeing each other when we got back home – we wanted to make it work. Our universities weren't that far apart, we could and would carry it on. I wanted to. We were in love, I suppose. Charlie was fun, and we laughed all the time. We were very alike. We didn't really delve into things, the way we were feeling, and we both liked it like that. He told me he loved me, and I didn't need to know when or why or how much. That was more than enough.

If I particularly wanted an intense conversation, I had Jake, or even Dale. He had got a little more serious than usual with this one girl he had been seeing, and I had seen a lot less of him. I was at Charlie's half the time, he was with his new, almost-exclusive girlfriend, even Joleen had managed to make a new friend, an equally unattractive girl on one of her courses. They went to the theatre together, to see strange contemporary dance pieces with lots of blood and incest. She seemed happier.

It got so that our little room, previously so claustrophobic and cluttered and stuffy, was frequently empty for hours at a time. On the occasions that I went back there, I could often find myself alone for a couple of hours before anybody showed up, and then mostly it was Dale. We talked about his girlfriend, and how Joleen was taking it quite well, all things considered, and I asked if he really liked this one.

'Well, you know, she's not you, but yeah we get on.' He smiled at me and winked, and I laughed back. Only ever in jest these days, the sleaze had stopped altogether.

'What does she look like?' I was curious.

'Jealous, are we?' he asked.

'Now, Dale, even if that were true, you know I would never admit it!' I batted it back to him.

'Well, let's see.' He sat down, and put his boots straight up on Joleen's desk as always, unbuttoned his jacket, loosened his tie. He obviously liked this girl, because he was looking much . . . cleaner. Instead of staying up all night writing, and then going to lectures in the clothes from the night before, Dale was now frequently going to his girlfriend's for his bedtime cookies, and his hair even started to look shiny, underneath the gel of his quiff.

I unpacked my books from the day and was laying out all the requirements for that night's essay – cigarettes, coffee, Maltesers my mum had sent me from home, and of course pens and paper and stuff. Take That were playing quietly on my CD player, and after at first grimacing, Dale had even started singing along; hearing it as much as he did, now he knew the words in spite of himself.

136

'Well, she's very bright.' He stared off into space, hands together thinking seriously about his answer.

'Is that it?' I asked, looking at him over my shoulder as I placed a highlighter next to a set of black biros.

'No, there's other stuff. I'm just trying to put it in order.'

I carried on arranging and then, realizing he had gone quiet, I looked over my shoulder, and caught him looking at me.

'What?' I asked him, confused.

'Do you know what I like about you?' he said.

'I thought we were talking about your girlfriend!'

'We are, we are, I'm just saying. You sing the music as well as the words. You sing the instrumental bits as well. Do you realize you do it?' He looked a little embarrassed as soon as he said it.

'I suppose, kind of, I don't know.' I was embarrassed as well. I hoped he wasn't about to say something serious, and nice.

'Well, it's the sign of a happy heart, you know,' he said, regaining his cool.

'Hurrah!' I said, and pulled at my top slightly, feeling it cling to me a little too tightly.

'Anyway,' he said, shrugging, 'she's very sweet. Doesn't understand jealousy.' He said it with an admiring look on his face, like he was picturing her in front of him.

'I've never understood the point in getting jealous myself. Waste of effort,' I said, partly because it was true.

'I don't think you understand jealousy unless it's part of your make-up. It's inherent,' Dale said.

'Maybe, or somebody makes you jealous. Anyway, I don't get jealous,' I said conclusively.

'Not even of Charlie, not even if he's flirting with a cheer-leader?' Dale asked slyly, trying to make me jealous.

'Nope,' I said. 'Not on my radar. If he wants to go off with

137

her he can, just means he can't go off with me again. I'm not going to worry about it.'

'Do you love him?' Dale asked, suddenly.

'Hang on a minute, I thought we were talking about you. Stop changing the subject!' I laughed, but turned away, trying a little too hard not to answer.

Dale went silent, and I could feel him looking at me again.

'Dale.' I turned round. 'Pack it in, you know I love him. Alright, now you, do you love what's-her-name?'

'Marie. No, I don't. I like her very much. But I don't love her. She's too nice for me. I need somebody a little darker – I need somebody with . . . a nasty streak.' We stared at each other for a second too long. I felt like he was talking about me. I felt like he knew that I knew. I pulled at my top again.

'Dale, you think you're nasty but you're not. Nobody wants nastiness anyway.'

'Maybe,' he replied.

Suddenly it had got very dark outside, and the lights needed to be switched on. The room felt very small, and Dale felt very . . . close. He got up suddenly and instead of turning on a light, he lit one of Joleen's candles on her desk.

'I've lost my highlighter, I need to get another one,' I said quickly. We both clocked the highlighter on my desk. I grabbed my keys and purse.

'I'll see you later on,' I said, hesitated slightly, and then grabbed for the door.

'Okay,' he said, as I shut the door behind me.

I took a large breath as I walked down the corridor, away from the room. I felt something terrible in my stomach. I felt nervous and strange.

I waited by the bus stop and had a cigarette. I saw Dale crossing the road a little way up, and ducked behind the shelter. He could see me out of the corner of his eye, and I saw him flinch slightly. I walked back to the room. I didn't see him for a week.

Swim When You're Winning?

Exhausted, shivering slightly, Charlie and I collapse onto our towels.

'I needed that,' I say, lying back.

Charlie looks at me strangely, and then turns, not understanding, and smiles at the sun, covering his eyes.

'Do you think it did you some good – cleared your head a bit? You seem a lot more relaxed,' I say. I am going to get control again. I am helping *him* out.

'Yeah, I feel a bit better,' he says, looking at me out of the corner of his eye.

'Do you want to go out for dinner tonight – we could go for an Indian?' I suggest.

'I'd rather get a takeaway. I don't really feel up to going out.' All of a sudden his face darkens at the prospect.

'Sure, we can do that as well. I quite fancy a nap first – I'm knackered. Shall we go back?' I ask.

'I think I'm going to stay here for a while, if you don't mind.' Charlie notices my nervousness at the thought of leaving him here on his own. 'Honestly, I'll be fine. I'm not the one who nearly drowned! I just want to do some thinking, on my own . . .' He is almost apologetic. I don't think it is a good idea to leave him on his own, or maybe I don't want to leave him on his own. All of a sudden it is more comfortable to be with him than not. But I can't start thinking like that. He is not himself. Once he's done his thinking we'll be right back where we started. It's just the sun, messing with my mind.

'Well, if you're sure you'll be ok, I don't want to act like your mother, but you know, you haven't been yourself,' I say, but he sits up and puts his hand on my thigh.

'I'll be okay, I just want to chill out, give you a break.' He smiles.

I get up and shake the sand out of my shorts and towel. I look down at him one more time, and he smiles reassuringly.

'Ok, well then, I'll go back, have a quick sleep, and then we can get dinner in for about eight.' He leans back on his towel and closes his eyes, his hands resting on his stomach. I trudge away in the sand.

Walking back to the cottage, I remember I still haven't phoned work, and it's nearly five o'clock. I speed up slightly, and as soon as I get into the cottage, throwing my towel on the floor, jogging into the bedroom, I check my mobile – nine missed calls. I start going through the messages – Phil, Phil, Amy, Nim, Phil, Phil, Jules, Mum, Phil. Oops.

I call Phil quickly, biting my lip with the guilt as the phone starts ringing.

'Hello, Nicola Ellis's office, Phil speaking.'

'It's me.' I grimace as I say the words.

'Nicola, where the hell are you?' He sounds panic-stricken.

'I'm in . . . I'm sick. I've been sleeping all day, just woken up. Sorry, is everything okay, have you covered for me? Did I miss anything massive? How did the shoot come out? What's the situation with the trailer – am I in trouble? It's nothing to do with me, you know that, don't you?'

'You had Tony in at eleven but I saw him instead, told him you hadn't turned up – he was pretty pissed off. He said you'd

142

told him the footage had to be done first thing, and he'd had to break his neck getting it done. And you were supposed to have lunch with Jess to talk about promotions, but I cancelled her beforehand. Badgergate has reared up – Publicity are fighting it, but it looks like it might make it into Monday's papers, and some mum is saying her three-year-old hasn't stopped crying since. Apart from that, everything's ok. What's wrong with you anyway?' Phil and I don't really have a boss/assistant relationship. We are too close in age, and I only ever order him to do anything if I am in a really bad mood. I have heard him tell people before that he knows how to 'play' me, which I don't take badly. He kind of does. He knows my moods.

'Women's things,' I say, knowing it will shut him up.

'Don't tell me!' he practically shouts down the phone. He doesn't like discussing anything to do with women's hygiene. He doesn't even like knowing that we shave under our arms. I had to tell him once what a hymen was. Phil is very private school, very . . . square-jawed. He has something going on up top, but his concentration is for shit. Work wise, he's fine if I ask him for something immediate, but anything with any longevity I might as well throw in the bin as soon as I ask him to manage it. But he makes me laugh, stops me getting too stressed, so he stays. Plus he knows the hours I keep, and that I am useless in the mornings, and to always cover for me with José. In return, I let him leave early on a Wednesday for football training. Football is still his life. He is slightly scared of women. He wouldn't know what to do with his time if he woke up one random morning to find competitive sport had been banned. It's all very concerning.

'So no real problems then – did José say anything?' Cunning bastard.

'No, he's in Spain for that conference.'

'So he is, fantastic. Look, call Tony, apologize to him for

me, make sure he didn't offend our old woman. Have you had a look at the footage – does she look scary?'

'I don't know – what's scary? I wouldn't want to snog her . . .'

'Jesus, you're useless. Okay, call Jess and apologize, and ask her to email me her initial thoughts, so we can discuss when I see her. Apart from that, I'll be in on Monday, anything you can't cope with before then, just call me, yes? The badger thing, well just make sure Operations make another master up, for when it all kicks off next week, and check it yourself. Actually go down there while they do it, smell the suite, if you even think they've been smoking marijuana, take it somewhere else. If José calls tell him I'm ill, but then call me, with his mobile number from Angela. Okay?'

'Absolutely,' Phil says, knowing full well he can leave early tonight if I'm not in the office.

'Have a good weekend, Phil. Remember to do that catalogue breakdown for me as well.'

'Doing it now!' he almost shouts. He hates it when I remind him to do something more than three times.

'Fine, I'll go. See you Monday. Don't leave before five-thirty.'

'See you.' Phil hangs up.

I sigh with relief, and feel exhausted again, all my adrenaline spent on the phone making sure I hadn't landed myself in it with José.

I lie back on the bed, holding my mobile, closing my eyes. It's still so hot outside. I like my job; it's not like Charlie's, it's relatively creative. Charlie just pursued the cash, I went after something that seemed, at the time at least, to be a little less mercenary. Male graduates gravitate towards banking, trading etc – it's where the cash is. Charlie wasn't particularly interested in computers or the media or medicine or law. He just wanted to make some money. The trouble is, the City doesn't just mean a different job, it means a different world.

Charlie is a broker. He sells things apparently. I'm not sure exactly what. I realize now that we have never really discussed his work properly, I have to admit to not being that interested. At first it was all very exciting, when we got our first decent pay packets, as we impressed our bosses, and did reports, and got promotions. But this was in the early days, when we still socialized with our uni friends, and were still essentially the same people we had been at college, before the atmosphere we worked in and the people we worked with had a chance to change us and, as a knock-on effect, to impact our lives. We hadn't turned bad yet, but our relationship had. I can't place exactly when our relationship morphed from two young carefree lovers into the train-wreck it resembles now. I remember the time we went away with my sister Amy and her then-fiancé, and some friends, for New Year's Eve. It was our first Christmas after America, and although we had experienced a difficult few months, we seemed to have passed through it. Of course nothing had been discussed, and little did we know what the eventual outcome would be. But we were still happy to be together, even if our sex had become a little awkward, a little cautious at times, always better when we had a few drinks inside us, and the recklessness set in. When sober, we skirted the issue: although each still dutifully making our way to the other's student house at weekends, we would lie together, kissing or hugging – sex that would end in an orgasm, but no penetration. Only when drunk would we revert to the bedroom exploits we had so carelessly pursued in the States, crossing back over the line we had passed on our very first night together, unthinking. We didn't discuss it, even then.

We trekked up into the middle of Scotland for our December 31st, and stayed in two remote cottages that used to be barns or milking houses. They both had log fires, and the boys fought over who got to stoke them the most. Charlie was always there first, but luckily nobody saw the irony except me. The skies seemed huge, as big as those in America, and the silence seemed vast, bouncing off the snow-covered trees and hills of the countryside. We did unusual things, like horse-riding on ice – Charlie fell off, but laughed about it and, after a dramatic silence, so did we. We went clay-pigeon shooting, with a farmer who wore a two bore shotgun on his hip as naturally as we wore our belts. We crunched our way through the white fields, wearing our sunglasses to protect us from the glare of the sun, and stood expectantly in ear defenders that doubled up as earmuffs. I screamed as I shot, but hit the flying discs of metal that flew through the air. We stood in a snow soaked field, and aimed at cold blue skies, and marvelled at the thrill of it, how naturally it came. Charlie and Jake managed to shoot nearly everything. A woman appeared on the horizon, on top of the hill we were aiming at, and I lowered my gun in shock, but the farmer told us to continue because it was 'only his wife'. Charlie laughed heartily, and I smiled at the farmer, only slightly concerned.

There was a pub down the road where we went drinking in the afternoon, after our morning's exploits and fried breakfasts, and we slammed shots and played darts, and downed drinks like the kids that we were. The locals were almost friendly, tolerating our money more than our conversation, and the fact that every day we drank them out of Aftershock and alcopops.

New Year's Eve itself was a strange affair. Amy and Andrew cooked all ten of us a meal, and we started drinking pina coladas at six, all dressed up and laughing, and hoping like hell we would be drunk by eight. Jake was there, with his new girlfriend, and two couples who were friends of Amy and Andrew, all teachers, all drinking more than the rest of us to make up for the responsibility they bore every day.

We started playing very drunken games at nine, and by

eleven fifty-five, three of the four teachers were asleep on the sofa, Amy and Andrew were curled up in front of the fire, Jake and his new girlfriend had mysteriously disappeared upstairs to see the New Year in rhythmically with the bongs, and Charlie and I were standing outside in the cold, with our coats on, arms around each other, looking at the sky, leaning on a wall that had been there for centuries.

'Four minutes to go,' I said, checking my watch and shivering slightly.

'Do you want to go in?' Charlie slurred.

'No, let's stay out here. It's nice, just the two of us.'

'We could always, you know, we could get upstairs in time . . . Jake seems to have the right idea.'

I shivered again, and Charlie went quiet.

'Let's stay out here, it's more . . . romantic,' I said. All of a sudden 'romance' had become something to endure, like some Japanese quiz show where they bury you in sand and shine mirrors in your face. Except here it was minus ten and the cold was making my eyes water.

'Three minutes to go.' I checked my watch again.

'Do you want to move in together, in the summer?' Charlie asked suddenly, and I gasped in cold air.

'What was that?' he asked, surprised, turning me around to face him. I leaned against the wall and defended myself.

'What?'

'That gasp – why, would it be so strange?'

'No, I just hadn't thought that far ahead.' I tried to meet his gaze, my eyes stinging.

'I have – we could move to London, rent somewhere – we don't have to buy straight away.' Charlie shook my arms a little bit, trying to persuade me it would be fun.

'Charlie, it really is still a long way off. I might have to move back to my parents' for a while, pay off some of these debts . . .'

He looked at me for a while, and to avoid his stares, I looked at my watch.

'Thirty seconds to go,' I said finally, almost embarrassed.

Charlie looked confused, and to stop him ruining the moment, asking questions I already knew I didn't want to answer, I kissed him. We kissed for a minute, and I deliberately counted the seconds.

'Happy New Year,' I said as we pulled apart.

'Yeah.' Charlie backed away slightly, but then reached out and took my hand.

'Shall we go back inside?' he asked.

'Happy New Year, Charlie,' I said again, taking his hand and pulling it slightly, to make him look at me.

'Yes, Happy New Year.' His eyes met mine briefly, and we walked back inside.

We went to bed, and hugged for a while, but eventually made our way to separate sides of our temporary bed. I remembered to hug him again, in the middle of the night, and he accepted it in his sleep. But by the morning we had drifted apart again. I suppose that was the start.

I did move back in with my parents after graduation, pleading poverty, and Charlie found a flat with some blokes he didn't know in Islington. It became a den of sloth. You stepped in the door, sat on the sofa, and didn't move for hours. It zapped your will to live. They had a cleaner, who swore at them in Polish for the mess they made, and the fact that it took her nearly the whole two hours each week just to do their washing-up, but she still came back for more. It was before Charlie became so house-proud, surrounding himself with high-tech gadgets and nothing else. His coffee table now has seven remote controls on it. He has a stereo that is wired up throughout the flat, which allows the music to come on in a different room when you enter it.

I commuted in from Kent, and spent a couple of nights a

week at his. But more and more, I felt inclined to catch the last train home, and more and more he filled his evenings, in my absence, with old university friends, but also with new friends, from work. These older guys took him under their wing, because they saw what a charmer he was; he attracted women he didn't want because he still had me, and they could pick up the surplus.

And so Charlie's job became the thing that made him go out on work nights, and eventually to strip clubs disguised as pubs in the East End, fifty pence in a glass for a full strip.

I moved out eventually, to Ealing, near friends, and my sister and Andrew, now her husband, but on my own, I needed the silence. Charlie bought his own flat, without any protests from me, on the opposite side of town. I bought my flat, without any protests from him, and we began to live our separate lives, punctuated with his arrival at my flat after heavy nights out, singing songs and slurring, tripping up and giggling.

Only in the last six months, however, did I sense that Charlie had started shagging around. We had grown apart, that was obvious, but to solve it, or confront it, was a bigger issue than I felt able to cope with. If he wanted to leave, eventually he would, and it didn't need emotional outpourings or digging up of the past on my behalf. And through it all I felt that deep down, I was at fault too, even if I wasn't the one having sex with other people. I wasn't a weak woman; I didn't stay because I had to. I stayed to see if he would stop, if things would get better without us having to thrash it all out. Maybe we could skip forward, forget the past, and get comfortable again. I didn't confront him about the affairs, the one-night stands, which surprised even me. Maybe it was the confrontation that he actually wanted. Typical me – good at getting angry about anything but our emotions, anything that might make me cry. We still attended the functions together, still did the rounds. But our sex became a drunken formality. And the christenings/weddings became more and more tiring, his behaviour more and more unacceptable. He became the perfect person not to take to a family occasion.

Of course Charlie got all the laughs and reinforcement from the boys in the City. You could split them into two groups – public school or Essex. Neither particularly was better or worse than the other; they were all obsessed with money and sex, but mostly money. One group was just more eloquent than the other. Not that they would be interested in having a conversation about anything other than money anyway, so the real difference was only whether you cared if they used the word 'fiscal' or not, and it's never really bothered me.

My friend Naomi went out with one of the Essex boys once; one of Charlie's crew. On the third date he had asked her to go back to his place, which in itself was a record in abstinence for a City boy, and she had agreed assuming he lived in a converted warehouse in Spitalfields. But she had somehow ended up on the last train out of Liverpool Street heading towards Southend, a train charmingly nicknamed the 'vomit comet'.

She eventually got off the train at Rainham, at which point her escort decided he would actually rather have a kebab than Naomi herself, and she ended up following him around freezing cold streets while his pissed up mates came rolling out of local pubs and greeted him with shouts of 'Oi Gary, you fuckin' bender, it's your round!'

Naomi finished it the next day. She rang him to tell him it was over, at which point he told her he thought she was frigid anyway. Besides which he was still in love with his ex-girlfriend, Kylie, and he didn't care whose baby she was having, he would love it like a brother. But essentially the only difference by then between Charlie, and Naomi's three-date Essex boy was that Charlie pronounced the 't' in 'slut'.

*   *   *

I realize I have fallen asleep when a phone begins to ring somewhere in my sleep, and eventually I realize it is my mobile, which has fallen off the side of the bed.

I answer it sleepily.

'Nicola speaking,' I slur.

'Sorry, did I wake you?' Phil asks, matter-of-factly. I rub my eyes, and glance out of the window at the sun setting.

'What? Yes, no, it's fine. What time is it, Phil?'

'It's . . . 7.30.'

'And you're still in work?' I ask incredulously, rolling my neck which has gone stiff.

'No, I left about . . . an hour ago. I just forgot to tell you that somebody called, and he said he was an old friend. Hold on, I've got it written down here somewhere. Hold that, mate.'

Phil passes the phone to one of his mates, and I hear him shuffling some paper, and music playing in the background, and the noise of a London pub on a sunny summer evening. I'm sure this can wait until Monday, but I'm not going to knock him for being conscientious. One of his mates is asking him if his boss is a 'bird' and I hear him say yes. He gets asked if he'd do me, and I hear him say 'shut up, she's on the bloody phone.' And then a whispered 'no'.

'Nicola?' he comes back onto the phone.

'Phil,' I say.

'Dave called.'

'Phil, I don't know anybody called Dave.'

'Sorry no, Dale, Dale called, American guy. He left a number, do you want it? Nicola – are you there?'

A thousand images flash through my mind.

'Nicola, are you there?' Phil asks loudly.

'Yes, Phil, I'm here. Have you got the number?'

The doorbell rings suddenly, and I jump out of my skin.

'Hold on, Phil, I've got to answer the door . . .' I walk,

151

dazed, to the door, holding the phone by my side. I answer it, bewildered. I look at the policeman.

'Can I help you?' I ask. I remember where I am, and who I am with. I look past the policeman into his car, and see Charlie, sitting in the front seat, wrapped in a blanket, looking guilty.

I can hear Phil shouting my name from the phone.

'Just one second,' I say to the policeman, and put the phone back to my ear. 'Phil, keep the number, give it to me on Monday, I can't take it now. But don't lose it. Phil, you mustn't lose it, okay?' I plead with him to be responsible.

'Alright! I won't.' He gets annoyed when I expect him to fuck up.

'No, Phil, this one is important, you mustn't lose that number.'

'I won't,' he says, a little calmer, realizing how serious I am.

'Okay, I'll see you on Monday.'

Turning back to the policeman, I see a second officer escorting Charlie out of the back of the squad car.

'Are you Nicola Ellis?' the first policeman asks, looking at his notebook, and then back at me.

'Yes,' I reply. 'What has he done?'

The second officer brings Charlie over.

'Again?!' I shout at Charlie. 'Why can't you keep your bloody clothes on?'

Two Inspectors Call

'Can we come in?' the policeman asks me, to break the silence, and stop my death glares at Charlie's head. Charlie stares at the floor and refuses to look me in the eye.

'Sure, come in.' I step back and hold open the door, and the policeman ushers Charlie in, while I growl at him. Charlie walks quickly into his parents' bedroom, and closes the door behind him.

The policemen stand expectantly by the sofa.

'Please, sit down,' I say. 'Can I get you a drink? We have wine, beer, whisky, gin, I think there's some port ...' Silence.

'Water?' I ask.

'Two glasses of water would be great,' the first officer says, and they both position themselves on the sofas, sitting forwards, on duty.

'I'll be two seconds,' I say, and move towards the kitchen, but instead duck quickly into Charlie's parents' room. Charlie has got dressed, and is lying on the bed with a pillow over his head.

'Charlie, you are not staying in here. Bloody come out.' I seethe under my breath.

'I'm too tired. They want to talk to you anyway. I've already spoken to them,' he replies. Muffled by the pillow, he is barely audible.

'Ahhhgggg,' I growl at him, and then storm back out of the room into the kitchen. I get the policemen their water, and sit on the chair opposite them.

'So, what do you need to talk to me about?' I ask, as they look at me expectantly.

'Well,' the first policeman pipes up again.

'Charlie didn't exactly do anything wrong. He was causing a bit of a disturbance, but nobody wants to press any charges. We just thought you might be able to shed some light on . . . why he was . . . doing what he was . . . doing.' The policemen both seem mightily embarrassed.

'So he's not really in trouble?' I ask.

'We just gave him a caution,' the second policeman says, apologetically, sipping his water.

'Are you sure a night in the cells isn't called for?' I ask.

The policemen look at each other quickly.

'I'm just kidding,' I say quickly, although quite obviously I wasn't.

'Look,' I sigh, 'what exactly has he done?'

The first policeman flips open his notebook, and just as quickly flips it shut again.

'There was a minor . . . assault,' he says, again apologetically. These guys feel really sorry for me, I can tell. I hate that.

'Oh my God, he hit somebody?' I ask, shocked.

'Well, not exactly,' they say in unison.

'I'm sorry, I don't understand – did he . . . kick somebody? I don't understand.' I am completely bewildered. I notice it is very dark in the room suddenly, and we are all talking to shadows. I reach over and turn on the lamp. Both of the policemen seem to relax a little. Charlie has obviously made them nervous.

'It was with a loaf,' the first one says.

'Sorry?'

'And a fish,' the other one remarks.

'That's right, once with a loaf, and once with a fish,' the first one says.

'A crusty bloomer, and a small haddock.' The second policeman refers to his notes.

I stare at them. My mouth is moving, trying to say something, but I don't know what. I take a breath. 'What? Sorry? He hit somebody with a small haddock?'

'Well,' the policeman puts his water down on the coffee table, 'it wasn't at close range. That's mostly why we aren't having to press any kind of charges.' He says this like it should make all the sense in the world. Which is ironic because I don't have a fucking clue what is going on.

'Look, I'm sorry if I'm being dense, but I don't know what you are talking about. What exactly did he do?'

'In total, he threw four loaves, and maybe, what, half a dozen fishes?'

'Yeah, about half a dozen,' the second one agrees with him, nodding his head.

'He threw four loaves and half a dozen fishes, and a couple of them struck some passers-by. From about thirty feet. No injuries, but you will have a dry cleaning bill, I believe.' He smiles at me slightly, as my head twitches from one to the other, trying to make sense of what they are saying. We all sit in silence for a couple of minutes. The policemen sip their water and put it down, rearrange the cushions behind them, tap tunes out on their legs. Eventually one of them coughs, and I look up, nodding my head.

'So he threw some bread, and some fish. Like a biblical thing? Where was this exactly; in town?'

'Yes, that's right, in the square.'

'Right,' I carry on nodding my head. 'Right.'

155

'So nobody is pressing any charges then,' I say.

'No, but we thought we should bring him back, because he seemed a little . . .' The policemen look at each other again, to try and find the right word, and not offend anybody.

'Insane?' I ask.

'No, no, no,' they both laugh, uncertainly.

'Sad?' the first one says.

'Yes that's it, sad,' the second one says.

'He seemed sad, did he?' I ask, nodding my head again. The policemen look at me with anxiety. They know I'm not happy. 'Is there anything you need me to do, officers? Do I need to sign anything?'

'No, no, it's fine, we just wanted to bring him home. He's a good kid is Charlie, I've played cricket with his father,' the first one says.

'Yeah, he's just great,' I say, sarcastically.

'Seriously, do you think he's okay?' he asks me, like I know.

'You know what? I don't know. I thought maybe he was just tired . . . but now, now I don't know,' I say quietly.

'And the bible thing – the fishes and loaves thing – I don't know what that's all about. He's not religious. He was singing earlier . . .' I stop myself. I don't think the bowling green incident, coupled with this, will look good. I don't know why I am protecting him.

'At what point did he start taking his clothes off?' I ask.

'Oh no, he was just in his shorts when we found him. He was using his top to carry the fish.' The policeman reaches down and picks up Charlie's top, which is next to him, and offers it to me.

'No thanks. You can just leave it there for now,' I say, all of a sudden smelling fish.

'Of course.' He drops it on the floor again.

The first policeman gets up, and the second one follows him to the door.

I follow them, and hold the door as they walk out.

'Thanks a lot, guys, I'll speak to him, calm him down,' I say, trying to sound calm myself.

'Look, don't be too hard on him,' one of the policemen says. 'I know how much stress these young boys are under, with these high-flying jobs – sometimes they just need to let off some steam. There's no real harm done.' He smiles at me weakly.

'Aha,' I say, and smile back, jaw set, anger flashing in my eyes. They climb into their squad car, and I wait at the door as they sit and chat for a minute, looking anxiously at me. I think they are worried about a case of domestic violence blowing up as soon as they drive off. I do really want to smack him, but that won't solve anything. And in the back of my mind, I'm worried. Maybe he really is having some kind of breakdown. Up until now I thought it was just a mini-crisis, an emotional outpouring, a little depression and a little shock. But it's getting out of hand. How easy is it to get somebody committed anyway?

Gone but not Forgotten

All our lectures finished the week before we left the States. We spent the last few days packing up, saying goodbye to people, playing tennis, going to the pub. I hadn't seen Dale for a while. The last couple of times I had run into him things had been awkward – if he was in the room when I got back, he would make an excuse and leave. I figured that would be it, and we wouldn't even say goodbye. Things had gone a little strange between us, we weren't comfortable with each other, but it wasn't mutual dislike any more.

Joleen packed up her stuff and cleared out the day after lectures finished, and it ended pretty much as it started, with an argument.

'I'm leaving now.' Joleen was loaded down with bags and coats, so I'd kind of guessed.

'Okay, well, bye then.' I looked up from my book.

'Dale won't come anywhere near the room now, you know that, right?'

Joleen followed this with a sly smile, as if somehow she had won a battle. I didn't even realize we were fighting.

'Okay, well, bye then.' I carried on reading this time.

'And if you do see him around campus, don't talk to him,

okay? His silly bitch of a girlfriend has slashed her wrists after Dale finally ended it. It was no fucking surprise, she's pathetic.' She followed this with another twisted smile that implied she had won that one too.

'Yeah, well, whatever.' I didn't look up, but Joleen didn't seem inclined to leave.

'I'm serious, Nicola, he won't have time for your shit.'

I snapped. 'What shit, Joleen? What actual shit is that?'

Joleen seemed to back down straight away. 'Whatever, I'm going.' Joleen swung open the door.

'Okay, Joleen. Fine. Bye.'

She stormed down the hall, leaving the door wide open.

No hugs, thank God. We weren't that shallow, we weren't going to pretend that both our years wouldn't have been a hell of a lot more bearable if the other hadn't been there. As soon as she left, I filled her side of the room with my suitcase and boxes in which I began to pack a year's worth of purchases.

Joleen had been oblivious to the shifts in my relationship with Dale – she hadn't noticed that somewhere during the year, and somehow, we had actually started to like each other, maybe even understand each other. I honestly didn't think I would see him, which made me want to say goodbye to him even more, and made me dwell on his absence more than I should have. I wondered how he was taking his girlfriend's drastic actions – whether he was, in fact, the evil little bastard I had him pegged for at the start and he actually didn't care. Somewhere in the back of my mind I didn't believe it, but I wasn't sure. He was, to all intents and purposes, a mystery to most people.

I was going straight home, as was Charlie, and we had agreed that we would work for a month, staying with our respective parents, and use the money we earned to bugger off to Greece or Italy for a couple of weeks and chill out together. It was all quite exciting, and yet terrifying, taking this relationship back home with me. I had never met his family, or friends in England, and yet we had practically lived together for most of the year. What daunted me most was the prospect of making it work at home, slipping back into old routines but with a new variable. I wondered how long we would last. Not that I wanted it to end, I was just nervous.

I had to return my last pile of unread books to the library and decided to get a coffee to warm myself up on a particularly breezy May day, and stopped off in the café behind our halls. As I walked in, I spotted Dale sitting in the corner, staring off into space, with a barely touched cup of coffee and a muffin in front of him. As soon as I saw him I knew that I *had* to say goodbye to him. I liked the idea that now, my leaving might actually mean something to him, might blip on his emotional radar somehow. He didn't notice me, as I ordered my coffee, but looked up as the door swung open with the force of the wind – you could hear the massive elms that lined the street struggling with their leaves outside. He looked over and saw me then, and he smiled. I paid for my coffee and went to join him at the back. The place was empty.

'Dale, I was hoping I'd run into you. I wanted to say goodbye. I'm leaving in a couple of days.' I felt flushed with the wind, and suddenly hot in my coat indoors.

Dale just smiled at me, intense and vacant at the same time. I sat down opposite him, and blew on my coffee.

'How's Marie?' I asked, knowing that if Joleen were there, she'd be screaming obscenities at me just for asking him.

'Joleen told you.' Dale shifted forward in his chair, ran a hand through his hair, which was wet for some reason, no sign of any gel at all, the quiff strangely absent today. It made him look younger, his hair falling at the sides of his eyes. I nodded, and blew on my coffee again.

We sat there for a minute, and he didn't say anything and just stared down at the plastic table, and his muffin.

161

Eventually I coughed, and stood up, as he showed no sign of moving.

'Dale, you probably want to be alone . . .' I started.

'Can we go somewhere and talk?' he blurted out, suddenly imploring me with tear-filled eyes, curtained by his hair.

'Sure, of course,' I said, and as he followed me out of the coffee shop, I felt a strange sense of pride, that after everything, he wanted to talk to me about . . . whatever he wanted to talk about. Joleen would be spitting chips.

We walked in silence for a minute, I kept blowing on my coffee, trying to cool it down, and so when I eventually sipped it, I wouldn't burn my tongue. I should have blown on myself. Dale gestured with his hands, as we walked, having a conversation in his head, without actually saying a word.

'I bet you wish Joleen was still here, to talk to,' I ventured finally.

'Yeah, I do actually,' he said. 'She means . . . a lot. You guys never really saw the best in each other.'

'I know,' I said.

'Joleen and I will end up together eventually. I just need to find her physically attractive first, but I'm working on it.' He gave me a wry smile.

'She loves you.'

'I know, I know,' he said, like it was a burden he just couldn't shake off.

'Is your girlfriend going to be okay?' I asked, as we turned in towards my block, my room, subconsciously.

'She's going to be okay. She'll be in hospital for a while. I don't know . . . what to do really.'

'About her?' I asked.

'Her, me, everything. I can't believe she did it. You know me, Nicola, I'm a shit. Why did she do it?'

'Probably because you aren't a shit. You aren't the shit you want to be. It just takes people time to realize it. She obviously has. But to do something like that, to try and kill yourself, it's more about her than you, Dale. You were just her reason, she needed a reason. A completely stable, non-suicidal person wouldn't have done it, even if you did break up with them.'

Dale nodded his head. My key was in the door, he leaned on the door frame beside me. I realized suddenly what was happening. But I turned the key without saying a word.

I opened the door and he followed me in, and shut the door behind him. I didn't turn the light on, even though the sun was almost down. He moved up behind me, and brushed the hair away from the back of my neck, and pulled my coat off from behind. It fell on the floor. He ran his hands down my arms to my hands, and kissed my neck, and the top of my back, and I felt myself let go, and let it happen. I turned around, and he kissed his way up my neck to the side of my mouth, and then stopped. So close I could taste the coffee on his breath, and a couple of strands of his limp fringe touched the skin by my eyes. I looked at him, and I knew he needed this, and he needed me. And then we were kissing, his tongue moving quickly and sharply in and out of my mouth, the way he smoked a cigarette, the way he spoke, the way he did everything. He kept stopping and taking deep breaths, and then kissing my shoulders, pulling my top off over my head, kissing the skin he found beneath it. I didn't try and slow him down, or guide him, I just leaned back and let him push me onto Joleen's bed. We pulled each other's clothes off, until I was wearing nothing but my knickers, and he was naked. He rolled me over on top of him, and laid back eyes closed. I moved down his body, and kissed him like a wife. I slipped his erection into my mouth, and stroked him softly. I crept back up his body, and took his face in my hands, peculiarly aware of his eyes now staring into mine. I kissed him harder on the mouth, so close that he couldn't focus on who I was, just my body next to his, moving with his, just a mouth kissing his, a tongue licking

163

his, hands holding his. He rolled me back over on the bed, and he slipped a hand between my legs, under my knickers, and into me, gently stroking, and then pushing his fingers in slowly, and then quicker, as I felt his dick ready against me. But he kept tickling, trickling his fingers just inside me, working around my last item of clothing, refusing to take it off. I reached down and slid my knickers down my legs, and he breathed heavily, as if I had just said 'yes'. He parted my legs with the weight of his thighs, as he guided his dick inside me, slowly, and stopped, as we both lay for a second, aware. Then he pulled back, and slowly, forcefully, pushed himself into me again, and then again, and I began to feel his need creeping, growing. I pulled his head into my neck and ground against him, faster, speeding him up. Dale pushed his hand into the small of my back, and arched me into him, and with no space between us, we urged each other on and on, and I felt an urgency inside me trawling through my body, a sweeping dread. Dale pulled back suddenly, but not quick enough. I closed my eyes, and brought my hand up to cover them.

We lay next to each other for a while, not saying anything, and then I got up and pulled on my top and jeans, over my naked body. Dale snatched up his shirt and trousers and did the same. I sat down heavily on the bed next to him, and he took out his cigarettes, lit one, passed it to me, and lit one for himself. We sat staring ahead, and I reached around smiling, and took his hand, to let him know it was alright.

'What are you doing tonight?' I asked him.

'I'm going down to the hospital. You?'

'Finish packing, I suppose.' I sighed hard, took back my hand, and massaged my neck. I could feel the tension.

'When do you go?' he asked, watching me.

'Saturday,' I replied.

He nodded his head, as if he agreed that I should.

He got up to leave, and I watched him move to the door.

I got up as he twisted the door knob, and took a couple of steps forward towards him. He turned and smiled at me.

'Have a good flight,' he said, and laughed a short sharp laugh, at the weight in the air, at this strange way to say goodbye.

'I'll try,' I said, and smiled back, raising my eyes to heaven, at us both, at our stupidity, and our misguided beliefs that we would make ourselves feel better, or lose ourselves in something so quick, and so small.

'Take my number, well, my parents' number,' I said suddenly. 'In case you're ever in London, and need a place to stay.'

I grabbed a scrap of paper and scribbled the number down quickly. He took it from me, and stuffed it straight into his pocket without looking at it.

'I'll see you,' he said, turned and spun out of the door, and I watched it close behind him. I heard him walking quickly away, his footsteps suddenly stop, then turn, and I could hear him walking back towards the door, and I prayed inside myself that he wouldn't open it. Somehow he sensed my prayer. I heard him stop, and then the footsteps make their way back down the corridor.

I had allowed it to happen, convincing myself that I was making Dale feel better. I thought I was helping him, like some Mother Teresa figure on heat. I realized in the seconds after he walked away that was not what I had done at all. I had simply helped myself. The phone rang, and I picked it up, not saying anything, numb.

'Nicola, are you there?' Charlie said.

Who Cares?

It takes me half an hour to get the fire going, but I don't give up piling on log after log, and far too many firelighters. I leave Charlie undisturbed – he hasn't come out of his room since the policemen left, and I imagine he's sleeping. By the time I have had a shower, moisturized, plucked my eyebrows, taken time on random stupid tiny things that require all my concentration but no thought, I am relatively relaxed. I pour myself a large glass of red wine from the drinks cabinet, sit myself down on the sofa in a huge sweatshirt I got free from work, clean jeans, and damp hair, and I feel ready to face anything. I smoke a cigarette smoothly, and sit back and think. I need to have a proper talk with Charlie, I think he is crying out for attention, crying out to talk, he just doesn't know how. For the thirtieth time since Phil rang, I mentally acknowledge that Dale has called, but in the same way as I have done for the last hour, I push it to the back of my mind. Charlie is my first, my only real concern. Dale is from a different world, Dale won't even recognize me now.

I dig around by the phone and find all the takeaway leaflets that have been collected and kept in an orderly manner by Charlie's parents. I find an Indian one and phone in our order. It's the same meal we always have, I don't need to ask Charlie what he wants. I potter about, turning lamps on, straightening cushions and throws on the sofa, tidying books on the table in the corner, putting paper down on the coffee table, getting cutlery, pouring myself another glass of wine. The temperature has dropped, there's a chill in the air, and I snuggle inside my sweatshirt, and close the back door. The sky is black. I look at my watch – it is nine o'clock. I see clouds creeping in from the wings, hanging over the cottage.

Somebody rings the doorbell, and I take my purse to the door, and accept two white plastic bags holding our evening meal.

I take the boxes out of the bag, put the naan bread on a plate, turn the stereo on, turn the volume down to low, press play on the Fleetwood Mac CD, one of Charlie's dad's, and move to Charlie's door. I knock quietly, and wait for an answer.

'Come in,' he almost whispers.

Charlie is sitting in bed, naked from the waist up. He has obviously been asleep – his eyes are a little red, and his hair sticks out in strange clumps on his head.

'Char, I've got us an Indian. Do you fancy a chat?'

Charlie just nods, and climbs out of bed in his boxers.

'I'll just put some clothes on,' he points to himself, and smiles at me.

'Absolutely – do you want a glass of wine?'

He looks up at me, debating it in his head.

'Sure, thanks.'

I close the door and move back towards the table. I remember some candles in a drawer in the kitchen, probably for power cuts. I take all three, place them in the empty candlesticks above the fire, and light each one. I turn off a lamp in the corner, leaving only one other by the sofa shining softly.

Charlie walks out of the bedroom. He stares at the scene in front of him for a moment, pulling down his sweatshirt distractedly.

'Come on, Charlie, it will get cold,' I say quietly.

He sits down on the sofa, and I pass him his wine, which he takes with a serious look, and then his plate, which he accepts with a smile.

'This looks great, Nix, thank you,' he whispers. I flinch as I see a tear appear in the corner of his eye – he can't cry yet; we haven't even started. But it disappears almost immediately, and he takes a tiny sip of his wine. For a while we eat in silence, looking at the candles, listening to the music, feeling the summer evening's chill, wondering how, in the midst of all our emotional turmoil and madness, we have found ourselves sitting in a parody of a romantic evening. I wonder how something that looks so calm, and promises so much romance, can actually be such a façade. I thought that if I made it look right, it would be right. But not a word has been said, and we both know that when it is, when one of us begins, and really talks, this calm room will be filled with all the madness again. Even if we whisper. You can't stop what's outside your door from coming in, you can't just shrug it off with your coat.

Eventually we find ourselves small talking, about the food and the wine, but it bores us both, there are bigger things to be said. Charlie, with a newfound frankness, begins.

'I'm alright, you know. Today, throwing that food in the village, I knew what I was doing. I just wanted people to . . . stop, to . . . look at me for a minute. A half-naked man in their midst, hurling fish and loaves, I wanted to wake them up. I wanted to, to break them out of their shopping, and their working, and everything! I wanted to affect them, make them think I was mad, shock them into doing something different. I launched a terrorist attack on their apathy. I just wanted them

169

to . . . care . . . about something, for a minute.' Charlie stops talking, deflated, looking down at his plate.

'Charlie, the thing is, your world isn't theirs,' I say.

'If you are feeling detached, or alone, it doesn't mean they are too. You are in a peculiar world, we both are. We work and play in a city that sits its homeless at ten-metre intervals on our way to our overpaid jobs, and we're numb to it – we've seen it all before. If I sat and thought about it, it would break my heart. But, Charlie, we don't, not because we don't have time, but because we don't have the inclination. We don't care. In a way we don't dare – how could we function?'

'It shouldn't be like that,' Charlie speaks through his anger.

'Why, Charlie, because you've only just realized it? All of a sudden you are ready to confront and condemn every social problem we have, you're going to clean the streets and clear the loneliness, because you've had some sort of personal . . . epiphany? People have been doing it for years, Charlie. There are more worthwhile people than us, thank Christ, and they've been trying to make us care for years. You can't go in to work every day with tears in your eyes, you can't spend all your time at the soup kitchen, or in the counselling centre, and have the life that you lead, the drinks, and the fun, and the car, and all the accessories of your life. And you can't see all the problems either. Those are just the ones that stand out. Everybody in London is kind of lonely, anybody in such a big city is – it's a choice you make, when you decide to live in a place that grand, that busy, when you accept that the people that pass you in the street may never pass you again. You can't have that, and a social conscience as well.'

I stop and take a breath, another gulp of wine. I am a little embarrassed that Charlie will think I am on my soap box, but when I get going, I find it hard to stop myself, I feel like I am an oracle. Of course it's only an hour later, when I've calmed down, when my passion for my subject has abated, that I remember every thought I've had has been had before. I remember that I don't really know what I'm talking about, just another taxi driver spouting on about politics, another bloke in the snug declaring the perfect England formation, another office gossip on the moral high-ground. It's always then, when I feel like a stereotype, that I feel like a fool, for while I am making my speech, in the middle of my monologue, I forget myself, and believe utterly in whatever comes out of my mouth. I can talk the big issues to death. It's my issues I can't voice.

'I want to go away then,' Charlie says.

'I can't live there any more.'

'Where do you want to go?' I ask, sincerely.

'Somewhere, somewhere smaller, somewhere people know me. I could live here – more people know me in this village than in town anyway.'

'You could, you could live here,' I say, and decide for a shot at the bigger issue.

'But, Charlie, why all of a sudden do you feel like nobody cares about you? Why now? You've always loved London, it's always suited you up until now, what's changed?'

Charlie shrugs quickly, turns his nose up, and looks down at his plate.

'So it's nothing then, no reason,' I say. Charlie shrugs again.

'Charlie, that girl, the girl being attacked – did you see more than you are telling me?'

'What? What do you mean? I told you everything I saw. It was horrible.' He looks up at me, pleading with me to believe him. I do believe him, but for the first time, something nasty clicks in the back of my head, some horrible thought that swims back with my memories, and song lyrics, and useless trivia, some terrible little question not yet ready to surface, that's just burst its shell. It nags a little, but then disappears.

But it leaves a slight uneasiness in my head, in the air between me and Charlie, that I might not know everything he has to tell. It hadn't occurred to me before that he might have kept something from me.

'I don't know!' he suddenly says, louder, more forceful than before.

'I don't know what I want to do, but I don't want to stay there – I don't want to heal the fucking world, but I don't want to be cold, I don't want to be cut off from everybody. I want to . . . feel something. It's just too easy, not to care. I get swept along, I got swept along.' We finished our food long ago, half-empty plates on the table in front of us, both sinking into the sofa and the wine. Charlie reaches over and fills up both of our glasses finishing the second bottle of wine.

'Charlie, you just have to make more of an effort. It doesn't have to be something dramatic. You just have to go after something that will make you happy. And if you know it's not what you've got, then, well you need to clear out the deadwood.' I half smile at him, knowing full well I mean me.

'You're drinking a lot, by the way, for a man who has given up booze.'

'I know.' He smiles and looks down at his freshly filled glass.

'It's okay, Charlie, it doesn't have to be all or nothing.'

'We've had trouble, haven't we?'

'Yes, but I think we've actually done quite well, considering what's been in our heads.' I look down at the wine in my glass.

'I think it was that summer. I think it was that early. We should have just let it go. But I didn't.' Charlie is still smiling at me while he talks, but my whole body has gone tense.

'Nix, don't you think it was that summer, after America, it was back then that it started going wrong?' He is still smiling at me, like we can talk about anything now, but I carry on staring at my wine, gripping the stalk of my glass harder and harder, digging my nails into my hand.

'Nix?!' He nudges me on the knee, almost laughing, wallowing in this new found honesty, wanting to say everything now. I look up and glare at him. He pulls back, like I've slapped him.

'What?' he asks. 'I need to talk about it. I know we were too young, but . . .'

'Charlie, stop it, I'm not going to talk about that,' I say fiercely. All my good intentions have come to nothing.

'Nix, you have to,' Charlie says quietly. 'I'm not the only fucked-up one in this room, you know. I'm not the only one with issues, it's just that mine . . . well, they've come to a head! Nix, you can talk to me about it. Surely by now, enough time has passed . . .'

'That is never going to happen, Charlie, enough time is never going to pass. You can't possibly imagine what it's like. Try, try and imagine it – how can you?!' I shout at him. But he just looks at me evenly. I slam my wine down, and get up to leave, but he lurches forward, and grabs my arm, pulling me back down.

'No, Nix, not this time. You'll never talk about it, you never say how you felt afterwards. What was I supposed to think? You were almost relieved, for Christ's sake, you wouldn't discuss it. How was I supposed to know? I just thought you were relieved, to have got it out of the way.'

'"It"? "It", Charlie, was a baby, and you thought I was relieved?! Are you fucking stupid? I didn't want to be pregnant, but I was never . . . relieved. You know, I've never told my mother – can you even imagine what that's like, or how she'd look at me if she knew? It didn't happen to you, Charlie, it happened to me!' I am crying now, tears streaming down my face.

173

'No, you're wrong. We both went through it; don't say it didn't mean anything to me, because it did! I know how hard it must have been, but you never spoke to me about it, you wouldn't tell me. I tried, but when a person pushes you away, well, what was I supposed to do?'

'You could have left,' I say, slumping back into the sofa.

'I know,' Charlie says, evenly.

We sit in silence for a while, smoking cigarettes, drinking more wine. Charlie opens another bottle.

'It was a strange summer,' he says. 'It was too early for us to have to go through something like that; we were both too worried about making it work, at home, away from America. I was so scared that we'd get home and you'd just see some little semi-detached house in Oxford, and think I was . . . different from what you thought I was. I thought you'd see my mates, and find me . . . ordinary.'

We lapse into silence again.

'How did we last this long?' I ask suddenly.

'*We* didn't really. You did, and I did. *We* was for America. We've had a six-year relationship, but we've both been single for five years. That's what happens when you get two good-looking cowards together!' Charlie leans his head on my shoulder, and nudges me in the ribs.

'Ouch! Who are you calling good-looking?' I laugh back.

'We should have talked more, we should have talked like this,' I say. 'Charlie, do you realize that this is the best conversation we've had in about four years?' I laugh. I know it's my fault, but Charlie tries to make me feel better.

'I know, I know. I've never really had that much to say, though, have I?'

'In all honesty, it was never your personality I was interested in, and once you lost your looks, well, it was all downhill . . .' We are both giggling now, slumped back on the sofa next to each other, a glass of wine each, feet up on the coffee table.

174

'It won't be like this when we get back to London, you know that, don't you?' I say, quietly.

'It could be,' Charlie says, under his breath.

'Charlie, in two months' time, we'll be back where we started.' I pull myself up to face him.

'You'll be going out with the boys, drinking yourself silly most nights, sleeping with anything in a skirt.' Charlie looks up at me quickly, as if somehow I wouldn't know about the others.

'Charlie, come on, I'm not stupid, and I'm no angel either, but obviously nothing on your scale.' He raises his eyes to heaven.

'No, come on, I'm serious, you don't talk to me like this usually.'

'I don't talk to you?! You drove me away. You made me feel like it was my fault, like everything was my fault. You were hard to pin down to a two-line conversation, if it was about us. Anything else was fine, everything else, you'd talk about anything but us. The only thing I wanted to talk about!'

'Maybe, or maybe I resented you for . . . the pregnancy, or maybe you didn't try hard enough, or maybe we just weren't meant to be. But whatever, Charlie, there's too much baggage now, no matter what we say, we couldn't go back to town together, I couldn't know that you've slept with half of your building, but this time actually caring! It would rip me apart.'

London flashes through my mind – Charlie's work, my office, and Dale . . . I don't want to see him, or speak to him. I hope Phil has lost his number.

Charlie is speaking.

'What if we didn't go back?'

'Sorry?' I ask, incredulous.

'I mean we'd have to go back, to hand in our notice, to get rid of our flats, but then – what if we went away . . . together?'

Charlie turns and grabs my hand, his eyes light up with the excitement, as the idea sparkles and glows inside his head.

'Charlie, don't be ridiculous – we can't just jack everything in. I don't have the money to go off . . . wherever.'

'I've got enough for both of us, it's not about money. You say we can't work in London, and maybe we can't, but what if we went away somewhere completely different – it could be like America again, just the two of us!'

'And two hundred million Americans,' I say, but he has me interested.

'You know what I mean. You said it yourself, how did we last this long?! Anybody else would have finished it years ago, but we both hung on – it counts for something!'

'Charlie, we've had too much wine!'

'No, we've had enough to wake up!'

I look at him seriously.

'Charlie, I'm not an easy answer to your problems. And you aren't a different person, neither am I. We can't just go off on two days of weirdness, and a half-decent conversation after a couple of glasses too many. It just wouldn't work out.' I hold his hand as the lights fade behind his eyes.

'I don't want to finish this, "us", now,' he says. I give him a sensible smile, squeeze his hand; you know it makes sense.

'At least think about it,' he says. I realize for the first time that he is slurring, and all of a sudden I feel the clouds in my own head, the taste in my mouth. I look around at the table and see four empty bottles of wine. We have been having this whole conversation half-cut.

'Charlie, look how much wine we've had.'

'I'm a different person now,' he says, reasonably. The candles have burnt down to their stubs, and are begging to be put out. I stagger up, and try and steady myself.

'I'm taking an executive decision to leave the tidying up

176

until the morning!' I declare, and manoeuvre myself around the end of the sofa, bashing my thigh nonetheless.

'I'm going to bed – are you going to be okay?'

'I'll be fine,' he says.

I walk over to the back of the sofa, and put my arms around his neck from behind.

'It is for the best, you know that, Charlie,' I say, and kiss him on the cheek, lightly.

He nods, and I go to my room. I hear him say 'Thanks,' as I close my door.

I sit in front of the mirror, and brush my hair, now dry, back into a ponytail, and put on a vest top and clean pair of knickers. I get into bed, and turn off my light. I stare at the ceiling, at the wall, at the window. I toss and turn for twenty minutes, and just when I start to doze off, and what I was thinking and what I am about to dream are beginning to merge, I hear a strange noise outside my door. I prop myself up, and listen for it again. It sounds like somebody is crying. I pull back the duvet, walk over to the door, and open it.

Charlie is sitting, hugging his legs, against my bedroom wall. His eyes and cheeks are wet with tears.

'Charlie?'

'I'm sorry,' he says, and he hugs himself closer.

I reach out my hand, but he doesn't take it. I kneel down in front of him, and push his hair out of his eyes.

'What's wrong? Please, Charlie, you have to tell me so I can help.'

'I'm a different person now,' he keeps sobbing into his hands. I pull his hands away from his face, and he suddenly clutches me around the stomach, and sobs into my belly.

'I know you are, I know you are,' I keep saying, stroking his hair.

He looks up at me.

'Can I stay with you tonight. Just next to you?'

'Of course.'

I take his hand, and pull him to his feet. He wipes his face with the back of his hand, and follows me into my room. I shut the door behind us.

I hug him from behind, and he cries quietly for a while, but it's soothing – it sends me to sleep. Somewhere in the night we twist and turn in our sleep, and we wake up in different positions, Charlie on his back, me with my head on his chest. His arm clutches at me tightly. When he wakes up, I am sitting at the end of the bed, looking at him. Thinking, what if we did go away? Could we do it – just up and leave? It wouldn't have to be forever, just the obligatory year that starts in Australia and ends in San Francisco, and leaves us both longing for home. And even if we didn't last past Sydney, it would be somebody to go with, it wouldn't be a town full of strangers. But now it's different. Now something makes me want to stay with him. Now I want it to last. Charlie looks at me sleepily.

'What shall we do today, you fruit loop? Let's fit the breakdowns in around fun!'

Charlie half laughs, rolls his eyes to heaven at his own predicament.

'We could just go for a walk.'

'We could do that . . . where, though?'

I mentally run through the shoes I've brought and whether I can go for 'a walk' in any of them.

'Let's just walk, see where we end up. Start as we mean to go on.'

Charlie hasn't forgotten last night's conversation. I feel my nerves tingling . . . with relief.

With jumpers around waists, plimsolls on, shorts and sun-glasses, we set off down the beach, over small rocks, round trees. We chat, but mostly we just walk. Every once in a while

178

we stop and catch some lovely view, and we both stare off in the distance, thinking our different thoughts about the same thing – could we go away? Eventually we sit and reapply sun cream from my backpack – ever the girl scout!

'We should head back early tomorrow, in case the trains are up the spout,' I say.

Charlie just looks off into the distance, then nods, without looking at me.

'What are you thinking?' I ask.

'I'm thinking about sex,' Charlie replies, unapologetic.

'What about it?' I laugh.

'Just that . . . it's strange. I mean, it's a weird thing to do. Especially with somebody you don't know very well.'

'What do you mean, weird?'

'Like, you actually let somebody into your body, or you actually enter into somebody else's body. It's just so – God, it's so intimate! So personal! Like somebody sticking their arm down your mouth.'

'It's pretty damn personal, yes. It's as intimate as it gets.'

'I'm never having meaningless sex ever again.'

'Charlie, I think you're getting carried away . . .'

'No, I'm serious, I'm not throwing it away. I'm going to get one of those books on the art of sex. My sex life is going to become legendary. Every single time is going to be different, experimental, deeply personal. No more average drunken sex for me.'

'Average sex isn't so bad. Just safe sex would be nice these days. If I could just completely relax, and not think about disease . . . the disease . . .'

We're the scared generation: we were just at the right age to be petrified of AIDS. We got pages and pages in the *Daily Mail* telling us we were going to die from a little bit of slap and tickle. I don't think I've ever coped with that. It still scares me.

'You should have a test. It'll put your mind at rest,' Charlie says matter-of-factly.

'Or yours, you mean. If I don't have it, you don't have it? Can I tell you something else? I still, STILL, don't get condoms. Even now, even after years of using the damn things. I still worry every time I open the packet that I'm going to rip it to shreds. And for your information, I have had a test. I had it a couple of weeks ago. I went for a Well Woman check, and they asked me if I wanted one.'

'Have you had your results back?' Charlie looks at me suddenly with a little more concern.

'Yeah, I got them a week later – you have to go back and get them in person, in case anything's wrong. I thought I'd be a wreck for that week – I thought the whole thing, the impending doom of it all, would get me, but I was okay. A few fleeting flashes when I turned the lights out at night, that it could be coming, but then I'd just tell myself not to worry, that I'd have had some kind of symptom, that I'd be fine. So all week I just convince myself it's okay, until the morning I have to go and pick them up. And even that's okay – I'm a bit twitchy, and I'm clockwatching because I have to wait until lunchtime, and the time is dragging. But then ten minutes before, I'm walking to the clinic, and I am absolutely freaking out. Physically shaking. Because it occurs to me that the only reason I've been fine for the past week is by convincing myself that I'm fine, and I haven't slept with anyone I know to be bisexual, or a needle drug-user, or from Africa – which are all the questions they ask you by the way, I'm not being a Nazi! But what if I'm just unlucky? What if, on one of the random occasions that I was stupid and drunk, I got literally shafted? I wouldn't be able to cope with it, if they told me I was positive. So then you start doing this terrible mind scan of every sexual indiscretion you've ever had, every stupid thing you've done. But it's only really stupid if it leaves a calling card.'

'So I'm guessing . . . you're okay, right?' Charlie ventures.

'Yeah I'm fine,' I shrug. 'I sat shaking in the waiting room for five minutes, feeling completely sick, and then they call you in, and the first thing they say is "You're negative." And I wanted to jump up and hug the doctor. And then they start going through all the other stuff you don't have – you don't have syphilis, you don't have thrush, and I'm just like "fuck the rest, I can get antibiotics for that lot, I don't have AIDS!" I'm actually considering creating a form, in Excel, that men have to fill in before touching me now – I want references for any distance less than three feet!' I'm laughing, until I realize that Charlie looks deadly serious.

'What?' I shove him in the arm.

'I'm promiscuous. I'm the definition. I sleep around. What if you got it from me?'

'Charlie, I just told you I don't have it! Don't worry about it.'

'You didn't have it two weeks ago, or a month ago, or whenever your test was, but you might have it now. From me.'

I drop my head, before explaining. It's going to sound insulting, but it was just self-protection at the time. I take a deep breath.

'Charlie, we haven't had sex without a condom for seven months. We've hardly had sex, but each time we've used protection. And since my test . . . Charlie we haven't had sex since I got my results.'

'Right.' Charlie looks like I've slapped him in the face. Like I've just branded him as some sort of walking health risk.

'It wasn't to be mean, but you admitted you've been sleeping around, Charlie, and I just . . . I just didn't want to take any chances. I'm not stupid, I knew it was going on, I just . . . never would have forgiven you if I'd caught something from you.'

181

'So . . .' Charlie searches for the words, 'are you saying that you'll never sleep with me again?'

I wasn't expecting that at all. We had decided to call it quits. I had decided never to sleep with him again. Not because of the disease thing, but because our sex had become painfully routine, an embarrassment of rehearsed moves performed time and time again. We barely even kissed any more, during sex. But stupidly, childishly, I couldn't say no to him, I couldn't say we wouldn't sleep together again. Because he seemed like a different person now. In two stupid, maddening days, he seemed like he needed me again, and liked me again. And if we could talk, if we could clear up . . . all our hurt, then maybe we could work things out.

There was another thing. Dale. Possibly in London. Dale phoning out of the blue. If I saw Dale, maybe I could . . . relax again with Charlie. Maybe we could be together now, but as two different people, better people than we were. If Charlie could change, then maybe I could to. I have baggage, issues I need to resolve. The truth is, this weekend, for all his madness, and all his stupidity and stripping, I have felt something for Charlie. And it was new, not the old feelings resurfacing, but new, definable feelings that made me want to get close to him again. I wouldn't go so far as to say I had fallen in love again . . .

'I don't know, Charlie. I'm not saying never. Things are . . . different now.'

Charlie turns and looks out at the sea, and I feel sunburn on the back of my neck, and my legs aching from the walk, and my bikini straps digging into the flesh on my shoulders like cheese-wire. I get up from the rock I'm sitting on and stretch. Charlie looks around and stares at me for an age.

'Shall we head back?' I ask, holding his gaze.

'Yeah,' he says, and I offer my hand to help him up.

He takes it.

We find the coast road – we are both too tired to scramble over rocks now – and we walk in silence, side by side, blinking at the sun, both thinking our own thoughts again, not dreaming of sharing them now. We have opened up to each other more, and it has left a residue of embarrassment, I feel like I have dropped my guard. All the romance that is suddenly racing around my head is foolish, childish. But I can't shrug it off; it keeps forcing its way back to the front of my mind, and I want it there, it makes me smile. I am so tired of being disappointed; I want to be surprised for a change. Does everything have to be so much of a challenge, does everybody, everything, have to let you down?

I start to hear a twisted tinkling music, and covering my eyes I look into the distance, and see a very small big wheel. It is a funfair, a permanent fixture, a tourist trap belonging to a different time, twenty years ago, when my parents took me on holiday, and we found a funfair, a miniature town, and an adventure playground. My mother held my baby sister in her arms while Amy and I ran around and around, climbing over rope ladders, jumping between tyres, hanging off poles. Around and around, as my parents took a well earned break. I would be wearing some oddity I refused to take off – my white holy communion hat with a swimsuit and trainers. Amy would be wearing her jumper dress, and we would race around the course, with stomachs full of Devonshire ice cream. We would only stop when we were forced, when my parents both needed a cup of tea, and we retreated to our holiday home in the middle of some wooded campsite.

As we walk closer, Charlie hears the music as well, which sounds ancient and sinister now, we have both seen enough horror films where these innocent destinations of fun have turned into psycho hiding death traps. But as we get closer, we can see little kids bobbing in the air on trampolines, squealing with delight, landing and launching themselves on different parts of their bodies. You can't walk past something like this.

'We have to go in,' Charlie says to me suddenly, with eyes wide.

'Thank God,' I laugh at him; I thought he would think me childish.

'Charlie, you're not going to flip out at a Punch and Judy show, are you?'

'No,' he says, a little too defensively, and I realize I have crossed a line. His madness is subsiding, as his brain allows him to rationalize his thoughts, and he doesn't want to be reminded of his actions over these last two days. It's not a joke any more.

We pay our pound entry each, separately, like school kids, and stop to survey what to do, where to go. There is paint peeling off every small building, but in the sunshine it looks charming – it shouldn't be too new, it makes it just right. We stroll around for a while, watching the parents of kids with too many additives roaming through their bloodstreams telling them to calm down. The parents look exhausted. There is a mirror arcade, and we walk through it, bored after the first mirror which makes me look tall and Charlie look short.

'Do you want to go on the big wheel?' Charlie asks, looking around for something to do.

'It's not exactly the London Eye, is it?' I say, and disappoint myself immediately. We are finding it difficult to enjoy these simple pleasures. London is starting to call. We have to manage our expectations. Bigger isn't always better.

There is a crooked house, but we both eye it suspiciously, not wanting to go in. We are both too big for it now.

We stop in the middle of the fair, and look around, disappointed that we couldn't make it more fun for each other, ashamed of how boring we both are, of how we must look in each other's eyes.

'You know the only thing I really want to do?' Charlie turns and says to me, and my stomach flips.

'No . . .'

'The trampolines.'

'No, Charlie, it'll hurt.'

'What are you talking about?' He tugs at my arm.

I give him a look, and then gesture to my bikini top – it's not exactly a sports bra.

'Oh right! Just hold them or something!' He starts to laugh, and drags me over to where the kids are bouncing. We peel off our shoes, and stuff our sunglasses into our backpacks, and wait for a couple of kids to get bored. There are only four trampolines, next to each other, pulled tight over concrete craters. I look at them dubiously – the kids bouncing on them, even the big kids, still weigh at least three stone less than me, and probably six stone less than Charlie.

'Char, are you sure these are going to hold us?' My nerves start to tingle slightly.

'Don't worry, it'll be fine!' he says, as two kids are dragged off by their respective fathers who, I swear, are both smiling at me as they gesture for us to have a go. I take a deep breath and, fixing Charlie with an accusatory stare, I step up onto the trampoline. Charlie leaps on with a bounce, and springs high into the air straight away, shouting 'Come on' at the world, and laughing, waving with his arms. I feel the trampoline beneath my feet, bending as I take each step. I look around and see both fathers eyeing me at a distance.

'Charlie?' I hiss.

'Come on, just bloody jump, it's great!' Charlie yells, as he lands on his arse, and bounces straight back up again.

I take another deep breath, and make sure I am in the middle of my trampoline. What if I bounce off onto the concrete? What if I have a faulty one, and it gives way – would I die from the fall, or from the embarrassment?

185

I watch Charlie bouncing away, making faces at the kids who stand with their dads watching us, who sneer back at the idiot having fun on something so childish.

I bend my legs and do a baby bounce.

'Shit,' I whisper, and stop myself. I am holding onto my bikini top with two full palms.

I try again, and bounce a little more, trying to let go of my self-conscious mind. I close my eyes to ignore anybody looking at me, and then open them again very quickly as I bounce a little higher, scared that I will drift out to the edges. And I bounce, for at least two minutes. I can't get the height that Charlie gets, because I can't use my arms – they are clamped firmly to my chest. But I laugh, at the unusual feeling, at Charlie, at the very fact that we are doing this. I watch the world bob up and down, and just as I feel myself getting too high, I tense my legs and bring myself back down to earth. You don't have to let go all at once. Small bounces are fine for now.

'I'm knackered,' Charlie says, and I turn to see him lying on his stomach, staring at me bouncing about in front of him. 'And I've hurt my balls,' he whispers, and starts laughing.

I stop my bouncing and sit down in the middle of the trampoline. We stare at each other. Is it just because of the bouncing, the redness of our faces? I can't pull my eyes away from him. We both know what happens next. We have managed, against all the odds of our cynicism, and our anger, and our mutual disappointment, to have fun.

I hear a kid behind me complain to his dad – I want a go, why won't they get off? – and I say,

'Shall we go?'

'Yeah.'

We scramble off, and kids replace us immediately, and start bouncing straight away.

We pull on our shoes, retrieve sunglasses from our bags

and force them onto our eyes, to shield us from the sun, and each other. We head for the exit, and start to walk quickly now, back towards the cottage. We stumble up the incline we edged our way down previously, and Charlie turns and offers me his hand to pull me up the final steps. I take it, and get tugged to the top. I am out of breath slightly, but Charlie doesn't step back. Our chests graze each other, and I look down rather than look at him. He pulls my sunglasses off, and I sigh deeply, knowing I shouldn't do this sober. Somebody in the wings should pass me a drink, some old farmer should whizz past on a tractor and pass me a bottle of red wine that I can neck in one. Because sober it's going to hurt when it goes wrong. But my thoughts are stopped, my whirring mind distracted by Charlie's lips touching mine. I feel my heart heavy in my chest, and try and catch my breath. It's like he hasn't kissed me for years. I can see his half-closed eyes, the blue and the brown, the light and the dark. I feel his hands – one in my hair, one on the bare skin of my back.

Starting Again

The sex isn't like before.

The rain falls down hard outside, and we are so close in bed, but not touching. The closeness of his thigh to my thigh makes my skin tingle, makes his hairs stand on end. Still we are not touching. We both slipped into bed without speaking, under the pretence of sleeping, and then turned and rolled towards each other. My breathing is fast, his is slow. I can almost feel his lips against mine, but not quite. My body reacts to the heat, and my limbs shake with an involuntary current that presses skin to skin suddenly, and Charlie leans forward and presses his parted lips to mine, slowly moving them around my mouth, letting his tongue creep into my mouth, letting it slide against my own, as we twist heads and hands twist into hair. His lips move down my neck, along my breastbone, my hands cradling his head as he moves it around my breasts, and then everything becomes one. With Charlie's hands in mine, and his legs between my thighs, and breast to chest, nipple to nipple, hands creeping around and holding my back, hands running down his back, nails slightly grazing the bottom of his spine, finding places to stop, and then moving on, with him on top and me on top and me on my side, and Charlie behind me, and slowly, slowly, with hands in my hair, and lips on lips again, eye to eye eventually, starting again, it's all new.

As the rain pelts the window, and we lie thoughtfully side by side, Charlie says, 'Are you alright?'

'I'm fine.'

Back to Life

We could go to Sydney – a lot of people start there – or South America: Cuba has become very popular. We could go anywhere, do anything. We could go scuba-diving in the Caribbean, snorkelling in Thailand, on safari in Kenya, we could drive Route 66. We could leave our lives behind, leave the people we have become. We could go and sit on top of mountains, look out at oceans, at seas of buffalo roaming the plains, and palm trees, and deserts. We could wear shorts all year round; we could trek through forests; meditate with Buddhas; taste monkey brains; pick berries in foreign fields; hear languages that sound like symphonies. We could walk, and get the bus, get the train, hire bicycles, fly in helicopters over canyons, charter boats, swim, sail, dive. We could drink, dance, sing, skip our way around the world. We could get carried away.

The train is both exciting and depressing. I lean my head on Charlie's shoulder and try to sleep, but I am too nervous. I am nervous that I will actually do it, that I will hand in my resignation. That I will phone my estate agent and place an advert to rent out my flat. That I will do all of this with a man I hardly know, not the man that I have been seeing for the last six years. Because Charlie is different now. I am convinced of that. He has his arm around me. He even smells different, tastes different. His eyes glisten, they've stopped dying, just in time, before it was fatal. He is clean and bright and full of hope. He wants to be with me again, and I want to be with him. I want us to be together, talking, looking at a picture postcard view.

There is something I have to do first, and I shift uncomfortably in my seat as I think of it. I need to see Dale. I need to tell him everything, sweep out the cobwebs that have been clouding my judgement, driving Charlie away. I need to resolve everything, before I go away, and now is the perfect time. The train speeds through countryside that seemed so alien to me just a few days ago. Before it was a world of pessimism, of cynicism, of people I would never know. Now I feel like every door has opened up for me – the places we can go, the people we can talk to, the dreams we can experience together are becoming a reality. In just a month we could be gone. I take a sharp breath, and Charlie holds me tighter. Charlie has realized our lives should be better thank God. Just in time. I was falling before, into a trap of monotony, of a dull average life experienced by too many people, but not me, not now.

We get back to London, and I feel elated.

'I'll see you later – I'll get a cab over.' Then I whisper something in Charlie's ear, and he smiles at me, surprised.

'I need to tidy up my flat!' he says laughing.

'Yes you do!' I kiss him softly, and he kisses me, with his hand in the small of my back.

'Nix, I can't believe you did this for me. I can't believe how . . . lucky I am to have you.' We stand so close it is a crime not to keep on kissing.

'You know what, Charlie, I feel like I should be thanking you. I feel like . . . I don't know, like you've woken me up. I feel like I've got something to look forward to! I can't believe we are going to do this!'

'We bloody are going to do it! You and me.'

'Damn right, you and me. Against the world!' I laugh and kiss him again, and pull away, picking up my bag, climbing into the taxi that has pulled up.

Charlie leans into the open window and kisses me good-bye.

'I'll see you later.'

As the cab pulls off, I feel so high, I barely even notice I am back in London, on the way back to my flat. The rain is coming down in sheets, the heat still hangs in the air between the raindrops. I wipe the sweat off my breastbone, and lean back, closing my eyes. I jolt upright as the taxi pulls outside my flat, and I hear thunder. My phone bleeps the arrival of a text.

Don't be too long, Char xxx

Two hours later, after a long shower, an inspection of my post, a change of clothes, I phone Charlie's mobile.

'Can I come over now? I'm all done here.'

'Of course. I'm just sitting here waiting for you to turn up, you fool!'

I hang up laughing. I'm smiling like a bloody school kid. I take the tube, and stop off at the market up the road from Charlie's flat to buy flowers and wine.

I get to Charlie's and let myself in with my key. He is sitting, naked on his sofa, staring straight ahead. I almost drop the wine. I stare at him mouth open, aghast.

'Charlie?' I ask uncertainly, 'are you okay?' I gulp back tears straight away.

He keeps a straight face for about a second, and then cracks the broadest smile.

'Just waiting for you, honey!' he laughs, and my shoulders droop with relief.

'You bastard!' I shout and laugh, as I hit him with the flowers, and he pulls me on top of him, kissing me forcefully on the mouth, unbuttoning my cardigan, reaching inside.

Closure, I Promise

Monday morning, and work is a nightmare, as I expected. I get in at ten, and Phil is already in his version of a panic as I walk in the door, but it's his usual laid back panic, which amounts to a slight look of tension just above his nose, resulting in an ever so slightly furrowed brow. That's why I like him as an assistant; he stops me worrying. Even when everything goes wrong, he never seems that fazed.

'And how are you, Philip?' I ask, as he slumps down in front of my desk and I shut the door to my office.

'Fine thanks – are you feeling better?' he asks, with no concern whatsoever.

'Yes, thanks.' I brush over it swiftly.

'Any political bombs drop since nine-thirty?' I turn on my computer and blow on my coffee simultaneously.

'Nothing really. The scriptwriter called, I didn't tell him about the old woman yet, in case we don't use her. He wants to know what's going on, and if he's going to get fired. He said he spoke to José on Friday, and he just went on about hygiene, and the need to wash your hair every day.'

'Oh for God's sake. How many emails have I got waiting?' I ask, flipping open my day book.

'One hundred and thirty-five.'

'Just from Friday? Jesus!' I almost get annoyed, and then I relax, and think, not for much longer!

I tap the code into my phone for my messages – 'your mailbox is full'. I can't wait to get away from this.

'Look, Phil, I've got something important to do first thing, so I'm going to close my door for an hour or so, and then we'll go through everything, get it all ready.'

'Yep'.

'Is that okay?' I ask – he seems a little weird.

'Yeah, fine. Why are you grinning? You look like a freak.' I realize I am smiling like the Cheshire Cat.

'Oh sorry, yes I'm fine. Just happy to see you as always, my little ray of sunshine.'

'Whatever,' he says, and gets up to go.

'Phil, one more thing, that guy that phoned, Dale – can you give me his number.'

'Yep.' And he walks out.

I look at my office, all the videos and scripts lying around, the old talent photos, the new talent photos, decisions that need to be made, piling high. I can't wait to get out! I realize that Phil is not returning with the number, and I get up and open the door, leaning out.

'Phil, the number?'

'Yeah, I'm just trying to find it. I think I may have left it in my football bag . . .' He is unconcerned. But I need it now. I feel a mild panic rise up inside my stomach. I have to have the number today, it can't work without it, my plan will fall apart.

'Phil!' I shout, and then lower my voice.

'Find the number,' I demand, and slam the door behind me and go back and sit at my desk, drumming my fingers on the desk, blowing on my coffee, clicking into Word, and just staring at the blank screen in front of me.

My phone buzzes.

'Yep?' I say to Phil.

'I've got it – do you want me to email it to you?'

'Please.'

I hang up, and wait for it to appear on my screen.

It pops up, and I read it quickly. Dale. And his mobile number. I put my phone on hands free – it's less personal, safer, from a distance. I dial in the number. The phone rings for ages, and just as I am ready to leave a message on an answerphone with a sudden relief, a lazy American voice answers.

'Hello?'

The sound of his voice startles me straight away, the years almost fall away, and I am a student again. I feel my stomach lurch, and my voice, when it comes, is an octave higher than normal.

'Dale, it's Nicola.' Silence.

He phoned me, how can he not know who it is? But then he speaks.

'Nicola. Nicola. How are you?'

'Yes I'm fine, Dale, how are you?'

'I'm fine too. Just dandy.' That is such a Dale thing to say, such a cliché. He says it like he is mocking me straight away, laughing at some private joke at my expense. I hope he hasn't reverted back to arsehole mode.

'You phoned! I'm returning your call! It's been . . . years. Are you in London?'

'Yes I am.' He is not sharing a lot of information for a guy who called me. This isn't what I had expected. I had expected nerves in his voice, not a smirk. I had expected a deep husky seriousness. Only now do I realize how long I have been imagining this call. How long I have been hoping or waiting to hear from him again. How I've pictured him, needing me, wanting me from afar. The one that got away!

How I have romanticized the whole thing in my head. It is not going to be like that now, I realize.

'So, Dale, what can I do for you?' All of a sudden my feelings are on the wire, my defences go up, I back away mentally. I turn on him with professionalism.

'Well, for a start, you could probably take me off speakerphone!'

'Oh right, sorry.' I pick up the receiver and I swear I feel it burn my hand.

'What can I do for you?' I ask again, hearing the closeness in the silence down the line. When he speaks I feel something rush down my spine.

'Well, I'm in London, finally. And I thought I'd look you up, seeing as you're the only person I know here.'

His voice sounds deeper than I remember. He sounds like he's smoked a million cigarettes since last we spoke, and it's probably not far from the truth.

'How did you get my number?'

'I phoned the number you gave me, it was your parents, they gave me this number.'

'God, you've kept it all this time? That's . . . organized of you,' I say, but thinking, that's devotion, that's . . . love.

'Well, it went into my address book, and I've always carried the names over. You don't mind, do you, me phoning?' But he doesn't sound like he'd care if I did mind – he sounds like he's enjoying himself, an old ghost creeping up on me, breathing down my neck, making me nervous.

'No, of course not. I'm glad you phoned. How are you, are you married?' I don't know why I ask this rather than any other question that could figure in the five years of his life I've missed out on.

'Well, yes and no. I'm . . . separated.'

'Oh, I'm sorry.' Am I?

'Look, I was wondering if you'd like to have lunch with

198

me. I was going to ask you to dinner on Friday, but now I only have today left. I'm off to Scotland tomorrow, and then over to Dublin for a few days, and then back to the States.'

'Oh, right,' I say, a little taken back. He just wants lunch. He doesn't want to tell me he loves me. He doesn't want to meet me at the Tower of London, or in the Dungeons, or under Big Ben, or anything else Dale-like. He just wants to have lunch?

'So, Nicola, are you free for lunch today?'

'Um, yes, well I'll have to check my diary, no actually it's fine, I'll just cancel if I have something on. Yes, I'm free for lunch. Where do you want to go?'

'You know London, not me. Can you suggest somewhere?'

I rack my brain and think of every restaurant in a two-mile radius of my work – nowhere too busy, nowhere too intimate, nowhere too expensive (in case he thinks it's my treat): Luigi's. Perfect.

'How about Luigi's – it's just around the corner from my office. Do you like Italian?'

'Yeah, that'll be fine.'

'Great, I'll see you there at one, shall I? I'll get my assistant to make the reservation.'

'Okay.' Silence. I am waiting for him to say goodbye, but nothing is forthcoming.

'Well, okay, I'll see you at one.'

'Nicola?' Still smirking at the other end of the phone. This whole thing is making me feel a little uneasy.

'Yes?'

'What road is it on? Or should I ask your perky little assistant? Having a man for an assistant! I always knew you were a feminist.'

'Oh, yes, no, I know, I mean, it's on Neal Street.'

'Fine, I'll see you there.'

'Okay, bye,' and I hang up before I get to hear him say goodbye.

I shout for Phil, and he sticks his head around the door.

'Phil, can you cancel anything I had in for lunch, and book me a table at Luigi's for one o'clock, please? Thanks.'

'You had me in for lunch.'

'Did I? Why?' I ask, surprised.

'For my appraisal; you moved it from last week, remember?' I can tell he is a little pissed off.

'Oh right, sorry, can we put it off till tomorrow? Is that okay – I really have to take this lunch. Do you mind?' I half plead with him.

'No but don't cancel on me then too.'

'I wouldn't dare! Thanks, Phil. Don't tell José, okay? We're already late with that.'

'I know,' he says, and closes the door behind him.

Shit, I've pissed him off. I punch a number into my phone. It rings twice, and then Charlie's assistant answers.

'Hi, is he there?' I ask – she knows my voice, although generally it's a lot more terse than this.

'Sure I'll just get him for you, Samantha.'

'It's Nicola.' I flinch. It doesn't count, I remind myself, nothing that has gone before counts now. He's different, after today I'll be different. It doesn't matter if he was unfaithful, because that was a different him and a different me. Nonetheless, I am still relieved to hear his voice sounding pleased to hear from me.

'Nix?'

'Yeah, it's me. Have you written yours yet?'

'Yeah, I handed it in half an hour ago. I can't believe how late you West End types start work.'

'Oi! Don't start. What do I write? I've never had to do this before!' We are co-conspirators.

'Just write that you've really enjoyed the experience, it's time to move on to a new challenge etc . . . don't burn your bridges.'

'Why not?' I ask, suddenly scared that this was all a pipe dream.

'Because someday, in twenty years' time, if we ever come back, you might want to think about getting another job,' he says, like a father to a child.

'Oh right, of course. Charlie?'

'Nicola?'

'You do still want to go, don't you?'

'Of course I do – I've handed in mine already!'

'I know I know, I'm just being silly. It's just a bit . . . scary.'

'I know, don't worry. Phone me when you've done it.'

'Okay.'

'I love you.'

'I know,' I say and hang up as I hear him laughing at the other end of the phone.

I start typing, Dear José. I didn't tell Charlie about lunch. I haven't told him about Dale. I should. This is the new us, a fresh start. Honesty and all that. I'll tell him tonight.

It takes me all morning, what with general phone calls, Phil interruptions and a quick meeting about whether it's feasible to work a Burger King promotion into *Evil Ghost: The Return* and whether they'd actually go for it if we did. We decide to manage our own expectations, and I send Phil off on a mission to check out all the breakfast cereals in our local Sainsbury's, to see if there's a crap one we've overlooked that needs some publicity. He comes back an hour and a half later, having popped into the pub for a cheeky half at eleven-thirty, loaded down with bags of Fruit Loops, and cornflakes, and porridge and bran. I tell him he could have just written their names down, and he looks perplexed. It doesn't matter. He lines them up on shelves around my office for me to look at, and I immediately throw anything with Kellogg's or Nestlé on it back out of the door at him. We have no chance with them.

Before I know it, I am throwing the letter at José's assistant, Angela, who takes it without looking, and I dash for the door and grab my coat before she has a chance to give it to him. If he reads it before I am out of the building, I will miss my lunch. I go down in the lift, checking myself in the mirrored walls. I stride out onto the street, desperately trying to project an air of confidence, but with nerves suddenly starting to eat me up inside. I walk into the restaurant, at one o'clock sharp.

By the end of today everything will be different.

Socrates Says

Wealth does not bring goodness, but goodness brings wealth, and every other blessing.

I want to be good. I don't want to be confused, lose my momentum. I don't want my judgement to cloud, my ideas to shift. I know I only really need one pair of shoes. Maybe two. I don't want to be confused by adverts, billboards. I don't need a 'lifestyle', I can't find happiness there.

So why, when I've been shopping all day, and I'm loaded down with bags, why do I feel so great? Why do I feel like I've achieved something? What am I looking for? What am I purging, why don't I feel whole – why do I know I'm still lacking?

You should be ashamed that you give as much attention to acquiring as much money as possible, and similarly reputation and honour, and give no attention to truth and understanding and the perfection of yourself.

Trouble is, money's easier. And reputation. In a world where goodness isn't even a virtue any more, why bother? Materialism is God, worship at its feet. There's a void in the soul that can't be filled with cash apparently, but fuck it, we'll be dead soon.

I alone am aware of how little I know.

Nobody else needs to know. There is no great need to publicize what I morally, spiritually lack. There is no need to draw attention to my own deficits, nobody else is doing it. Everybody else is buying shoes without a heavy heart and a screaming subconscious, why can't I?

A Date with Disaster/Destiny

Dale is there already, seated at our table. He doesn't even say hello, he just kind of stands up, and sits down, and smiles a lazy smile.

My nerves vanish suddenly, I just feel that this is how we should do it, slip straight back into it. He is wearing the same suit I have seen a thousand times in college, perched on a chair with feet on a desk. I suddenly realize that Dale and I share something completely – we share memories of that year. It happened, we can't erase it. I was there and so was he, no matter what happens, at some point in his life he'll remember a conversation, or a time when I was there. We share a year of our lives, while trying to share nothing at all.

'Dale,' I raise my eyebrows, 'you've had that suit cleaned since the last time I saw you, I swear!'

'December '99,' he says, smiling.

'Well, we all celebrated the millennium in different ways, I guess.' I sit, and Dale sits down a moment later.

My phone rings as Dale opens his mouth to speak, and I grimace and apologize. I grab at it to turn it off – it is only José – but am secretly pleased that he knows I am needed somewhere, by someone at the end of the line.

'That's a m-o-b-i-l-e phone,' I enunciate the letters slowly. 'You can walk and talk and everything.'

'And there was I thinking it was one of those new fangled transistor radios.'

'No.' I shake my head at his mock stupidity. I don't know what to say next. I cough uncomfortably and glance around the room. Dale just smiles knowingly at me, and I feel transparent.

'Well, what are you doing in London?' I ask him, to stop this moment seeming so intimate, to stop us believing we can read each other's minds.

He takes a breath, a cough, like I've spoiled something, and replies, 'I always knew I'd come . . . and now the kids are with their mother . . .'

I gasp slightly, a swift intake of breath. He knew that would floor me. I think this whole conversation, this whole meeting, may have been designed to make me feel as uncomfortable as possible. I am floored.

I realize now that I expected Dale to be slicked-back hair and middle-aged bohemia, I thought he wouldn't have moved on somehow, would have stayed the same as I had, but he's had a life, had kids, been married, and I have to ask.

'You're married? What fool accepted that job?' I realize that my sarcasm is sounding cruel, and that I also meant to be slightly cruel – that I am jealous, jealous that he didn't hold out for me, when quite clearly I would never have said yes, but nonetheless. I see a flicker of hurt in his eyes, and feel bad.

'Anybody I know?' I say quickly to brush over my last comment.

He looks down, and slightly ashamed, as if that one line has penetrated the armour, and I realize what he has done. He is just as cruel.

We both know he's going to say her name before he does, and we both know the massive connotations of him saying it to me, and yet he is brave, and doesn't deny it, and then he says,

'Joleen.' With a gesture of his hands he shrugs off the fact that he did it, while holding his hands up to every guilty feeling encompassed in doing it. He wrecked her life, knowingly, in a weak self-pitying moment of 'I do'.

I take a sip of my drink, and look around, and try and disguise the look in my eyes, be it pity or contempt or jealousy.

'She got pregnant. I couldn't leave her. She was carrying my baby.'

'Oh my God, Dale, you don't have to explain it to me – Jesus, I'm sure it was great – I'm sure you were very in love.' I try desperately to pretend that I think it's fine that he married her, and that he must have loved her. And that things must have changed dramatically after I left.

'It wasn't like that – if she hadn't been pregnant . . .' He looks down again, and pushes his cutlery around.

'If she hadn't been pregnant . . . you wouldn't have got married?' I ask, I don't know why. I don't have to voice it; it's obvious.

'Well . . .' Within minutes we appear to have crash landed into a nightmare of a conversation, and I am making assumptions about a man and a life I have no right to make, but yet I feel I am on the money here, and that this is, even partly, the reason he came, and he called. He wanted this conversation to happen. It's like I'm the person who can absolve him. And him me.

'But what about your girlfriend, the one when I left, the one who tried to commit suicide – I thought you were going to try and sort that out.'

'She died the month you left.'

'But I thought she didn't kill herself.' I am shocked again. Somebody's life ended and it didn't even affect me – I thought she had carried on living like the rest of us.

207

'You left, you wouldn't know,' Dale says, almost an accusation.

I need to wring the emotion out of this conversation – we'll either be killing each other or fucking on the table in the next five minutes if this keeps up. We need to talk about something less 'fraught'. Something non-violent, non-sexual, non-explosive. 'So how many kids?' I ask with a smile, praying they are all alive and well.

'Two.' He looks at me seriously – he wanted to carry on the killing or fucking conversation.

'Two kids? That's impressive, for a man of your diminished stature at least.'

He ignores my attempt to lighten the conversation; Dale has serious things in mind. He doesn't want a lunchtime of sarcasm that brushes the surface, he wants to face things, and get his penance.

I don't know what he expects to come of this. I don't know how he thinks this will make things better. I'd rather have a conversation about air travel, about the sights he's seen. I check my watch, I have been sitting here for fifteen minutes and it seems like hours. I realize nobody has taken our order. I shout 'Waiter', at the same time as Dale says, 'I wanted to see you.'

We are both embarrassed for a moment, and the waiter is at our table before I can acknowledge his outburst. So instead I order a salad, no starter, and Dale does the same. The waiter makes the usual requests about bread and oil and olives and we accept. He leaves us eventually. I dust off the napkin on my lap, and compose myself, and look up at Dale who is looking back at me seriously.

And I realize I can't say the same thing back. I didn't want to see him. I just wanted the mess to be cleared up. I wanted to feel better about all the things that had been making me feel lousy for all this time, about feeling bad for a man that

208

I convinced myself I pity screwed, about the periods I missed from then on. About a decision I made without him, about resenting Charlie for making me feel worse, just by being nice and supportive, thinking it was his of course. I never told Dale. He thinks he is sitting opposite some wisecracking English girl that he developed a crush on for a year, and this whole thing could be so romantic if we could pick up where we left off, now he is done with the first half of his life. He thinks we can find each other now we are older and wiser and all the youthful things that drove us apart aren't important now. He has romanticized me without even knowing that for nearly every day since I left he has crept into my thoughts as the man who ruined my chance with Charlie, and the man whose child I threw away.

But to look at him: he looks like an old man. Foolish old man dreams.

'I'm a teacher,' he says. 'Poetry.' Out of the blue.

'I knew it,' I say. I want him to share himself, if he wants to. I don't want to burst his dreams, not yet.

'You and your dark poetic centre,' I say, and he smiles like I understand him better than anybody. It makes me want to cry.

He was so much older at college, nearly seven years older than me. He should be sorted by now, but his life is falling apart. He's scared, and he thinks maybe I'm his lifeboat. At least he has his kids.

'Do you have a picture . . . of the kids?'

He reaches into his coat pocket and pulls out a bashed-up old wallet, and takes out a photo. A photo of a beach and a holiday. Strange-looking kids. I say they are 'adorable'.

Our food comes, and time goes on, but nothing is really said now.

Mine isn't another trauma to add to his list, to add to his sadness. I thought I might tell him everything, dump it all on him, and make myself feel better, clean my own slate, and not worry about his. But Dale's slate is too full already.

We order coffee – I have to get back to work.

'Can I call you?' he asks suddenly. And I realize that lunch wasn't about me at all – but about his expectations and his thoughts. I'm sitting here thinking I've ended something, and he's thinking it's the start of something.

'Where are you going to call me from? You're going back to the States aren't you?'

'I could come back, after Ireland. I could . . . rent a flat, you can teach anywhere.'

I should just say no, I should say I'm with Charlie now; for the first time in years, I'm with Charlie again. But I give him my number anyway, and change the last number so it's wrong. I am a despicable coward. I don't want to upset him, but in fact I just don't want him to be upset in front of me. He can be upset later, when he tries to call and realizes I've given him the wrong number. I shake my head and close my eyes, trying to discard my weaknesses. I hate myself, still.

He gives me his hotel number as well, and I take it and put it in my wallet. I get up to go so quickly I knock a plate on the floor, and as Dale leans down to pick it up, I back at least three feet away. He looks up to see me backing away, shouting,

'Have a great time in Scotland – it's great, I'll speak to you when you get back, lovely to see you.' I turn quickly and only glimpse the look of confusion on his face. I leave the restaurant, and look back to see him plugging numbers into his phone. Then he smiles very sadly, and he knows and I know.

I keep having visions of Dale grabbing me from behind and kissing me as I steam back to the office. I just want to phone Charlie. My mobile dies as soon as I try and turn it back on to retrieve his number. I practically run back to work.

I ignore Phil and storm straight into my office, shutting the

210

door behind me. It's not only that I can really do this now, go away with Charlie, but I want to do it. I want to run away, play with dolphins, climb mountains, get fucked on a beach on some potent local cocktail of smoke and spirits. I can turn everything around and simultaneously leave everything behind. But I dial Charlie's mobile and it is dead. I phone his work, and it rings and rings and nobody answers. I hang up and dial again. Charlie doesn't answer, and neither does his assistant. I slam the phone down and swear, pick up the receiver and hit redial. Phil knocks and sticks his head around the door, and I practically scream 'not now', and he swears under his breath and closes the door again.

I hear José shouting outside my office, 'She will not say not now to me!' and the door bursts open.

'What ze fuck is zis?' he shouts, waving my resignation letter in front of my face.

I slam the phone down again.

'That's my resignation, José,' I say, through clenched teeth. I don't want to go through it all now, or remind myself that I have done it.

'I know what it fucking is, I want to know why!'

'Then why didn't you ask "why the fuck are you resigning" instead?'

José's forehead goes a little red, and I can see him trying to keep a lid on what will be a massive Mediterranean storm when it hits. José pulls back one of the two chairs in front of my desk and sits down, crossing his legs, regaining his cool.

'You cannot resign. It is in your contract.' He says this seriously – he just doesn't understand how these things work.

'José, of course I can resign, don't be ridiculous. I'm giving you a month's notice. It's perfectly legal.'

'Well zen, I will sue.' He smiles at me like he has won.

'Jesus, José, you can't sue! It's perfectly legal, I'm allowed to leave if I want to, I don't owe you my life.'

211

José changes his tack.

'What about *Evil Ghost?* All your 'ard work, somebody else will claim the credit.' He smiles at me, knowing full well he'll claim it anyway.

'I really don't care, José, honestly.'

'It says 'ere you are going travelling?'

'Yes. With my boyfriend.' The three little words stick to my tonsils as they surface, and I practically gurgle them. I am worried. It is needless worry: he is probably just out to lunch, but something knocking at my subconscious tells me things aren't quite as rosy as I have made out. Trusting him is proving harder than I thought.

'You 'ave a boyfriend? I did not know.' José spits at me, abandoning any sense of professionalism, and just insulting me instead.

'Oh piss off, José, if you have just come in here to be nasty you might as well leave.'

'I do not believe zis story about travelling. I zink you are going to a competitor. I zink I should clear your desk now.' He thumps my desk with his fist, but bullying is not going to work today. I try to keep my cool, calm.

'Fine, do it! Please, be my guest, but you still have to pay me for another month.'

'For fuck's sake . . . We shall see, Nicola, don't 'old your breath.' José stalks out and slams the door behind him, and I throw a pack of Post-its on the floor in frustration, my nerves getting the better of me, losing control of a situation that was never going to be controlled.

I try and compose myself, and ignore the bitter bile feeling in my stomach that is rising up my throat. Every few seconds the nerve endings in my fingers tingle in unison, and then abate.

I press the speakerphone button, and try to push the redial button as calmly as possible. What is wrong? I know something is wrong. I sit with my head in my hands and listen to the rings in the distance as I drift off into my head. Finally, after thirty rings, somebody answers, agitated:

'Hello?'

It is Dan, one of the guys Charlie works with, sounding weird.

I try to stay composed although I want to scream. My heart is pumping dread-infused blood to every part of me.

'Is Charlie there? It's Nix,' I say in the most controlled voice I can muster.

'No, Nix, he's not around. Hasn't he called you?'

'No, not since before lunch. Do you know where he is? Why isn't he there?'

There is silence for a moment at the end of the phone. I mutter 'Jesus' under my breath, involuntarily, and in response Dan says,

'I should let him tell you.'

'No, tell me now. Please.' My breath is coming in gasps.

'He's with the police.' Dan sounds embarrassed.

'Why?'

'He's been arrested.'

'What for?' Dan and I speak quickly, knowing the other's question and answer before they say them.

'Assault.'

'Somebody in the office?'

'No, it's a girl.'

'A girl?'

'Look, Nix, you should really speak to him.'

I hang up.

After ten minutes of ignoring my phone ring and my computer bleep, I register a thought – get through the day. I know I should call him or his parents, or his brother. But I'm not going to. I'm going to get through the day.

What's Wrong?

When I was young I used to go to confession. I remember lying even then. Making things up to please a priest who wanted to hear the bad things I had done, when in truth I had done nothing – how much can an eight-year-old really do?

I remember saying things like 'I was nasty to my sister', or 'I was rude to my parents' when I wasn't. But I knew that the priest wanted to hear something, I didn't want to waste his time, or mine, so I made stuff up. Maybe I had been fighting with my sister, over dolls or games or sweets, but it was over before it began. It was absolutely and completely harmless. But I said it nonetheless. As soon as I said it however, I felt like it was right for me to confess it. It gave it a gravity it shouldn't have had, a depth that didn't previously exist. It made it worse than it was. I was a normal eight-year-old apologizing for things that didn't need to be apologized for.

Who makes an eight-year-old go to confession? Who tells a child to be sorry for being a child, and forces them to rack their brains for some trace of naughtiness that previously they had been fine with, had not thought of as wrong? You can always be sorry was the lesson, you should always be feeling bad for something. You will never be perfect.

I went away and said my two Hail Marys, and my three Our Fathers, not really feeling absolved of anything, just knowing, now, that I had done something that needed punishing, even if I hadn't realized it at the time.

I sat in a booth, at the age of eight, and made myself feel guilty just for being me.

What, in God's name, were they thinking?

Completely Nuts

I go to the supermarket after work and wander round the aisles, picking up onions and tins of rice pudding and minutes later seeing them in my basket, realizing I don't even eat them. A shelf-stacker spots me stuffing a pack of frozen sweetcorn among the fresh bread, and we do a ten-minute dance around the shop as he follows me and picks up a Battenberg cake that I try and stuff among the carrots, and a bottle of Special Brew I dump among the takeaway sandwiches.

I get to the tills and place my basket down in front of a middle-aged woman who obviously thinks she has better things to do than pack my shopping. She starts to empty my basket, and I wake up a bit. She runs a tin of fruit cocktail over her scanner.

'I don't want that,' I say.

She puts it to one side and runs a loaf over her scanner. She picks up a tin of dog food, and it bleeps as she pushes it past the computer.

'Oh I don't want that either.'

'Then why is it in your basket?' she asks me, with a definite tone in her voice.

'I made a mistake, alright?' I say back. I don't think much of her attitude.

'What about this?' she asks pointedly as she picks up a tub of crème fraiche.

'That's fine.' I glare at her, and she codes it in.

She picks up a jar of pesto but maintains eye contact with me as she bleeps it in, and I raise my eyebrows at her. I definitely don't like her attitude.

She picks up a bag of pecan nuts.

'Not those,' I yelp at her, just before she pushes them through.

'Oh for God's sake – are you taking the piss?'

'No, I have a nut allergy, I can't eat them.'

'Then why the hell are they in your basket? There are people waiting here.' She gestures to a young bloke standing behind me, but he looks away embarrassed.

'I think you are being very rude. What ever happened to the customer is always right?'

I challenge her with my stare but she just mumbles something under her breath and takes a magazine out of my basket. I ignore her and look away. The magazine won't bleep for her scanner, however, and she can't seem to find the code.

I sigh heavily and she scowls at me.

'First day?' I ask her pointedly.

'That's it!' She slams the magazine down and presses a bell by the side of her till.

'What are you doing?' I ask, knowing I have gone too far.

'I'm calling my supervisor.'

'Why – I haven't done anything wrong.'

She just looks around, and then starts shouting 'Bob' at the top of her voice, as a young guy, no older than twenty, hurtles towards the till at breakneck speed, with his head leaning so far to the right that it would appear he is missing some necessary vertebrae.

218

Before she gets a chance to speak, I pipe up, 'I don't like . . .' I lean in to read her name badge, 'I don't like Eileen's attitude, Bob. She's being very rude. Isn't she being rude?' I turn around to gain reinforcement from the guy behind me, but he has moved to the next queue.

'What's wrong here?' Bob musters his most authoritative manner, which is pretty poor. His voice should definitely be lower than it is.

'She doesn't want to pay for half of this!' Eileen gestures towards the pile of food next to her.

'So? It's not illegal is it, Bob? I'm distracted and I made a few mistakes, you can't call the police about that!'

'Eileen, just give the lady her bill.'

'Thanks, Bob.' I smile sweetly at Eileen who tuts loudly and finally locates the code on my magazine and stuffs it into my bag.

'Sorry, madam. I hope everything is okay now.' Bob practically curtsies.

'Yes, it's fine, thanks, Bob, although on a separate note I think Eileen's rings –' I gesture towards the fingers full of gold sovereigns on her hands, '– may have been adding money to my bill. I swear I heard the till beep a few extra times.' I shrug my hands at him like it's not my fault.

Bob, replies, very seriously,

'They couldn't activate the till, madam.'

'Fair enough, if you say so. Thanks, Bob. How much do I owe?'

I pay my bill under both Bob and Eileen's watchful glare, and make a meal of adjusting the products in my bag, and leave. As soon as I am out of the shop I feel like a spiteful kid. My forced smile drops from my face, and I walk slowly towards the tube station. My mind wanders back to Charlie, and I quickly shrug it off. I'll think about it later.

I get home and make dinner, munching on an almost empty

219

bag of peanuts (Eileen would be cursing if she could see me now!) while the water boils for my pasta, and then watch a soap with my plate on my lap. Every time my mind starts to wander, I force it to go blank. And still I don't call.

The thought that keeps creeping back into my head uninvited, the thought I keep trying to shove out again without acknowledgement, is: Oh dear God, what have I done?

Phil was pissed off at hearing of my resignation as José screamed it through the wall, when I had meant to take him out to lunch and tell him myself. But as usual, it took the form of a sulky two minutes, and then he was right as rain again – he had football training that evening. He did admit, unprompted, that I was the best boss he'd ever had, which was the nicest thing he'd ever said to me. I think I might be the only boss he's ever had, but I didn't feel like pointing that out.

Charlie has been arrested on assault charges, and I know I should go to him, I should do something, but I just want to go to bed. I'll sort it out tomorrow. I fall asleep straight away.

The phone wakes me at two; I can hear it ringing in my sleep. I know who it is even before I wake up, as the noise reverberates around my dream world.

'Nix, it's me,' Charlie says down the line, with a voice that sounds battered by a night's worth of talking and the odd cigarette.

I just say, 'Okay.'

He says, uncomfortably, 'You won't believe this,' half-knowing that I will.

'The problem is I kind of do,' I say before he says anything else, and we both go silent.

I don't know what route to take, so I just say,

'You shouldn't have called me.'

'You have to help me,' Charlie says dramatically, and I get

220

the impulse to hit him, punch him down the line somehow. He sounds so pathetic, so small.

'I don't know what you expect me to do.'

'I don't get to make any more phone calls now,' he says quietly.

'You shouldn't have called me then,' I say.

'Nix,' he says quietly.

'I'll come down tomorrow,' I say, and hang up.

I get up the next day and call Phil at work to cancel my meetings.

'Looks a bit funny,' he says in an off-hand way, as he brings up my diary on his computer.

'I don't care what it looks like,' I say sharply, and he shuts up.

We go through everything on the phone: José has seen the footage of our smoking old lady, and has decided it will only work with this particular old lady, and that the scriptwriter should meet her for inspiration. He has also seen all the boxes of cereal lying around my office, and told Phil that we should be pitching for Coke or Pepsi instead. Even Phil understands how ludicrous this is; José is only doing it to fill up poor Phil's time with useless PowerPoint presentations for a pitch we won't even get a chance to make, to ultimately piss me off. I give one-word answers to the last of Phil's questions. I can tell he is beginning to feel nervous about the next month, my resignation month, and the fact that he is going to be lumbered with everything, cutting into his 'pretending to play cricket with a ruler by his desk' time.

'What about my appraisal?'

'Oh, Phil, I'm sorry I really am. We'll definitely do it next week, Monday lunchtime. Put it in, you're booked, it's a date.'

Phil just sighs.

'What if there's something I can't handle?' he asks, and I feel a little sorry for him.

'Tell them I'm sick. Completely sick,' I say, and rather than ask what I'm going on about, he takes this as his cue to say goodbye.

I hang up, and just sit for a moment, staring ahead, before reaching for my address book.

I phone Charlie's brother.

'Hi Peter, it's Nicola, how are you?' I ask, trying to start off with some kind of pleasantry, instead of launching into 'what police station are they holding your brother in?'

'Yeah, I'm okay. How are you?' Peter asks in a worried voice that I read as pity.

'Great, thanks,' I say with sarcasm, but realize that Peter doesn't need it; it's not his fault Charlie is his brother.

'Do you know where Charlie is?' I ask, before he can react.

'Dad called, said he's still at the station.' Peter sighs heavily – I hear the sound of his kid's music in the background – the little sod has just got into heavy metal.

'Which one?' I ask, and write down the name.

'Charlie told Dad you guys were kind of, well, you were going to go away together. Back together, you know what I mean,' he says almost apologetically.

'Yep, I know what you mean. We'll see.' I say goodbye, and hang up again. After a few minutes I get up, put on my coat, stuff my keys and my wallet into my bag, grab my mobile, and head out.

I see him straight away. He walks over to me, and we don't say anything. I just feel tears welling up in my eyes.

'When's your flight?'

'At three. It's fine, I've got time.'

I feel myself start to cry, and he guides me through to the

222

bar, and a big sofa in the corner. He motions to a barman and I don't see what he orders, but he sits me down, takes my coat off me.

'It's too hot out for this,' is all he says, and throws it onto the chair.

I lean forward and put my head in my hands. I don't know why I am here, but it seemed like the only reasonable place to come. I had pulled up the numbers of all of my friends one after another, picturing them on the end of the line as I told them, and their reactions, every time in my head, were the same. Nim would ask me what the hell I was doing; Jules would try and be nice and say everything she could to discourage me without upsetting me; Jake would wonder where it had all come from, and hadn't Charlie become a bit of a loser recently? I had stared at my sister's number long and hard, and envisaged her answering the phone in her office, and trying to work out what to say. I knew every single response would be the same: 'He's an arsehole/twat/wanker/child/prick (that would be the boy's answer), just finish it, he doesn't deserve you etc . . .' I couldn't bear to hear it. And then it had come to me. I had searched madly through the receipts in my purse for a minute, and pulled out Dale's hotel number. Even as I plugged it in to my phone on the bus, I knew he would be there. When he answered, and I heard his voice, it was like a weight off my shoulders, absolute and utter relief.

After a couple of minutes, I realize there are two scotches on the table in front of us, and Dale is sitting on a chair opposite me, contentedly, waiting for me to talk.

'I'm so sorry,' I say and sit up, wiping my eyes, trying to gain my composure.

'Why, what have you done?' he says softly, and smiles.

'No, this,' I say, gesturing at my red eyes and puffy, tear- and mascara-stained face.

223

'It's fine,' he says, and leans forward to take a sip of his drink. He holds it in his mouth, and then swallows it smoothly. I follow his lead and take a sip and try and knock it back just as cleanly. Unfortunately I cough most of it back up, and perform a couple of minor convulsions as it hits the back of my throat. Not quite as slick as Dale. It crosses my mind to pretend to be having an emotional outburst, but I just can't be bothered. I regain my composure, sit back and sigh, and let my hands fall heavily at my side.

'So,' Dale says.

'So,' I say.

'So,' Dale says again.

'Charlie's at the police station,' I say.

'Why?'

'You don't want to know.' I sigh.

'Okay.' He takes another sip of his drink.

'Oh, it's such a long story. I don't know what to do.'

'How is he?'

'I don't know,' I say guiltily, 'I haven't seen him yet.'

'Right.' Dale looks down at his glass, then necks the final remnants of his drink.

'He attacked somebody, a woman. Well, he might have. I think he's claiming he didn't do it. I don't know! Some woman was attacked outside his house, not sexually, I mean she was punched or something.' Like that makes it all right.

'And he told me all about it, said that he saw somebody do it. Then we get back – we'd been away for a weekend, kind of – and he gets arrested for it. I don't know what to think.' A thousand thoughts rush in and out of my head and I bang it against the back of the sofa to try to get them to stop.

'Hey, hey, stop.' Dale gets up and walks over to the sofa, sits down next to me.

I look over at him, and he stares back.

'Do you still love him?' he asks quietly.

'I don't know,' I say.

'Well, I suppose that's all you need to know.'

'You're right,' I say.

'I'm glad you called me,' Dale says.

'I'm glad too,' I say. Dale leans over, lifts my slumped head up and pulls it onto his chest, and pushes his arm behind my shoulders. I stare ahead, as I recognize the starch and soap and aftershave mixture of smells on his shirt. He relaxes completely and leans back.

'Look at us,' I say after a while, without moving.

'I know,' he says, with a smile that I can't see. I take his hand and hold it, wrapping his arm around me.

'Can we just sit here for a while? I'll go and see him then,' I say.

'Sure,' he replies, and I think he may have closed his eyes.

'Have you missed your flight yet?' I ask.

'Almost.'

'Can we still sit here for a while?' I ask again.

'Sure,' he says.

'Can you still stay here, instead of Scotland?' I ask.

'Sure,' he says.

I wake up when I realize Dale is gently stroking the hair away from my forehead, and I feel slightly uncomfortable. In fact, I feel terrible. I have to go and see Charlie, and I haven't. I'm sitting here using a man who doesn't deserve it, mucking him about.

I lurch up and Dale is startled.

'I should go,' I say quickly, and leap to my feet, grabbing my bag and coat. The sweat trickles down my back where it has been lurking for the last half an hour.

'Of course.' Dale jumps to his feet, looking a little confused, and I see a hurt in his eyes that I try and ignore.

I feel awful. I feel responsible for him, and Charlie, and this whole mess, as if they have no free will, no minds of their own. As if they are not accountable for any of their actions, and I am directing their movements and scenes and monologues, and if the performances are bad, if things go awry as they have done, the buck stops with me. I feel like I should just tattoo my forehead with the words 'sorry, for everything'. They are grown men, both of them, not retarded or incapable, and yet their letdowns are my fault. Somehow Dale's divorce, that is my fault. They aren't blaming me, and I'm not playing the martyr, believe me. I can just manage to trace everything back to me.

I wonder if it's because I think I can make it right that I choose to accept the blame for all these things. If I can just help Charlie, love him enough, explain everything, he will be fine. If I can be more supportive, more communicative, he won't need to look for his love elsewhere. Simultaneously, if I can just have a quick fling with Dale, and put an end to our drawn out international sexual chemistry and misplaced longing, show him that we are not meant to be, and send him back to America with self-confidence and renewed belief in love and life, then he will be able to start his life again.

'Will you call me later, and tell me how it goes?' Dale asks. I realize I have just been staring at the floor for about thirty seconds.

'Of course,' I say, and smile. I lean in and kiss him quickly goodbye on the cheek, and dart off towards the door again before he even has time to realize what has happened.

I hail a cab and check my watch – quarter past two. I head for the police station.

Confession Time

I feel like a criminal just walking in. I check my hair in the swing doors, as if having a hair out of place is itself a criminal offence. And my mind is whirring, thinking, 'don't swear, don't touch anything, don't look at anybody too long. Eyes down, hands in pockets.'

I head towards the desk and wait behind a teenage boy who is talking with the desk sergeant about parole. Don't listen, don't make judgements. You could be arrested for any of these things. I turn around and look at the noticeboard to distract myself from their conversation, and see Charlie sitting just around the corner, holding a cup of tea. He feels somebody looking at him and looks over, and smiles ever so slightly. He is indeed pleased to see me. I feel a rush of relief. I'm on my way. I can make this right.

I gesture to him, asking whether I can come over to him, and he beckons me over, nods his head and smiles again.

'What are they doing? Is it over?' I ask straight away, but three feet away from him, no physical contact, not in a police station. Indecency or something; they could get me on that.

'Well, no. They've questioned me already, I haven't been arrested. I can go home. But I can't leave the country,' he says. Normally that remark would have seemed like a joke, but not when you are about to apply for visas to countries on the other side of the world.

'Oh right. Well, let's go home then.' He offers me his hand and something stops me taking it, an impulse not to touch him surges through me. I am not afraid of him, I think.

We go back to his in a cab, and I make a cup of tea, and he slumps down on the sofa.

Explanations are required. I need to understand what exactly is going on, but he doesn't look in any fit state to talk. He has a face full of stubble, and tired red eyes. His suit looks crumpled, and it occurs to me that they went and got him from his work. But I need to know what he has done. I want a confession, of guilt or innocence, something, and I want it now. I need to know how to feel about him now. I need to know if I can stay here tonight.

I say, 'So?'

Charlie sighs heavily and turns to face me on the sofa. I stand gripping the side of the counter, watching the droplets form on the side of the kettle, and I realize I am digging my nails into the surface.

'You have to believe I didn't do this, Nix. I need to know that you know I'm innocent.'

'So why did they fucking arrest you then?' I surprise myself with the sound and the volume of my voice. There has been a scream waiting to come out, and now it has. But I can't stop, even looking at the alarm and the hurt in his eyes. 'They don't arrest people without proof, Charlie; they don't arrest people on a hunch, it's not allowed. Why do they think you did it? And what exactly are you supposed to have done?' I think this is what it must feel like to have your blood boil. Steam seeps from the kettle.

'I didn't do anything,' is all he says.

'Yes, but what do they think you've done? What are they accusing you of?'

'Assault,' he says.

'What kind of assault? Spitting, slapping, punching? Fucking rape?'

'Don't be ridiculous!' he shouts and stands up, wide-eyed.

'Should I be scared, Charlie?'

'Of me? Of course not. Jesus, Nicola, I'm not a different person from this morning. They've made a mistake. I can't believe you don't believe me.'

'Ouch!' I flinch as I realize I have pushed my hand against the metallic side of the kettle, and my skin is starting to stick to it. Charlie rushes over but I put my other hand up.

'No, don't come over here yet,' I say, and run my hand under the cold tap.

We both stand still and watch the water gushing, and Charlie loosens his tie. I flinch again slightly. My nerve endings are on red-alert.

'So what now? It kind of disrupts your plans,' I say quietly.

'Our plans,' Charlie replies, walking over and leaning on the other side of the counter, pouring hot water into a mug with no tea or coffee in it.

'No, Charlie, your plans, you, running away. You using me to get away.'

Charlie slams the kettle down on the counter.

'I didn't fucking do anything!'

I just want to hit him.

How could I just throw my life away after a couple of days? It's a problem when somebody you think you know suddenly turns on the charm, says they've changed – your guard is unintentionally dropped, familiarity draws you in, and almost without question you can be duped, or fooled. Charlie was at the bottom of my wish list last week, and then a bit of sun and the South Coast let me believe we could be

229

Romeo and Juliet after all. I was too easily fooled. I wanted him to be different. Six years of not being able to say goodbye, despite all the reasons in the world, proves, if nothing else, that I was having difficulty facing a life without him.

The thing is, I really was convinced that he had changed, that he cared again, and I let myself show that I cared. I let myself get swept along and this dream that I had only dared dream in the last few days now seemed just as impossible to give up. Charlie seemed right again.

The thought that is whizzing back and forth around my head, the thought that I have to acknowledge, is whether I can forgive him if he did do it? I loved Charlie before, I had just stopped liking him. Now, I like him again, and it's hard to willingly give that up. If he made a mistake, was it a different him? Was it a final act, a last desperate measure to get my attention, to make me open up to him, that drove us back together? Was it the old Charlie, the one that I had created by blocking him out and driving him away, but refusing somehow to let him go? If I made him what he was, if my having sex with Dale resulted in me becoming pregnant and feeling guilty for terminating it, feeling guilty about not telling Dale, feeling guilty about not telling Charlie it wasn't his, then am I responsible?

Had my hating Charlie for not being able to tell him pushed him to do something awful that shocked his whole system back to life? Did he do it partly so he could seek my forgiveness, for everything that he had done to me, all the unfaithfulness? If I had forced him to do something truly big, to make us even and let us forgive each other, then I should forgive him. We are as bad as each other: we deserve each other. Charlie forced an issue I wasn't brave enough to force. Whether he did this or not, I should forgive him.

I turn to face him, and there are tears in his eyes.

The kettle has cooled and I notice beads of water that have

formed at its base on the counter. I reach out my hand to him. He looks at me, unsure, and his eyes widen, in disbelief. He reaches out and takes my hand. I let out the breath I have been holding, and he pulls me in. We stand in the kitchen and hold each other for a while, and I rest my face on his neck, and his hair. I smell him almost subconsciously, it is so familiar. We go to bed, and sleep curled tightly into each other, barely speaking, getting up occasionally for a glass of water, or to open a window. My phone goes a couple of times in the other room, and I ignore it, and snuggle back into Charlie. I know who it is.

Small Truths

Every now and then I am seized by the fact that I am stuck in my head. This is me, I can't ever escape. Suddenly I feel claustrophobic. I want to scramble out of my head, out of my body. I want to be somebody else. I just don't want to be me.

The world has got so shallow; being with somebody means so little now. If I could have anything, I'd have romance. But what is romance other than the atypical, and why would that be easy? Even when we get close, things slip through our fingers before we realize what's happened. Living, insecurities, pride get in the way of the ideal we want our life to be. And we end up clinging onto people in vain as they pull and tug away, to get their head above our emotional water, and shrug off our neediness to concentrate on their own.

Everybody has an ordinary life. Even the people that we think have extraordinary lives just have more money. I am living in a dream world. Magic isn't going to happen. I just have to learn to depend on somebody, and let somebody depend on me, instead of fighting off normality and wrecking myself and other people in the process. If I could photograph my life, I'd realize how great things are, how good I have it. Maybe I'd be positive and optimistic. I get to mostly spend my life how I like. If I can't really lose myself, it's because there are so many people that are trying to tell me that they love me, and I don't really let any of them say it, comfortably.

It's very easy to look around to see what you don't have, but it's not so easy to see what you do have. You beat yourself up about things that really don't matter. I don't have to be perfect. I can't be everything to everybody. Repeat that a hundred times. Write it on the blackboard until your wrist aches and your fingers are dry and bruised by chalk. I may not be what I thought I'd be, but that's okay.

Starting Again, Again

Charlie and I wake up to the sound of the phone ringing. We are entangled in each other and I pull my hair free as he leans over to answer. He answers a couple of questions curtly and hangs up. I pull the duvet up around my neck and lay my head on his chest. He kisses the top of my head and hugs me a little too tight.

'Who was that?' I ask, wide awake.

'The police station – they want me down there again at eight-thirty,' he says quietly, like just saying it might rock the boat we're on too much, and send one of us overboard.

'Well, that gives us time enough for breakfast. Let's have it on the balcony.' I crawl out of his grasp and sit on the side of the bed, pulling my hair up into a ponytail. I grab his dressing gown and pull it on.

'Shall I do the coffee?' he asks, stretching. He seems so fragile, it seems like his whole world depends on me.

'No, hon, you stay there for a minute. I'll do it.' I lean over and, holding my weight on my arms, give him a soft kiss. He kisses me back, and I pull myself away. I leave him sitting up in bed, thinking.

I scramble some eggs, toast some bagels, pepper everything,

pour the juice and the coffee and head out to the balcony. The early morning summer chill hits me slightly as I lay everything out, and I feel Charlie come up behind me and put his arms around me.

'Thank you,' he says quietly, and I rub his forearms as they are wrapped around me, and just smile. We eat our breakfast like honeymooners, passing each other food, me sitting between his legs, our feet propped up, resting on a chair in front of us, leaning on his bare chest, looking out at the early morning sun. We both pretend everything is fine. I almost believe it. I pass a bagel over my shoulder and he takes a bite.

And as the sun warms us up I look down over the balcony at the street below, the street where the girl was hit, and where Charlie phoned the police. I look down at the news-agent's where Charlie was evicted in his dress. I don't say anything, but I wonder whether Charlie is thinking the same things as I am. A few cars go past, cabs mostly. I shiver for a moment, and Charlie hugs me tightly. I close my eyes as the sun begins to blaze, even this early I feel it burn into my skin. Yes, this is certainly a strange summer. The sun keeps coming back for more. The word 'heatwave' gets muttered and whispered during the spring months, as if to say it too loudly would scare it away. It never actually seemed to fulfil its promise. And yet here we are, slap bang in the middle of an unlikely season, an unfamiliar air lending itself to every-body's actions. I can't decide if the air is heavier or lighter with the heat, whether emotions are charged or relaxed. I feel myself warming up, and I can't decide whether the sun is boiling my blood or warming my heart.

I look up and back at Charlie's profile, so close to me, and I smile and moan a small sigh of agreement. Charlie's dick grows harder against my lower back, and I take his hands and slip them gently inside my robe. I turn my head and we kiss slowly and softly. Anybody glimpsing us would say we were in love. I get up and turn around, still wearing Charlie's robe, undone now, and slide myself onto him. We kiss and rock and kiss as the sun steams up the sky. I hear the cars passing below us, and doors closing. I hear alarm radios clicking on and breakfast DJs announcing to the waking that it's going to be another spectacular day. And as Charlie and I time ourselves, working against each other, each clinging to the other's neck, looking into each other's eyes the way we used to, we know we have forgiven each other – but it's a small easy forgiveness, a sex forgiveness.

When it Rains, it Pours

Charlie and I go our separate ways at the train station. I make my way back to my flat, and he heads towards more questions. I have a quick shower, slap on some make-up and set off for work. Even in my jeans and a vest top I feel over-dressed for the heat, and Charlie, hoping it will make a good impression, is wearing a suit. I've phoned his work on my mobile and explained to his boss that Charlie will phone him later. He seemed fine about it, even nonchalant, which I took to be a good sign. He obviously didn't believe it, or maybe he didn't give a shit about Charlie. I wasn't sure which was better.

My biggest surprise as I walk into the office is to see Phil in a shirt. My first thought is that he must be going for another job, and a wave of affection hits me, at the thought that he can't bear the idea of working there without me.

'What time's your interview?' I ask, and take a swipe at the back of his head with my newspaper. I can be social, my spirits seem to have lifted, shifted somehow, towards optimism. Phil ducks out the way of my paper, and raises his eyes to heaven.

'I wish. No, they made me go to two of your *Evil Ghost* meetings yesterday, and I figured you wouldn't be in today

239

either, so I'm going to have to start dressing up for work now.' He sighs, like he carries the weight of the world on his shoulders for a matter of seconds, and then as usual, it lifts.

'But Phil, I never dress up for work, I mean unless it's really important,' I say, and beckon him to follow me into my office.

'Yes, but you are overlooking the very important fact that you know what you are talking about, whereas I –' he golf swings with an imaginary club, and follows the imaginary ball with his eyes – 'do not.' He slumps down in the chair in front of me.

'Are you going to miss me then? I bet you never counted on that,' I say as I dump the contents of my in-tray onto my desk.

Phil doesn't answer, just golf swings again in his chair. He seems a world away from me, another generation, when in fact he is only three years younger than I am. 'Do you want a coffee?' he asks as he makes his way out of my office.

'Yes please, and then can we have a quick meeting, half an hour, current status etc?' I hear a faint 'yep' as he walks towards the kitchen.

I turn on the TV with the remote, and switch to the news, but it's just another report on the weather. More heat this afternoon, breaking tonight with a storm. Thank goodness, I think as I wipe the sweat off my neck, the air needs clearing.

Phil returns with my coffee, and shuts the door behind him.

'Are you seeing anybody at the moment?' I ask suddenly – it occurs to me that Phil doesn't seem to be troubled like the rest of us, with matters of the heart.

'Only lady palm and her five lovely daughters,' he says, and I raise my eyes to heaven while he chuckles to himself. Lucky, innocent, naïve, immature Phil. Still living with his grandfather, completely untouched by the responsibility and guilt of a relationship that lasts more than a night. I still wouldn't want to be him though. Nothing can be that bad that I'd wish my life away to a world that revolves solely around the FA Cup, the Premiership, and Sunday League football. I once accused Phil of being insensitive, after he showed a complete lack of interest in the death of Angela's cat. He got quite angry, and informed me he had cried 'when Fulham went down.' Enough said.

My mobile rings again, and I note the number before turning the phone off completely – it is Dale, for the third time this morning. I will phone him later, I have to see to Phil, I tell myself guiltily.

We spend the next hour going through stuff I think he should know. The scriptwriter will need to cut his hair at some point, because José will fire him otherwise with me out of the way. We still don't have a lead, the model we used in the teaser will need to be in the production somewhere, but don't let José convince her to go nude, because we won't get it past the authorities. The sales team needs more brochures, music needs clearing, contracts need drawing up, and somebody needs to monitor the budget, because José won't. Phil seems petrified at first, as I reel off the things I do, but relaxes into boredom after the first twenty minutes; it is too much for him to take in all at once. I make him listen nonetheless, hoping some of it will sink in. He really doesn't have any ambition at all. On my departure he will either have a very rude awakening, but throw himself into it and get himself a promotion, or else he'll just get a bar job and have the time of his life. Yes, I am back to going away again. Charlie has my faith, if not my complete trust.

My office phone rings and I pick up, as Phil spies an opportunity to make a dash for the door and hovers by the handle waiting for the nod from me to say he can go. After a couple of seconds I shake my head and point back at the seat in front of me. He sighs heavily and slumps into it, arms crossed, practically horizontal, staring off into space.

I hang up, and decide I have to tell Phil, if nobody else.

'Look, Phil, one last thing.' His mood noticeably brightens at the word 'last'.

'I have to tell you something, but it is completely confidential, and if I hear that anybody else knows I'll know it came from you, okay?'

'Yes, yes, yes,' he says quickly, and tries to hurry me up with his hand, anxious to know what it is. I raise my eyebrows annoyed, and he sits back and waits for me to tell him.

'I have to go out now.'

He sighs heavily.

'I have to go to the police station,' I say to get back his attention.

'Why, mate, what have you done?' he asks, concerned.

'It's not me, it's my boyfriend – you remember Charlie, you've met him a couple of times.' I watch his face drop slightly. I know that he thinks Charlie's a wanker. He had done everything short of saying it to my face, some kind of misplaced concern on his part for me, the little brother I never had.

'Look, he hasn't actually done anything, they are just questioning him, but now they want to question me, so I'll be gone for a couple of hours, okay? Are you going to be all right – can you cope if I pop out?'

Phil's persona changes instantly, and his gentlemanly side takes over.

'Absolutely, you go.' I smile and say thanks.

'But take your mobile with you, just in case,' he says quickly, before shutting my office door behind him. I don't have a chance to say anything back. I resolve to phone up Nim and Jules, both of whom Phil fancies, and bribe

242

them to go with him to his next football 'do', as a thank-you.

As I head down in the lift I think about where I am going for the first time. I have never had to speak to the police, officially, before last week, and now I can't seem to get away from them. What do they want to ask me anyway? It crosses my mind that Charlie might have given my name as an alibi for the night of the attack. I feel my face flush just at the prospect – I can't lie to a policeman, it would be like lying to a priest – it's not allowed, but then it's never stopped me before. Maybe they just want to ask me a few questions about Charlie generally, where we went in Devon etc . . . It is only this non-threatening thought that gets me to the station. I chain smoke the whole way.

I sit in reception on a hard, plastic chair waiting for the officers to call me through, and read the various pamphlets pinned to the noticeboard. They are all don't drink and drive, or have a smoke alarm, put locks on your window, don't inject heroin . . . all sensible stuff, and I comply with them all. So far, I am faultless. I feel a slight sense of relief. I wonder where Charlie is, somewhere in the building, in an office, or even a cell, being asked whos and whats and whens about a night he just wants to forget.

Eventually an Officer Brown comes and introduces himself, and asks me to follow him. He doesn't look any older than Phil, and his clothes seem a little silly on him, a kid in a grown-up's uniform, but I follow him nonetheless. I am not about to tell him he looks stupid. He leads me into a room at the back of the station full of desks and paper and filing cabinets, and asks me to sit down in front of one of the desks. A couple of other policemen mill about at the door, chatting. I expected it to be more organized than this, tidier. I also expected to be locked in a room with a two-way mirror with the suggestion of somebody lurking behind it, watching my every move. But instead I just sit where I am told, among the piles, and watch him as he shuffles through some paper to find a notepad. He stares at the pad for a while, and I cough uncomfortably as the silence drags on. He looks up at me, and I realize that he is actually trying to get a word out, but struggling. I narrow my eyes slightly, and nod my head at him to go on, but it doesn't appear to make much of a difference. He is having real trouble. Stutters are the strangest things, so hard to understand, and yet so hard not to laugh at the awkwardness of it all. There is a song, by the Bare Naked Ladies, I think, where it talks about being the kind of person who laughs at funerals, and this is exactly the same thing. The compelling need not to laugh at all, the tragedy of the thing, sometimes seems like the biggest incentive to collapse into hysterics. I make a real effort not to, however, and also fight the urge to tell him to 'just sing it'. Finally when the word arrives, I am shocked to hear the noise come out of his mouth.

'C . . . C . . . C . . . CCCCan I ask you a few questions?' he asks.

I want to say 'you may, but whether you can or not remains to be seen.' But I just say, 'Sure.'

He asks me about Charlie, how long we've been together, but he seems to focus on the fact that he has just resigned. I explain that I have done the same thing, that we have decided to go travelling. He seems happy enough with this answer, and then asks if Charlie has spoken to me about a woman being attacked outside of his apartment on the evening of Wednesday last week. I say yes, and try and remember what Charlie had told me about the night itself. I start with Charlie going out on to his balcony and looking down with a beer, and finish with him phoning the police. I leave out the part about him having sex with her, or the dress-wearing incident the next day – after all, he didn't ask me about those bits. Again, he seems quite happy with the answers. I have forgotten all about the stutter by now, as he seems to have completely forgotten himself. But as he stands up, it starts again.

'T T T T T TTTT . . .' is all he is saying, and I stick out my hand to shake his to break the silence. He shakes my hand but carries on with the 'T T T T TTTT' in rhythm to our hand shaking, and after a while my arm actually begins to ache. Again, as if my growing tired and or bored is the trigger that he needs, he blurts out,

'TTh Th Thank you for meeting with me, it was good of you to spare the time. Your boyfriend will be out front by now, so you are both free to go together.'

Out front Charlie is indeed waiting, by the noticeboard, reading a pamphlet on littering and the fact that it is just rude, and I dig him in the back with my finger.

'You ready to go then?' I ask, with a smile.

'I can't believe they called you down here,' he says with sincere concern.

'Are you okay? Did they ask you horrible questions about me?' He wants to know everything, I can tell, and I want to tell him everything.

'No, not really. You told them you've resigned, and he only seemed interested in knowing if I had done the same thing. I think they were just corroborating your story. It was fine, I promise,' I tell him, and rub his back.

'Okay.' He looks away, and then back at me.

'You really are great, Nicola, you know that, don't you?' he says, and I am taken aback by the affection in his eyes. It makes me feel like a fraud.

'Yeah, I'm bloody marvellous,' I say, and try and conceal the sarcasm, directed right at myself.

Charlie announces that he wants to head into work, put on a brave face, spread the word that he's done nothing wrong, and that everything is fine. We kiss at the tube, and make arrangements to meet that night. I have a work thing I have to go to, some clients taking us out to a restaurant in town, which I had completely forgotten about, and which I desperately don't want to go to, but have to really, seeing as it's kind of for me, and if not Phil will just feel uncomfortable all night.

I say I'll be over to his late, and he should eat without me, and I jump on the tube. I check my watch as I get off at Leicester Square, and realize the battery must have died hours ago. I switch on my mobile knowing there will be messages. There are three, all from Dale. The first is concerned, the second is agitated, the third is kind of angry, and why not? I have stopped him going to Scotland, and now I won't even take his calls. I check the time – it is three o'clock. I shiver slightly, and check the sky. I can see clouds creeping in from the west.

Back at work Phil has told everybody about my imminent departure, and they are all very anxious to hear about where I plan to go on my travels, and good for me, how they wish they were going etc . . . 'Just go then,' I say, 'just jack it all in and go.' But they make their relevant excuses: debt, kids, career . . . I sit there thinking how great Charlie and I are, and how brave. We are seizing the day, we are throwing caution to the wind.

I head into the kitchen to get away from the feigned sincerity of some of the younger bitchier secretaries, who are just using me as an excuse to hang around Phil's desk. I think it's his shyness that they mistake for aloofness that attracts them. And he is a very good-looking young man. If only they knew that they petrified him, they'd have him tied to the desk in no time.

As I fill my mug with instant hot water, I hear somebody come in behind me, and turn to see José blocking the doorway.

'Hi, José,' I say wearily; another confrontation.

'Just to let you know, I am checking the security cameras. I zink you 'ave been stealing from zese offices, and I intend to call ze police.'

He exhausts me, but, at the same time, I can't stop myself laughing. 'What is it you think I have stolen, José?'

'Stationery,' he says in a cool voice. The top three buttons of his shirt are undone, and chest hair is sprouting out all over the place. But there is no sign of sweat on him.

'What kind of stationery?' I know this is complete rubbish, but he is playing every card in his pack. It's almost admirable, in an idiotic way.

'General stationery. Angela tells me zere is 'ardly a stapler left in ze building, and I 'ave noticed your bag bulging in ze evening.' He smiles at me; he knows this is ludicrous.

'What exactly do you think I have been doing with all these staplers?'

'Car boot sales.'

'You think I've been selling staplers at car boot sales? If I was going to steal something, wouldn't I steal something a bit more profitable, like phones? Or laptops?'

'Ahhh, so you admit it!' José leans back against the door frame and smiles again.

'José, for God's sake, get out of my way,' I say as I push past him, and manage to spill a couple of drops of my coffee on his beige loafers.

'Beetch!' I hear him swear as I walk back to my office.

'Jesus Christ,' I mutter, and close the door to my office, divert all my calls to answerphone, and begin the unenviable task of clearing my inbox.

At around six, I raise my head, and check my mobile – another missed call. I close the door and redial the number. After one ring, time enough for me to pat my hair down but not to compose myself, Dale answers.

'Nicola?' He sounds relieved.

'Dale, hi, I'm so sorry.' I mean it as well. I feel terrible. But not terrible enough to have phoned before.

'What's going on, has he been charged?' he asks, still concerned. His accent is becoming familiar again, his voice not alien, but soothing.

'Oh, no, well, they let him out yesterday.' I feel guilty as I say it.

'Oh right,' and Dale jumps to all the logical conclusions, I can hear it in his voice. The disappointment is glaring.

'Yeah, so he's okay. I don't really know what's happening, they just seem to be questioning him. And I've been down there today. It doesn't even look like much will come of it. I don't know for sure, of course . . .' My voice trails off as I realize for the first time that I don't know what will come of it. I should know that at least, what exactly is going on. I feel suddenly anxious, in the dark.

I realize that neither of us has said anything for a while, and I know I should ask about him.

'So what are your plans now, then?' I try to sound curious, and not guilty.

'I phoned the airline today, I didn't know what would be happening . . .' Dale sounds guilty too.

'And?'

'Well, I've missed Dublin now as well, but I can get a flight back to the States whenever I want.' He is waiting for me to tell him what to do.

'So are you going to book it for the weekend?' I ask, telling him what I think, without actually saying it.

'Yeah, I could do.' The sadness is almost seeping down the phone now, and I shiver, as I start to hear the patter of rain outside against the window. It's only light now.

'Well, then you have another day to look around town, tomorrow, and you can fly back on Friday night. You must be missing the kids like crazy.' I pretend to sound like I mean all of this, and ignore the fact that I have stopped him going where he was going.

'Yes, I could do that,' he says, and then quickly, before I have a chance to say anything, 'Can I see you, before I go?'

'Oh Dale, I have to work tomorrow. What with resigning and everything, they are watching me like a hawk.'

'What about tonight then, just for a drink, just to say goodbye?'

'Well, I have this work do that I have to go to, and . . .' Charlie doesn't even know he is here: I have deliberately kept it from him, not because of the circumstances, but because I really don't want him to know. Charlie would probably have liked to say hello, but I've kept him to myself. Another secret. Just rack 'em up.

'I suppose I could meet you before going to the restaurant, it is on my way. Just for a quick drink – I have to be there for eight, so if I leave now, I can make it – okay?' I make it sound like I was going to come all along, that I hadn't even considered not seeing him.

'Sure, I'm here. I might pop out later, catch a play or something.'

'Great, well, I'll be with you in about half an hour then.'

'Great, I'll see you then.'

We hang up on each other at the same time.

Outside the rain starts to hammer down, and even though Dale's hotel is not more than ten minutes' walk away, I try desperately to catch a cab – I don't have an umbrella. But it's always the same in London, as soon as a cloud pops into the sky, hailing a cab is the hardest thing in the world. I gradually start to make my way down the street, stopping to look both ways and see if I can glimpse a rare orange light, but they all shoot past me with their smug inhabitants dry inside. My paper, held pathetically above my head, is soaked through and starting to stick to my hair, and my vest top is soaked. I make a run for it.

I get to the hotel more wet than dry, having given up the hope of looking like anything but a drowned rat about a minute after I'd started running. It is actually quite refreshing just to say: 'Fuck it I'm going to get wet, so come on rain, do your worst.' It's strangely liberating.

I shake the rain off, half laughing, in the foyer while the receptionists and busboys look over at me in shock and disdain. Fuck 'em. My phone starts ringing and I fish it out of my bag, trying desperately not to drip all over the rest of the contents.

'Hello,' I almost shout as I get to it just in time. I am elated, still half laughing at how I must look, how I feel.

'Nix, it's me,' Charlie says breathlessly down the phone.

'Char, where are you?' I wipe my dripping hair away from my forehead, and pat the rain off the side of my face.

'I'm at work, just about to leave now – where are you?'

'Oh, I'm at the restaurant, just about to be seated.' I am lying, again.

'Well, have a drink for me, and get home fast – they're not taking it any further – I'm not being charged. I fucking told you!' Charlie almost screams it down the phone, sounding like a man who's just won the lottery.

'You're kidding, that's bloody great! That's great.' If I am honest, I can't quite believe it.

'What happened?' I need to know the details

'The girl said she didn't know who it was, but it wasn't me. She'd just mentioned my name when she'd first woken up because I was the last person she'd seen. She just said we'd had a coffee and a chat and then she'd left. But she's fully conscious now and she's told them she can't really remember what happened.'

'Charlie, that's brilliant,' I say, as I try and hide the incredulity in my voice.

'I want to be with you, now,' I continue. I want to hold him and make plans and tell him I believed him all along.

'I know, can't you get out of this bloody thing – tell them you feel ill or something? Sod it, just tell them what's happened, I don't care, they'll understand. Please?'

'Oh Charlie, I wish I could. I'll be quick though, I'll just have a starter and then I'll come straight round.' I'll just say hello and goodbye to Dale, have a quick drink, and then blow out the dinner, and go straight round to his.

'Great, well, get home as soon as you can. I love you.'

'I love you too.'

'We're going away, just you and me!'

'I know, I know.' It's the first time we've both really believed it since we've been back.

'I'll see you soon,' and I hang up.

I feel unbelievable. Outside the rain has stopped and the sun is coming out again, at seven o'clock at night, one of those late red suns that really shouldn't be there. I feel over the fucking moon. I want to sing and dance and jump for joy. I can't remember feeling this good, forever, since uni, since America.

I phone Dale and tell him I'm downstairs.

'I'll come straight down,' he says, not happy at all, business-like even. I just need to do this, have this drink, and say thank you as well – he helped me through it. I need to send him on his way with a dignified goodbye that lets him know that I'm glad I saw him, and that everything, me, him, Charlie, his kids, everything will be all right.

I can't sit down because my jeans are soaking, so I linger at the door while I wait for him to come down. I watch the stairway for him, but he doesn't appear, just a youngish guy with a shaved head in jeans and a sweatshirt, who walks towards me with a serious look. He stops in front of me.

'Oh Jesus, Dale?! What happened?' I instinctively rub my hand over the top of his head and feel the freshly-shorn bristles. 'What butcher did that to you?' I laugh, and he smiles back. You can really see his face, but it looks completely different – squarer somehow, and his eyes bluer, almost Irish.

'Time for a change,' he says, laughing at himself, and feels his head.

'You look great, I mean very different, but . . . oh my God, it really suits you! I didn't even recognize you! And what's with the jeans? You look like something out of a GAP advert!'

'Is it that bad?' He looks serious for a minute, and then smiles again.

'I just thought it was time I relaxed, I went shopping today – I've never owned a pair of jeans in my life. Thought it was time I gave it a try – you can't really knock it till you've tried it.' He crosses his arms, and looks away, almost embarrassed.

'No, it really suits you, you look great, honest. I just didn't recognize you that's all.' I laugh again, and then we realize that we are staring at each other for no real reason.

'Well, I, unfortunately do not look quite as good,' I say, and gesture towards my soaking wet hair – I can still feel the water on my eyelashes, but can't wipe them because of the mascara streaks that would be left behind.

'You got caught in the storm,' he says.

'And you are a genius,' I reply, and ring out the bottom of my top, which actually leaves a puddle at my feet. I shiver slightly.

'Well, you need to get dry, and nowhere is going to let you sit down in those,' he gestures towards my jeans which are two shades darker with damp.

'Let's go upstairs and get you dry, and we can have a drink there.'

'Oh.' I am taken aback slightly, I don't know why, it's not as if I can't trust myself; I am completely sober. I realize I haven't eaten all day, but I am only going to have one drink. And what I want to do most is see Charlie. I won't stay long.

'Of course, if you don't mind. It makes sense.' I sound like I am justifying it to myself.

'Yes it does, come on it won't take long.'

Dale walks off towards the stairs and I follow, and the disapproving receptionists' looks follow me.

'Ahhh, it hurts, my legs are too tired,' I say as I drag my soaked denim-encased legs up the last flight of stairs to the third floor.

'Come on, stop whining,' Dale says, and grabs my outstretched hand and drags me up the last few steps.

'Sadist,' I say, smiling.

'Flattery won't get you anywhere,' he replies, and with that his key is in his door.

I stand uncomfortably by the bathroom while he grabs some towels, and passes me the complimentary bathrobe that hangs behind the door.

'Not worn once,' he says, as he hands me a pile of fluff, and flips on the bathroom light.

'You can change in there,' he says, and motions towards the bathroom, which is huge and marble and white and old-fashioned. He walks over and throws himself onto his bed, and grabs a newspaper from the side, leaving me standing stupidly by the door.

'Thanks.' I feel like a kid, being supervised by a teacher. I thought the sexual tension would be too much for us and we would be ripping each other's clothes off like the last time we had been in a bedroom together, albeit six years ago. But Dale is all grown-up, and I am the kid; he just wants a drink, and to read his newspaper, I am the one being childish, and unforgivable. I towel dry my hair and peel off my jeans with some effort, pat myself dry, and think about Charlie, waiting in his flat with a bottle of champagne for me to come home and celebrate. I am fine, I am in control, I am not going to do anything more than have a drink and go. Besides, Dale seems like a different person now, with his lack of hair and his new jeans. It's like the control has shifted somehow, and he who previously needed me to prove he was still young and attractive just doesn't any more. His haircut has performed the reverse Samson effect, and now he has the power. No, I am completely in control, and not about to do anything silly. I double knot the dressing gown.

One Step Forward or Two Steps Back?

My feet feel particularly naked stepping out on the carpet of his room, and as I look down at the starting to chip red nail varnish on my toes, I jump at the knock on the door behind me. Dale springs up and without even looking at me, brushes past to open the door. I hurry further inside, so that the waiter won't see me, and think we are doing anything we shouldn't. I have a guilty conscience, and I haven't even done anything . . .

I position myself on a chair, moving a familiar-looking suit onto the side of the bed, and adjust the bathrobe so that it covers my knees, and no bra or cleavage is showing. Dale catches me doing it as he walks back from the door with a bottle of red wine and a couple of glasses. He looks away and pretends he didn't see, and I stop immediately. I am embarrassed enough for the both of us, with my presumption. He is making me feel like a fool.

'You do drink red, don't you?' he asks, as he puts the two glasses down on the side.

'Absolutely.' I try and sound bright and breezy. I just don't want him to come any closer; he needs to stay on that side of the room.

'I spoke to my kids today,' he says, as he pours the wine, and I feel all of my adrenaline pour out of me. He really does want to go home, he really does just want one last drink. I am being stupid, thinking like a child. I am nearly thirty, for God's sake. I need to get a grip. I concentrate on the voice of cautious conscience in the back of my head, the one that always persuades me against doing silly things. The one that has been kicking around for a while, since the last time I did something really stupid. I will rely on it now, not to let me blurt out something inappropriate. To talk about his kids, and his trip, and then let me leave, emotionally in one piece. I do not need to hit the self-destruct button every time. I have self-control, I can use it. Not every opportunity is one to be taken – not everything has to end in some fated romantic disaster.

'How are they? They won't recognize you when you get back.'

'I know, I know,' he says, rubbing his head again, with a look of simultaneous pride and regret.

'And the kids at school! All the teenage girls are going to fancy you now.' I laugh, and relax a little.

'"Fancy"? That word always makes me laugh,' he says. 'They "fancied" me anyway,' and I notice his accent, remember he's not from these parts. He is a world away, and he is going home soon.

A thought slams me. 'For God's sake, don't tell Joleen you saw me, she'll think I made you do it!' I say, and then catch the look on his face, a serious look, at the mention of her name.

'I wasn't going to tell her I saw you; it would only upset her.' He takes a large gulp of wine, and I follow suit. He sits on the end of his bed, legs apart, cradling his wine glass in his hands, head down. Even the pose doesn't seem like him, seems too young for him somehow. He looks like a footballer, not a poetry teacher.

'Even now, after all this time, she'd get upset if you talked about me?' I ask, incredulous.

'Oh please, you love that it would upset her, don't sound so shocked.' He is being confrontational, and I rise to the bait.

'Why would you say that? I was barely even there, just a year, and you never had any feelings for me anyway, you just pretended, to wind her up. She must know that by now.'

'She isn't stupid, don't talk like she is.' Dale turns and snaps at me, with flashes of anger in his eyes.

'Sorry, God, I wasn't saying she was stupid, I'm just saying that it was, you know, so long ago, and we were at college, and, it was nothing.'

'It wasn't nothing.' Dale rubs his hand from the front of his head to the back, he has acquired a new habit, in a day.

'Oh, Dale, come on.' I try and laugh it off.

He necks his drink, and pours himself another large glass, which almost spills over the top. I take another gulp. I don't like where this is going. I meant it to be light-hearted, a fond farewell, not some massive deep and meaningful. Dale is a man of passion, no cutting off of hair can get rid of that. He wants to feel great things, romantic things. He wants to be Shelley and Byron rolled into one. He wants his life to be fated, he believes in destiny, he wants drama and tears, he wants to see me cry. An anger rises up inside me. Is this some game that he and Joleen concocted before he came away, some malevolent way to get back at me for ruining their year at college, gate-crashing their party of two? I bet they haven't even separated – she's probably hiding in the wardrobe, waiting for me to make a fool of myself. But they're out of luck today. I've come for my drink, and then I'll go.

I have worked myself up into a state, and I gulp my wine, and put my glass down, ready to leave.

'Do you know what Einstein said?' Dale asks me, assuming of course that I won't know.

'No, what did he say?' I ask, angrily, waiting for some deep pearl of wisdom that Dale thinks will go right over my head. So what if it does? I'm sick of this.

'He said, "When I was young I found out that the big toe always ends up making a hole in a sock, so I stopped wearing socks."'

What? Dale starts to laugh to himself, and I just sit there looking confused for a second.

'What are you talking about?' I try not to laugh, all the anger oozing away.

'I'm just saying, big toes make holes in socks.'

'No, you're not, you bloody know you're not. I learn from my mistakes, Dale, we all do.'

'I don't.' He turns and looks at me and the smile fades.

'We made a mistake, didn't we? You didn't mean to do what you did, and I didn't mean to let you leave.' This is the conversation he's been waiting to have since they checked his passport at the airport.

'Oh Dale, Jesus, let's not get into it all right, let's just finish our drinks, and say goodbye.' I realize I am out of wine, and get up and walk over to get the bottle, pour myself another large glass. As soon as I take a sip, I feel slightly unsteady, but walk back to my chair and sit down carefully. Dale takes a pack of cigarettes out of the back of his jeans, and lights one, offering the pack and the lighter to me. I do the same, and breathe out smoke carefully, watching it curl up towards the ceiling and disappear.

'Don't you ever think about it?' Dale asks quietly, head down again.

'No, I don't. It was what it was; saying goodbye, getting rid of the tension. I don't know, we just wanted to do it so we did. We were kids.' My lies are even bigger than me now, they sound convincing. I am amazed how easily it comes.

'I wasn't a kid. It was more than that,' he says seriously.

'No, it wasn't, you just think like that because you were going through a hard time: what's-her-name had just tried to top herself.' I feel my words slur slightly, and an insensitivity creep into my voice, and I concentrate on sounding nice.

'And you know, I was leaving, you looked so sad . . .'

'Don't you dare call it a pity fuck.' Dale jumps up and walks back to the bottle, picks it up and slams it down again, and drops fly out of the top.

'Well, don't dress it up as something it wasn't,' I shout back, stubbing out my cigarette, and glaring at him.

'Dale, we shagged once; it doesn't matter, it hasn't changed our lives. For God's sake, not everything has to be riddled with some fucking meaning that's not even there.' I am almost convincing myself.

'Not everything has to be for a reason.' I quieten my voice.

'We've moved on, we're grown-ups, you have kids, for Christ's sake. Let's not make a drama out of it.' I sit back against my chair, and let my head fall back, with the exhaustion of the conversation, of trying to think straight. I feel the room spin slightly, and open my eyes wide, and sit up. Even now, even after everything, I can't admit it. It would do more harm than good. He doesn't want my confession; he needs to hear me say it didn't matter.

'I have to go,' I say quickly, and finish off my wine in a gulp.

'Do you still love him?' Dale asks, ignoring what I say.

'If you are talking about Charlie . . .' I don't answer. I want to say yes, I really do, but I don't want to lie any more than I have to.

'Well, there's my answer,' Dale says in response to my silence, and indignation sweeps me.

'Yes, yes I do. We fit, we've stayed together, through everything.'

259

'Yeah, I bet there have been some really tough times – did his football team lose a game? Did you put on a couple of pounds? You really are a pair of survivors!' The sarcasm in Dale's drunken voice is tangible, and I bite my tongue.

'Look, this has turned nasty, so I'm going to go. I'm sorry it had to end like this, I really am, and it was very nice to see you, but this is bloody stupid.'

I get up and stumble my way towards the door, but Dale jumps up and stands in my way. I expect him to grab me but he doesn't.

'Even after what he did, you're going to stay with him? He attacked somebody! A woman! And you're going to forgive him?' I am shocked, but that is all. Dale really thinks we are something, his feelings are running deeper than they ever should have.

'Dale,' I say quietly, in a whisper, 'he didn't do it. The police have cleared him of everything, the girl herself admitted he didn't do it. And you know what? Even if he had done it, even if I had left him, it still wouldn't have been about you and me. You think there is an "us", Dale, but you're just clinging to it, some wild idea of what I am, and what you could be with me, when it's not either of us at all. Not everything is romantic, not everything is destined to be. Sometimes,' I reach out and touch his arm, 'we just want things to be different, to entertain ourselves, to kid ourselves that we're different. But we're just normal, we're two people who met, had sex, and then didn't see each other for a while, and just because we share some kind of sexual tension, it doesn't mean we're . . . I don't know, meant to be.'

'Don't patronize me.' Dale grits his teeth, and I am suddenly exhausted again.

'Then calm the fuck down, Dale, this isn't sodding Shakespeare.' I try to push past him, but he grabs me and spins me around.

'Don't talk to me like I'm a kid – why did you even come, if you had nothing to say?' He seems absolutely bewildered that I could just leave like this. I am not fitting into his plan of what tonight was supposed to be.

'I came to say goodbye, I came because I wanted to say thanks – no, you know what? If you want honesty, I came because I thought I had to! I came to make you feel better about yourself, to send you on your merry way with a happy heart. Jesus, I just came to say goodbye, Dale. That's it.'

'It was more than that.' We are standing too close, I can feel his hands digging into my arms, and I know I should break away.

'All right, I came to prove that I could trust myself. That Charlie and I are fine, because I could trust myself with you. I didn't want to run away from this one. I wanted to . . . get closure or something stupid. There you go – is that American enough for you?' I laugh slightly, at my own words.

Dale stares at me hard, and then smiles. 'Closure? Are you sure about that word?'

'I know, I sound like an idiot. White trash all along.' I sigh and laugh. I feel Dale lean in and his lips brush mine.

'No, Dale, Jesus!' I pull away from him, fighting myself and the urge to make another fucking huge mistake.

We stand and stare at each other and I know for a fact that if he kisses me again, I won't say no, but does he know that? It's the red wine, and the drama, and the tears, but mostly the wine, I tell myself quickly. But still I just stand and stare at him. I don't think he will do it – how much rejection can one man take? But it's like he knows what I'm thinking – maybe I give it away, maybe my mouth isn't saying anything, but my hands are signalling to him, kiss me again, and I won't say no. He takes a step forward, and puts his hands on either side of my face, and kisses me softly. I feel his tongue lick my upper lip, but no part of me moves, except my mouth,

261

kissing him back. I feel his hands move down to the knot on my robe, but he keeps kissing me, and then after a couple of seconds, he steps back and looks at the double knot that is refusing to come undone.

'Jesus,' he laughs, and it is almost enough to bring me to my senses, but as quickly as an image of Charlie darts through my head, the knot is undone and his tongue is on my breasts and his hands are up and down my back, and I feel myself pulling his sweater over his head. I push him down onto the bed, but he pulls me with him, holding a breast in each hand, pushing my legs apart with his knees, and my hands are at his jeans, unbuttoning them quickly, and pushing my hand inside. I run my tongue down the hair on his chest, and then up again, licking his nipple, kissing his neck, meeting his mouth again as he kisses me hard and takes my face in his hands. I so want to kiss him, and impress him, and have him want me more than anybody that has gone before, and make him believe that this was the sex he has always wanted, and I am the person who can make him feel more than anybody else. I want him to want to be inside me more than he wants anybody else in the world. And an urgency creeps into his movements as he kicks off his jeans and I see how hard he is already, how much he wanted this, but I want to slow him down, and make him realize how great this is, what we are doing. But I feel him spread my thighs, and guide himself inside me with an urgency that says he couldn't slow this down. I reach down and try and hold his dick, try and slow him up, but he pushes my hand away, and presses himself back inside me, and I resolve to kiss him for all the time it takes, and to hold him for as long as I can, because I don't know what will happen when this ends.

Sleeping on It . . .

I wake slowly, and the unfamiliarity of the room confuses me for a moment. I lay still and listen to the heavy breathing next to me, feel the arm tucked into my stomach, and the legs behind me cradled into my knees. Dale is holding on for dear life. The clock on the table next to the bed reads 10.04. It hasn't hit me yet, what I've done, why I'm here, but I shudder slightly, and convince myself it's the cold, and not the icy blood running through my veins. I don't feel bad yet.

As the minutes tick on, and Dale leans in even more, sleeping deeply, and I somehow drift in and out of sleep, expecting to wake with a start at any moment and shout Charlie's name, I realize nothing is happening. I don't feel bad at all.

I wake again, and check the clock, it seems like only minutes since I checked it last, but it reads 11.58. I force my eyes to stay open for a minute, wait for the dread or the guilt or the fear to come, but still nothing happens. I move Dale's arm from around my waist, and slither out of bed.

'Where are you going?' he asks, lying in the same position.

'To the bathroom,' I say, and grab my bag on the way in. I close the door, and fish my mobile out of my bag: two missed calls. I check my messages. One from Phil, asking desperately where I am. And one from Charlie.

'So obviously you are getting drunk, and fair enough. It's been a rough couple of days. Enjoy yourself, I'll be here when you get back. Wake me when you get in.'

He doesn't sound drunk, or pissed off, or angry. A bit tired maybe, but that's it. I turn my phone off, and chuck it back into my bag, and then run the cold water, splash water on my face, and peel out my contact lenses. I run my fingers through my hair, and flatten it down slightly, a makeshift makeover.

I creep back out into the room, and gather up my clothes – my bra and knickers and vest top lay on one side of the bed, my jeans on the other.

I put them all with my bag, on a chair.

I flip off the light . . . and get back into bed.

Dale immediately rolls over to me, and I push my head under his arm, onto his chest. I can tell he is awake, his breathing sounds uncomfortable; I am not sure if he is relieved at my staying or not.

'Go to sleep, I'm not going anywhere,' I tell him, and he kisses me on the top of my head.

I close my eyes, kiss his chest once, shift myself so the hairs on his chest aren't in my mouth and I can breathe, and drift away.

Should I Stay or Should I Go?

Where do I go from here? The light blazes through the window, the clock flashes again, 06.52.

The obvious thing, the impulse that strikes me most, is that I should be on my own. I shouldn't be scared to do my own thing, admit that my feelings either run too shallow or too deep for both of these men, and walk away. I can't always run away from being on my own, some time has to be the time to try it out. I should just get up, look at the day, today is as good a day as any, bright or cloudy, rain or shine, and stop making excuses, and decide that today is the day to go it alone. But the mere thought of it scares me silly, and not the independence, or the self-reliance that it requires. The idea that I could lose both of them, in the same day, and be left standing, numb and stupid, is the worst part of all. Just thinking about it is merely an emotional exercise in exposing my fears, on some kind of erratic impulse, scaring myself to try and prompt the swell of guilt that usually comes.

We all know the right thing to do, the nuns know it, the priests know it, the good and just know it – I should end it with one, and start it with another, properly and wholly and honestly. Or finish it with them both.

Even if I reject the moral route, or the religious route – if I try and look at this thing philosophically, I am caught failing.

Socrates talked of the keys to a worthy life, a healthy soul, and pinpointed the virtues we should aspire to: Courage, Moderation, Piety, Wisdom, and Justice. I am striking out on all counts. In the Socratic Virtues World Cup I am Luxembourg – I'm not trying very hard, and my shorts don't match my socks.

The sensible thing, for now, is to leave, and go to work. Dale is sleeping deeply, and rolling out of bed doesn't wake him.

I grab my stuff from the chair, pull on jeans – knickers can wait, and pull on my top. I close the door behind me, and as I walk down the hotel corridor and put my sunglasses on, I actually feel quite glamorous, until I notice my bouncing bra-less breasts twanging about in front of me, and just feel like a slut. I cross my arms as I walk through reception, and take care not to make eye contact with anybody, in case I see looks I won't like.

I step outside and it's a beautiful morning – the rain has cleared the air, and the sun is up, and a whole group of people who are used to functioning at this hour are going about their business – I feel like a gatecrasher. I'm not usually awake at this time, let alone out and about in central London. I decide to walk to the gym and get a shower, wash my hair, generally clean up. By the time I emerge it is nearly half-past eight, and I make my way into work. It still seems so early. I have left a message on both phones. To Dale:

'Sorry I didn't say goodbye. I need to think about things. I will call you tonight, if you are still here. Bye.'

To Charlie:

'Charlie I got caught up, and I drank too much. Hope you didn't wait up. I'll call you later – I need to talk to you about some stuff. Sorry. Bye.'

I didn't mean to apologize – it just came out. I impress myself with my honesty – no cover-ups; I have intentions of telling the truth.

I hang around outside the building and finish my cigarette. It's quiet, for Covent Garden, but it's lovely – like some kind of secret world. I resolve to get up earlier more often, and experience this again. I've only got a month left. I shudder slightly at the thought of it. I need to decide, today, what I'm going to do. I need to make some calls. This one needs advice, and expert opinion. This one needs to call in the girls.

I take the lift up to the sixth floor, and let myself in. I grab a coffee, and walk through the open plan desks to my office – not for much longer. I remember how great it felt to get it, this ten foot by fifteen foot room that was mine, on loan, at least, until I really fucked up, which somehow never happened. How strange it felt at first to be shut away from all the gossip, and how wonderful it felt to be able to shut the door and actually get things done. It's the least of my worries, but I'll be sad to leave it. It's my first office. I walk in and shut the door, only raising my eyes slightly as I walk past Phil's desk and spot two rulers taped together which are the most prominent thing on it, his new and improved work cricket bat.

I open up my email, and check the clock – five past nine – the hordes will start flooding in soon, and then my silence will be gone. I get to work fast. I grab my mobile and drag up Amy's number, and plug it in to my work phone.

'Hey,' she says, sounding like she's walking to work.

'Hey, it's me,' I say. 'Look, I need to ask you something, it's a bit complicated, hon, and I'll explain it later, but what would you say if I said I was thinking of going away with Charlie, for a while, travelling.' I wait as the phone goes quiet for a couple of seconds. 'Amy?'

'Yeah, I'm here. Bloody hell! Are we just speaking hypothetically?'

'Yep, hypothetically, what would you say?'

'I'd say don't.'

'Why?'

'Because he's an arsehole.'

'Okay, but what about if he'd changed, what about just the travelling thing? What do you think about me just going travelling?'

'You've never wanted to go before.'

'I know, but what if I want to go now?'

'Where, what, working or backpacking or what?'

'A bit of both.'

'I'd say don't.'

'Why?'

'Because you've just bought your flat and now you're going to go off travelling. I think you'll get sick of it in two months. And I don't trust Charlie. Have you spoken to Mum?'

'No.'

'I don't think she'll want you to go.'

'So, you think I shouldn't do it.'

'Not right now, maybe next year, maybe with a bit more thought. Where would you go?'

'I don't know, Australia, South America.'

'You see, you don't even know that. We need to talk about this properly.'

'Okay, I'll call you over the weekend – lunch on Sunday?'

'Sure, I'll call you on Sunday morning.'

'Is the baby alright?'

'Yeah, he's great.'

'I'll speak to you later, lots of love.'

'You too.'

'Bye.' I hang up, and write 'Yes' and 'No' on a piece of

paper, and put a mark under the 'No' section. I pull up Jake's mobile number and plug it in.

'Miss Ellis!' he answers.

'Hey, baby, are you okay?'

'Yes, but where the bloody hell have you been? I tried to call you at the weekend.'

'Yeah, I know, I'm sorry. I was away . . . with Charlie.'

'Oh how is he, all right?' Jake sounds dubious. They used to really get on, but now Jake thinks he's a shit; they barely even talk any more. Jake is now very much my friend again, not shared between Charlie and me.

'Yeah, he's fine, look, what if I said we were going to go away?'

'What, like on holiday?'

'Yeah, sort of. Well no, more like . . . travelling.'

Silence again, at the other end of the phone. But this time I don't say anything. If I prompt him he'll just say what he is going to say, but quicker. I hold my pen, poised, over the 'No' section of my piece of paper.

'Nix, he's a . . . he's a prick. I'm sorry, but you should get rid of him, he's turned into an absolute arsehole. A City boy.'

'No, you see, you're wrong. I mean he was, but he's changed back, or rather he's changed, he's woken up to himself.'

'When did this happen?'

'At the weekend.' I hear myself saying it, and I know I sound ridiculous.

'Listen to yourself! What did he do, buy you some flowers, spend the night?'

'Jake, don't be an arsehole, I'm serious.'

'Well, Nix, don't be an arsehole yourself! What are you thinking? Don't fall for it, believe me, I know men, I am one, and we can turn on the charm when we want, but Charlie's too far gone. He's done too much. Stop forgiving him.'

'I'm not forgiving him. I'm just forgiving myself.'

'Poetic but rubbish.' Jake has a frankness to him that cuts through small talk. But sometimes he is too adamant. He can be wrong, even if he won't admit it. However, I don't think this is one of those times. He thinks he knows me, which annoys me. He does know me, which annoys me even more.

'Okay, well, it was just an idea, I'll talk to you later.'

'Look, don't be pissed off with me, you asked me for my opinion. I really, really don't think you should go.'

'Okay, how are you by the way, still with, what's-her-name?'

'Rebecca? Nope, done, dusted, she was a freak. She wanted to go DIY shopping at the weekends, and she asked me to put up shelves. I'm a simple bloke, Nix, I can't play those kind of games after a month.'

'Fair enough, anybody new on the scene?'

'On a date tonight actually, found some number in my wallet yesterday, must have got it a couple of weeks ago. Sounds like a nice girl. Sarah.'

'Well, have fun, I'll speak to you soon.'

'Yeah, take care, Nix,' and we hang up.

Jake is a simple bloke, he likes his fun, hates commitment, but Monogamy is his middle name. He doesn't shag about on anybody, he will always finish whatever he's in first. It's almost admirable these days.

Another mark is made on my paper. I dial Jules. She comes on the phone, hushed voice, sounding sweet.

'Hello,' she whispers, and I can picture the smile on her face.

'Jules,' I whisper back, 'why are you whispering?'

'I'm about to go into a meeting with Princess Anne.'

'Oh shit, I'm sorry, I'll call back.'

'No, it's fine, I've got a couple of minutes, is anything wrong?'

I don't bother with the travelling bit, we don't have time,

and she'll want to talk about where, and not why. I just ask the question.

'Do you think I should stay with Charlie, if he told me he'd changed?'

'Oh Nix. I don't know, what do you think?'

'I don't know, that's why I'm asking you.'

'Oh Nix, I think you could be happier . . . I'm sorry.'

'No, don't apologize, it's fine. I wanted you to be honest.'

'Yes, but I haven't seen him for a while, I mean he might have changed. I haven't seen him since, well, that strip club.'

'Okay, thanks, hon. Look, haven't you met them all yet?'

'What, the Royals?' I can hear her smiling at the other end of the phone again, instead of the concerned look I know she will have been wearing for the rest of our conversation. 'Nearly! But Princess Anne's a good one, wish me luck!'

'Okay, speak to you soon.'

We whisper our goodbyes, and I picture Jules beaming at the princess, winning her over.

I punch in Naomi's work number.

'Naomi speaking,' she spurts out after only one ring.

'Can you talk?' I ask quickly, she flies about at work in the morning; something to do with 'her markets' that I don't understand. I hear the noise of her office in the background, it sounds like a football match.

'Yep, quickly.'

'Charlie's changed, shall we go travelling?'

'Changed how?' I feel her full attention snap to me and the phone.

'He's nicer.'

'Nicer how?' she asks. She needs the facts to make a decision.

'He's had a . . . a life-changing experience . . . he's changed his focus.' Every time I try and explain this to anybody, I sound like an idiot.

271

'Drugs?' she asks.

'No, not drugs, something else.'

'Nope.'

'Do you want to expand?'

'Well, I don't really have time, and we can discuss this later, but, briefly, he was your university boyfriend who's hung about too long, and I know the stuff that he gets up to, as I am sure you do too, and a man who does that cannot really care about you, and you are being too nice, and I work with lots of nice men if you are worried about being on your own.'

'Nim, if you work with so many nice men why aren't you going out with them, plus, you don't work with nice men, you work with bastards!'

'I know, forget that bit. But Charlie is one of them.'

'I get it.'

'No, I mean, he really is, you really do deserve better.'

'Stop, I get it. I'll speak to you later.'

'Okay, bye.'

I put a mark on my piece of paper again. My 'Yes' column is looking lonely, with just my line on it. I know I should call Mum, but I don't feel brave enough for that conversation yet. She'll be upset if I even mention it. She likes to have her family close to her, and she'll tell Dad, and he'll just worry about guns, and dangerous animals, and getting mugged in a foreign country. I'll talk to them when I've decided what to do. Everybody has told me not to do it – they all know me better than I know me. I try and convince myself that I can be young and carefree and not give a damn about hot running water or electricity, but they remind me that these things are important to me. Jake actually laughs at the idea of me and a backpack, which is unfair, I think.

So I can at least have one more tick in the yes box, I decide to call my little sister. She is still at university, not quite twenty-one, and the most irresponsible person I know. She would tell me to go for sure. I check my watch, it's half past ten. I've been doing this for an hour and a half. I know that I am going to wake her up – she is at college, she keeps a whole other body clock. If I wanted to call her at three in the morning, I'd catch her wide awake, but any time before noon is pushing it. Her phone rings five times, and I decide to wait for the answerphone. But then a boy answers, sleepily.

'Hello?' I am slightly confused, and I hear Charlotte, my little sister, mumbling in the background, and then a sharp 'give me that!' and she comes on the phone.

'Hello?' She, too, is half-asleep.

'Little one, it's me,' – we have called her that since she was a baby; I don't know why, it's more of a mouthful than Charlotte, her actual name, but it has stuck.

'Oh hi, I'm asleep.' I hear her fighting the battle between speaking to me, and going back to sleep straight away.

'Who answered your phone?' I ask, coming over all big sister – I still can't resolve the issue I have with my baby sister having sex, and especially casual sex.

'Oh that's Jon, my gay friend.'

'Oh, right.' And I believe her, partly because she wouldn't bother to lie to me about anything; it would require too much effort on her part, and partly because it makes me feel better.

'Can I call you later? I was up writing an essay until five.'

'No, honey, just talk to me quickly and I'll put a hundred quid in your bank account this afternoon.' And lo, I have her attention.

'What can I do for you,' she says, the pound signs in her eyes holding them open like matchsticks.

'Little one, what if I said I was going away for a while – travelling.'

'On your own?' she asks, confused.

'Not exactly, with Charlie.'

I have no idea what she thinks of him, we don't really talk about things like that. She is my little sister, and I give her money, and hugs, and expensive presents at Christmas. I love her huge amounts, even when she is being a thoughtless little bastard, but I would never really ask her opinion on something like this. I think maybe this is why we are both a bit bewildered by this conversation.

'Are you still with him? I thought you broke up,' she says.

'Why would you think that, I never told you that,' I say, a little defensively.

'No, I just thought you didn't talk about him any more, I haven't seen him for ages.'

'Well, we're still together, but we're thinking of going travelling – what do you think about that?'

'Do Mum and Dad know?' I get the same response from both my sisters, we are all conditioned to think first of what our parents will say. In a way, we are all still kids, asking for permission for everything. It's not that we wouldn't get it, we invariably would, we are just always slightly nervous about asking.

'No, well, I haven't decided to do it yet, and I don't want to worry them. But what do you think? It would be great, wouldn't it?' I am putting the words into her mouth, making it easier for her just to repeat them back to me.

'I suppose.' She doesn't sound so sure. Why does everybody but me think this is a bad idea!

'What? Charlotte, what?'

'It's just, you've just bought your flat. And Amy said you and Charlie weren't getting on that well . . .'

'When did she say that?' I snap.

'I spoke to her at the weekend.'

I feel jealous – I haven't spoken to Charlotte enough, and Amy has a baby and still finds time to call her, and gets a conversation out of her without having to give her any money.

'Oh right, so you don't think it's a good idea then.'

'I don't know, do you want to go? What about work?'

'What about work? I don't have to stay in the same job for the rest of my life!' Why is she asking all these mature questions – why is she being the reasonable one? Why do I suddenly feel like the twenty-year-old? I sense her dozing off at the other end of the phone as I go quiet, and decide to hang up.

'Hon, I'll put that money in this afternoon, okay?'

'Oh thanks,' and then to somebody in the background, 'make me a blackcurrant?'

'Hon, I'll talk to you at the weekend,' I say.

'Okay, love you,' she says, and I can sense that she's falling asleep as she hangs up.

I sit, with my pen in my hand, and then screw up the piece of paper without putting Charlotte's mark under the 'No' section. What am I doing?

Phil bursts into the office.

'Shit, sorry, I didn't think you were in yet!' he exclaims.

'Why would I not be in? It's nearly eleven o'clock!'

He averts his eyes, rather than replying that that wouldn't be so bizarre.

'I've been in since eight-thirty actually,' I say, and shuffle some papers on my desk. Obviously I've been working all this time, and not making personal phone calls.

'Bloody hell.' He is mildly impressed.

'Where did you get to last night – you didn't even turn up!' I realize he is pissed off with me. He doesn't like to be left alone at work things, he feels out of his depth, or fraudulent, embarrassed that he is not important enough to be wined and dined, and he is wasting a client's time, a client who is too nice to say so.

'I got caught up, I'm sorry about that. Was it okay?'

'Yeah, it was alright. Well no, it was bloody boring actually.' He shrugs, and turns to leave.

'Did you want something?' I ask, and he turns around, still a bit pissed off.

'No, I was just going to turn the cricket on – on your TV – but don't worry.'

'No, Phil, stick it on, it's fine. It's not like it's noisy.'

'Cheers,' and he isn't pissed off with me any more. Mental note: set up Phil and my little sister before going anywhere. They have a depth of feeling and attention span only otherwise found in goldfish. They are cheerfully shallow. Of course, if it worked out, and they made a relationship of it, they'd end up as fucked up as me. Mental note: do not set up Phil and my little sister.

Phil fiddles with the TV, trying to find the right station, and I pick up the remote and try and help him, but nothing happens.

He turns and looks at me.

'That's for the stereo.'

I pick up the three other remote controls and try and work out which is which.

'Do you want to just give them to me?' he asks with a not so patient smile.

'It's fine,' I say, and hit some buttons. The screen goes black, and a DVD starts to play.

'Can I just have them?' His voice raises slightly.

'No! I can do it!' I hit another button, and the TV goes off.

'Oh, just take them.' I push them in his direction. Phil presses a button and instantly the cricket comes on. Sod this office. Sod technology. I need to get back to basics.

Starting Again, Part Three

I spend the rest of the day actually working, which distracts me at least. Every time I feel the impulse to dwell on things, and every time one or the other creeps into my head, I answer an email, or pick up the phone to a writer. The day goes, if not quickly, then productively.

I call the scriptwriter in, close the door to my office, and nail *Evil Ghost 2: The Return*. We decide that our practically naked heroine lives in a old house, a house that was once the scene of a terrible fire, in which perished Tony's OAP. Thus whenever she appears, she is surrounded by the smoke of the fire, and she coughs a lot, because of the smoke inhalation. Our hero is going to be the model-cum-actor who has just moved in downstairs, who recently lost his girlfriend, who he thought was the love of his life, to a terrible bush fire in Australia. He will have flaming flashbacks. His dead girlfriend will be seen perishing beneath a particularly burning bush, and she will be very plain, so that we know that he really did love her. However, this will allow people to understand why he can fall so quickly for our naked model, who is much prettier. The old woman will stalk the halls at night, killing off any pets in the building first, which alerts our hero and heroine to the otherworldly presence. That and the smoke in the hallways just after she's gone. If we have the money we might use an effect in post-production where fire creeps up the walls of any room she has just been in. Then she will burn all the clothes of our heroine who can then be practically naked for the rest of the film. When she finally makes herself known she will be surrounded by the smoke, but also the ghosts of all the pets she has killed, and she will be able to talk to them, like a kind of arsonist Doctor Do-Little. She will appear at breakfast time, after our heroic couple have spent their first night together, and they can both be eating supermarket Bran Flakes of some kind, which helps them keep their looks and youthful figures. Finally, after much running about, our hero will put our old woman out with a bucket of water, the only thing she cannot overcome. It is a complete rewrite, but we are both pleased with it. It takes the whole afternoon.

I check my watch as I see the sun setting outside my office. It is quarter to eight. I realize that I don't know where to go tonight, and I don't know who with. I have spent all day trying so hard to ignore the problem, ignore both of the men in my life, that it only dawns on me now that they have both been ignoring me. Neither one of them has called me, or left a message, or tried to talk to me about last night. Where are they both? A nasty daydream shoots through my head that Dale might have done something rash, and tracked down Charlie, and told him everything, although it would save me doing it. No, that would be a bad thing. An even nastier thought creeps into my head – what if Dale has gone? What if he has had enough of my indecision and got a flight back to the States?

I look at my monitor – my in-box is clear, for the first time in weeks. All my calls have been made, my work here is done. I should go now. But where? I pick up my mobile, and go with my first impulse. I phone Charlie.

'Hey you,' he says as he picks up the phone. The mobile phone has erased any notion of a surprise call. You cannot answer if you don't want to speak to somebody, because their name comes up. Or you can let the answerphone take it safe in the knowledge that that person can wait until later. Or you can pick up, if it's somebody you don't mind talking to. At least Charlie has picked up.

'Sorry about last night,' I say instantly. I still feel the need to apologize, even though I've decided, now, in a moment, what I'm going to do.

'It's fine – are you hungover?' he asks, concerned.

'No, I'm okay.'

'Are you – you sound strange,' Charlie says, and I realize I am still thinking, even now, if my decision is the right one. All these doubts.

'I'm okay – are you at home?'

'No, actually, I'm in a cab, I'll be there in about ten minutes. Gorgeous day, huh?'

'Yeah, it's been lovely. Can I come over?'

'Of course.'

'Shall I bring anything – do you have food?'

'Is Thai all right? I'll do a curry.'

'Great, I'll see you soon.'

'Bye.'

'Bye.'

As I leave work, I realize I am still in the clothes he saw me in yesterday. I dash into the nearest shop, and pick up a white cotton summer dress. Then I put it down and pick up the same thing in black. I pick up the white one again, and head to the till with them both. I go back to work and change, dumping my jeans and T-shirt in a bag under my desk.

On the tube, I am overwhelmed with the need to have it all sorted out already, to have had all the necessary conversations, and be resolved with the outcome. The kind of

279

nervousness that makes you want to scream and bury your head under a pillow grips me, and then subsides, and I realize I am fine, and strong, and I can cope with all of this.

Charlie opens the door to me – I don't know why I don't use my key, it just feels better not to.

'Did somebody die?' he asks me, looking at my dress.

I smile, and kiss him hello lightly on the side of his mouth, and dump my bags on the sofa, heading straight for the kitchen.

'Can I have a drink?' I ask him as I pour myself a large whisky.

'Yeah . . . go ahead.'

'Do you want one?' I take a massive gulp that shudders through my system.

'No, I've got a water, thanks.' He looks at me, confused. I don't look back.

I head towards the balcony. Charlie has the doors wide open.

'How was work?' I ask him.

'Good, great. They were great about the whole police thing.' He is chopping onions and smashing garlic and coconut on a board in the kitchen. He looks really relaxed, like a young gorgeous celebrity chef, with his sleeves rolled up, and a camera smile.

I don't answer, just stand by the door, and let the sun warm me up, and kill the shivers down my spine.

'They confirmed my leaving date – I can go at the beginning of next month.' Still I don't say anything.

'Nix, are you okay?' he asks, and I hear the knife stop its chopping behind me.

I turn and face him, and my eyes adjust to the light inside of the flat.

'Yes, honestly, I'm just tired. Is dinner nearly ready?'

'Fifteen minutes – put your feet up.' He goes back to his

chopping. I take a deep breath, and wander out on to the balcony. Brave and strong.

'Can you just watch these for a second?' he shouts out from the kitchen, and I stick my head around the door.

'I want to get changed, it's nearly done.'

'Sure,' I say, and trip over the doorstep into the living room.

'Easy,' he laughs, and gives me a sideways glance over his shoulder as he goes into the bedroom, which I ignore. The whisky has gone to my head.

I hear the shower come on, and Charlie makes appreciative noises as he jumps under it.

I prod at the simmering mush in the wok, and light a cigarette.

'I feel great,' he calls from the shower.

My head hears 'good for you' in a different tone to the 'Good for you' that comes out of my mouth. Charlie has somehow pole-vaulted onto some higher plain – some relaxed, confident sure of itself mindset. I am a bag of nerves.

I stir the rice, which is sticking slightly to the bottom of the pan.

'Charlie, I think this is ready,' I shout, and then laugh at the strength of my own voice as Charlie appears from around the door, dressed only in a towel around his waist.

'Sorry, this is almost done. Shall I dish up?'

'Sure, if you don't mind.' He pads over and drapes a hand around my shoulder and kisses my forehead.

'Get dressed, you're all wet,' I say, and shrug him off, scared that he'll tell me to just let it burn and pull me with him.

He pads back into the bedroom and I hear him pulling on his jeans as I lump the curry onto two plates. I'm not hungry in the slightest. I stuff the bottle of whisky under my arm, and take the plates with me outside.

Charlie comes after me with the cutlery, dressed like an

advert for Ralph Lauren, all starched and clean and crisp in a white polo shirt.

We sit on opposite sides of the table, and Charlie takes a couple of mouthfuls before realizing I'm not eating.

'Aren't you hungry?' he asks me, surprised.

'Yeah, no, I mean, I need to tell you something.'

'What?' he asks, and puts another forkful into his mouth.

'Charlie, I don't think I'm going to come away with you.'

'What?' He puts his fork down, and looks at me seriously.

'I don't think I . . . want to. But I think you should go.' I look at him apologetically, and even pull back a little, not entirely sure what his response will be.

'Why not – I mean, what's made you change your mind?' Charlie talks evenly, like an adult, a reasonable man. I feel like a lying kid.

'I don't think it's the right time for me to go running off, and I know I said I'd go with you, and I'm sorry. But I just . . . I don't think I want to go. I'm really sorry.' I look down at my plate, and push some onto my fork in case Charlie decides to throw it at me. But I am kidding myself – he's not going to throw anything. He's not angry, he's hurt. My conscience wants him to be angry, but he isn't going to react like that.

'What about your work? Will they let you take your resignation back?' he asks me quietly.

'I'm . . . still going to leave work, Charlie.'

'What?'

'I'm still going to leave work, I'm just not going to go travelling . . . with you.'

'You're still going to . . . I don't understand . . . you're . . . this is you finishing it, isn't it?'

'Yes, I'm sorry. I don't think we are . . . ready to go travelling.'

'But last week, in Devon, you said you wanted to go, you gave your notice in at the same time! You had no intention of

282

coming with me?' I feel like I have broken his heart, but that can't be true. Last week his heart wouldn't have been broken, and feelings can't change that much in a week.

I don't say anything, just look down at my plate, and wait for him to talk at me. He pushes himself back from the table, and walks over to the railings, placing both hands firmly on them, and we both wait in silence.

Finally, he speaks.

'Nix, is this about the thing, with the girl? It's madness – the police have cleared me, everybody's cleared me, except you!' His voice gets louder, and I can sense that I have broken through his whale noises and rainforest sounds veneer of calm.

'It's not about that! But, it kind of is as well. Charlie. Last week I would never have doubted that you did it; I would have assumed you were guilty. How can you be that different, change that much in a week? And even if you have changed, even if it's only a bit, I can't risk my life on it! Charlie, people don't change overnight – they don't put on a dress and find the Lord. It takes years. Last week, I was going to tell you it was over, and now . . . now I am. We just put it on hold for a while.'

'This is fucking insane.' Charlie storms towards the table and I flinch as he picks up his plate, but then strides through the doors and into the kitchen. After a couple of minutes to let him calm down, I follow him in. He is standing by the sink. I put the bottle of whisky down in front of him, and pour myself a glass.

'Do you want one now?' I ask him.

'Don't flatter yourself,' he says, and turns away.

'Charlie, I'm really sorry, but we were just kidding ourselves, really, weren't we? You know that . . .'

'Where are you going to go?' he asks, ignoring my pleas for him to agree with me.

'I don't know . . . I thought I might go somewhere a bit more permanently, live somewhere for a while.'

'Like where, Australia? You can go to Australia, just not with me?' His voice is filled with hurt and accusation.

'No, probably not, more like . . . I don't know . . . more like America or somewhere.' I don't need to tell him everything, but I can still be honest.

'America? We've already been there, hell, we've lived there!'

'Well, I wouldn't go back to the same place obviously, I could go to New York, or Las Vegas . . . I don't know where exactly yet, I just fancy going back.'

'When will you go?' He stabs at me with questions.

'In a couple of months, I suppose, when I've got everything sorted. I don't know how long it takes to get a working visa, and all the other stuff. I might ask work if I can get a transfer – there's bound to be something going out there. How about you? Will you still go?'

'Yeah, in a couple of weeks, I suppose. It doesn't make any sense not to. I'll be fine.' Charlie hastily picks up his plate and scrapes the contents into the bin, and then throws it into the sink.

'I should go,' I say quietly.

'Yes, you should.' He has turned his back to me, and is barely audible.

I grab my bag and head for the door.

I close it behind me, and hear a crash of plates and pans behind me, inside the flat, Charlie letting me know how he really feels.

Almost Romantic

On the tube I am in two minds – to call Dale or not to call Dale. To wait until tomorrow, when I'm feeling less emotional, needing less to be hugged and consoled, or to bite the bullet and grab the bull by the horns. I get off the tube at Covent Garden, almost by accident, thinking I am going to work. I decide to go and have a coffee, sober up completely, and then make a decision.

The big question, ladies and gentlemen, is 'do I want him to go?'

Charlie will be fine, or maybe he won't. I know I have let him down hard, but that whole weird spell was short lived, a reaction to something terrible as opposed to a sustainable reality – even Charlie couldn't have kept it up for much longer. He'll survive, he'll pull through, we weren't going to work out.

But Dale? Dale has crash landed into my life at the most confusing point for years, at a time when Charlie is making his exit, I'm getting bored with my job, and I can clearly see thirty just over the horizon. Is the promise of Dale, and a little unexpected excitement and an unfamiliar continent, the real reason I could go to him now? Or is it because I actually want to see, as he does, how we could be together, whether we could fit? He is unlike any man I have ever known, and now is the time for something new and brave. If I am going to take steps to change my life, why not take massive ones? Why not step all the way across the ocean?

I sip a coffee in a coffee shop, I don't even know which one; they all blend into each other these days. The high street is like one giant cappuccino, broken up occasionally by a clothes shop. You can't swing a cat for hitting a low-fat sugar sachet. But they are good places to think. You rarely see couples in there, or anybody being social – it would never occur to me to arrange to meet somebody in one of them, they all seem so transient. They are 'in and out' venues, not a place to stop and chat – they have no atmosphere. But because of that, the people who do end up there seem alone, by accident. They always seem to be waiting for somebody, or thinking about somebody, or missing someone. Actually, they really just look like losers. As do I, now, sitting in this coffee shop, alone. I try and down my coffee so I can leave, and end up spilling half of it down my dress. I swear loudly, inviting stares from all the other people sitting on their own around me, thanking God they are not as conspicuous as I have just made myself. I can't go and see Dale now, even if I wanted to, I am soaked from the bra to the waist. I remember the dress back at the office, grab a handful of napkins, and dash back to work. I change quickly, and head out again. Checking my watch, I see it is a quarter past ten. I walk towards Dale's hotel, convincing myself I can turn back or get on a tube any time I like. I can just walk and think.

The streets are packed with people holding glasses, spilling out of pubs and spilling their drinks, pissed on the summer sun and the warm night air. I stop and start along the crowded streets, full of tourists walking around in ill-fitting shorts that they've had to buy in Marks and Spencer's, because they had been reliably informed it wouldn't be hot in London, and all they'd packed were sweaters and jeans. And tourists somehow need to wear shorts. And they need to carry cameras, and they need to talk very loudly to each other on the tube. Actually, they mainly just seem to need to annoy the shit out of me.

I linger outside the hotel for a while, and have a cigarette, and think. What is it exactly that I want to say, where exactly am I going with this? Shit, I am thinking way too much, and this is a night for impulses, and I just need to follow those impulses, go in there, and say whatever it is that springs to mind, even if it's just 'have a good flight'. Although it won't be that, I already know it won't be that.

My phone starts to ring as I get near the steps of the hotel and I drag it out of my bag quickly – it is Charlie. I want to turn it off, but I can't. I deserve whatever he wants to say to me, and I have to take whatever he wants to throw my way – he is the one hurting right now, and I am the one on the way to a new beginning.

'Hey, are you okay?' I ask him as I answer the phone.

'Jesus Christ, I'm fine! Stop asking me how I am! You really think a lot of yourself, don't you – do you know how patronizing you sound? You haven't ended my world, you know!'

I didn't expect any of that. I thought maybe he'd be tearful, but he's skipped that bit, and gone straight for the anger.

'I'm sorry, I was just trying to be . . . nice, or something.'

'Where are you?' Charlie demands, and I suddenly get indignant. I don't have to be a doormat to his feelings, I don't have to be his sounding board. He doesn't get to order me around.

'I'm out.'

'Out where?' he slurs. Obviously he has hit the whisky after all.

'Just out. On my own. Thinking.'

'I'm really sorry, I didn't mean to shout at you. I just, I need to speak to you. You can't just say that, and then walk off, and not give me a chance to talk to you.'

'Charlie, we can talk, just not tonight, it's not the time.'

'When then? Tomorrow? Will you call me?'

'Maybe tomorrow, maybe next week. We should have a bit of time to think.'

'Will you call me? If I don't call you, will you call me?'

'Yes, of course, I'm not cutting you off completely, Charlie, I'm just saying we should, you know, not be a couple any more. I'll speak to you soon.'

'Are you going home now?'

'Soon.'

'Why, where the fuck are you?' Charlie's anger boils over again.

'I'm nowhere, just walking, Charlie, please, for God's sake.'

'Are you with somebody else?' The question I've been waiting for finally comes, and even though I've been expecting it, it still hits with the force of a bullet at close range. This is the one I don't want to answer.

'Well, Nix, is there somebody else? For fuck's sake, there is, isn't there!'

'No, no there isn't! Please, just go, I'll call you soon.' I hang up, and turn off my phone, flustered and red, and I feel like my heart is getting a little more bruised with every word I say to him and each step I take towards the hotel reception. But I go in anyway.

I wait at reception while they phone upstairs, but it just rings. Dale isn't in. But he hasn't checked out. He is here, in London somewhere, I just don't know where. I want to grab a car, and circle the town, hail a cab and get him to kerb crawl every short man in town, until we find him. But these are not the thoughts of a reasonable person. A reasonable

288

person would just wait in the bar with one eye on the door. So that is what I will do.

I sip my drink, arrange my hair, check myself in my compact, and just sit back and think. I haven't been so very brave. I have managed to tell Charlie it's over, but it's not like I'm forging some brave new world on my own. I haven't conquered any fears, nothing really changes. I've bounced from one man to another, like I need them to lead me to my life, as opposed to going there myself, or letting some outside force take me there. When I was young, I used to think by seventeen I'll be this, by twenty-one I'll be this. Now I'm thinking about thirty, just around the corner, it will be here before I know it, and then forty. It's a challenge to meet it, to grow up and face it. I have just bought a flat, my first flat. But I'm not ready for kids, I'm not ready for marriage. I'm not even ready to stay in the same job for the next month. I have no concept of commitment; the only thing that appeals to me is running off into the great blue yonder and wasting another couple of years, not making any major decisions if I can help it.

I feel my head nod, and realize I am falling asleep, and have not been watching the door at all. I get up and stretch my legs and yawn. Maybe I should just go home – I check my mobile – it's half past twelve. I wander out to reception, and they've turned down some of the lights. I feel déjà vu; here again, at the wrong side of midnight. I head to reception, trying not to stagger with sleep, and ask the new people who have started working since I sat down to phone Dale's number. They check his box. The guy behind the desk comes back to me, looking slightly embarrassed, and practically whispers, 'I'm afraid he's checked out, Miss.'

'What? He can't have, check again.' I am sure it is a mistake and I only feel slightly worried, waiting for it to be resolved.

'No, Mr Curse. He checked out about half an hour ago.'

289

'But how can he have? I've been here, I didn't see him.' I look around, and point at the bar, and the door, and the stairs, not really knowing what I'm proving.

'I'm sorry about that.' He looks mortified.

I am mortified. How has Dale crept past me, and out again, without my even realizing? Without seeing me sitting there, waiting for him. Stupidly, I hadn't left a message for him; I thought I would see him. I turn back to the desk clerk, and I am truly scared – I don't have a number, or an address, I can't write to him in two weeks and ask if it's all right if I come and stay. If he goes, he really goes. I can't decide what I want to do if he's not here, it doesn't work like that – he needs to be here to hear what I decide. He needs to be here.

'Do you know where he went?' I sound like an idiot just saying it.

'He was heading to the airport – he's the only person that's checked out since I've been on.'

'Do you know what airport?' I can't believe I am asking these questions.

'Well, no, but Heathrow, I guess, that's where the transatlantic flights go from mostly. But I don't know for sure.' He looks apologetic.

'No, you're right. Of course it's Heathrow, thanks,' and I am off and running. I don't know where. I skid to a stop at the hotel entrance, and spin around to find the concierge, who must have got him a cab. How could he just leave, without saying goodbye?

I spot the concierge, who is down the steps by the tree with all the sparkling lights hanging from it – I've often thought how pretty it is, driving past, but not now.

'Excuse me, hello!' I shout and bound towards him.

'Yes, madam.' He is old and wise-looking; he will help me.

'Have you called a cab for an American guy, a short

290

American guy, in the last half an hour? He was staying here, going to the airport.'

'No, madam, I can't say I have.' Not the answer I expected again.

I spin on the spot; where now? I feel tears of frustration welling up in my eyes.

'I am looking after his bags though.' I turn and face the concierge again. 'Sorry?'

'I'm looking after his bags. He said he'll need a cab a bit later. He's just gone for a stroll, I believe. His bags are in my holding room. If it's the same man.' He smiles at me in a gentle way, and I know that he is a very good man.

'Do you know which way he went?' I ask.

'Well, he went towards the park, but I don't suggest you go running off in that direction at this time of night, madam. Why don't you just wait in the bar?'

'Nope, been there, done that, fucked it up. Oh sorry.' I apologize for swearing, he could be somebody's granddad.

'That way?' I ask, backing away from him and pointing over my shoulder in the direction I'm headed.

'Well yes, but I strongly suggest you just come back in and wait, it's not safe to go running off.' But I barely hear his last words, I am skidding down the road. There are loads of people about, I don't know why he thinks it's not safe – it's busier now than at midday.

I get to the entrance of the park and stop suddenly – it is very dark inside. I actually don't want to go in on my own. I've always been a little afraid of the dark. But in all honesty it's not that. I'm not scared of the dark, I'm scared of being alone in the dark. I'm scared of being on my own.

I take a couple of steps forward, but I really, really don't want to go in there. I have a flash of inspiration – like a dick, I have ignored my mobile phone, and I whip it out of my bag. It is almost out of battery, but it should last a phone call. I press

291

'call' and wait for it to connect, jumping up and down with all this surplus nervous energy that has found its way into my system. It clicks through and . . . starts to ring. And instantly I can hear a phone ringing. I hear Dale saying hello down the phone line, but I can hear him saying it as well, close to me, in real life.

'Hold on,' I yell down the phone, and take a couple of quick steps into the dark, thinking, if I do this fast, it will be fine. And there he is, sitting on a bench just inside the park, with his silly shaved head, not looking like himself. A wave of relief sweeps me, and then fear again – what do I even want to say?

I walk over to the bench, and sit down next to him, and he keeps looking at the grass in front of him, without looking up at me, and I am cold.

I sit shivering next to him for a minute.

'I thought you'd gone, without saying goodbye.'

'Nope,' is all he says.

'I'm glad I caught you before you left.' I wait for him to ask me why, but he just sits there, staring at the grass.

I take a deep breath. I realize I haven't spoken to him since I ran out on him this morning. It's nearly one o'clock in the morning now. I think about where we were this time twenty-four hours ago.

'I spoke to Charlie. I'm not going travelling.' Still nothing.

'I told him it's over.'

'Did you tell him about last night?' he asks, the first words he's said to me, in his familiar American drawl.

'Well, no, I didn't think there was any need to go into that, I was telling him it was over, that was enough, I think.'

'Right.' He still won't look at me.

'Dale, are you okay?' I can't believe he is showing no reaction whatsoever – no emotion at all.

'Dale?' I ask again.

'Did he ask you if there was anybody else?' he asks.

'No, no, he didn't ask,' I say, and gulp.

We sit there for a couple of minutes, and I shiver again. He takes off his coat, and hands it to me. I slip it on, and snuggle into his borrowed warmth, and the smell of it.

'I have to go soon,' he says quietly.

'That's the thing,' I say, and turn myself to look at him. He still looks at the ground, but speaks quickly.

'I am going. I'm not staying,' he says, and I am thrown.

'Okay, well, I just thought we could talk about the possibility of, well, if you won't stay, maybe I could come and see you . . . or something.' I feel like a useless kid. All my courage has gone out of the window. He is non-responsive.

'Why would you do that?' he asks, and looks up finally. I can really see his eyes, feel them searching for the right answer from me.

'Because, I'd like to see you . . . or spend more time with you . . . it would just be a shame if that was it.' I trail off.

'What, like last night? Do you want to come and see me, sleep with me, meet my kids, say hi to Joleen?' He is being cold, and I don't know why. Somehow I have hurt him all over again.

'Why are you being like this? Don't you think it would be nice to . . . keep in touch?'

'I don't know that it would. You don't know what you want. I came here, I thought I'd say hello, and look what's happened! You've split up with Charlie – you shouldn't have done that!'

'I didn't do it for you! I did it because I was always going to do it! I did it because we were running on empty, and you being here, well, it just made me realize that I didn't have to be with him because I felt sorry for him, or felt guilty about something, and besides you didn't just come to say hello, you came with every intention of . . .' He looks at me too deeply, and I look away.

'Well, for whatever reason, Dale. I just think that we get on, you know? Maybe we could just see what happens.'

He stands up, and takes a couple of steps forward.

'I have to go.'

'No, no, you can't just go like this!' I shout and jump to my feet.

'Why not? Because you aren't in control, because someone is rejecting you for once? This is how it feels! I'm going.'

He takes a couple of steps away from me, and I run towards him, but stop myself short before actually touching him. He senses me behind him and turns around.

'What, Nicola? Are you going to tell me that you love me? How desperate are you going to get here, to get the upper hand?'

'What? No, well, I wouldn't say I loved you, but . . . I feel fondly for you.' I sound pathetic.

'Fondly? You are joking.' He turns and walks away again.

'Why are you being so cold – I don't understand what I've done wrong? I was in a difficult situation!'

'Well, so was I – I came here and sought you out, and put myself out on a fucking limb for you, and you weren't even going to give me the right phone number, for Christ's sake, but then Charlie fucked up and you needed a shoulder to cry on, and you let me coerce you into bed, like you had no say in the matter, and were doing me a favour – I felt like we were back at college again! And then you sneak off, and I spend a day waiting around for you to call, thinking, I won't call her, she'll turn up. And now, now that I've made up my mind, you want me to change all my plans for you! Tell me, if I told you I'd stay would you want me to go? Is it just somebody leaving YOU that you can't take? Because if that is it, you are pathetic.' He looks at me icily, and I want

294

to shout something at him, shout that he's being unfair, he isn't even trying to see it from my perspective, but I'm scared that if I open my mouth I'll cry.

'Well?' he says, and takes a step towards me, and looks into my eyes.

He takes my face in his hands, and wipes away a tear that rolls slowly down one side of my cheek, and then says softly,

'Do you think that you are so fucking irresistible that no one, especially not me, could walk away?'

I shake him off and take a step back, and start to cry. I rip his coat off and throw it on the ground in front of me. He practically chuckles at my immaturity, and picks it up, brushing it down, and throws it over his arm.

'Oh stop fucking crying, you'll be over this in a week.' And he turns to walk away.

'You know what?' I yell after him, through my tears my words sound distorted, and I sound young, eighteen again.

'You know what!' as he carries on walking away.

'I'm glad I did it. I'm glad I got rid of it! It could have turned out like you!'

As soon as I say the words, I regret them, and I put my hand over my mouth to stop myself saying anything else. The worst things are said in the heat of the moment, horrible things that you don't for a second believe, you just want to hurt somebody as much as they have hurt you, make them feel as bad as you are feeling. But there are some things that should never be said, that are too bad to take back.

Dale turns and looks at me, and takes a few steps forwards. I am suddenly very aware of where I am – in a park, in London, at one o'clock in the morning with a man I have just told I killed his baby. I am scared, and I look around quickly to see if I can spot anybody else, but we are alone. The only light is from the street-lamps behind Dale, which he is blocking out with a frame that seems to have grown bigger in the last few minutes.

'What did you say?' he asks me quietly.

I stand still, and hope he will just walk off.

'Is that it? Is that what this has all been about? Did you get . . . were you pregnant?'

'No, I didn't mean that,' I say quickly, and try and make myself seem bigger.

'Nicola, did I get you pregnant, all those years ago?' Dale has a strange look on his face, almost a smile. My eyes widen at the situation I am in. I am actually starting to fear for . . .

'No, Jesus, just go if you're going. I'm not keeping you. I'm sorry, I'm sorry if you had a shit time in London, and I'm sorry if I wasn't the princess you thought I'd be. Please, Dale, just go. Don't say anything else.' I hug myself tightly, try and protect myself from his eyes, which are stabbing into me.

'Did I get you pregnant?' he asks again and takes two more steps towards me, within striking distance now. I shake my head and start to cry, and hope he will just leave.

Dale leans in towards me, and I feel my body tense up, but I am rooted to the spot. He whispers in my ear,

'Would have been a lucky kid, if it had its mother's looks and its daddy's brains. But the other way around could have been terrible.' He lingers for a second, and I can feel his breath on my face. And then he does something unexpected; he kisses me softly on the cheek, a cheek wet with tears.

'See ya,' he whispers, and turns and walks away. I look up after a minute, and see him over the road, climbing into a taxi. I think he looks towards me, but I'm not sure. The door closes, and the driver pulls off. The cab turns around, and drives towards me. I walk towards the road, and wait on the pavement on the other side of the road. The cabbie waits for a motorbike to pass, and then pulls off, past me. I look into the darkness, but I can't see his face. How could he just brush it aside like that, how could he not be affected by something like that, something huge? How could he leave, after what I'd just told him?

I walk back towards the hotel – I need to get a cab, I need to go home – and then my mobile starts to ring. I reach for it in my bag, and see Charlie's name flash up on the screen, and my battery bleeps at me to be charged.

'Hello?'

'Nicola, why are you still up? Where are you? Have you been crying? What's going on, are you alright?'

'Yeah, honestly I'm fine,' and I fight off the tears from starting all over again.

'Where are you?'

'In the middle of town.'

'Get in a cab, and come here now.'

'Charlie, how can I? I can't, not after tonight.'

'Yes you can – get in a cab, come here now. You were there for me, I'm going to do the same. I've got money, just get a cab. And not a dodgy one either, a black cab.'

'I can't.' My phone goes dead. I walk over to the concierge.

'Are you okay, Miss, you aren't hurt, are you?' He notices my tears.

'No, I'm okay, can I get a cab please?'

The concierge whistles for a cab, and one pulls out from a street down the road.

'Thank you,' I say, and get in.

'Ealing please,' I tell the cabbie, and sit back in the dark. It's time to go home.

Perspective

The weekend drifts and drags by; every time I turn on my phone there is another message from Charlie, angry or upset or apologetic. I don't call. It wouldn't do him any good at all. My moods fly about like juggling balls, and my thoughts range from getting on the next plane to the States, to going round to Charlie's, to just sleeping all day every day for the next year. The fact that I now have three weeks before I leave my job and I have done nothing about travelling, or finding myself another job, panics me slightly, but then I just push the thought away, and sleep again. I need to pull myself together. I need to see my friends, who all seem to sense that something is wrong, and are leaving messages constantly as well. By Sunday night, I know that the right thing to do is get up tomorrow – no more sleeping all day! – and go to work, and log onto the internet, and look for cheap holidays. I also need to phone up Jake and tell him he can rent the spare room in my flat for the next few months if he wants, if he doesn't mind me coming and going. That way I have the mortgage covered, and I can use my savings just to go away, come back, decide what I want to do. As exciting as the prospect of this should be, breaking the routine, the world is my oyster and all that, I am not remotely excited. It feels like a chore just to make a decision. I am distinctly . . . numb. The problem is, I can't work out who it is I'm missing, Charlie or Dale. I convince myself it can't be Charlie, given that I have ended it with him, and I know I shouldn't go back, and I am practically convinced that he hasn't really changed, and he can't really love me like he says he does. But how can it be Dale? He was only here for a week.

I get into work early with washed and dried hair and a face full of make-up, and make quick phone calls to everybody, including Amy, who was worried as I had not phoned yesterday and had lunch as agreed. I fill up my diary with meals and the cinema and drinks, and coffees with Jake and Jules and Amy and Naomi, to keep myself busy. But when the last call has been made, and I put the phone down, I still feel numb, and quiet. I turn on the computer and start making lists of the work I need to do before going onto the internet and searching for holiday destinations. I think it's true – nothing is as much fun on your own. Everything is better shared with somebody you like, or love.

My phone rings, and I answer it, wondering why Phil isn't in yet.

'Hello, Nicola speaking.'

'Oh Nicola, it's Terence Sewell, Phil's granddad.' I have met him a couple of times, lovely bloke, like a much older Phil with decent conversation. Phil has lived with him for a couple of years, since his parents moved to Barbados.

'Hi Terence, is he chucking a sickie and getting you to call for him again? He really can phone himself you know,' I say.

'Nicola . . . Phil died yesterday morning. He was in a car crash, on the way back from football.'

'What?' I ask, bewildered. I don't understand what he is telling me.

300

'Phil died, yesterday. He won't be . . .' His voice breaks and I hear him sob, and try and control himself. I manage to hold onto the phone, but I am out of breath suddenly, and my body feels like it is collapsing on the inside.

'I can't . . . I don't know . . .' I can't speak. I want to be sick.

'The funeral will be on Thursday, I think. I'll give you a call and let you know.'

'Oh Jesus,' are the only words I can say, completely involuntarily.

'I'm very sorry, dear, he liked you a lot, he liked working for you . . .' His voice goes again.

'Thank you for letting me know. Is there anything I can do?' I say the words without focusing, on autopilot.

'No, his parents arrive at midday. If you could just let people know, at work, that obviously he won't be in.' I hear him cough to stifle the sobs in his throat.

'Of course, thank you, for phoning . . .'

The phone goes dead.

I stare at the wall, and the door, and drop the phone. I can't breathe at all. I feel sick, and giddy, and all I can think of is Phil's face, playing cricket with his stupid ruler, and laughing at some terrible, politically incorrect joke. I run to the bathroom, past people flooding into the office, trying to stop me and ask what's wrong, but I don't make it in time, and I throw up all over the toilet floor. I slump down the side of the wall, and start to cry and hold my head in my hands, and shake with tears.

After an hour of people walking in and out on me in the bathroom, of dragging my hands through my hair, of crying myself to pieces, and when I am hoarse, and can physically cry no more, I push myself to my feet, and walk back into the office. I don't look at his desk as I walk past, the organized

301

mess that was his way of coping, and make my way down to where the MD's PA sits. People look at me weirdly, and stop and stare but I ignore them. I mumble out the necessary words to her in monotone and do not even note her reaction, the tears that immediately spring to her eyes – I think she had a thing for him, all the younger girls did, and I ask her to send an email to everybody in the office, let them know what's happened. I tell her I am going out.

I grab my cigarettes and my sunglasses from my desk, and have to look away at the photocopier as I walk past his desk again, and head out into the bright blazing sunshine. All I can think is that now, now I need to be on my own. Using shaking stiff fingers, I manage to light a cigarette on the third, fourth, fifth attempt, and walk to the square, which is half full already of people sunbathing and laughing and soaking up another day that they got. I sit on a bench in the shade, and cry again. Images of Phil just keep pushing themselves to the front of my head. I want them there. I want to cry, I want to keep on crying. Every time my crying stops, and I get tired, and rest my head back, my mind makes me focus on him again, like some masochistic urge, and I start to cry again. Occasionally people walk past, and look away rather than look at the girl crying on the bench in the sunshine: something must be terribly wrong, they think. Something is. The sound of an ice-cream van penetrates my head, and I think that it is strange for it to be playing its tune in the middle of Soho. I want to punch anybody that comes within ten feet of me, and fight anybody whose voice I can hear talking about rubbish, about boyfriends, or the one who didn't call, or how drunk they had been the night before. I want to make the whole world shut up, just for a while. He was a friend, and he saved my arse time and time again. And he worried about work without seeming to worry at all. Everybody has a death day – a day that they live through year in, year out.

If they knew that that was the day they would die, I wonder whether they'd have a 'death day' party, and mark it with the significance it deserves. Get drunk at least. And then in the next couple of days they'd be reminded how important it is just to live out each day properly, and wholly. Then, in the following weeks they'd forget it, and carry on as normal, having pointless arguments and doing pointless boring things, and worrying needlessly about trivial nothings, the way we all live.

I get back to the office at lunchtime, and now everybody is hushed as I walk through, and conversations stop around me. I feel the odd arm stroke my back as I pass , but I ignore it. I look at Phil's desk outside my office, and pick up his ruler and carry it with me into my office, and close the door. I phone my mum.

'Mummy, it's me, can you talk?' I ask, as I hear the noise of her office in the background. She works in a solicitor's, has done since Charlotte was old enough to go to secondary school.

'Of course, what's wrong, darling?' she asks.

'Mummy . . .' I feel the tears come again, the way they only can when you are talking to your mother, and through my tears I manage to say it.

'Mummy, Phil died,' and the tears flow again, and I feel like a child.

'Oh Jesus,' she says. It must be where I get it from. I had often told her about his stupid exploits, his silly stories, she had met him every time she had come up to town for lunch with me, or to the theatre in the evening. He had made her cups of tea while she waited for me to get out of over-running meetings.

'Come home,' she says, instantly knowing what I need.

'Can I?' I ask, stupidly.

'Of course, come home now.' She says it with an urgency

that the word 'died' causes in any mother. She wants me home, and I want to be there.

'I'll be home in a couple of hours,' I say.

'Okay, I love you.'

'I love you too,' I say and start to cry again, and hang up.

I get a car to take me back to my flat, and I throw things in a bag, and then head back out in fifteen minutes to the train station. Every moment I spend, waiting for the train, sitting on the train, staring out of the window, going home to my parents, I feel like the people around me, the strangers, should know what has happened, should know that somebody had died. But I don't say anything. I just sit in silence until I get to my parents' house. My dad is retired, plays a lot of golf, goes to the gym, but he is there when I get in. He takes my bag, makes me a cup of coffee, and quietly calls my mother, and talks in whispers. My mum's car pulls up ten minutes later, and she hugs me for a while, asks me what happened. I tell her I barely know. I go to bed, my old bedroom, full of all my teenage things and colours, and sleep for a while. When I get up it is getting dark, and I can see the sun setting, beautifully, outside the hall window as I walk downstairs, and hear voices in the garden. I walk through, and see Amy, sitting chatting with my parents. My dad smokes a cigarette, and my mum sips on white wine. I walk out and sit in a chair by my daddy, and reach for his cigarettes and light one. Charlotte has phoned apparently, but has exams this week, so can't come home. Of course she can't, I say, of course she should stay where she is. Amy had come straight from work, phoned Andrew her husband, and told him he had to kiss the baby goodnight for her, and she would be back tomorrow.

We sit in the dark, and the garden lights come on. My mum puts a plate down in front of me and I pick at it for a while, and my dad gets a bottle of red, and pours me a huge glass. We sit in the garden and talk until midnight. Sometimes I go quiet, and sometimes I start to cry again. It is important to be here. These are the people who really love me, the people who drop everything when you need them to, because they want to. I am so lucky to have them here. They are the rock my life is built on. So many people don't have it, and I am so busy going about my time that sometimes I forget how lucky I am. I raise a glass to Phil, and so do my parents and Amy.

'To Phil – he would have wanted me to cry!' I laugh slightly, and wipe my eyes.

Everybody goes quiet, and we take a sip of wine.

Good Grief

The funeral is packed with young boys in black suits – Phil's two football teams, and his cricket team. A couple of boys have slings and scratches. They were in the car with him apparently. He was driving, but a van had lost control and just ploughed into the driver's side, Phil's side, so unprotected by the thin metal car door between him and the hurtling tonnes of metal throwing themselves fatefully towards him. He had died in the hospital an hour later. His granddad had been there in time. I give him a kiss hello, and he thanks me for coming. All the wreaths are shaped like footballs, and I wear my sunglasses throughout. I see his mother's shoulders shaking softly in the front row, and I clutch Amy's hand tightly.

It is so long since I have been in a church, I have forgotten how much the atmosphere overwhelms me, how my current beliefs and my rational objection to everything that it stands for cannot combat the reverential way I behave within its walls. The priest didn't know Phil, but he is peculiarly appropriate nonetheless, in the face of this outpouring of grief, the kind of grief that overwhelms you completely. I didn't realize that Phil was the real man in my life, the one I spent the most time with, relied on, who made me laugh, and who I argued with on a regular basis, without it mattering. The fact that I worked with him now seems secondary to the fact that he had become a friend. I couldn't fully understand the massive depth of my emotion until I admitted this to myself. The candles burn by the altar, and the procession comes. Neither my sister nor I take communion, even though we have done a thousand times in the past, in our youth. It would feel completely fraudulent. People use their tear stained tissues to wipe the sweat from their foreheads, and the back of their necks. The footballers all shift uncomfortably in their heavy suits, as the incense lingers over our heads and mixes with the heat that is already there, to suffocate us. By the time the doors are opened at the end of the service, and everybody spills out into the glaring sunshine, we all have to adjust our eyes, a congregation of young boys throwing on designer sunglasses to hide rare tears.

We make our way in Amy's car to the subdued reception at Phil's grandfather's house. It is clean and old, and I can picture Phil with his feet up on the coffee table, eating his dinner off his lap, watching the footie, and shouting at the television. I can't imagine he ever sneaked any girls back here. We find a corner of the room, and sip on lemonade. We are surrounded by all these boys who spend their time getting pissed, going on tour, joking and laughing, now standing solemnly, on their best behaviour, in their best suits, munching on prawn sandwiches.

I don't talk to Phil's family, apart from the obligatory hellos and goodbyes. Their loss is so much greater than mine, and yet I feel cheated somehow. It would have been nice to see Phil with a girlfriend, growing up finally, settling down. He always let me talk for him, let me say what he was going to say, because he knew that I would. Eventually he would have been great at being somebody's other half. It would have made him.

We leave after a couple of hours, and Amy drives me home, through the sunshine-soaked streets. It feels incredibly lonely to be this sad, to have come from such a muted occasion, and pass people lying out in the sun, radios blaring out music. You almost feel deprived, knowing that you can't enjoy something that is usually such a blessing, this bizarre London summer sun that seems to have infiltrated my life, and scorched everything, scarring it forever. Because now everything has really changed, and there is no turning back. I cannot feel somebody slip out of my life for good, completely, and not act upon it. It would be insulting. So today I'll sort myself out.

Growing up, we dream of our life ahead, and what we'll do. Sometimes we cling onto those dreams when they are already lost, until they become all that we are. We become bitter as they pinch at our eyes, fire our brains, and crease our clothes. We project our young dreams onto seemingly unfulfilled lives, and label ourselves a 'failure' in a life we've yet to live.

It takes something huge to move us on. Sometimes, unfortunately, huge things happen. But we should thank God that they do. It's just different to the way we thought it would be.

We pull up outside my flat, and Amy turns off the engine.

'Are you going to be okay?' she asks me quietly.

'Yeah, I'll be fine. Honestly.' I give her hand a squeeze.

'You can always come and stay with me and Andrew, you know that, don't you.' And she means it.

'Honestly, hon, I'll be okay. I just need to . . . I don't know what I'm going to do. I finish work in a couple of weeks, and I've done nothing.' I sit back against the seat and close my eyes, and fight the tears this time.

'What about Charlie?' she ventures.

'What about him?' I ask quietly. I have thought of him. I

have thought of asking him to come over, to lay next to me in bed, to come with me to the funeral. But somehow none of it seemed fair.

'He's called me a few times – he called Jake, and he told him about Phil. He sounds really worried about you.'

'I know, I know. But, Amy, I was so horrible to him.'

'Well, he was horrible to you too,' she says quietly, not angrily, 'but people change. Maybe he has. He called me for God's sake, and he knows what I think of him; he must be desperate to talk. It's up to you, of course. But if you call him . . . you might feel better.'

'I know, I will. Kiss the baby for me, I'll be over one night this week.' I kiss her goodbye, and climb out of the car.

I go up to the flat, and pick up all the cards lying on the mat. I change into a vest top and shorts and make myself a large Martini and lemonade, and sit down at the kitchen table, light a cigarette, and start to sift my way through them. There are a few words in each one, from the girls, telling me they are there if I need them. I think they feel I need prompting to lean on them. But I'm okay, I'm working through it. I don't want to talk about Phil any more, say what a waste it is again. Everybody knows it; I don't need to tell them. I spot Charlie's handwriting on one of the cards, and leave it until last. I'm worried what it might say. I don't think I will be able to understand any begs or pleas for contact at the moment. I tear the envelope and pull out a card – it has a picture of Elizabeth Taylor and Richard Burton on the front. I open it, and brace myself for what it says, and mentally warn myself not to get angry at anything he has written, preying on me when I need a shoulder, the way Charlie is. But I smile as I read it.

'You know where I am if you need me, Charlie'. That's it, no sentimental words, no tugging on my heartstrings. Just a note to say he's around. Nothing I can take badly, nothing that can be misconstrued, not telling me I need him now, or how much he loves me. I walk through the flat with my phone in my hand. I lean on the balcony, glass in the other hand, and feel the sun on my face. I feel a hundred. I look at my phone, look away, and call Naomi.

'Nim, it's me.'

'Are you okay?'

'I'm okay. What are you doing tomorrow night?'

'Whatever we're doing.'

'Can we go out, have a few drinks, see how it goes?'

'Absolutely. I'll call Jules.'

'I'll speak to you tomorrow.' I press a button on the phone and lean back on the balcony. I don't have time to play games any more, to second guess what's out there that I'm missing out on, to mess anybody around. If I want something, I just have to admit it. I put on my Van Morrison CD – Phil hated Van Morrison – and it makes me laugh, and I brush away today's last tear. I run myself a bath.

I watch TV on my own until it's dark, and when I wake up on the sofa it is eight o'clock in the morning. The sky is cloudy, and I can hear the rain scratching the windows. I turn on the radio just as the newscaster tells us all that the summer is over, and London breathes an internal sigh of relief. The heat was fucking with everybody's minds. Another month of sunshine and the city wouldn't have been the city any more. It would have been an industrial Ibiza. And you can't live like that . . . that's just for holidays.

It Could Be So Different

I walk towards the bar, desperately trying to keep my umbrella from blowing inside out, and ruining my freshly dried and straightened hair. My feet, naked in strappy sandals, are freezing, my toes wet and glistening, as I try to dodge the puddles that have been spreading across the pavements since this morning, since the rain started to pour down. My jeans protect my legs from what is now driving rain, but I am still clammy inside my coat: the heat hasn't vacated with the sun.

Tonight I need to drink and dance and laugh, and be a fully paid up member of the strappy sandal army, and forget my problems, drowning in a shallow puddle of how life could be if only this was all it took to really make me happy. I have powdered over the imperfections for the night. It's part of moving on. For Christ's sake, it's only for a few hours, I haven't emotionally dodged anything for weeks, and tonight, well tonight, I just need to revert to type, just for a little while.

Jules and Nim are already in the bar on Wardour Street, sipping on cocktails, chatting and laughing. I am met with hugs and kisses, slightly anxious looks shared between the two of them which I catch, and I assure them that for tonight I just want to relax, and not think, and not get upset about anybody or anything. Nim starts talking straight away,

'I don't think people should be allowed to die.' Jules practically spits out her drink and glares at her, and I laugh, it is her way of dealing with it.

'Jules, honestly, it's fine, I'm fine.' I rub her arm as she continues to look at me anxiously, and Nim looks at her as if she's making a fuss.

'Nim, go on,' I say, sucking on my straw.

'What I meant is that we should live in some benevolent science-fiction type arrangement, some *Logan's Run/Brave New World* place, and that you just get moved on to another stage, instead of dying; another planet every now and then, so you can't really miss anybody, because you know you are going to see them still.'

'Have you been playing Dungeons and Dragons again?' I ask, and Naomi laughs with us.

'No, I'm not being geeky, I'm talking about relationships, and grief and not having to deal with people leaving you behind.'

'So you think they just move onto another stage of life somewhere else, and we'll meet up with them again at some point? But isn't that supposed to be Heaven?' I ask.

'Yes, but we should be able to phone them, conference them in or something, so we all believe it.' Nim is not religious in the slightest, her parents might have been Protestant, even they can't remember.

'Go away,' Jules says over her shoulder to some drunken twenty-year-old boy who is trying to buy her a drink.

'So in Nim's new world, if people don't die, they just "move on" to some kind of big boardroom. I think love should be different too. I want to have a fantastic boyfriend in Nim's world!' Jules finishes her sentence, and swears at the bloke behind her who moves his hand off her back quickly and walks off.

'Yes, but meeting people would be entirely different,' I say. 'Some weird night would be compulsory date night – Tuesday night would be compulsory date night, so you wouldn't be able to opt out and be too bloody scared to meet somebody new. And it would all be organized through sci-fi personal columns. It would be the only place to meet people, and if you met somebody any other way you'd be ashamed to admit it, it would be too sad. Because you wouldn't know if you matched or not. Everybody would think you were really desperate if you went out with somebody you met in a bar, for instance, because it would be looks that attracted you, and that would be really sad.' They nod their heads in agreement, and I flatten my hair. Naomi grabs her bag and heads to the toilets to sort out her lipstick.

'Are you sure you're okay?' Jules asks as Naomi clicks away in three-inch heels.

'I'm okay, I just . . . it's just funny when somebody at work dies, you know? You make a list in your head of the people that mean something to you, that you care about, that you are scared about losing, and work people don't even figure on your list. But then something happens, and you realize how much some of them mean to you . . . I don't know. But I don't want to talk about it tonight anyway.'

Jules rubs my arm, and I look away quickly, and then back again, composed.

Nim clicks back, and throws her bag down. Jules goes to the bar to get more drinks, and Nim and I both light cigarettes.

'Have you spoken to Charlie?' she asks.

'No . . . I got a card, it was sweet, but I don't know, Nim, it doesn't seem right, or worth it, or something.'

'Well, it's up to you,' she says, and sucks on her straw.

315

'Don't touch me,' I say to a bloke who has just propped his chin on my shoulder, and shrug him off, and carry on talking to Nim. 'I tell you another thing, in "Nim's world", I wouldn't bloody cry as much. It's a joke. My eyes are permanently red, my throat hurts, I'm going through mascara like water.'

'Yes, but sometimes you just feel like a really good cry,' she says.

'I know, but you could have, like valves, in your neck or something, to control all your emotions. And if you fancied a cry you could just turn your valve on, get it out of your system, and then turn it off again. Controlled emotions, that's the way forward.' Nim looks at me strangely, and Jules, with her purse tucked under her chin, balances three glasses on the table.

'Where did we get to? Cheers!' Jules says as we clink glasses.

'Nix wants a valve in her neck to make her stop crying,' Nim says.

'Oh Nix.' Jules holds my hand.

'I'm not crying now, Jules, it's fine. I'm just saying it would be nice not to be at the mercy of my emotions, not to be so sodding up and down all the time. And not just when . . . you know, when something huge happens. But all the time, all the bloody tears, all the anger, the frustration. It would be nice just to turn it off for a while, just bob along evenly. It would be a break.'

'It's called being single,' Jules says, raising her eyes to heaven.

I laugh, but then Jules qualifies,

'Actually that's a lie. I'm quite happy. I'm happy on my own, happier than I would be with somebody awful anyway. I'm independent, I'm in control, I don't have to take anybody's shit, I rely on myself completely. It's only at night that I really miss somebody, and even then, you get the bed to yourself.'

'I know,' I say, nodding.

'Falling in love, getting hurt, being mucked around, being confused, having to commit, being scared you're going to change your mind, it's just not worth it. Any of it. We should just be on our own, it's much more sensible. It's not just sensible, it's preferable.' I am adamant.

'Nix, I didn't say that.' Jules looks at me sadly, as if I am suddenly without hope, and I could not be more wrong. She talks as quietly as she can over the music pumping from speakers at either side of the bar,

'The day goes much quicker if you have somebody to daydream about, or focus on, or think about. Somebody to think about before you fall asleep. It is worth it.'

'It just has to be with somebody who is worth it.' Jules reaches out to rub my arm again, and I feel like a fool.

'It's better to be on your own than to be with somebody who isn't worth it, but if they are, then . . .' Nim trails off. I have been simplistic. I have tried to smile my problems off and Nim and Jules won't let me, because that means I am brushing theirs off too.

'Well, what if you don't know if they are worth it or not?' I ask, trying to recover my cool, trying to look less naïve.

'I think you always know,' Jules says, and refuses to break eye contact with me, so I look at Nim, and she is nodding her head and sucking up the last of her Pimms from the bottom of her glass, hidden behind the mint leaves.

I look away, and Jules must feel bad, because she changes the subject.

'So, are you still going to go away? I mean, are you still resigning?'

'Hell yes,' I say, relieved to be right about something. 'I can't do that any more, stupid films, sodding *Evil Ghost 2* –

The Revenge should not be a source of stress for me. Nobody is going to see it, and even if they do, it is just not important enough to stress me out as much as it does. And work is going to feel weird now anyway . . .' I don't have to explain.

'So what are you going to do?' Nim asks.

Silence. I want to answer, I just don't know. I sit and shake my head for a while, and eventually laugh.

'I haven't got a fucking clue,' I say.

Everybody cheers as a song comes on, an old song, a song that reminds everybody in the bar of being young, and we collectively wish we were nineteen again.

'Shall we dance?' Jules asks.

'Absolutely,' I say, and Nim nods her head. As I stand up, the cocktails in my bloodstream bubble towards my head, and we dance for the rest of the night. At one point I am laughing uncontrollably when a very short guy wearing white socks and slip-on shoes that glare out with the effect of the strobe won't leave Jules alone, and she tries to run away from him on the dance floor. A few more cocktails, and everything gets pushed to one side, just for the night.

Doing the Maths

I believe everybody has a formula for their own happiness. Constituent parts, important to the individual, or maybe the group, that equal the sum of a happy life, both physically and emotionally. I've worked out mine, the letters as symbols that when put together make what would work for me. I don't think it's a meaningless exercise. I think it helps, if only to enable me to see where the formula is breaking down, the bits that are lacking in my life, and are defying me in my search for relaxation, and the need not to constantly apologize for myself, or strive for something better.

I need my health, that's a constant. We pretty much all do. To be healthy or at least be coping physically with whatever condition Fate has thrown at us. And I need to be secure financially, not destitute. I have lived with debt; it seriously affects my state of mind, and is one of the greatest causes of depression. The other big thing that I can admit that I need is love. I need to feel loved, it defines my self-worth. I need the love of my family, and my friends, but increasingly I have inwardly admitted that I need the unconditional love of somebody who just doesn't have to love me, but does. I need somebody that puts me first, without question, without thinking. This kind of love only comes from your partner. And I need that, I'll admit it. Once you have felt it, and lost it, it feels like your oxygen has been cut off, and that somehow all of a sudden you are just not as important in this big old scheme of things as once you were. As much as love, I need trust. I need to know that the rug is not going to be whipped out from beneath me at any given moment, and that person whose body I am hanging my life on is not going to shrug me off like an old T-shirt tomorrow.

And I need to feel good about the future, positive about what's in store for me and mine. Finally, FINALLY, I need to lose the guilt. I need to shake off the bad stuff, and not be preoccupied, controlled even, by the past, and things I can't change, things that I know in my heart of hearts are not hurting anybody any more but me.

So that's my formula, or in short:

Security + Optimism (Health + Love / Trust) - Guilt = Happiness. I have tried to minus cigarettes from the health section, because they really do make me happy, but then I just feel guilty, and that outweighs the nicotine, so the cigarettes lose out. I don't think my formula is particularly unique; I think a lot of people, a lot of women perhaps, could take 'Formula Nix 1' as it shall now be called, or a version of it, substituting Security for Excitement or whatever. But that's what I need.

What you can see from my formula, however, is that I can't just rely on me to be happy. I need somebody else in there, playing their part, for me to be in a place where I can finally put my emotional feet up. And maybe Charlie could have been it. Early on, in America, we had the makings. But it went wrong and by the time he flipped out, the only thing Charlie knew to do with a woman was fuck her. And it is just too soon to know if he has changed, and reasonably, and not living in a fucking romance novel, I can't take that chance.

What I need to know, in my heart, is that Charlie's winning formula is similar to mine, and I can't leap back into anything when deep down I feel it could still be so different. More along the lines of,

Beer(Curry + Football / X-box) + Sex = Happiness.

Ring any bells?

I can't bet my life on that.

What is There to Think?

I get up at eight and survey the remnants of my tan, and finally admit to myself that it is long gone. All that remains is fake, straight from a bottle, but an expensive bottle, professionally applied, and it looks good so I am fine with it. I do the maths in my head, and calculate that I have in fact been home for three months. Soon my friends are going to realize that it doesn't matter how long I was abroad, you don't stay golden for this long without a little help from some chemical concoction and a Costa Rican woman in the gym by Piccadilly who doesn't even know what a streak is.

I hang over my balcony and suck on a plastic tube that is supposed to trick my mind into thinking I am smoking. It doesn't work, it hasn't yet, and I pad into the bathroom, apply my morning patch, and take my coffee out onto the balcony with me. If I can't have nicotine, caffeine is the next best thing. It is hot already, and I kind of know the déjà vu is coming before it even hits. When it does, I laugh. I have been here before, but my world was different then. I look up at the sky and wonder how thin the ozone layer must actually have got over London now, what with the sun making regular spring appearances. But I smile, good things should happen on sunny days, and toast the air, to Jake and Sarah, the bride and groom, on their big day.

I flip the radio on in the living room, and dance over the papers lying all over the floor, my homework from last week. I have my first exams a week on Monday, and I am actually looking forward to them. I want to prove to myself that I am as good as I think I am. I am pretty happy.

An hour and a half later I jump in the car with a jacket and an overnight bag, and a present that I bought Jake in Havana – twenty Monte Cristoes, especially for the groom. Jules has the proper present, and I am picking her up on the way.

I flip the radio on in the car, and beep the horn outside Jules's place twenty minutes later. Deciding that I could do with another mirror check, I run to the door just as Jules pulls it open with wet hair and an apologetic grin.

'How long are you going to be?' I ask.

'Ten minutes,' she pleads, and I carefully place myself at her kitchen table, and open the post that came just as I was leaving. There is a letter from an elderly couple I met in Brazil, who actually live in Yorkshire, and who like to keep in touch. A credit card bill that I peek at gingerly and try and forget the amount I owe as soon as I see it. That was my running away money, my sorting myself out money, I don't feel bad that I spent it, I just don't actually need to see it written down. The final envelope looks like a card, and as I pull it open an electronic shriek leaps from the inside.

'Jesus,' I say as I yank out the invitation, and Jules comes running out in a short skirt and bra.

'What was that?' she asks, surprised.

'It's an invite, to the premiere of that film I worked on before I quit, *Evil Ghost 2*, it's being held tonight. I think maybe they are trying to fill some seats.'

'Well, you can't go, we're at the wedding.' Jules looks at

me with concern, as if there is actually a decision to be made here.

'I know that, Jules,' and then, 'Is that what you're wearing?'

Jules looks down, and then runs back towards her bedroom, shouting,

'Part of it!' over her shoulder. At least her hair looks dry now.

Looking at the invite again, I realize the old lady we found on the bus is on the front, looking over-made-up and petrified herself – I hope they paid her more than extra's money, although I doubt she got any actual lines. It's her moment of fame though, even if it has come a little late in life. Staring at her picture, I imagine the office briefly and sigh mercifully that I have left it all behind. Phil's face darts into my mind before I can stop it, and I smile again, a different smile, fondly, only a little sad. There's cricket on today, England versus Australia. He wouldn't have gone to his own wedding if it meant missing a Test. I went around to his granddad's a couple of weeks after I came back, and we sat and had a coffee, as I sucked on my plastic cigarette. I didn't stay for long, I just wanted to say hello. I had a bit of trouble with the photos that still stood on his fireplace, of Phil and his brother smiling out from a football pitch. I left so soon after he died, I had almost convinced myself he'd be around when the travelling bug finally worked its way out of my system, and I felt the need to see my parents, my sisters, my nephew, my friends again. As I said goodbye to Phil's granddad at the door, I promised to go and watch the cricket with him over the summer, and it occurs to me that we are going in a couple of weeks. It's in my diary, I won't forget.

I walk over to Jules's bin, press the lever with my foot, and the lid springs open, but something stops me throwing my invite in with the remains of last night's dinner. I go back and put it into my bag, as Jules dashes out of the bedroom, with two different shoes hanging from each hand.

'Nix, are you wearing sensible or strappy?' she asks, waving each one frantically.

'Strappy, but sensibles are in the car for later. Just pack them in your overnight bag,' I say with a smile, and she dashes back into her bedroom muttering, 'Of course, Jesus, I'm an idiot.'

We pick Naomi up half an hour later, and I put my foot down on the M11 to get us there on time. I have borrowed Amy's car, and debates about putting the roof down are abruptly concluded when we all realize we won't have time to rectify convertible hair. But it is a gorgeous day, and the girls suck on champagne ice-lollies that Nim made last night, and which I politely decline because I am a) driving, but more importantly b) wearing cream. Jules is in fuchsia, Nim is in pastel blue. We consulted heavily before we bought our outfits.

By the time we get to the church, which is hidden down some country lane in the middle of deepest Norfolk, and we have congratulated ourselves on the fact that we have only had to turn the car around twice, and only once illegally, the congregation appear to have taken their seats, and we run as fast as we can in heels on gravel to the door. We squeeze into the back pew, and I take a breath, looking around at this beautiful church, and the gorgeous pale pink flowers hanging on the walls, and the rose petals on the floor. The organist starts to play almost immediately, and we are on our feet again, relieved that we made it inside before Sarah turned up, and we didn't have to follow her in, in shame. I lean around what must surely be an uncle, and see Jake standing nervously at the front of the church, looking back towards me, as Sarah's dad nearly takes my head off marching past. Apparently he's a police commander or something; we all whistled when Jake told us, and I reminded him that smoking marijuana was, of course, still illegal, strictly speaking, and there would be no more of that with the threat of his new in-laws popping round for tea. He said if he had to he'd fake the necessary disease and say he was taking it for medicinal purposes. But right now he looks nothing but happy, over the moon, watching Sarah being marched up to meet him, smiling through her veil – 'bad headgear,' Nim whispers to me and Jules, and we nod our heads ever so slightly in agreement. It's her day, we'll let it lie just this once. Jake doesn't care.

I remember the tissues in my purse halfway through the ceremony, after standing up and sitting down countless times, and singing hymns, and not quite kneeling for the kneeling bits like a proper Catholic should, because it'll leave a mark on cream trousers so it just ain't gonna happen. I'm fine with it, I've worked through some of the guilt, and not kneeling down because my trousers don't permit it is not going to get me sent to hell. I blot the tears before they fall down my cheeks, and gulp loudly as I hear Jake's voice break at the front of the church during his vows. I remember the last time I was in a church, for mass, not just looking around, which I did a lot of in South America, seeing the beauty of the buildings and not absorbing the fear and the loathing that I so associated with them in the past. I say a little prayer to Phil, say hello, how you doing, that kind of thing. That's the bit I'll hang on to, the belief that he's up and about somewhere above me. I can pick and choose if I want, it doesn't have to be all or nothing, wearing a cassock or burning a bible. I take the bits that I need now.

I realize Jake is being told he can kiss the bride and I am broken from my daydream, and clap and smile with the rest of the congregation as he walks back down the aisle towards us, arm in arm with Sarah, a married man. He smiles and raises his eyes at me as he walks past, and

I grin eagerly back, and wait for the rest of the pews in front of us to pile out behind them – church rules: last in, last out. But I gasp suddenly as I see a man walking towards me, chatting to Jake's brother, casually laughing and smiling, not looking ahead. It is only at the last minute that Charlie looks forwards and catches my eye, and sees me mouth 'Oh my God' and hold my breath as we lock stares. It hadn't even occurred to me that he would be here, and now I can't break his gaze. We both look petrified for a second, before simultaneously gaining our composure, and I murmur 'Hi' as he brushes past me, fumbling for his sunglasses in his pocket, to protect his eyes. I take a deep breath, and turn to face Jules and Nim, who both look equally as stunned.

'I swear I didn't know he was going to be here,' Jules says to me quickly, and I take a deep breath.

'It's fine, I can cope with it, it's not a problem,' I say, and fumble in my bag for my sunglasses at the same time.

Outside, as the photographer dances around Jake and Sarah who have people to talk to and hug, I try my very best to talk politely to Jake's family, and a couple of guys from university who I haven't seen for years. But my eyes keep roaming the crowd to spot Charlie, until finally I see him on the opposite corner of the grass, looking directly at me. I look away quickly, and then back again, and he has looked away. And then Jake arrives with a hug.

'Oh my God, congratulations, this is so huge, you are actually married!' I babble at him as he smiles, almost serene.

'I know, it's bloody great.' He is beaming, the happiest I have ever seen him. 'Still got your tan, I see.' He prods my arm, and gives me an accusing look.

'Yeah, well, I was away for eight months you know, it's a long time.' Jules and Nim say their hellos, and we stand and make small talk for a couple of minutes, before Jake pulls me aside, and the girls are distracted by a guy who has really blossomed since college.

'You know Charlie's here, right?' Jake asks quietly.

'Yeah, I saw him just now. Could have done with a bit more warning.' I try to laugh but the honesty of it sticks in my throat.

'It's not a problem is it?' Jake says.

'It's just, he called me after the Phil thing, trying to speak to you, and when you went away we kind of kept in touch. I see him quite a lot now, we play football at the weekends, and I just hadn't got around to mentioning it to you, what with organizing the wedding and everything, and I've hardly seen you since you got back. He's really changed, grown up or something . . .' Jake trails off.

'No, Christ, it's absolutely fine. My God, it's your wedding, of course it's fine. It's been nearly a year, Jake, I'm a big girl.' I convince Jake at least, who smiles, hugs me again, and then gets grabbed by one of Sarah's aunts and dragged sideways into a photo. The gap he leaves reveals Charlie, thirty feet away, but staring directly at me again, and I want to run and hide. I do the first thing I think of, and smile and nod my head, and when no response comes I spin on my heel and grab Naomi, dragging her towards the car.

'Have you got any cigarettes on you?'

'Yes.' Naomi reaches into her clutch bag.

'But aren't you wearing a patch?'

'Sod the patch.' I pull my jacket off and rip the plaster from my arm.

'Jesus Christ!' I cry out a little too loudly, just as the priest wanders past towards the gates, and I am met with a disapproving holy glare.

'Sorry, Father,' I mumble. I feel like I am regressing by the minute. How can this be? This morning I was so serene, so confident, so happy. But now? Now I feel like a bloody train

329

wreck. Nim is reluctant to give me a cigarette so I grab them out of her hands, and spark up just as Jules rounds the corner.

'Nix, no!' she shouts and starts to run towards me as if a bus has suddenly come swerving in my direction. Defensively, I pull the cigarette from my lips and hide it behind my back where she can't get at it.

'Oh Nix, why? You've been doing so well!' The look of disappointment on Jules' face could rival the priest's.

'It's just one day, and besides, Jake made me promise I would smoke at his wedding, and I can't argue with the groom.' I wince at my own lie, and Jules turns her attention to Nim.

'How could you give her a cigarette?'

'I didn't give it to her, she took it, and anyway I think Charlie is stressing her out. It's not your ex-boyfriend giving you evils from across the car park.' Nim gestures behind Jules, who spins round and I follow her gaze to where Charlie is standing at the edge of the crowd, looking towards us. We instantly turn and look in three opposite directions.

'Fuck. I thought I would be fine with this but I am so obviously not. What am I going to do if he's on our table? He looks like he hates me, I can't handle this. Jesus, eight months of therapy, dossing about in South A-bloody-merica is ruined in one afternoon.' I suck on my cigarette and shake my empty hand with nerves.

'Look, you're going to be fine, it's only one day. And we're here.' Jules grabs my hand and shakes it to get my attention.

'Isn't she going to be fine, Nim?'

Jules looks towards Naomi for back-up, but just gets a feeble, 'Yeah.'

'You know what, it is going to be okay. If he ignores me, I'll handle it. If he starts screaming at me, I'll handle it. If he knifes me, I expect one of you to rugby tackle him, and the other one to stop the bleeding with one hand, and phone the police with the other.'

People start to walk towards us, and we realize that the 'formal' photos, of which there are going to be few apparently, are over. Much trendier to get them naturally and in black and white later. We turn and stroll towards the car, while Nim and Jules fight over who is going to navigate to the reception. Nim messed it up the first time, Jules is trying to say in her nicest voice, and she should take over. Nim counters with the fact that she is now familiar with the way Norfolk roads work. I start the car as Jake and Sarah drive past us and Jules, in uncharacteristic fashion, lunges for the passenger seat, leaving Nim standing, gob-smacked on the gravel. I drive off with Nim staring at the back of Jules' head in disbelief, and Jules staring straight ahead, refusing to look back. It seems we've all changed a little in a year; it's amazing what you can do if you try.

The reception is being held at Sarah's parents' house, off another country lane in deepest Norfolk, but ten miles from the one we were already on. This time we follow the stream of cars in front of us, which get stuck behind a tractor, but at least we don't get lost. For the extent of the journey my mind replays Charlie standing in front of me outside the church, not meeting my smile with his. I am petrified that he has reverted to type, ditched the new Charlie who was just finding his feet as I left for South America, and now, now he only sees me as a hindrance to him pulling at the wedding. And I think about the strange sensation in my stomach, the nerves kicking about like a baby, and the knowledge that I won't be able to eat at the reception, my appetite deserting me, so I should be careful and not drink too much.

'Don't let me drink too much,' I blurt out as I park the car in the grounds of an overwhelming farmhouse, near what look like the servants' quarters.

'Okay,' Nim and Jules say in unison.

As I walk across the lawn, making tiny stiletto holes, carrying the present, wearing massive sunglasses, I feel I must look the picture of calm, but all I can think is 'must see seating plan, must see seating plan.' Jules and I accept a Pimms from a tray and wander towards the back of the house and Naomi dashes off to find a toilet. Fifteen minutes later, I see her strolling back, chatting to Sarah's mother, smiling as she makes her way towards us.

'I checked out the seating plan in the marquee, and I couldn't see his name, but he's definitely not on our table,' she says as soon as she reaches us.

'Thank God,' I sigh, but feel bitterly disappointed at the same time. Is it just prolonging the inevitable argument, or do I really want to speak to him? I survey the lawn, and Charlie is nowhere to be seen. The thought suddenly occurs to me that he might have left, said his goodbyes to Jake and explained that he didn't want to make things awkward, or that he had another wedding to go to, or any other feasible excuse. And my stomach kicks again, with a feeling I know is disappointment. Please God, let him still be here. But as the sun starts to drift towards the horizon, and the master of ceremonies announces that dinner is served, and we stumble towards the marquee on three glasses of Pimms and no food since yesterday, my intentions of not getting drunk appear to be slipping away with the sun, and Charlie has still not turned up.

I notice Jules stagger slightly in front of me and realize that I cannot count on her to keep me sober. I grab Nim's hand, squeeze it tightly, and beg her, 'Please, please, control my drinking.'

'I will, don't worry.' She squeezes it back, wrinkles her nose and smiles. I am in safe hands.

The meal is uncomfortable, as I try desperately to take a sip of water for every sip of wine, and make small talk with one of Sarah's brothers, while keeping an eye on the door in case Charlie arrives. By the time Jake is standing up to make his speech, Nim and Jules are both whooping and cheering, completely pissed, and I know that I am the only person to be relied on to keep me from getting trashed. If only we hadn't booked a cab from here to the hotel, and I had agreed to drive back, instead of picking the car up tomorrow. What an idiot I am. I look around the tables one last time, and finally acknowledge that Charlie isn't coming back, and as Jake asks us to toast his beautiful new wife, I neck my glass of wine. It's going to be all downhill from here. I shouldn't have worn cream.

Jake's speech seems to go on forever, or for at least an entire bottle of red, which disappears into my glass and then into me by the time he is 'wrapping up'. I try and focus on him standing at the top table, and listen intently to what he is saying, as my head becomes increasingly cloudy, and my eyes swirl.

'And lastly, I would just like to say that I think we make a beautiful couple, in fact, to be honest, I think I make a fantastic groom, and I know I am going to do my damnedest to be the best husband I can. But I know that, working for the paper, there are going to be some nights that I will be home late, and I don't want you to feel like I am not with you. Sooooo, I've come up with a reminder of this fantastic day, and more importantly, me on this fantastic day, that can keep you company on any cold night when I can't get home to watch you fall asleep. Charlie, if you wouldn't mind.' I can see Jake looking towards the door, and I register Jake saying his name, and swing my head towards a new commotion and laughter that is emanating from the corner of the room. At first all I can see is two Jakes – one at the top table and one moving across the room to meet the first. But my drink-addled brain manages to register that it is in fact a life-size cardboard Jake gliding towards the top table, in his morning suit, holding a pint of beer aloft in front of him, and then I realize that the cardboard cut-out is on wheels, and being pushed by Charlie. I gasp, not only at the drunken realization that he is back, and how happy this makes me, but also at the realization that I am of course now very drunk.

The laughter dies down, and Jake continues, as Charlie takes a step back, and accepts a drink from a waiter standing to the side of the room.

'So, cheers, darling, here's to us.' Jake raises his glass to his new bride.

'And thanks to Charlie, a mate, for sorting this all out, and missing a good feed in the process. We saved you a canapé!'

All of a sudden everybody seems to be on their feet, and I push back my chair uncertainly to stand, steadying myself on the table, and make sure to raise my water glass, as we shout,

'Cheers!' and, 'The happy couple!'

I down my water in one gulp, and sit down quickly. People seem to be moving about around me, up out of their chairs to talk at other tables, but I am reluctant to go anywhere. The only person I want to talk to is on the other side of the room, and I'm not sure if I'll make it intact.

Neither Nim nor Jules appear to have registered that Charlie is back, they are hammered and giggling at something that I am sure is not funny.

'Girls, girls, he's back,' I whisper too loudly.

'Who is?' Nim asks, wiping her eyes.

'Charlie.'

'Oh, where?' Jules looks around wildly and then back at me, confused.

'In the corner, for Christ's sake, he just pushed the cardboard Jake thing in! How pissed are you?' I look from one to the other, and they stare at me with glazed eyes.

'I'm pretty pissed,' Nim says after a silence.

'So am I,' Jules says seriously.

'But you were supposed to be stopping me from getting drunk!' I practically shout, aware that I have already forgotten most of the conversation we've just had.

'Don't drink any more then,' Nim says practically, and takes away my glass.

'That's water!' I say, and put my head in my hands. This is all going horribly wrong.

'Look, it'll be fine, he doesn't even seem to want to talk to you,' Jules says, thinking she's being nice, I am sure, but cutting into me like a butcher's knife.

'But what if I want to talk to him!' I wail through my hands.

'Do you? Oh, I didn't realize.' Jules takes a giant slug of white wine.

'Well, I just can't. I'm just going to have to keep out of his way. I'm nearly as hammered as you, it'll all go wrong. I must look like shit,' I wail again.

'You look fine!' Nim says into her glass.

'You can't bloody see, what would you know?'

'This is true,' she says, and necks her drink.

I push back my chair suddenly, and make two grabs for Nim's cigarettes on the table.

'Where are you going?' they both shout at once, like a pair of drunken synchronized idiots.

'I'm going to get some fresh air, and try and sober up.'

'Well, take this,' and Naomi tries to pick up the huge jug of water in the middle of the table.

'It's really heavy,' she says, unable to lift it, and collapses forward onto the table, giggling, and Jules starts laughing as Nim's hair dangles into some coffee.

I smile at the two of them, they are out of it, they can't help me now, and it's not their fault. I can take care of myself.

'I'll see you in a little while,' I say, and stagger towards the marquee curtains, prodding them with my hand, trying to find a break in the material.

It is dark outside, and cloudy. I stumble away from the sound of music and laughter and towards the back of the house. My heels stick into the lawn heavily, and I get stuck twice, before I take them off and turn up my trousers, swaying dangerously with my head by my knees, trying to ensure my hems don't get dirty but painfully close to falling over completely. I manage to make it upright again, and spot a bench at the bottom of the garden, before it turns into fields. When I get there, I survey it closely, trying to spot any evil mud marks, but it looks clean, and I slump down, my head spinning less, the air penetrating my eyes, my nose, sweeping through me. I am pissed, but not beyond help, this is a rectifiable situation. I just have to stay out here for another couple of hours, and I'll be fine. I consider a nap, but know that in a cream suit on a garden bench that is a dangerous idea. I look back at the marquee, the dark shadows of people moving around outside of it, and the laughter reaches me again. I can faintly hear the music, an old eighties song, and I know Nim and Jules will be staggering around the dance floor about now, scaring the children, and getting disapproving looks from grandmothers. So what, we're just drunk, there are worse things you can do. Besides, everybody does bad things. They aren't hurting anybody with theirs at least. I realize the song has changed, and Lionel Ritchie has come on. I close my eyes quickly to see if I can without throwing up, and surprisingly the world doesn't go into orbit. I start to sing quietly to myself, I can just sit here for a while, and sober up. It might be cold, and dark, and I might be sitting on my own in a stranger's back garden, but it could be worse. I could be throwing up. I sing, not that quietly any more, and wait for my head to clear.

'Alright?'

I snap my eyes open, and see Charlie standing in front of me, holding a beer.

'Oh shit,' I say before I can stop myself.

'Nice, thanks,' he says, and looks at his feet.

'Sorry, I didn't mean it like that. I'm just, Christ, I'm really pissed, Charlie.' I venture a smile, and he smiles back. His tie is pulled down from his neck, and his top button is undone. He looks great, familiar, a little heavier since the last time I saw him, but great nonetheless.

'Can I sit down?' he asks quietly.

'I'm hoping you will,' I say, smiling again, closing my eyes so I don't have to think about how much I have missed him.

We sit in silence for a couple of minutes, and I can hear Charlie taking sips of his beer. It is just bloody great to know he is sitting next to me; I feel like I've dreamed it.

'That was a nice thing you did for Jake, the big cardboardy thing. Looked a bit scary to me, but I'm sure Sarah will like it.'

Charlie doesn't answer, and I turn my head deliberately to look at him.

'Oh, your sideburns have got long!' I say in shock.

'I've been cultivating them,' he says evenly.

'Well, they look good.'

'Thanks. So how was South America? Got any photos?'

'What on me? No. Only just moved out of that stage, mind. A week earlier and you would have had the slide show.' We both smile, knowing it's true.

'But it was good, it was great, really . . . good for me. It feels like I've been away forever.'

'I know,' Charlie says quietly, and we turn to look at each other.

'I'm not in the City any more,' he says, and I know that this is information that he is desperate to pass on.

'Oh, right. Not in the West End?' I ask, incredulous.

'No, I'm training to be a teacher, well, I've just qualified actually. I am a teacher.'

'Bloody hell!' This is out of left field, and I am impressed, and floored, and massively surprised. No wonder he wanted to tell me.

'And I've been seeing a counsellor, since about the time you left actually.'

'Bloody hell!' I say again, shocked. This is a lot of information to take in, drunk as I am.

I realize he is feeling open, uncomfortable, so I jump in. 'Christ, so, Sir, what do you teach?'

'P.E.'

'Right, so not quite as worthy as it first sounded then,' I say.

'No, I generally tend to leave that bit out.'

'All the girls will fancy you, you know that, don't you?'

'Only reason I'm doing it.' And we both laugh slightly.

'How about you? Have you gone back to work?'

'No, actually. I've gone back to college. Got my first exams next week. Thought it was about time I tried something I really wanted to do.' I am proud of myself, I can hear it in my own voice. I have moved on too. We haven't wasted our year apart, Charlie and I.

'Bloody hell! What's the course?' Charlie asks.

'Social work.'

'Jesus!' Charlie looks amazed as well he should, social work is just so not me.

'No, I'm just kidding. It's philosophy.'

'Right, not quite as admirable as it sounded then.'

'No, that's why I say social work,' I say, and we both smile.

'I'm really enjoying it, though.' I run my hand through my hair, and feel myself sobering up slightly. But I am still pissed.

'Are you seeing anybody?' Charlie asks with his head down, his elbows resting on his knees, bottle in both hands. It seems like a mammoth question, and despite myself, and the way I thought I would feel answering this question, when Charlie eventually asked it, I am relieved to say,

'No.' We sit in silence for a second, as I wait for his reply, and only when it doesn't come I realize I haven't asked the question.

'Oh. You?'

'No. Haven't met anybody. Well, not anybody that comes close to what we . . . had.' Charlie turns his head to look at me sideways, and I meet his eyes.

'I know what you mean.' My nose scrunches up on its own, involuntarily. It's true, I haven't.

'I was shocked, you know, that you went, and you didn't even say goodbye or anything.' Charlie cuts to the chase.

'Oh God, I know. I feel bad about it. But it was a funny time. I just had to get away. And I told Jake to say goodbye to you for me.'

'It's not quite the same, is it?' Charlie looks hurt suddenly, and we have both been doing so well to keep control.

'I know, it's not, you're right. I'm sorry, Charlie.'

'Was I really that bad? Actually, don't answer that, I know I was.'

'Charlie, it was me that was confused, you were sorting yourself out, but I was all over the place, and I didn't know what I wanted . . . you weren't that bad. By then.'

339

'So do you know what you want now?' Charlie looks at me again, and I realize he has just put his feelings on the bench between us, for me to crush if I want. He is being brave.

'Yes,' I venture quietly.

'What do you want then?'

'I want to be a philosopher.'

There is a second of shocked silence, and then he laughs loudly, at the relief of such a trivial answer to such a massive question.

'Sorry, sorry, that was easy. Do I know what I want? I guess I do. It's quite hard to admit it though.' I understand what I'm saying now. The drink is still there, dissolving in my bloodstream, but my mind is clearing by the second. What is there to think about, really? When you fall in love, well, that's it. It's the thing I learnt. Everybody does bad things, you can't expect them not to. I did a bad thing, so shoot me. I'm still allowed to be in love. It's part of my equation.

Charlie is looking back down at his bottle again, and I get the feeling he is about to ask the last awkward question between us. Because when I answer, and we both know, we can relax again.

'So . . .' Charlie seems to be feeling the pressure. But I want him to ask it. It's going to make me feel loved, and that's what I need.

'So?' I ask.

'So, I've moved on, I teach football now,' he laughs slightly. 'And you've moved on, you . . . wear black, sit and think in cafés or whatever.'

'Oi!' I shove his leg with mine, and it is the first time we've touched for over a year.

'Well, you do whatever philosophy students do, and we both seem to know . . .' he trails off again. He is finding this hard-going. And his insecurity makes me feel loved enough, his complete inability to form the words. I don't want to make him suffer.

'I think I know, Charlie, I mean, as much as I can.' I reach out, feeling the nerves in my arm as I try to hold his hand, and he lets me, and studies our hands together for a second. And looking at my hand, he says,

'God, I really, really fucking missed you.' He says it in bewilderment, as if he never knew he could.

'Thanks. I missed you too.' I pull his hand slightly, and he sits up.

'Jesus Christ, I can't believe I'm going to do this. I feel like one of your class. I feel like I'm bloody fifteen again.' I gulp, and hope I'm not too flushed by the drink, not clammy and cold and horrible-looking.

Charlie leans in, and I lean in, eyes open, and our lips touch each other's while my heart seems to bang about in my chest. I can't believe how amazingly, overwhelmingly happy I feel to be kissing him again. Gradually, softly, I feel his tongue and I put my hands on the sides of his face, feeling the cultivated sideburns. I feel his hand in my back. It is a slow kiss, and we pull apart slightly. We are sitting face to face.

I breathe out my nerves with a sigh, and flex my neck slightly, shrugging my shoulders free of the tension.

'Limbering up?' he asks quietly, and I laugh in surprise.

'So is this a clean slate then?' I ask, suddenly scared that it might not be.

Charlie wipes a strand of hair off my face, and whispers,

'Completely.'

Epilogue – After All That

Soho Street, 11.15, Wednesday night.

The queue for POP, a late night dancing bar.

Charlie, six of his mates, a boys' night out.

'Charlie, check it out.'

'What, mate?'

'Check it out, over the road, the blonde.'

'Where?' There's a sense of urgency in Charlie's voice.

'Over the road, mate, by Starbucks. The blonde, mate, the blonde!'

Charlie spins around on one foot, and spots the blonde.

'Nah, mate, look at the conk on her – druids worship that nose every solstice. And I'd like to check her cuffs – bet they don't match the collar.'

The boys laugh. The blonde looks over self-consciously, and knows they are laughing at her. You can always tell who is laughing at who. The boys are taking no care to be discreet. She pulls her jacket a little closer around her neck, and puts her head down slightly, trying to shrink her nose into the shadows. It is always her nose. She's going to get the surgery, she's sick of this shit.

Charlie turns back to the queue, bored with laughing at the

blonde. Slapping his hands together, he dances on the spot to the music coming from the pit of the club, seeping out into the night. If only they could be down there. The anticipation of the queue. He knows he doesn't need to be queuing, he could slip the bouncer a fifty, and they'd be in, but it's a warm night. The women may be downstairs, shaking their tits and arse in bikini tops and tiny skirts, and the bar may be downstairs, with all the ingredients for his favourite cocktails. But for the moment Charlie is content to get this last breath of street air before descending into the heat of the club for the next four hours. And they're in no rush, there are women on the street as well.

It has been an unnaturally hot May for London.

You can feel the heat not just in the air, but in the people. A restlessness presided over the city's singles. The girls wore their clothes like smooth silky invitations for sex. Shirts clung to torsos, skirts stuck to thighs, faces shone and heels clicked through offices beating out a thrusting rhythm as they went. The mornings were filled with a clean promise, in a much needed early shower, who knew what these strange days would bring, after sweating out another night under the sheets, with whoever he had brought to his bed, familiar or unfamiliar, Nicola, or somebody else. More often than not, somebody else. Walking the streets to work, watching the air rise from the streets, and the day begin, everybody wearing relieved smiles, that the sun had decided to stick around for another day at least. And so what if you had to be in the office? There was always the weekend. And Bank Holiday season was underway.

Windows open at work, the phone rings non-stop, but a swift one at lunch, sunglasses on, still psyched for the afternoon, flirting, sunbathing, music spilling out from the radios of soft tops rolling past. Jamaican funk in London town. A strange time. And everybody up for it. The evenings, heat holding into the night, into the bars, ties loosened, sipping something long and cool, sitting outside bars by the river, the heat willing you to stay out all night, swaying home eventually, a little something on the arm picked up in the bar, an unnatural blonde, loving the summer just as much and loving the vibe of middle of the week sex, and telling you about plans for the weekend. In the summer, everybody has plans for the weekend, and this year summer had definitely come early.

Charlie was getting a lot of sex. The weather was his friend, and proving to be the most powerful aphrodisiac known to man. Charlie knows, if the sun is out, and you turn on the charm, the women don't say no. No talking, no tomorrow, just sex.

One in, one out. The bouncer beckons them forward,

'How many of you?'

'Seven.'

'Four now, three in a minute.'

'Cool.'

Turning to the boys at the back, Charlie talks and walks backwards at the same time,

'Boys, we'll get the drinks in.'

The boys nod, as Charlie turns and is slapped in the face by the heat of the club as he jogs down the steps into the basement. The music is thudding out from behind the big swing doors, and the tune is muffled. Something about joy and pain, sunshine and rain.

'Don't leave now, ladies, the party's just starting!' Charlie turns on the charm for three average girls in high street sequins, his arms open wide, palms facing the ceiling, blocking their exit, their make-up running slightly down the sides of their faces, sweat trickling into their cleavage from the backs of their necks.

'It's too hot in there!' offers one of the girls with a smile, as the other two ignore him and push past to get out.

Charlie carries on walking towards the big swing doors, and as somebody pushes them open from the inside, the heat and the music jump him at once. The boys are behind him, as he dips his head into the bar.

This is the night.

At the bar, Charlie does the drinks.

'Boys, boys!' The lads are already surveying the scene, the music, the women, the competition, the vibe, the atmosphere. Sizing their night up from these very first seconds.

'Boys – what are we drinking?' Charlie shouts over the music, as the boys turn back to face him at the bar, and Charlie gets his wallet out from the back of his jeans. He feels his mobile vibrate at the same time, but ignores it. People are already pressing him to get to the bar. The place is moving, the dancing has spilled out from the volcano of the dance floor, and girls are already standing on the sofas, a couple on tables, dancing at their girlfriends. Charlie has observed in the last couple of years a tendency in women to dance suggestively with each other, shaking up and down behind each other, holding eye contact with their mates, turning every man on within ten metres. And that's exactly why they did it. They weren't lesbians, they were just showing their slutty side, without putting other blokes off.

'I'll get a round of beers to start, it's too fucking hot in here,' Charlie tells the boys, and is distracted immediately by two girls in the corner running their hands up and down each other's thighs, looking over at a group of blokes next to them.

Charlie, getting out a twenty, trying to attract the attention of the girls behind the bar, he holds it out in his hand and leans on the bar. The music is pumping through his head, as a hip hop beat kicks in and he nods his head in time. The air is thick with noise and drink. Charlie closes his eyes for a couple of seconds, and feels the pain in the back of his head ebb towards the front. He pushes it back, tries to ignore it.

It comes and goes, just a headache. A product of the heat, and the treadmill at the gym, and the deal he's trying to cut with PWC. The pain throbs for a couple of seconds and then recedes again. Charlie opens his eyes again, and it is gone completely. A barmaid comes over, black bra under a white shirt, he doesn't even notice her face, and leans forward for her ear.

'Four Stellas.'

'How many?'

Charlie holds up four fingers, and the barmaid turns around to the fridge, and Charlie turns around to see if the boys are still with him, which they are.

Josh is already chatting up some brunette, Josh likes the brunettes – kids himself they're the ones with the brains. Charlie has explained to Josh a thousand times that if his intention is only for the night, which it is, then what is the point in going for a girl who can hold a conversation. Besides, conversation is overrated, unnecessary. She hasn't got to meet the parents. But Josh just likes the brunettes. Charlie doesn't care – blonde, brunette, redhead, whatever. He's not looking for conversation, not on nights like these. From the corner of his eye he can see lights flickering over dancing bodies, and he wants to get over there, get into the action, stop hanging about for this fucking waitress. Charlie scoops up the beers, and turns awkwardly as the queue at the bar heaves towards the space he vacates, and he manages not to spill any beer, holding them over a short fat Chinese girl's head to avoid bumping her.

He dishes out the beers, then gestures to the girl with his head.

'Too many spring rolls.' The boys laugh, and the three of them head over to the dance floor, leaving Josh with the brunette, as the other boys come through the doors, and Charlie tells them he didn't have enough hands, and they're on the beers. The new boys make their way to the bar, sticking their heads over Josh's shoulders and leering at the brunette he's chatting up. Charlie leans back against a sofa facing the dance floor, with about thirty centimetres of personal space to drink his beer in, and surveys the scene. Luther Vandross, an eighties classic, is pumping out of the speakers from every corner, and Harry and Deacon are standing slightly in front of him, swigging their beer from bottles, checking out the action. One group of girls has caught their eye – office girls all of them, no lads with them as far as Charlie can see, all very do-able, all completely in his league. He notices the blonde first, in a bikini top and low cut jeans, riding on her hips, hair pulled back off her face, not too much make-up.

Charlie doesn't trust girls with it caked on – he doesn't get to pretend he's better looking than he is, so why should they? And besides, he has gone to bed with some stunners and woken up with some pigs before now, and it's always the ones with bright red lips and shit all over their eyes that stain his pillowcases black and powdery. Charlie sizes her up, sees her dancing with her mates, stopping and laughing every now and then, and taking the piss out of a group of blokes with no rhythm dancing behind them. She catches his eye just as the song changes. Looks away, and then back again. And Charlie holds his gaze.

She smiles. He's in.

Charlie is paying his dues, putting in the groundwork, chatting to his bikini top girl, pretending to listen, but dipping his head so that she can talk into his ear and staring straight at her tits. The flat bit in between them, her breastbone, has a trickle of sweat running down it, and Charlie wonders if it would scare her off to move in right now, and just lick it up . . .

Waiting for a cab, 1.15 a.m.
The blonde and Charlie hail a cab, and leap in the back. Straight away his hands move under her bikini top and feel

her tits, damp with sweat, and his tongue is so far in her mouth their faces are a blur.

She sits astride him, and unbuttons his jeans, while he sucks her neck and her chest, and as she reaches into his pants and feels how hard he is already, she pulls back and gives him an impressed smile. Because Charlie is very drunk.

The taxi driver checks them out in his mirror, but decides to look elsewhere, and concentrates on the road, as they move horizontally to get the blonde's jeans off. The cab stops at traffic lights and drunken clubbers bang on the windows and shout out obscenities, but Charlie is in a fucking trance and ignores them. The blonde seems to get embarrassed, however, and jumps off him, just as he was fumbling with his dick, trying to get it into her. Charlie lays back, dazed and confused. He had hoped she wouldn't even have to get out of the cab. Pushing himself up on his elbows, his erection standing between him and the blonde who is pulling her jeans back on, he feigns sincerity.

'What? What's wrong?' he sighs.

'I'm not gonna shag ya in the back of no fuckin' taxi – I ain't like that. Let's wait till we get back to yours.' Her voice rings nastily in his ears – she is young, twenty maybe at most, and common. She doesn't pronounce her words properly. She looks suddenly grotesque to Charlie. Some little tart who buys her clothes down the market, and makes ten grand a year as a hairdresser's apprentice. He knows the type – he knows every type. Nicola's underwear drawer flashes through his mind quickly, full of expensive bits of silk and lace. He shakes the thought off.

'Look,' he says, pulling himself up, but not bothering to put himself away. 'I thought it would be fun, exciting.' He reaches over and massages one of her tits. The boys would love this. How much had he bet them that he could have her in the cab anyway? A twenty? A fifty? A ton?

'Nah.' She pushes his hand away, and pops herself back into her bikini top

'Let's wait till we get back, yeah? It'll be nicer.' Charlie almost laughs out loud. 'I don't want it to be nice, love. I just want it to be . . .' Charlie sees her face dropping, her angry little jaw setting in front of him, and the prospect of not actually getting a fuck in the next half an hour.

'I wanted it to be exciting, didn't I?' He smiles over at her, but now he is getting increasingly fucked off himself, for having to try so hard. This was supposed to be an easy one.

The blonde smiles and leans forward and pecks him on the mouth, and then nestles under his arm, trying to get a hug. Charlie freezes – what the fuck is she doing? Jesus Christ, he'd picked wrong tonight.

'What number?' the taxi driver yells into the back. Charlie's erection has abated, and he tucks himself away.

'Just by the entrance is fine,' he says. What now?

The blonde jumps out before him, and he sees the tight little arse in her jeans, and the curve of her back. Fuck it, he'll fuck her.

Charlie pays the cabbie, and pushes her into the stairwell, spins her round and sticks his hands down her jeans. She pushes him back.

'Not yet, wait till we get upstairs!' She laughs like she's the ultimate, the fucking bee's knees, like she can keep him waiting. Charlie considers pushing his hand straight back down there again, but changes his mind, and walks off ahead of her, up the stairs to his apartment. The blonde follows.

Charlie's flat, 2.04 a.m.
Charlie's erection has gone. Rolling around on his bed with this little blonde tart, grabbing her and tossing her from side to side, they had both got naked within seconds of getting into his flat. But nothing is happening downstairs. His dick is limp,

even though he is tugging it himself, guiding it into her little mouth, lipstick smeared all over her face now. But the more she sucks, and moans, and moves up and down him, the more he sticks his fingers into all her openings, the less difference it makes. Charlie flips her over suddenly, and tries to guide his limp dick into her arse, but she jumps off him, and he lays back, defeated.

'Can't you get it up no more?' she asks, angry.

Charlie lays back in silence. She stomps her skinny little foot.

'Charlie, can't you get it up now – what about in the taxi? It was up in the taxi!' she screams at him.

'Just fuck off, okay,' Charlie says, and closes his eyes.

'I'm sorry? Excuse me? Did you just tell me to fuck off? Charlie, did you just tell me to fuck off – did you?'

'That's right. Fuck off. Shut the door behind you.' Charlie rolls over and stares straight ahead. This is the third time in two weeks.

'You bastard. You can't just fucking chuck me out!' The blonde's tiny, tinny voice shrieks at him. Charlie just stares ahead, naked; he pulls the sheets over himself.

'You can't just chuck me out, you fucker – where am I supposed to go?' She walks around and stands naked in front of him. Charlie is repulsed.

'Just leave. The phone's through there if you want to phone a cab.'

Charlie rolls the other way – he doesn't want to look at her ugly skinny little frame now; spot-lit from behind, she looks like a child.

'You cunt,' she whispers, and spits on him. She grabs her clothes, and storms out of the bedroom. Charlie hears her swearing and a vase smashing in the lounge, and then his front door slams shut.

Charlie sits up, and pulls on his jeans from the floor. He walks

351

into the kitchen, rubbing his eyes, pushing a hand through his hair. He feels sick, with the heat, and the sweat creeping down his back. His flat is quiet. He steps over the glass of the shattered vase that Nicola bought him, then changes his mind, leans down and picks up the pieces, and places them on the side by the kettle. He grabs a beer from the fridge, pulls open the door to his balcony, and steps out into the night air.

Leaning over the balcony, he stares out at the street. He tries to clear his head of the day. Nicola flashes through his mind. He wonders if she's home. He pictures her asleep in her flat, oblivious to everything, to what he's doing. If she cared she'd know. Or does she? She knows. She won't say anything though. And he's starting to hate himself. Thinking of her, lying in bed, he feels something rise slightly in his trousers. He can hear a tiny clicking below him, and he sees the blonde emerge from the front of his apartment block, and struggle down the steps. She is still adjusting her top. She looks like a prostitute stumbling down the road. Charlie watches her try and hail a passing cab without a light on that just speeds up and drives straight past. He hears a muffled high-pitched curse. She was laughing at him before. Goading his lifeless dick with her giggles. It's not lifeless any more. Charlie feels it stiffen in his jeans. The blonde flops down on the side of the street. Two drunken blokes on the other side stagger past and shout out abuse. She screams at them to fuck off. Charlie walks back inside, grabs his keys, and leaves the flat, his erection growing harder by the second, throbbing slightly in his jeans. He hits the button for the lift, which comes straight away. His mind whirls at the thought of catching her up.

The music in the lift is straight off some hand-held organ. It tinkles along annoyingly as Charlie paces the lift, waiting to get to the ground floor.

*   *   *

352

The blonde is still sitting on the floor as Charlie walks towards her purposefully. He is within shouting distance.

'Now, I'm ready now,' he shouts at her as he gets closer and closer.

'Eh?' She turns around to see him getting nearer by the second, and tries to scramble to her small feet, to run, but he is on her, grabbing her arm.

'Get off me, ya fucking asshole.'

Charlie and the blonde grapple for a few seconds. 'Get off me, ya fucking queer. Get the fuck . . .'

Something snaps behind Charlie's eyes. A pain shoots through his head, and he grabs it with his hand, letting go of the blonde's arms. Instantly, she lashes out at him and misses, but Charlie reacts and strikes back with the back of his hand. Her tiny head hits the wall, and her eyes close. Her body goes limp in his hands, and he drops her to the ground. The pains shoot through his head, and Charlie looks around himself, trying to work out how he got here, where he is. Who is this young girl lying at his feet – what was he going to do to her? The tears start to pour out of his eyes, and he reaches down to shake her, but she won't wake up. He feels like he is going to be sick, to pass out, his breathing comes quick and fast. Charlie runs, as fast as he can, back to his flat, leaving the girl lying out in the middle of the pavement. He gets back to his flat, and grabs the phone, and heads out to the balcony. He can see her still lying there. The pains in his head begin to subside as he dials 999. As the phone rings, Charlie has the sensation that the lights are going out.